DARK
ROOM

ANDREA

DARK ROOM

KANE

wm WILLIAM MORROW *An Imprint of* HarperCollins*Publishers*

DARK ROOM. Copyright © 2007 by Rainbow Connection Enterprises, Inc. All rights reserved. Printed in the United States of America. No part of this book may be used or reproduced in any manner whatsoever without written permission except in the case of brief quotations embodied in critical articles and reviews. For information address HarperCollins Publishers, 10 East 53rd Street, New York, NY 10022.

HarperCollins books may be purchased for educational, business, or sales promotional use. For information please write: Special Markets Department, HarperCollins Publishers, 10 East 53rd Street, New York, NY 10022.

FIRST EDITION

Library of Congress Cataloging-in-Publication Data

Kane, Andrea.
    Dark room : a novel / Andrea Kane.—1st ed.
        p. cm.
    ISBN: 978-0-06-074134-1
    ISBN-10: 0-06-074134-1
    1. Murder victims' families—Fiction.   2. Parents—Death—Fiction.
3. Loss (Psychology)—Fiction.   I. Title

PS3561.A463D37 2007
813'.6—dc22   2006049101

07   08   09   10   11   WBC/RRD   10   9   8   7   6   5   4   3   2   1

To ANDREA CIRILLO, the ultimate professional gyroscope, whose instincts, energy, and integrity are incomparable, who always gives her all—and then some—and who can't be fazed and can't be foiled—not even by egg salad. Thanks, AC, for your guidance, your partnership, and your uncanny ability to keep me moving in the right direction.

ACKNOWLEDGMENTS

With tremendous gratitude to those who generously shared their time and expertise, and whose efforts helped make the creation of *Dark Room* possible.

Maureen Chatfield, founder of M. Chatfield Ltd., for graciously allowing me a bird's-eye view of the inner workings of running a boutique social agency. Special thanks to Karen Cooper for our "mock consultation." I can see why M. Chatfield Ltd. has earned its well-deserved reputation.

Amanda Stevenson, for taking me "behind the camera's lens" and introducing me to the art, science, and technology of modern photography and photo image enhancement.

Detective Mike Oliver, who never ceases to amaze me with his "day in the life of" an NYPD detective stories. There aren't many people who can keep me riveted, make me cringe, and make me laugh all at the same time. It's that very combination of qualities that made him a great cop, and helped me do the same with Monty.

Hillel Ben-Asher, M.D., who not only taught me all the medical information I needed to write this book (and there were countless examples as "the thick plottened"), but who helped me weave them into the story in precisely the right places and ways. After the medical school education he provided me—I may not be a doctor, but I'm pretty sure I could play one on TV!

Caroline Tolley, who jumped in the instant she was needed, made editing *Dark Room* her top priority, and invested all the time, care, and skill it took to make the book—and me—the best we could be.

Metamorphosis Image Consulting for an education in body language, style, and haute couture.

Lucia Macro for plunging wholeheartedly into the chaos with me, for seamlessly tightening without compromising character or plot, and for becoming my instant cheerleader.

And to my family—no words are enough to suffice. Fortunately, none are needed.

ONE

The nightmare crept through her like a slow-acting toxin, paralyzing her as it insinuated itself into the darkest recesses of her memory. There was no escaping the devastating finale, no looking away from the horror.

She couldn't bear to see them. Not their broken bodies. Not their vacant stares. And not the pools of crimson blood that kept oozing beneath them as their lives drained away.

With a low moan, Morgan forced herself awake, jerking upright. Her muscles were rigid. She pressed back against the solid oak headboard, letting it cool her perspiration-drenched skin. Her heart was slamming against her ribs, her breathing fast and shallow.

This was a bad one.

She squeezed her eyes shut, concentrating on the muted sounds of predawn Manhattan. The intermittent *thump-thump* of cars making their way down pothole-ridden streets. A distant siren. The hum of 24/7 just outside her brownstone window. It connected her to life, to the comfort of what was real and familiar. She drank it in, fighting to drown out the images of her nightmare before they engulfed her.

It was an exercise in futility. The nightmares might be sporadic, but the vivid memories had been seared inside her head for the past seventeen years.

She shoved back the covers and swung her legs over the side of the bed. Her nightshirt was damp and clinging to her body. Her hair was plastered to the back of her neck. She gathered it up, twisting its shoulder-length strands into a loose knot and pinning them to the top of her head with the clip she kept on her night table. A winter draft blew past her, and she shivered.

She'd half expected tonight's episode. It was that time of year. The nightmares always came fast and furious around the holidays. But exacerbating the situation had been her own damned fault.

Morgan glanced at the clock on her night table: 5:10. No point in trying to go back to sleep. Not that she could if she tried. But it wasn't even worth the effort; not with only fifty minutes until her alarm went off.

She pulled on a robe and padded into the dimly lit hall, crossing over to the spare bedroom. The contents of the box she'd been going through were on the ottoman just as she'd left them—memorabilia in one pile, photos in another, and the working journals she'd only recently discovered off to a side.

Still haunted by her dream, she flipped on the light and went straight for the photos, kneeling down beside the ottoman to peel back a layer of history.

The top snapshot meant the most and hurt the most. It was the last photo of the three of them together. Wistfully, Morgan studied it. Her mother, gentle and elegant. Her father, intense and dynamic, one arm wrapped protectively around his wife's shoulders, the other hand gripping the shoulder of the skinny little girl in front of him—a girl who had her mother's huge green eyes and fine features and her father's sharp, probing expression.

Morgan turned the photo over. The handwriting at the bottom was her mother's. It read: *Jack, Lara, and Morgan, November 16, 1989.*

She'd penned those words a month before the murders.

With a hard swallow, Morgan put down the snapshot and sifted through the others. Her mother in college, posing with her best friend and roommate, Elyse Shore—then Elyse Kellerman. Law school graduation day for Morgan's father, both her parents standing in front of Columbia University, brandishing Jack's diploma. Their wedding day. The day Morgan was born. Family photos of happy occasions, from Morgan's first birthday to summers at the beach with all the Shores—Elyse, Arthur, and Jill. Last were the photos Elyse had developed for Morgan months after the funeral—photos taken at Daniel and Rita Kellerman's lavish Park Avenue penthouse on Christmas Eve, where Morgan's parents had dropped by for the holiday party being hosted by Elyse's parents in honor of Arthur and those who'd contributed generously to his political campaign.

Those were the final photos taken of Lara and Jack Winter alive. The next ones were snapped in a Brooklyn basement later that night by the crime-scene unit.

With a shiver, Morgan put down the stack of photographs and rose, tightening the belt of her robe. Enough. She was allowing herself to be sucked into that emotional vortex all over again. Her mental health couldn't withstand it. Dr. Bloom had cautioned her about this very thing.

Time to listen to his advice. Be proactive. Focus on the present.

She'd get a jump start on the day; brew a pot of coffee, shower and dress. Then she'd head downstairs to the office. She had a slew of early morning phone calls to make in the hopes of catching her clients before they left for work, and a mountain of paperwork to attack. At eight-thirty, it would be time for her therapy session—which worked out well since Dr. Bloom's office was just a block away from the Waldorf Astoria Hotel, where she had an eleven o'clock new-client interview. After that, it was back to the office for a one o'clock follow-up appointment with Charlie Denton—attractive, forty-four, married to his job in the Manhattan D.A.'s office. With very specific criteria and a crazy-busy life, he was still looking for Ms. Right. And it was Morgan's job to find her.

She turned off the light and left the room—and her past—sprawled out on the ottoman behind her.

———

THE DEAL WAS cut.

No one in the Brooklyn D.A.'s office was happy about it. Another scumbag who'd turned on a fellow inmate to save his own neck. Another case where the rule of law converged withcut Darwin's survival of the fittest.

Having to go easy on that drug-dealing punk, Kirk Lando, was a rotten break. But they had no choice. He'd given them a cop killer in exchange for a lighter sentence. The NYPD was happy; Nate Schiller would pay for killing one of their own.

Schiller would probably have his throat slit once word got out at Sing Sing why he'd lied about shooting Sergeant Goddfrey. Normally, killing a cop would have made him a hero there. Not this time. Schiller had screwed himself—bad. When he'd tracked Goddfrey down in Harlem and blown him away, he'd also blown away the perp Goddfrey had been cuffing at the time, figuring he was eliminating the sole witness to his crime.

Bad move. That perp had been gang leader Pablo Hernandez. Once the gang members inside Sing Sing got this news, Schiller could kiss his ass good-bye.

The whole trade-off sucked—for bigger reasons than leniency for Lando or the inmates taking out Schiller. Lando's story was true. It had been corroborated by a couple of neighborhood teens, now adults, who'd spotted Goddfrey's killer fleeing the scene. Originally, they'd provided a description. Now they'd each picked Schiller out of a lineup. So there was no doubt that Schiller had killed Goddfrey and Hernandez. Which meant he couldn't have committed the double homicide in Brooklyn he'd been convicted of as part of his killing spree.

The ripple effect was going to be felt far and wide. The daughter. The congressman. The staff over at the Manhattan D.A.'s office.

And one really pissed-off retired cop.

TWO

Pete Montgomery swerved his car into the driveway, glaring at the semi-attached house that served as his office as if it were the enemy. He was in one foul mood. He'd purposely left Dutchess County at eight forty-five to avoid rush hour. Still, it had taken him three hours to get to Little Neck. It should have taken half that time. Except that it had started snowing—just a dusting with the threat of an inch or two to follow. But that was enough to transform all the drivers on the road to pitiful, scared-shit wimps who drove with their noses pressed to the windshield and crawled along at a snail's pace.

He hopped out of his faded maroon 1996 Toyota Corolla, which had a hundred thousand miles on it and had been put back together again more times than Humpty Dumpty. Still, Monty—as everyone called him—insisted that it had another good decade of life left in it. Besides, it was the perfect car for a private investigator—ordinary, unpretentious, the kind of vehicle that could blend in anywhere.

His phone was ringing as he unlocked the office door, and he strode over to grab it. "Montgomery."

"Hey, Monty." It was Rich Gabelli, his old partner at the Seventy-fifth Precinct in Brooklyn. They'd worked together for a dozen years, right up to Monty's retirement at age fifty. Gabelli was younger—and more tolerant—so retirement for him was still a ways off.

"Yeah, Rich, what's up?" Monty was already shuffling through his files, putting his cases in priority order.

"You working half days now? I called your cell three times, and there was no answer. I guess being a newlywed takes up lots of time. And energy."

Monty grunted. He'd been taking good-natured flack from his buddies since he'd remarried his ex six months ago. "I wasn't home with Sally. I was on the Cross Island, cursing out the other drivers. Besides, I saw your number pop up. I ignored it. It's time to get a sex life of your own and stop living vicariously through mine."

"That's easy for you to say," Gabelli retorted. "Sally's still a babe. Have you taken a good look at Rose lately? She's put on twenty pounds."

"And you've put on thirty. That gut of yours needs its own desk. So be grateful Rose doesn't dump you. Now what do you want? I've got work to do."

"I called to give you a heads-up." There was a somber note in Gabelli's voice that Monty couldn't miss.

"About?"

Gabelli blew out his breath. "The D.A. cut a deal with Lando. He gave them the name of Goddfrey's killer."

"Good. It sucks about Lando, but Goddfrey's killer deserves to rot."

"I agree. But there's more."

"I'm listening."

"The guy who shot Goddfrey—it was Nate Schiller."

"Nate Schill . . . Shit." Monty ground out the word. "Are you sure?"

"Yeah. Schiller was bragging at Sing Sing about popping a cop. He was dumb enough to mention it was Goddfrey. Which means he killed Hernandez, and figured out who he was too late. There's evidence to corroborate it, so he'd confessed to killing Jack and Lara Winter. Killing an A.D.A. would mean rotten treatment at Sing Sing, but killing a gang leader would mean being carved up like a chicken. And since Goddfrey was killed that Christmas Eve in Harlem around the same time as the Winters were murdered in Brooklyn, Schiller couldn't have killed them."

"Son of a bitch." Monty slapped his file on the desk.

"You were right all along."

"I didn't want to be. I still don't. But I won't lie and say I'm surprised. The Winter double homicide didn't follow Schiller's pattern. The crimes felt too personal. And the Walther PPK? Not exactly Schiller's style."

"You know he loved throwing us off track. Anyway, the Manhattan D.A.'s pushing to reopen the Winter case."

"Big surprise. Jack Winter was their golden boy. They'll want to nail his killer's ass. Problem is, the ball was dropped the minute Schiller confessed. Now it's seventeen years later. No matter how much noise the Manhattan D.A. makes, who's gonna jump? With no leads, no witnesses, and a skimpy list of potential suspects—most of whom are either dead or vanished into the woodwork—they might as well try pulling a rabbit out of their ass. Talk about a cold case."

"You're right. We already dug out the file. There's nothing. But the captain wants us to go through the motions."

"Of course he does," Monty agreed drily. "He's got his ass to cover. Man, he must be thrilled I'm gone. He knows I'd be all over this if I were still on the force." Abruptly, Monty broke off, his voice taking on a rough note. "What about the daughter—Morgan—has she been told yet?"

"That's the reason I'm calling. This whole deal just went down. The D.A.'s office is scrambling to get their shit together. They're not looking forward to the fallout. But they can't risk a leak. So they're notifying her today." A pointed pause. "As soon as our precinct finishes dotting our *i*'s and crossing our *t*'s to give them the okay. Which I'm doing as we speak."

Monty got the message. "That gives me time to get to her first."

"Right. If that's what you want."

"It's what I want." Monty fell silent. He could visualize the hollow-eyed child who'd grown old in the space of a heartbeat just like it was yesterday. Even now his gut wrenched when he pictured the scene he'd walked in on.

Most cases didn't get to him. This one had.

And still did.

"She was in bad shape," Gabelli murmured. "You were the only one who was able to reach her."

"Yeah, well, I was in pretty bad shape myself at that time. That's why she and I connected."

"I remember." Gabelli cleared his throat. Partners or not, there were still some subjects he shied away from. That bumpy time in Monty's life was one of them. "You'd better move fast. I can only hold up the process so long. And I don't need to tell you that you didn't hear this news from me. The captain would hand me my ass on a platter."

"Not a problem. We never spoke." Monty grunted. "But between you and me, I'm doing him a favor by being the messenger. I might be able to do some damage control."

"With Congressman Shore, you mean."

"Hell, yeah. He's going to have a cow. When the murders went down, I'm the only one he didn't threaten to sue."

"He wanted answers. I can't blame the guy. He and his wife had just lost their best friends, *and* been handed custody of their kid."

"Blame him? He was more controlled than I would have been under the circumstances. Seeing that poor little girl, what she was going through—hell, I would have resorted to more than threats to get my answers." Monty shoved his pile of paperwork aside and grabbed a pad and pen. "What's Morgan Winter's address? I want to get to her before anyone, including the press, does. She's going to be freaked out enough by this news without being ambushed by reporters."

The rustle of paper. "She lives in that brownstone her parents left her on the Upper East Side. She runs a business out of there, too—some kind of high-class matchmaking service." Gabelli read Monty the address.

"Thanks, Rich. Give me an hour. Then let the dogs out." Monty blew out a breath. "I hope Morgan Winter can handle this."

"She's not a kid anymore, Monty. She's a grown woman. She'll be fine."

"You think so? I'm not so sure. She didn't just lose her parents that night. She found them, murdered. The kid was traumatized. The only thing that kept her from going completely over the edge was knowing the killer was caught, locked up, and given life without parole. Now I have to tell her he wasn't."

———

IT WAS ONE o'clock, and Morgan's stomach was growling as she hurried back into the brownstone. She hadn't eaten a thing all day. In fact, she hadn't had a minute to breathe since she'd unlocked the doors to Winshore LLC five hours ago. Business at the boutique social agency was hopping. The phones had been ringing off the hook when she left her newest employee, Beth Haynes, and dashed out for her eight-thirty therapy session. They were still ringing when she called to check in a short while ago. The good news was that Beth had informed her Charlie Denton was running late and had pushed back his appointment until three o'clock. That gave Morgan a window of opportunity during which to cram down her sandwich—assuming it was delivered in the next hour.

She brushed the snowflakes off her coat and hung it up, rubbing her arms as she glanced around. Done in rich woods and Oriental rugs, the ground floor was the business hub of Winshore. The second floor, also designated as part of Winshore's office space, was equally elegant but much cozier. It consisted of a cushy sitting room for interviews and a large, airy living room for photo shoots and fashion consultations.

Upstairs was for relaxation and comfort.

Downstairs was all business and bustle.

Well, not *all* business. There were personal touches, too: recent client wedding photos on the credenza, some funky art pieces on the desks, and—thanks to Jill Shore, Morgan's partner and dearest friend—an array of eclectic holiday decorations purchased on her travels. This included an eight-foot Christmas tree that barely cleared the ceiling, a handcrafted Hanukkah menorah Jill had found in Israel, and a Kwanzaa display.

Morgan smiled as she squeezed by the tree to get to Beth's desk. "No one can accuse us of shortchanging the holidays."

"That's certainly true." Beth blew a few pine needles off her pink cashmere sweater. "And Jill's still not finished yet. She said something about bells to commemorate the winter solstice, and books to explain its ancient roots."

Morgan's amused gaze flitted around the room, settling on the nook beside the fireplace. "Well, we do have one empty corner. I guess that's the one that'll take on the winter solstice theme." She grimaced in response to a loud growl from her stomach. "Any idea if Jonah's on his way?" she asked hopefully.

Jonah Vaughn was the delivery guy for Lenny's, the best *and* the busiest kosher deli in New York. Located on Delancey Street, Lenny's delivered overstuffed sandwiches to offices all over the Lower East Side and Brooklyn. And while Winshore was clearly outside that delivery zone, Morgan and Jill had a special "in" with the owner. Lenny was Jill's grandfather. And since Morgan had grown up as a member of the Shore family, he was like a grandfather to her, too.

Beth gave her the thumbs-up. "You're in luck. Jonah called from the truck right before you walked in. He should be here in ten."

"Thank goodness. I'm about to pass out from hunger."

"Well, hang on. Reinforcements are on their way." Beth swiveled her chair away from the computer and stretched. She was a fresh-faced young woman of twenty-two with a sharp mind, great people skills, and a psychology degree from Northwestern. Morgan had met her at a seminar and snatched her right up. After six months of training, Beth was well on her way to being a fantastic interviewer.

"Anything urgent I should know about?" Morgan picked up the stack of phone messages and began sifting through them.

"A slew of new inquiries." Beth jotted down a few additional notes. "Speaking of which, how was your meeting at the Waldorf? Rachel Ogden is barely older than I am, but she sounded like a dynamo on the phone."

"She is." Morgan handed Beth the information forms Rachel had filled out, together with Morgan's notes from their interview, ready to be organized in a new client file. "At twenty-five she's already a high-powered management consultant. I have a few guys from our database in mind for her. Starting with Charlie Denton. He's in his forties, but Rachel prefers that. I think they'd really hit it off."

The phone rang again, and Beth blew out her breath. "Break over. Probably another new client."

"Part of why these calls are coming in fast and furious is Elyse's doing," Morgan replied, grinning. "She makes commercial announcements before every spin and aerobic class, and pitches Winshore while perched next to every Lifecycle and treadmill." Affection laced her tone when she spoke of Jill's mother, Elyse Shore. The woman was a pistol. She ran an upscale gym on Third Avenue at East Eighty-fifth Street, where the term "word of mouth" took on a whole new meaning.

The front door of the brownstone opened and Jill burst in, shaking snow off her coat. "It's coming down hard. That's the bad news. Now the good news. I saw Jonah's truck. Lunch has arrived. Not a minute too soon, either. My stomach's growling like something out of a horror movie."

Shrugging off her coat, Jill continued to talk as she ran her fingers through her hair to dry it. She was more striking than beautiful, with red-gold hair, dark eyes in contrast, and a wide, sensual mouth. And when she smiled—which she did often—her entire face lit up.

"It's a good thing corned beef has renewing powers," she informed Morgan. "My afternoon's going to be crazier than my morning. Back-to-back meetings, first with our accountant, then with our new software designer. Pushed to save money, then pushed to spend it. By six o'clock, my brain will be fried." She waved away any outstanding concern. "Not to worry. I'm picking up the winter solstice decorations on my way home. The last of the office will be decorated tomorrow morning. Oh, and I'm meeting Mom for dinner. We're going over the final party details."

Jill rubbed her palms together for warmth, her eyes sparkling as she contemplated the holiday celebration Winshore was hosting for its clients. "You won't even recognize Mom's gym when we're through with it. Lighting, music, decorations. And enough food to sink a ship. It'll be fantastic. Before I forget, Dad left a message on my cell. He's flying in from D.C. tonight. So save some time."

At long last, Jill stopped to catch her breath, and Morgan found herself marveling, yet again, at her friend's tireless energy. That was Jill—the whirlwind. She lived life to the fullest, and pushed all the boundaries in the process. She was all about reveling in whatever the world had to offer, and if anyone existed who didn't like her, Morgan didn't know about it. Jill was a proverbial breath of fresh air, a sister in all ways but blood, and Morgan adored her.

"Morg?" Jill was eyeing her speculatively, her brows knit with concern. "You okay?"

"Fine. Just hungry."

With a quick sideways glance, Jill verified that Beth was on the phone with a client. Then she crossed over and pulled Morgan aside, lowering her voice as she spoke. "No, you're not just hungry. You're exhausted. It's no wonder Dad's worried about you. Which, in case you haven't figured it out, is why he's coming here straight from the airport. Did you have another bad night?"

Morgan shrugged. "I've had worse. Then again, I've had better. It's par for the course these days."

Jill frowned. "Maybe I should cut back on the whole decoration thing, at least for this year."

"Don't you dare. Your holiday spirit has nothing to do with my night-mares. If anything, it diverts me."

"Not really. You're a mess."

"I know." Morgan didn't try denying it. "I'm not sure why they've hit me so hard this year. Dr. Bloom says it's a subconscious vicious cycle. Reading my mother's journals triggered a stronger-than-usual connection to her and my dad; that connection prompted me to delve deeper into her journals, which, in turn, triggered more nightmares."

"But the nightmares were worse than usual even before you found those journals buried in that box of your mother's things. It's been weeks since you were yourself."

Morgan sighed, massaging her temples. "I just have this weird, creepy feeling. I can't seem to shake it."

Before Jill could reply, the front door buzzer sounded, followed by a rhythmic knocking and a bark of "Lunch!"

No second announcement was needed. Jill hurried over and yanked open the door. "Hey, Jonah," she greeted the teenager who tromped in.

"Hey." Tall and gangly, Jonah was swallowed up by his down parka and boots, with only a lock of sandy hair and the puffs of cold air he was exhaling visible. But the telltale aromas of deli meat wafting from the brown bag he carried were the only ID required.

"You're a lifesaver." Jill snatched the bag, opening it for an appreciative sniff. "Corned beef on rye with mustard, and a Dr. Brown's cherry soda. All's right with the world."

Shoving back his hood, Jonah acknowledged Jill's statement with a nod. "I've heard those words about ten times in the last hour."

"I'll bet." Jill dug around in her purse and pulled out a bill, stuffing it into Jonah's gloved hand. "Get some pizza instead."

"Thanks." Gratefully, he pocketed the tip. "But I already ate. I had two pieces of your grandmother's noodle pudding—*kugel*—" he amended, using the Yiddish word Lenny had taught him. "After all, I have a reputation to uphold.

"I'll bank this," he murmured on that thought.

Despite being Welsh, Jonah had been gobbling up Rhoda's kugel since he was old enough to take the subway to Lenny's by himself. Everyone teased him about it, but his addiction had landed him this delivery job. Lenny had hired him on the spot, offering him decent pay and unlimited kugel, while affectionately labeling him "The Kosher Kid."

But the best perk of his job had been Lenny introducing him to Lane. Interning for a photographer with Lane's skill and notoriety was the opportunity of a lifetime.

"Ah," Morgan ventured. "Another donation to your camera fund."

"Yeah." Anticipation flickered in Jonah's eyes, and his customary monotone took on new life. He was a quiet kid, and a bit of a geek. But he was a whiz at computers. As for photography, Morgan knew that was his passion, as was this new internship of his. Anytime those subjects came up, he lit up like Jill's eight-foot Christmas tree.

"I saw a cool camera on eBay," he announced. "A Canon Digital Rebel XTi. It's got everything—even a self-cleaning sensor—anyway, if it's still there after Lenny pays me on Friday, I'm bidding on it."

Jill waved her arm at the three computer stations. "If you need extra money this month, our system could use a few software updates and a maintenance check. How about it?"

"Sure." He scratched his head. "I've got two weeks' vacation from school starting next week. I can put in a few days here."

"Great."

Jill and Jonah lapsed into computer jargon, and Morgan used the opportunity to pluck her sandwich out of the brown bag and head for the kitchen.

She was halfway there when the front door buzzer sounded again. She looked over her shoulder in time to see Jonah open it. A tall man in a wool overcoat stepped inside. His features were concealed by a turned-up collar, but he had dark hair and a no-nonsense stance.

He folded down his collar and unbuttoned his coat. There was something decidedly familiar about him. Which meant he must be a client. And *that* meant she could kiss her pastrami good-bye.

"Hey, Jonah," he greeted the boy. "Making a lunch delivery?"

"Yeah." Whoever the guy was, Jonah looked surprised to see him here. "I've got a couple of extra sandwiches. Did you want one?"

"Nope. Already ate. But thanks." The man's dark gaze eased from Jonah to Jill. "I'm looking for Morgan Winter. Is she in?"

"Do you have an appointment?" Jill responded in her friendly-but-noncommittal tone that said Winshore didn't accept walk-ins.

"No. But it's important that I see her. Is she around?"

His voice—Morgan recognized it. And it didn't belong to a client. Or a walk-in.

It was a wrenching memory from the past.

"I'll check," Jill was carefully saying. It was obvious she'd picked up on the urgency in his tone. "May I ask your name?"

Morgan had already begun retracing her steps when he replied.

"Yeah. Tell her it's Pete Montgomery."

THREE

Jill looked baffled.

The name meant nothing to her. But it meant a life-altering moment to Morgan; the end of childhood, the beginning of a nightmare.

"Detective Montgomery." She approached him on autopilot.

"So much for that scrawny little girl," he said, extending his hand. "I
feel old."

"You don't look old. You look the same." Morgan's mind was racing.
She wouldn't jump to conclusions. Maybe his visit had nothing to do with
the past. Maybe he was here for himself, to seek out the right someone.

Doubtful. He wasn't the type. Plus, the way he'd announced himself—
it smacked of police business.

She glanced down at his left hand. He was wearing a wedding ring. So
much for partner seeking.

He followed her stare, awareness flickering in his eyes. He knew she
was seeking confirmation—and why. "Can I speak to you alone?"

"Of course." Nodding, she led the way to the first-floor conference room. She could feel Beth's curious gaze and Jill's anxious one. She probably should have offered them an explanation, or at least an introduction. But she was having trouble holding it together.

She shut the door behind them and turned to face him. "How are you, Detective? It's been a long time."

"Long enough for you to grow up and start your own business." He eyed her for a moment, then glanced around the sleekly decorated conference room. "Nice setup. I checked out your website. It says that Winshore is a boutique social agency. What's that—a high-class dating service?"

Morgan sensed he was trying to put her at ease, and she forced a smile. "It's a specialized matching agency. Jill and I started it up for busy professionals who are looking for a life partner, but whose lives and careers make it impossible for them to invest the time and the energy necessary to find the right person. We provide one-on-one screening, and sophisticated methods of personality analysis and matching. We've got dozens of success stories. Marriages, happily-ever-afters, lifelong partnerships."

"Okay, then, a matchmaking service for rich CEOs who want you to weed out the crud for them." Detective Montgomery shot her a wry grin. "Sorry. I'm just yanking your chain. I didn't mean to offend you."

"You didn't," Morgan assured him. "Believe me, I've heard just about every comment there is to hear—from curiosity to good-natured teasing like yours to outright insults. I can handle them all."

"Sounds like you love your work."

"I do. We benefit a large chunk of the New York population who are comfortable professionally and financially, but are still very lonely." She paused, then found herself sharing the rest. Somehow she needed him to know—because of who he was, because of how he'd factored into her life. "That's the bulk of our business. But recently I started up a separate branch, in honor of my mother. It's composed of women who've survived abusive relationships and are looking for healthy ones. For those clients, our fees are waived."

He got it. She saw understanding flash across his face. "That's a great tribute to your mother. I'm sure she'd be proud."

"I hope so."

"You said your partner's name is Jill—I assume you mean Jill Shore, the congressman's daughter? Which would explain the name 'Winshore.'"

"Yes." A nod. "You know that Elyse and Arthur became my guardians. I grew up with Jill. She's like a sister." Morgan broke off, fiddled with the raglan sleeve of her sweater. "Detective Montgomery, please forgive me for being blunt, but you picked a really awkward time to drop by. The holidays are still very painful for me. This year's worse than usual. And now you show up . . ." She swallowed. "Please tell me how I can help you."

"Why is this year worse than usual?"

His gruff question caught Morgan off guard. It was almost as if he knew something she didn't.

"I've been sorting through some memorabilia," she replied carefully.

"Is that the only reason?"

She'd forgotten what an intuitive man he was. There was no point in supplying half-truths.

"Actually, no. But it's the only reason that makes sense. The rest—it's just a feeling. A creepy, unsettled one that's been hanging on for weeks. There's no basis for it. I just can't shake it."

"Oh, there's a basis for it. It's called a mental connection, or a sixth sense, or whatever the hell you call that inexplicable link that sometimes exists." Detective Montgomery dragged a palm over his jaw.

There was no denying where this was headed, and a cold knot formed in Morgan's gut. "The reason you're here—it has something to do with my parents' murders?"

"Unfortunately, yes." He shoved his hands in his pockets, his mouth thinned into a grim line, his brows drawn. "Nate Schiller didn't kill your parents."

Morgan stared at him blankly. She'd heard what he'd said, but his words might just as well have been gibberish.

"You're wrong," she said at last. "That's impossible. He was convicted. He confessed. Plus, the pattern . . . it fit his MO. The prosecution proved it. He's guilty."

"That's what everyone working the case thought. They were wrong.

The same night your parents died, a cop and a gang leader were shot to death in Harlem. The times of the two crimes were concurrent. Which means two separate perps. The D.A. just got new evidence to support that. Nate Schiller was in Harlem that night, which means someone else killed your parents."

"Oh my God." Morgan leaned back against the wall, using its solid weight to brace her. "But why would he confess if he didn't . . ."

"He knew he'd be doing time no matter what, but perps who kill gang leaders don't fare well at Sing Sing." A tense pause. "Are you all right?"

"No."

He scowled, looking pained and disgusted. "I didn't mean to blurt it out like that. But frankly, I don't think mincing words would make it any easier to bear."

"You're right. It wouldn't." Morgan forced out the next question. "Do the police know who *did* do it?"

"Not yet. But they're working on it."

"They?" Her head came up. "Not you?"

"I'm not with the department anymore. I retired five years ago. I'm on my own now; a PI."

"Yet you're the one here, telling me the news."

"That was my choice. You'll be getting official word from the D.A. this afternoon. A contact of mine tipped me off. Your parents' homicides were my case. I feel responsible."

"You felt responsible then, too," Morgan reminded him.

She hadn't forgotten. She'd never forget. He'd been a true hero; a knight in shining armor to a little girl faced with a horror that no amount of time could erase.

She'd been in shock when he'd arrived at the scene. Elyse and Arthur had already been notified. They'd gotten there in a heartbeat. It didn't matter. She couldn't respond to them.

Arthur had summoned a grief counselor. But it was Detective Montgomery who'd taken charge. He'd handled things just right, wrapping a blanket around her to stop the shivering, speaking to her in gentle but steady tones. When she'd balked at the Shores' overtures to take her home, he'd suggested they give her some space. And when she'd stuck to his side like glue, he'd advised Elyse and Arthur to get in their car and follow him to the police precinct.

He'd put her in his car and driven her to the Sutter Avenue police station. She remembered the sign, because its bold-lettered designation: 75TH PRECINCT, POLICE DEPARTMENT CITY OF NEW YORK had looked so official and intimidating.

Detective Montgomery had guided her past the seedy-looking people and up the stairs to a skinny kitchenette that looked like her school cafeteria, only smaller and messier. He'd brought her a hot chocolate and sat down beside her. Then, he'd talked—about his kids, about how he wasn't living with them right now and how hard that separation was for him, about how no distance could ever break the bond between parent and child.

He told her that her parents would always love her. Always be with her. No matter how far away heaven was from earth.

That's when the dam had broken. She'd cried—no, sobbed. Big, gulping sobs that racked her body and tore her heart into fragments. Once the tears started, they wouldn't stop. She'd cried until her body was too exhausted to continue, at which point she'd slid down, curled up across two tattered chairs, and fallen asleep. Vaguely, she remembered Detective Montgomery carrying her into a small, musty room with stacks of files and storage boxes—and a cot. He'd placed her on it, and tucked a blanket around her before he left. He'd made sure the door was ajar so she could hear voices—his included. He'd even left on a light so she wouldn't be scared.

Months later, after dozens of therapy sessions that enabled her to begin dealing with that night, Morgan had started taking emotional baby steps. She let Elyse in enough to ask questions to fill in the blanks. She'd learned that Detective Montgomery had worked with the Shores and the counselor. He'd called several times over the intervening months to check up on her, to make sure she was holding up.

She hadn't been surprised. She'd been touched. He was a good, kind man. She'd tried to express that in the note she eventually wrote to him.

But that first night, she'd felt nothing. She'd been numb. She'd stayed with the Shores because they were the closet thing to family she had left, and because that was what her parents had wanted. Anything more seemed impossible. Love them? No way. Not when she was so filled with pain and anger. All she wanted was to turn back time, wave a magic wand and have her parents alive and with her again.

Elyse and Arthur had been wonderful. They'd tried so hard, offering her everything from time and tenderness to the best medical care and the finest crisis counselors and child therapists money could buy.

She was grateful. That part had come easily. But the rest had taken longer.

"Remembering?" Detective Montgomery interrupted her musings to ask.

"Yes." Morgan raised her head and met his gaze. "I was remembering how astute you were. You never pushed. You never told me what I was supposed to feel. You let me grieve. You didn't intrude, but you didn't walk away. Without you, I'm not sure I would have gotten through that night."

"You're giving me way too much credit. You had a lot of people in your corner. Besides, you were a trouper."

"I didn't feel like a trouper. I felt like my life had ended."

"It had. You've rebuilt it."

"I suppose." Morgan folded her arms across her breasts and rubbed the sleeves of her sweater with her hands. She suddenly felt cold. "But scars like the ones I have don't go away. Not completely. So hearing this bomb you've just dropped—it's like the wounds are being ripped open again."

"Yeah." He acknowledged that reality with a scowl. "I wish like hell I could make this go away. The last thing I want is to deprive you of your peace of mind. It took long enough for you to find it."

The sincerity of his words touched her. "You're still a very kind man."

"I'm a very *pissed* man. Don't kid yourself. I want this case solved. I plan to keep close tabs on it until the real perp is caught."

"What makes you think that'll happen?" Morgan bit out. "The case got botched when it was new. Now it's old. Plus, you're out of the picture. To me, that says the odds of solving this are next to nil. The real animal who cold-bloodedly shot my parents to death will keep walking the streets a free man—just like he has been for the past seventeen years." Morgan's voice quavered, the impact of her own words sinking in. "God," she whispered. Her eyes filled with tears, and she pressed her hands against her face. "How can this be happening?"

"I don't have an answer. But it sucks." Detective Montgomery didn't insult her with placating words. He just walked over to the sideboard, picked up the pitcher of ice water that was sitting there, and poured her a glass. "Here." He pressed it into her hand.

"Thank you." Morgan took a deep swallow. "I didn't mean to lace into you like that."

"You didn't. You're frustrated and in shock. You have a right to be. You also have a point. This case has been closed for ages. But don't underestimate the clout that Congressman Shore wields. He's a high-ranking member of the House of Representatives, a big shot on the House Committee for Financial Services. New Yorkers love him. So does most of the country. He's got pull—and visibility. And he's sponsoring a high-profile bill. The noise Congressman Shore is bound to make will give the powers that be the incentive they need to hang in there until they get it right."

The censure in Detective Montgomery's tone was hard to miss—as was its meaning. "You never were totally on board with the findings of the previous investigation," Morgan realized aloud.

"I had my doubts," he replied bluntly. "But that's all they were—doubts. I didn't have a shred of proof. Then Schiller confessed. So I assumed my instincts were unfounded."

"You assumed wrong."

"Yeah, well, hindsight is twenty-twenty."

Morgan studied his expression. She wasn't fooled by his flippant remark or his stoic facade. "You're still beating yourself up for not exhausting all the possibilities."

"I wasn't given a choice. Am I kicking myself? Sure. But regret is part of life."

"It doesn't have to be. Not this time." Morgan set down her glass. "Handle this investigation. Find my parents' killer."

His brows arched slightly. "I already told you I'm off the force."

"You also told me you're a PI. Well, I'm a client. Name your price. I'll find a way to pay it. I don't have faith in the cops, or the D.A. I have faith in you."

"That's flattering. But the D.A. thinks I'm a pain in the ass. So does my old boss. I wouldn't be doing you any favors by taking this on."

"Yes, you would. You're not the type to be intimidated by people, or by protocol. You'd get around both."

"You think so?" He looked amused. "Maybe sometimes. But this isn't one of those times. Believe me, no matter how low I fly under the radar, I'll still show up on their screen. The sparks would fly."

"A part of you would relish that," Morgan guessed shrewdly. "You'd take on the system—and you'd win."

He chuckled. "You're a pretty good judge of character, Ms. Boutique Social Agent. But you're giving me way too much credit."

"I don't think so." Morgan drew in a breath, sparks of recall flickering in her mind. "I remember. I might have been a child, but that night is engraved in my mind forever. You took charge. You were ten steps ahead of everyone else. And you didn't play games. You were a straight shooter. And, yeah, maybe a maverick."

"There's no maybe about it. I'm a cowboy. That's why I left the force and went out on my own. Playing by the rules is not my strong suit."

"Good. Play by whatever rules you want. Bend them. Break them. I don't care. As long as you get that bastard." Morgan grew more intense, taking a step forward and pressing her palms tightly together as she gazed straight at him. "Please, Detective, I'm begging you. Do this. Do it for your own peace of mind. For whatever made you go that extra mile all those years ago." Her lips quivered and she swallowed, hard. "For the little girl you held together and the haunted woman she's become. Please."

A myriad of emotions crossed his face, and Morgan could tell she'd reached him. He was reliving the past, remembering the same agonizing moments she was.

"You believe you can get this guy," she determined, reading his expression. "I believe you can, too. In fact, I know it. So I'm pleading with you—do it. Take me on as a client."

He nodded, his jaw set. "All right," he said gruffly. "You've got yourself a PI."

FOUR

Morgan sat alone in the conference room for a long time after Detective Montgomery left. Her whole world had been turned upside down. Mixed with the shock and pain was anger. And, on some level, there was also a sense of emotional reinforcement—a confirmation that her feelings of uneasiness and apprehension were founded in reality.

Her parents' killer was walking the streets—and had been for the past seventeen years.

There was a light tap on the conference-room door, and Jill eased hesitantly inside. "Morg?"

"Come in." Morgan answered her friend's unspoken question, even as she continued to stare off into space.

Jill walked over, perching at the edge of the conference-room table. "What's going on? Jonah says that Pete Montgomery is a detective."

"He is." Morgan tilted back her head to meet Jill's worried gaze. "He was with the NYPD. Now he's a PI."

"That much I know. He's apparently a regular at Grandpa's deli. He has been for years—with his precinct buddies and with his family. His son's the photographer Jonah's working for. What did he want?"

"To forewarn me."

"About?"

"A major screwup. One that's going to affect us all and push me beyond what I can handle."

"Morgan, you're scaring me." Jill sank down into a chair and leaned forward. "You obviously know the guy. Judging from what I overheard, he hasn't seen you since you were a kid. Was he part of the team that investigated your parents' murders?"

"He was the lead detective. He was also the first cop on the scene, the one who saw me through the initial trauma, and the one who gave your dad updates from day one until Nate Schiller's arrest, trial, and conviction. As it turns out, it was all for nothing."

Jill's eyes widened. "You're not telling me they're letting that animal out on parole?"

"No. He's definitely locked up for life."

"Then what?"

A shaky exhale. "Schiller's not the one who killed my parents. He committed all those other murders, plus two more—a cop and a gang leader. But my parents weren't among his victims."

"What?" Jill stared. "I don't understand. They're just finding out about this *now*?"

"It's a long story. But, in a word—yes." In a tone that was devoid of emotion, Morgan filled her friend in. "So we're back to square one," she concluded. "No—worse. Now I have to live with the knowledge that whoever really killed my parents is still out there. That he's been out there all these years. That there might have been other victims since. That there might be more yet to come—" Morgan broke off.

"Stop it." Jill wrapped a supportive arm around Morgan's shoulders. "Don't let your mind go there. Focus on the fact that this screwup's going to be fixed."

"Oh, it's going to be fixed all right," Morgan agreed. "Because I'm going to make sure of it. I'm not ten years old anymore. I plan to take steps to resolve this—on my own and by choosing the right pros to do what I can't."

Jill absorbed that thoughtfully. "Do those pros include Detective Montgomery?"

"They start with him. He's key. I hired him on the spot." As Morgan spoke, her shock and upset began rapidly transforming to proactive determination. "Is Charlie Denton here yet?"

"He just arrived. Do you want me to take the appointment for you?"

"No. I want to talk to him. He works at the Manhattan D.A.'s office. He came on board several years before my father was killed. He knew and respected him. I'm guessing that by now word's gotten around the office. Maybe Charlie will have an update on what's being done to reopen the investigation into my parents' murders. I want to know how riled up his office is, and how much pressure they're going to exert to get at the truth." Morgan rose.

"What can I do to help?" Jill asked, spreading her hands in a helpless gesture.

"Just give your mom a call. Ask if you can postpone your dinner. I'd like us all to sit down and discuss this situation as soon as Arthur's plane lands. Is that okay?"

"Absolutely." Jill looked relieved at being given a concrete task she could wrap her hands around. "I'll call Dad first. Maybe he can catch an earlier flight. The sooner he hears about this, the better. If anyone can light a fire under the right asses, it's him. But, Morgan, in the meantime maybe you should wait before jumping in with both feet."

"I can't." Morgan squeezed her arm, already heading for the door. "Your heart's in the right place, and I love you for it. But if I don't *do* something, I'll fall apart."

Jill nodded mutely, watching her friend hurry from the room, shoulders rigid with purpose. She wasn't fooled by Morgan's burst of adrenaline or show of bravado. The blow she'd just been dealt was crushing. Her emotional state had been fragile enough before Detective Montgomery arrived. And now? Now her one source of comfort had been obliterated.

Reaching over, Jill scooped up the telephone and punched in her father's number.

———

SEATED IN WINSHORE'S cozy waiting room, Charlie Denton shifted in his chair. The espresso Beth had brought him offered little appeal. For the conversation he was about to have, a few shots of whiskey wouldn't be strong enough.

He'd been a prosecutor for almost twenty years. He was tough and thick-skinned, with no problem about going for the jugular. It took a hell of a lot to rattle him, and rarely did confrontation throw him off balance.

This time was different.

It hit way too close to home.

Setting down his cup, he reached around to massage the back of his neck. The sooner he got this over with, the better.

From across the hall, he heard the intercom on Beth's desk sound.

"Yes?" she asked, having picked up the phone. "Of course. Right away."

A minute later she appeared in the doorway. "Mr. Denton? Morgan's ready for your meeting. I'll show you up."

"Thanks, but that's not necessary. Second-floor sitting room, right?" He waited for Beth's nod. "I had my original interview there. I know the way."

With that, he hustled up the staircase, stopping only when he'd reached the second door on the right.

It was ajar, and Morgan was seated on the taupe microsuede sectional, her forehead creased in thought, an open file on her lap.

She was a beautiful woman. Fine-boned, delicate, with a rare combination of gentleness and intensity that was both reassuring and sexy. Ironic that she could be so oblivious to it—oblivious to so many things—she, who was highly intelligent and intuitive when it came to reading others.

He stepped into the room, shutting the door behind him. "Hi."

"Hello, Charlie." She looked tired. And pale. The anniversary of her parents' murders was coming up. She had to be hurting.

He was about to shove that pain in her face.

"Sorry about changing our meeting time," he began. "It's been a day from hell."

"I hear you." She gestured toward the overstuffed club chair situated diagonally across from the sectional. "Have a seat."

He perched at the edge of the cushion, gripping his knees and leaning toward her. There was nothing to be gained by delaying the inevitable. So he plunged right in.

"The reason I pushed back our appointment today is that I'm not here to discuss my social life. I'm here to discuss a plea bargain the Brooklyn D.A. struck this morning. It directly affects you. It concerns your parents' murders and who did—or didn't—commit them."

She went very still. "Go on."

"Nate Schiller's confession was bogus. He didn't do it; he was too busy killing a cop and a gang leader at the time of your parents' homicides." Charlie paused to gauge Morgan's reaction, interpreting her silence as initial shock. "I'm sure this news is hitting you like a ton of bricks, and for that I apologize. As for why you're hearing it from me, there was a daylong political haggling session between my office and the Brooklyn D.A. Our side argued professional courtesy; theirs argued professional jurisdiction. Our side won. So here I am."

To his surprise, Morgan gave a humorless laugh. "Your side won. But you lost. What happened—did you draw the short straw?"

"Huh?" Whatever he'd been expecting, it hadn't been this.

"Who am I kidding?" She answered her own question. "The D.A. just handed you your instructions and showed you the door. It makes perfect sense. You and I are acquainted. We have a comfortable, positive working relationship. Plus, you knew my father, maybe even worked a few cases under his direction. Therefore, you were the logical choice to break the news to me. How civilized of both D.A.s. Or how self-serving, depending on how you look at it. Is it *my* reaction they're worrying about, or is it Arthur's? Because I'm stunned and unnerved. I have been for the past few hours, since I got word. As for Arthur, he doesn't know yet. But if I had to venture a guess, I'd say he'll be infuriated to find out that my parents' murder investigation was botched and that whoever really killed them is still out there walking the streets."

Charlie stared. "You already knew about Schiller?"

"A friend told me. He wanted to spare me the pain of hearing about it from a stranger, or worse, from the press."

"I see." A long pause as Charlie regained his composure. "You either have a very well-connected friend, or we have some serious leaks. This news wasn't supposed to get out before you were told—personally."

"I'm sure that's true. But at this point, it's immaterial." Morgan forced a tight smile. "Stop looking like you're about to face a firing squad. I don't believe in shooting the messenger. The news is out, its initial impact over, and I'm still in one piece."

He eyed her speculatively. "We've never really spoken about your parents, other than the niceties. You know I was fresh out of law school when I came on board at the Manhattan D.A.'s office. Your father was an icon. Every newbie hero-worshipped him, including me. He was a brilliant prosecutor, with dead-on instincts. I never met your mother, but I heard she had a heart of gold."

"She did."

Charlie blew out his breath. "Their murders sent shock waves through the entire system. I can't imagine what it did to you. You were a ten-year-old kid. Not only did you lose your parents, but you were at the crime scene."

"I found their bodies," Morgan supplied tonelessly. "And you're right. You can't imagine. But you can guess. It changed me forever."

"And now you've got something new to deal with—this news about Schiller."

"True. But my coping skills are a lot stronger now. So's my will. I'm not going to sit passively by and let the job of finding my parents' murderer become another item on someone's to-do list. I'm going to move it along."

That got Charlie's attention. He went very still. "Meaning?"

"Meaning I'm going to start out by assessing just where this matter stands in the various law enforcement offices." It was her turn to lean forward. "Tell me, Charlie, how ticked off is the Manhattan D.A.? Angry enough to push Brooklyn to initiate a whole new investigation? Or is this a back-burner case, icon or not?"

He was walking a thin line and he knew it. "I'm not sure how this will play out. The old-timers are ripping. Especially the ones who were close to your father. They want resolution. The younger crowd's a different story. They only know Jack Winter as a name. Bottom line is, reopening the investigation will require resources. Lots of them. It's been seventeen years. The trail is cold. So is the case."

"We could heat it up. Or rather, *you* could." Morgan reacted to the wary expression on Charlie's face. "I'm not suggesting you play Deep Throat. Or even that you step on toes. I'm just asking that you dig up a little information for me about what cases my father was working on at the time of his death."

"Who might have had it in for him, you mean."

"Exactly. It would be a start."

"I'm sure Brooklyn's Cold Case Squad will kick in and cover that territory."

"Eventually. Once the turf war is over and the files are dusted off. I don't want to wait for that. I want to cut through the red tape. Starting with the old-timers, as you put it. You could talk to them, see what you could find out."

"There are two problems with that strategy. For one thing, whatever cases your father was handling are now spread out all over the place—from solved and filed away, to cold and in storage, to wide open and reassigned. And for another thing, you're assuming this crime was a personal vendetta. It could still be a robbery gone bad."

"We won't know until we check. But that brings us to the third problem—or rather, the *fundamental* problem—the one that's really causing your reluctance. Politics. The battle over which jurisdiction gets—or wants—this case. Till you're sure of that, you run the risk of pissing people off. Well, relax. I'll take care of it. I'll talk to Arthur. He'll make sure you're given the green light, and that just enough of the powers that be are made aware of that."

A hollow laugh. "You make me sound like a self-serving bastard."

"No. Just a guy who values his professional future. I don't fault you for it. Now, will you help me?"

Charlie steepled his fingers in front of him, lowering his gaze to study them. He couldn't look Morgan in the eye and remain unswayed. Actually, he couldn't remain unswayed even without eye contact. Too many personal feelings were involved here—complex, multifaceted personal feelings. Staying impartial was an impossibility. It had been then. It was even more so now.

He lifted his gaze to meet hers. "I'll see what I can find out."

HEATHROW AIRPORT WAS a zoo—wall-to-wall travelers all scrambling to get to and from their destinations.

Lane Montgomery just wanted to get home.

He shifted in his seat, glancing at his watch to see how much longer it would be before boarding time. As far as he was concerned, it couldn't be soon enough. Talk about jet lag. He'd been to Beirut, Istanbul, Athens, Madrid, and now London, all in ten days. He was cranky, bone-weary, and overtired. All he wanted was an hour in his Jacuzzi, and eight more between his sheets.

He leaned back, shut his eyes. He loved his work. But this part of it was starting to get to him. The life of a paparazzo had been exciting as hell at twenty. At thirty-three, covert photo ops that felt all too similar to his tabloid days in strategy and execution—despite the fact that they were CIA-sanctioned, being done for an entirely different, noble cause—were getting old. The crazy schedule, the requisite secrecy, and the subsequent isolation—all of that was eroding the thrills and excitement and replacing them with a new kind of restlessness.

Life on the edge was great. But a little more normalcy would be a welcome relief.

His cell phone rang just as the overhead voice announced that his flight was starting to board—*finally*, after an hour plus of delays.

He stood up, slung his camera bag over his shoulder, and dug his cell out of the pocket of his leather bomber jacket. He was already walking toward the boarding line as he glanced at the caller ID.

It was Hank Reynolds, the editor he worked with at *Time*.

He punched on the phone. "Hey, Hank."

"Hey. Where are you?"

"About to hop on a plane at Heathrow."

"Heading away or home?"

"Home. And not a minute too soon. The flight's already been pushed back twice. I've worked twenty hours a day for the past week and a half. I'm wiped. I plan on sleeping the entire way to Kennedy. I'll wake up just long enough to get through customs, get home, and get from my bath to my bed."

Hank chuckled. "Understood. Tell you what. Give me a call tomorrow. I've got an assignment for you."

Lane groaned. "Where and when?"

"Next week. That gives you plenty of time to rest up. And it's right here on your home turf—New York. No travel. No time change. No long days without food or sleep."

And no dicey undercover work, Lane added silently. *Just a nice, normal photojournalist assignment.* "You sold me. What's the subject?"

"Congressman Arthur Shore. You've worked with him before, right?"

"Yup. During his last reelection campaign, I did a photo essay on him and his hobbies—rock climbing and bungee jumping—for *Sports Illustrated*. What's he up to that would interest *Time*?"

"Obviously, you haven't had a chance to pick up a newspaper this week. Shore's fighting to push through some pretty cutting-edge legislation. He's also still living the daredevil life of Indiana Jones. Skydiving and zooming down the Rockies' most treacherous ski slopes are his newest things." A pause. "Plus there's another high-profile aspect of his personal life that just exploded onto the scene. I'll get into details tomorrow. The bottom line is, I want a comprehensive photo essay on the personal, professional, and recreational risk-taking, boundary-pushing daredevil congressman. You're the perfect guy to give it to me."

"Yeah, okay. Count me in." Lane was only half absorbing Hank's words. "I've gotta sign off now. The plane's boarding and I'm really out of it."

"You sound it. Go home and get some sleep. The last thing you want is to burn out."

"Funny. I was just thinking the same thing."

FIVE

Dinner at the Shores' Upper East Side apartment was Chinese. It was quick, it was easy, and it caused no interruption to the heavy discussion taking place in the living room.

Seated on the sofa, Morgan filled Arthur in on the day's events. He grew more furious by the minute, pacing around the room, brows drawn together as he processed the information. Nothing unusual there. Arthur never sat still. And when he had a problem to mull over, he paced. Jill never left her post by the floor-to-ceiling windows—where she'd been scowling at the cluster of reporters still camped outside the building, hoping for a personal reaction from the congressman.

When the food arrived, she and her father joined her mother in the kitchen. Elyse had already set the table and made a pot of green tea, although she had one ear cocked toward the living room, listening to what was going on. She wanted to gauge her husband's reaction, see how much he could do to bring closure to this nightmare, keep it from wreaking havoc on their lives again.

No one felt like eating. Still, for the sake of sustenance and a shred of normalcy they sat around the kitchen table, going through the motions. Conversation ceased, the only sounds in the room those of rustling cardboard and clinking silverware as portions were doled out. The silence continued as they picked at their food, sipped at their tea.

"I still don't believe a screwup like this went through the whole criminal justice system unnoticed," Arthur muttered at last, pushing back his chair and giving up on his meal. He rose, a tall, handsome, charismatic man who exuded energy and passion in everything he did. "Such gross incompetence is inexcusable."

Elyse pursed her lips, glancing over at Morgan to see how she was holding up. Her own food remained largely untouched—and not, in this case, because of her preoccupation with healthy eating and staying young and fit. After seventeen years as Morgan's surrogate mother, she knew how much Lara and Jack's homicides had cost their daughter. She had genuine doubts over whether Morgan could hold up under the strain of reliving that entire chapter of her life. "It's appalling," she agreed. "We've got to resolve it as soon as possible."

"That's easier said than done." Jill's forehead creased. "A wrongful conviction that's almost twenty years old? Unraveling it to get at the truth will be a bear."

"It'll be done," Arthur pronounced. "That's a given, not an if. But that doesn't change the fact that the whole situation's indefensible. Not only because it's Jack and Lara we're talking about. Or even because Jack was such a high-profile A.D.A." A muscle worked in Arthur's jaw. "I was kept up-to-the-minute during those homicide investigations. I knew every move the cops made, every avenue they were pursuing."

"I remember," Elyse murmured. "You checked in with Detective Montgomery every day by phone. And you met with him once a week at your dad's deli to go over the status of the investigations."

"Yes, well, those conversations are what's bugging me now. Detective Montgomery was never a hundred percent on board with the idea that Schiller was guilty. He kept saying it felt wrong, that there were inconsistencies nagging at him. Then Schiller confessed. That nipped Montgomery's theories in the bud. The investigation was wrapped up. Schiller was tried and convicted. Case closed."

"That's the way the system works, Dad," Jill reminded him.

"But it's not the way *I* work. I shouldn't have been so damned accepting. I should have made them review every piece of evidence even after the confession."

"Arthur, don't do this," Morgan interrupted, speaking up for the first time since the meal had started. "Detective Montgomery ran through this same thought process in my office today. You're both blaming yourselves, and that's absurd. You pushed as hard as you could. A killer confessed. There was no reason to doubt that confession. End of story."

Arthur shoved his hands into the pockets of his slacks and regarded Morgan with a brooding expression. "You said you hired Montgomery. That was a shrewd move. As a PI, he'll take more risks than he could have as a cop. I'll get in touch with him first thing in the morning, offer him whatever resources he needs. As for this Charlie Denton, I'll place a few calls and make sure the decks are cleared for him to get whatever he can on the cases Jack was handling."

"Thank you," Morgan said gratefully.

The taut lines on Arthur's face eased. "I don't want thanks. I want *you* to do something for *me*. Ease off. You look like you're about to collapse. I'm home now. Leave this in my hands and in the hands of professionals like Montgomery. You made great strides. You started the ball rolling. Now take a step back. You're having a hard enough time coping with the anniversary of your parents' deaths. Don't ask more of yourself than you can handle."

"I told her the exact same thing," Jill chimed in. "Maybe she'll listen to you."

Morgan forced a strained smile. "I listen to all of you. I realize you're worried about me. I'll try to gain some perspective on this, and pay attention to my own limitations. But tonight's not the night to do that. In fact, tonight's not the night to do much of anything. I'm beyond wiped out. All I wanted was to fill you in ASAP. Now that I have, I really need to head home and get some sleep." She rose, weaving a little as she did.

"My driver's parked around back," Arthur informed her. "He'll take you home."

"That's not necessary. I can walk."

"Right, and faint in the street. Forget it. You'll take the car. Besides, it'll help you dodge the press." He glanced at Jill. "You, too. You'd never be able to walk by them without spouting your opinion on invasion of privacy."

Jill's nose wrinkled. "You know me well."

"We know you *both* well," Elyse amended. "We know your weak spots and we know when you've maxed out." She hugged each of them in turn. "Now go home. Get some sleep."

"You don't have to twist my arm," Morgan assured her. She sent Arthur a questioning look. "Can we talk tomorrow, after you've made those calls? Do you have time?"

"I'll make time."

"What about your meetings?" It was no secret that Arthur was swamped.

"It's all under control," he replied. "I'll have plenty of time to reach out to everyone I need to. Remember, Congress is in recess until after the holidays, so nothing's getting done in Washington. Which leaves me free to stay in New York and concentrate on my home base. I've got a dozen or so irons in the fire. In terms of national publicity, I've agreed to do a story for *Time*. 'The Daredevil Congressman,' I think they're calling it. That's a great angle. So stop worrying."

He studied Morgan's pale face, the dazed look in her eyes, and a flash of fierce determination crossed his face. "None of this means a damn. Your situation takes precedence over everything. I'll make those calls first thing in the morning. After that, I'll head over to Winshore. You can make me a cup of espresso with that fancy machine of yours."

This time Morgan's smile came naturally. "You've got a deal." She felt like the weight of the world had been partially lifted off her shoulders. "Thank you, Arthur. This means the world to me." She turned to Elyse. "Will you forgive our running out and leaving you two with the cleanup?"

"What cleanup?" Elyse waved away her concern. "Stacking plates in the dishwasher and putting cartons of uneaten food in the fridge? That should take all of ten minutes." From the corner of her eye, she spotted her husband whipping out his cell phone, turning away to check his messages. A wistful expression crossed her face. "I think I'll turn in early, as well. We all need to recharge. Any way you look at it, the road ahead's going to be rocky."

IT WAS 2 A.M. and Monty still hadn't slept.

He rolled onto his back, giving up the fight and reconciling himself to a sleepless night. He glanced over at Sally, feeling a surge of peace and contentment at the sight of her lying beside him. They'd been remarried for six months now, and he still felt like the luckiest man alive. After three decades in law enforcement, he'd seen more tragedy and ugliness than he let himself dwell on—certainly more than enough to know that Sally encompassed everything that was good and beautiful. And this time around he had the maturity and wisdom to hang on to that.

Sally's deep, even breathing told him she was sound asleep. Carefully, so as not to disturb her, he slid out of bed, yanked on a pair of sweats, and headed down to the kitchen. As always, during his restless nights, he followed the same counterproductive but enjoyable routine—counterproductive because every aspect of it was guaranteed to prolong his insomnia. He brewed a pot of strong, black coffee, found a relatively fresh donut—which he microwaved for precisely nine seconds—and plopped down at the table to snack and think.

Tonight's thoughts were all about the resurrection of the Winter homicide cases.

Gabelli was a good guy. During the quieter part of his workday, he'd managed to make a copy of the entire original file—from interviews to written reports to crime-scene photos. After that, he'd packed it up and left the precinct for the night, making a quick detour to Little Neck. According to the voice mail he'd left Monty, he'd slid the file under Monty's office door, so it would be the first thing he tripped over when he walked in tomorrow morning.

Monty couldn't wait to get his hands on that file. Not that he needed it to remember the crime-scene details; those were forever etched in his mind. But he did need it to review and reevaluate each investigative step they'd taken, this time with a fresh eye and the more sophisticated forensic tools at their disposal.

Checking for a DNA match would be easy—provided the perp was already in the system. But if he wasn't, if the murders had been, as Monty suspected, personal and committed by someone without a record, there'd be zip to go on.

The crime-scene photos were another matter. True, they'd been taken in the late eighties. But their quality had been pretty decent, and the area and angles they'd covered had been comprehensive. Which was a good start. Because, as luck would have it, Monty knew the best damned image-enhancement and photo-retouching expert in the business. A pro whose skill at interpreting photos had earned him respect within the law enforcement community and beyond.

Monty took another belt of coffee. It was the middle of the night. If he remembered his dates right, his poor son had just gotten home from Europe a few hours ago. He was probably sprawled in his bed, dead to the world.

Okay, Monty would give in to his paternal instincts—for one night.

But tomorrow Lane was getting a phone call.

MORGAN JERKED AWAKE, plagued by that gnawing feeling in the pit of her stomach–the feeling that something was wrong, but not quite grasping what it was.

Abruptly, she remembered, and everything inside her went cold.

She sat up in bed, pulling up her knees and wrapping her arms around them. Arthur would set things in motion. And Detective Montgomery would be on this case like a bloodhound. Still, it wasn't enough. It was *her* parents who'd been shot to death, and she couldn't take a passive role in figuring out who'd really pulled the trigger.

There had to be something more she could do.

She scrambled out of bed, went back to the spare bedroom, where she'd left her parents' memorabilia. Maybe there was something here that could help her. The problem was, all the photos were personal, as were the mementos. And the newly discovered journals were her mother's. They dealt with plans to aid abused women, to offer them counseling and medical care.

That had been Lara's passion—and why Morgan had initiated the pro bono branch of Winshore. If she could help women who'd survived abusive relationships find healthy ones, she'd be contributing to her mother's dream.

As for her father's things, there were no notes, no old date books, nothing personal other than the framed photo of her and her mother, and the handsome pen set he'd kept on his desk.

However, along with the stack of photos her mother had collected were newspaper clippings, tributes to major cases that Jack Winter had prosecuted and won.

Carefully, Morgan laid out the articles. She'd been reading through every one word for word. The names and convictions didn't ring any bells. Then again, she'd been a child when they occurred. The fact was, any of those criminals could have had outside contacts or angry family members who'd "take care of" an A.D.A.

Bottom line—any of these articles could contain *the* kernel of a motive, one she didn't have the knowledge or expertise to spot.

Damn. Morgan sat back on her heels, swamped by a sense of frustration. She was grasping at straws. But at least she was grasping. No matter how worried about her Arthur and Elyse were, how insistent they were that she stay out of the line of fire, she couldn't. She had to take an active role in this investigation.

Her posture rigid with purpose, she refolded the articles and slid them into an envelope. She'd give them to Detective Montgomery. Maybe the names would mean something to him. If not, maybe they'd ring a bell with Charlie Denton, or with another attorney who'd been with the Manhattan D.A. at the time.

It was a potential avenue.

One she had to take.

SIX

As luck would have it, Hank Reynolds reached Lane before Monty did.
Lane had just finished his workout and was gulping down a bottle
of water when the phone rang.

He draped a towel across his shoulders and walked across the room he'd
converted into a home gym when he renovated the Upper East Side brownstone he'd bought from his brother-in-law, Blake. The place was great, roomy
enough for an extensive digital photo lab, a gym, and a media room.

With a quick glance at the caller ID, Lane picked up. "I must admit,
you've got balls," he informed his editor. "I know that *I* wouldn't mess with
me this soon after the ten days I just had and the bed I've barely slept in."

"Well, I would," Hank replied. "Plus, I know you. You always swear
you're going to be zoned for a week, then you're bored after eight hours.
You sound out of breath. Bet you're just back from the gym."

"Nope. I worked out at home." Lane grinned, polishing off the water.
"But you're right. I bounce back fast. And bed gets boring when you're by
yourself."

"Yeah, well, get out your BlackBerry, pick a name, and click for company. That'll solve your lonely bed problem by tomorrow."

Chuckling, Lane tossed aside his towel and sank down on the padded bench against the wall. "I think you're exaggerating just a little. But I like the image, so I won't argue. Now, tell me about this piece on Congressman Shore you're so hot to run. And skip the current political events update. I might globe-trot like a lunatic, but I do have Internet access."

"Fair enough. But there's a new scandal in the congressman's life—one that has nothing to do with politics."

Lane groaned. "This isn't going to be an exposé is it? I've heard all the rumors about his younger women. I've read the blogs on 'Arthur's Angels' claiming he has—and enjoys—the best-looking interns in D.C. I couldn't care less."

"This is *Time*, Lane, not the *Enquirer*. The piece has nothing to do with his sex life. It has to do with his best friends' murders, which happened seventeen years ago. Apparently, the killer who confessed didn't do it."

"What?" Lane's head came up. "Are you talking about Jack and Lara Winter—*those* murders?"

"The very same. There was a major screwup. It's just now surfaced. Who knows how many asses it'll come back to bite."

"My father worked that case. He was the lead detective."

"I know. So does the congressman. Which makes him twice as eager to have you be the one assigned to do this photo-essay piece."

"Why?" Lane was instantly wary. "I was sixteen when it happened. I wasn't privy to the case details. And I wouldn't pass them along if I had been."

"Take it easy. He's not looking for a mole. He doesn't need you to pry information out of your father. He hired him. Actually—it was the Winter's daughter who hired him. But it's the same difference. She's been Shore's ward since her parents died. Anyway, the point is, Shore is a busy man. Meeting with you about the article, while he touches base with your father about the case, will save him time and give him peace of mind."

"How's that?"

"Trust. He wants to have editorial approval over the photos and text we use to portray this angle."

"'This angle'—meaning the reopening of the Winter's homicides?"

"Yup. Given that Pete Montgomery is your father, Shore feels comfortable you'll respect his wishes and limit your coverage. In other words, you'll depict concern and intensity, but nothing more."

"He doesn't want to blast the system—at least not publicly, and not yet."

"Right. He's restricting his media appearances to discussions of his proposed legislation. Nothing on the Winters' murders. No interviews. No official news conference. He's deflecting any questions on what he considers to be a highly sensitive and personal issue. If pressed, he'll say only that all inquiries should be directed to the authorities. So, with regard to this subject, you're it."

Lane rubbed the back of his neck thoughtfully. "Fine, so I'm getting a preliminary exclusive. I'll hear the lowdown on the homicide investigation, take a few candids of him and my father." A pause. "We should do this at Lenny's. It'll add a familial touch. The shots will be homey but earnest. Not to mention that I'll be well fed. My father and I have been regulars at Lenny's since I was a kid."

"You and the rest of the five boroughs. But you're right; it's a good idea. The subtle reminder of the congressman's humble roots will play out well in contrast to the charismatic and successful politician he's become."

"I can pick Shore's brain about his proposed legislation there, too. Afterward, I'll take some shots of him among his constituents. Now, what about the thrill-seeking angle? Where does that come in?"

"I was wondering how long it would take for you to get to that," Hank replied wryly. He knew Lane, and how he'd be chomping at the bit to strike out on some high-risk adventures. "Not to worry. From what he said, the congressman has great plans in store for you. He mentioned heli-skiing in Colorado's San Juan Mountains, and skydiving in the Poconos—not the run-of-the-mill jumps you've done a dozen times, but some accelerated free falls. He'll tell you all about it tonight."

"Tonight?" Lane interrupted. "What's tonight?"

"Oh . . . that." Hank cleared his throat. "I sort of promised him you'd drop by his place for cocktails. He wants to run through the key points of the photo essay and go over the itinerary for next week."

"And he wants me to take some at-home shots of him and his family. That way the public will see for themselves how well the Shores are coping with this bomb that was dropped on them. At the same time it'll show their solidarity, and portray the congressman as a loving family man. He could use that now; it might just neutralize whatever negative impact those rag magazines are generating by running nonstop pieces on his extramarital affairs with twenty-five-year-old women."

"You got it."

Lane shrugged. "Works for me. I would have appreciated having a little more than six or seven hours' notice, but what the hell. What time does he want me?"

"Six o'clock."

"I'll be there."

MONTY SPENT THE entire morning poring over the file Gabelli had shoved under his door, updating notes and making a list of every possible ball the NYPD had dropped.

His analysis was interrupted first by the expected phone call from Arthur Shore and then by the less expected visit from Morgan Winter.

The congressman offered Monty every means of support he had and all the resources that were at his disposal. He said he'd be speaking to both the Manhattan and Brooklyn D.A.s, using his political clout to ensure their cooperation. And he requested weekly meetings between himself and Monty so he could act as a liaison between the official and unofficial investigations and, at the same time, protect Morgan from taking the brunt of this traumatic situation.

Their phone conversation was interrupted when Arthur got a return call from the Manhattan D.A., which he signed off to take—but not before arranging an initial meeting with Monty. Monday. Noon. At Lenny's. For lunch.

Barely had Monty agreed and hung up, when his doorbell rang. Morgan was standing on the front step, hands shoved in the pockets of her wool overcoat. She came in long enough to proffer an envelope of articles regarding convictions her father had won, then asked what else she could do.

Monty cleared his throat. "Look, Morgan, I'm going to be honest with you. I got my hands on a copy of the case file. It's not pretty. The details are gory and the photos are graphic. I'm not sure it's a good idea for you—"

"I want to see it." Her fists clenched and unclenched at her sides. "I *need* to see it."

He had to admire her pluck. He also understood the basis for her resolve. But he knew better than she what she was letting herself in for, and the emotional preparation she needed to face it.

"Here's the deal," he told her. "I need time to scrutinize every report, every interview, every lead. In the meantime, you need time to steel yourself. What you're about to see will be hell. So let's each take a couple of days to prep. When we're both ready, we'll walk through that door together. Just understand that that not only means digging up painful memories, but reliving a nightmare. I'm sorry—but there's no other way."

"I understand," she said tonelessly. "I knew what I was signing on for when I hired you."

"Maybe. Maybe not. I spoke with Congressman Shore. He's worried about you, and your ability to handle the repercussions."

"I know he is. And I'm grateful to him for it. But this is something I have to do. If that means living through more intense and frequent nightmares, so be it."

A terse nod. "Fair enough. Give me a day or two."

"Then we'll talk?"

"More than talk. We'll get into a detailed recap. You were there that night. Till now, you've been fixated on the scene you walked in on, the memory of discovering your parents' bodies and all the horror that went with it. Now you'll have to think beyond that. You might have seen or heard something that could amount to a clue. And that's just the beginning. I want to go over whatever you remember about the weeks leading up to the night of the murders. Telephone calls your parents received. Conversations. Arguments."

Morgan's eyes widened. "Detective, I was ten years old—hardly privy to the details of my parents' lives or their marriage."

"You'd be surprised. Kids pick up on a lot more than they realize."

"Where are you going with this?"

"To the same place you were going when you collected these newspaper clippings for me. Was this a random killing or was it personal? Your father was a prosecutor. He put away criminals. That means he made his fair share of enemies. Did one of them go after him and your mother for revenge? If so, there might have been warning signs. Signs your parents discussed, and you overheard."

"So back to square one." Morgan raked a hand through her hair. "With all our digging, this might still turn out to be a burglary gone bad."

"Yeah. It could. This personal vendetta angle could be a dead end. It's just as likely that some strung-out junky killed your parents for their cash and jewelry. But, no matter who's responsible, I plan to find him."

"*If* he's still alive."

"Even if he isn't, I want to find out who he is—was. We all need the closure."

PONDERING HIS OWN words after Morgan left, Monty admitted to himself that they were bullshit. There was only one way to find real closure. And that was to find that son of a bitch alive and make him pay. Anything less would leave a gaping void—for him and, more important, for Morgan.

He opened the file again, studied the photos of the murder scene. Christmas Eve, 1989. Lara and Jack Winter shot dead in the basement of a renovated building on Williams Avenue where Lara ran her women's abuse center.

The murders had taken place between 7:30 and 8 P.M. At the time, Lara and Jack had been there alone—except for Morgan, who'd begged to come along and help decorate for the center's first annual holiday party. They'd come straight from a Christmas Eve political bash for Arthur, hosted by Elyse's parents in their posh Park Avenue penthouse. Talk about a modern *Tale of Two Cities*—Manhattan at its most affluent and Brooklyn at its most indigent. But from what Monty had learned, the Winters' hearts had been far bigger than their egos.

And their reward? Being shot dead, left crumpled in pools of their own blood on a filthy, broken-up cement floor, only to be discovered by their ten-year-old daughter, who'd come down to see what was taking her parents so long to carry up the paper goods.

His gaze darting from one photo to the next, Monty reached for the phone and punched in a number on speed dial.

"Hey, Monty. Your ears must be burning," Lane greeted him.

"Huh?"

"My editor at *Time* and I were just talking about you. He told me you're working with Congressman Shore. That means you and I will be having lunch together on Monday. Pastrami on rye at our favorite deli—just like old times." Lane paused, cleared his throat roughly. "Actually, once Hank told me you were taking on the Winter case—*again*—I was going to give you a call, make sure you were okay. I know that investigation was a tough one for you. This news must have hit you hard."

"I'm fine." Monty frowned. Of his three kids, Lane had been the only one who'd been old enough, mature enough, to sense the parallel between the splintering of their own family and the wiping out of the Winters'. And Monty had sucked at hiding it from him, at protecting him from his father's inadequacies. Actually, he'd sucked at pretty much everything back then—everything but polishing off a six-pack and being a cop.

"Monty—you still there?"

"I'm here. I'm just confused. I spoke to Shore an hour ago. He didn't mention anything about your joining us on Monday. Then again, he didn't have time to. He had to grab a call from the D.A. He fired out the when and where for the meeting, and hung up."

"The where was my idea. Lenny's is a good meeting spot—it's home base for the congressman and good food for us. Why are you ticked off? Is my being there a problem?"

"That depends on why you're coming. It's sure as hell not about doing a magazine spread on the screwup surrounding the Winters' homicides, not when Shore is busting his ass to keep this low profile. So why would he want a photojournalist there?"

"Face time for him and media coverage for his bill. I'm covering the legendary congressman who's living on the edge again—professionally, stirring up conflict between different special-interest groups over this new legislation he's proposing; personally, striking out on brand-new thrill-seeking adventures. As for the shocker about the wrongful conviction in the Winters' homicides—let's say I'm being given the job of censoring what does and doesn't leak out about it."

"Clever thinking on Shore's part," Monty muttered. "Getting the best photojournalist in the business, who also just happens to be the son of the PI he hired. He gets skill and discretion all in one package. He also gets you stretched too damned thin for my purposes."

This time Lane reacted bluntly to his father's rankled tone. "Okay, Monty, spit it out. What's bugging you?"

"Time. How long will you be working on this photo essay?"

"A week, maybe ten days."

"No good. I need you on the crime-scene photos."

"Fine. You got me. I'll do whatever you need me to."

"Yeah, when? While you're jumping out of planes?"

"No. I don't do my best work when I'm free-falling." Lane blew out a breath. "Listen, Monty, give me a little credit. The minute Hank told me there was a glitch in the Winter convictions, and that you were involved in the investigation, I assumed you'd want me for the photo interpretations and image enhancement. My assignment for *Time* is based in New York. If my out-of-town time amounts to several days, it'll be a lot. Which means I'll be home almost every night, right here in my house with my state-of-the-art equipment."

"Right—your state-of-the-art equipment and your other twenty-five assignments."

"Not to worry. This one's top priority. Besides, I've got Jonah working for me now, remember? He can handle a lot of the routine work for my nonclassified projects. Which will free me up for the critical ones like yours. So why don't you swing by my place over the weekend and bring me up to speed. That way I'll have a better idea what I'm looking for. If there's anything in those photos that'll help lead you to the real killer, I'll find it."

"Okay." Monty was somewhat mollified, but still wound up—a state of mind that wasn't vanishing anytime soon. "What's your schedule?"

"I've got cocktails at the Shores' tonight. The congressman wants to brief me on next week's itinerary and adventures. Other than that, I'm flexible. Jet-lagged, but flexible."

"How was the trip?"

"Successful. Manic. Long."

Monty didn't push. He was well aware that some of Lane's assignments were government-sanctioned and that any discussions about them were off-limits. Still, there was something about Lane's tone this time that was different. It smacked of weariness, and maybe a hint of something Monty recognized from personal experience—something that had eventually made him walk away.

"You could use some time off," he remarked casually. "And I don't mean traveling on some godforsaken assignment, or jumping out of planes for the thrill of the plunge. I mean downtime. Chill-out time. I tell you what—why don't you spend Christmas up at the farm? Bring whoever you're dating these days. The whole family will be there—Mom and me, Devon and Blake, Merry . . . oh, and that law school kid she's seeing."

Lane chuckled. "His name's Keith. And he's a nice guy. Intelligent, self-assured enough to withstand your interrogations, and crazy about Merry."

"*Too* crazy about her. She's sweet, young, and trusting—way too naive to know what Keith has on his mind. But none of those traits apply to me. I know just what part of his body he's thinking with."

"So do I. And I'm no happier about it than you are. But Merry's not nearly as naive as you think. She's almost twenty-two. She's got a definite mind of her own. Besides, she's graduating from college in May. What are we going to do after that, lock her in her room?"

"Sounds good to me."

"Yeah." Lane found himself agreeing. "Me, too."

"In the meantime, what's-his-name, almost-attorney-at-law, is getting the guest room at the opposite end of the house."

"I never doubted it."

"So you'll come?"

Lane hesitated, but only for an instant. "Sure. Sounds great. A dose of home is just what I need."

"Think you'll be bored?" Monty asked drily. "A long weekend at the farm can't compare to cocktail hour at the Shores'."

"I'll manage."

"By the way, who's on the guest list tonight?"

"The congressman and his family, I assume."

"If Morgan Winter shows up, you can tell her you'll be analyzing the crime-scene photos for me. If not, keep it quiet. I'm not sure who, besides Arthur, she's sharing the details of this case with. I know she's close with his wife and daughter, but that doesn't mean she's giving them a blow-by-blow. And technically, Morgan is my client, and my work for her is confidential. So use your judgment."

"I will. As for Congressman Shore, I doubt the news that I'm on board would come as a shock to him. He knows my areas of expertise. And since he wants me at your lunch meeting Monday, he obviously expects me to be in on your discussion. You'll fill him in on the progress of the investigation, and I'll provide my analysis of the crime-scene photos firsthand. There's no conflict of interests, if that's what you're worried about. Shore opened this door himself. If anything, my *Time* assignment is his way of making sure I'm involved."

"I'm not worried. I'm sure you're right. Shore might not want this case publicized, but he does want it resolved. If he can maneuver you into taking part in my investigation—either by asking you directly or hoping I do—he'll be thrilled."

Still eyeing the photos, Monty brought the conversation to a close. "Anyway, I should call your mother, let her know you're home in one piece and that you'll be joining us for Christmas. That'll make her day. I'll skip the part about your playing daredevil with Congressman Shore next week—at least for now. She'll have plenty of time to start worrying about that on Monday."

"Good idea. Peace of mind is not something I offer Mom too often."

"That makes two of us. Living a risk-free life is not exactly my strong suit, either." Monty paused, then gruffly continued. "Listen, Lane, I'm glad you'll be working with me on this case. I'm getting the right guy this time.

I'm not walking away until I do. I don't expect you to fully understand, but—"

"I do understand," Lane interrupted in that tone that reminded Monty how wise beyond his years his son was. "And, Monty—I won't let you down."

SEVEN

Charlie Denton sat in his cluttered office at the Manhattan D.A.'s, watching the sun disappear behind the New York skyline. Another day. Another backlog of cases. And one monstrous problem that wasn't going away.

Congressman Shore hadn't wasted any time. By 10 A.M., the decks were cleared for Charlie's in-house investigation. Finding out who'd inherited Jack Winter's cases and what their status was—now and then. Checking with a handful of long-term employees whom Jack had worked with to see if they remembered anything. Even contacting Jack's former office staff— lawyers, paralegals, clericals—who'd long since left the D.A.'s office, to see if they recalled anything that might lead to the real killer.

What was that expression? The pigeons had come home to roost.

What had been a ticking bomb seventeen years ago was now a heat-seeking missile aimed at his head.

It wasn't just Arthur Shore. It was Morgan Winter, too.

Charlie swung his chair around, picked up the envelope Morgan had given him a half hour ago. It was filled with photocopied articles of her father's court victories. Morgan didn't recognize any of the felons' names. Charlie recognized all of them. One in particular made his skin crawl.

He wished he didn't have dinner plans tonight. But he did—with one of the women on his match list. Karly Something-or-other. The manager of a top New York modeling agency. He was taking her to La Grenouille, because they both loved French food. He was sure she'd be lovely, intelligent, and great company. But his mind would be on his work.

COCKTAIL HOUR AT the Shores' was more laid-back than Lane had expected.

He was met at the door by Arthur's petite, gracious wife, Elyse, who greeted Lane warmly. If the rumors were true about Arthur being frequently involved with women younger than his own daughter, it was hard to understand why. Elyse was attractive, vivacious, and as well toned as any twenty-five-year-old. She also had an innate refinement and class that went far deeper than any cosmetic surgery she might have had.

Then again, she came from money. Her father, Daniel Kellerman, was the CEO of Kellerman Development, Inc., a major real estate developer. It was no secret that he'd helped launch Arthur's political career. He'd made his new son-in-law corporate counsel of Kellerman Development right out of law school—a lucrative and high-visibility job that eased Arthur into the right professional and social circles. Between his own sharp mind and charisma, and his father-in-law's contacts and financial resources, Arthur had been elected first to the New York City Council, then the New York State Assembly, and finally the U.S. House of Representatives.

Elyse herself was an undeniable asset to her congressman husband, even in a setting as relaxed and homey as the one Lane walked into.

Dressed in an emerald-green velour Lacoste running suit, with her frosted blond hair cut fashionably short and wispy, Elyse invited Lane in, took his coat, and asked what he'd like to drink. Judging from the tomatoey color and consistency of the contents of her highball, Lane assumed her cocktail of choice was a Bloody Mary.

He quickly found out otherwise.

A loud whirring noise had been emanating from the kitchen since he'd arrived. A younger female voice called out, "Second round of tomato-carrot-celery juice, coming up."

Lane blinked as a pretty strawberry blond in her late twenties with the energy level of Road Runner burst out of the kitchen, carrying a pitcher of her homemade concoction. "Hi." She didn't miss a beat when she saw him standing with her mother. "You must be Lane Montgomery. I hope you're ready for the best combo of beta-carotene and lycopene you've ever tasted." She flourished a glass. "Can I pour you some?"

"Sure." Lane's lips twitched. "I'm guessing you're Jill."

"Guilty as charged."

"Don't let my daughter intimidate you." Congressman Shore strolled into the hallway, wearing a caramel-and-black-print crewneck sweater and black slacks. He stuck out his hand to shake Lane's. "We actually have normal drinks here, too—everything from a full liquor cabinet to beer to Diet Coke. So don't panic if you're not a health freak. Just speak up."

"Actually the juice sounds good," Lane replied, setting down his camera bag and taking the glass with a nod of thanks. "I'm always up for trying something new."

Arthur led Lane into the living room. The L-shaped sectional and matching armchair were sand-colored brushed twill with thick down cushions and sage-green throw pillows. The entire room had a cool, natural feel to it—Elyse's touch, Lane suspected.

"Have a seat," Arthur invited, gesturing toward the sofa.

Lane complied, taking a sample taste of his vegetable juice. "This is excellent," he called out to Jill, holding up his glass. It was, too. Refreshing, with a kick.

"Good—a man of taste." She gave him an enthusiastic thumbs-up. "I'll make more when Morgan gets here." With that, she glanced at her watch. "Where is she, anyway?"

"She called," Elyse supplied. "She said she had an errand to run and she'd be a few minutes late. She should be here anytime now." A flicker of concern crossed her face. "I hope she ate lunch. She hasn't had a decent meal in two days."

"This morning I coaxed half a muffin down her throat," Jill murmured.

"And I coaxed down the other half when I dropped by the office," Arthur added. "But you're right. She's not eating."

"Or sleeping," Jill added.

"I'll get the fruit-and-cheese platter." With a burst of nervous energy, Elyse headed to the kitchen. "We can start nibbling while we wait for Morgan." She returned a moment later, placing the platter on the coffee table and giving Lane a rueful, self-conscious look. "Forgive us for the familial worry. This is a difficult time."

"No apology necessary." Lane weighed his words carefully. "I can't begin to imagine how hard this must be. I'm sorry this whole painful chapter in your lives has to be dredged up again."

"So are we." Arthur spoke frankly, not mincing any words. "This news was a shock to us all. But the one hit hardest was Morgan. My goal is to protect her as much as possible—starting with our topics of conversation. Tonight, let's discuss lighter topics, like next week's itinerary. There'll be a time and place for getting into the nitty-gritty of the investigation."

"Understood." Lane nodded, hearing the message loud and clear. He had to respect the congressman's show of paternal protectiveness. "Speaking of next week's itinerary, I can't wait to hear what you have on tap for us."

Arthur relaxed, and a flicker of amusement lit his eyes. "You won't be disappointed. As I recall, you were no slouch when we did that *Sports Illustrated* spread. You were quite the rock climber and bungee jumper. Are you still in top shape?"

"Better than that." A corner of Lane's mouth lifted. "I've been doing double duty at the gym so I can keep up with you."

"You can try." A broad grin. "How good are you on skis?"

"I took my first lesson when I was six. I've tackled pretty much every expert slope in the U.S., plus a handful in the French, Swiss, and Austrian Alps. This year, I was thinking of hitting the Canadian Rockies, going straight to British Columbia and taking on Whistler/Blackcomb's legendary vertical drop."

"Excellent. After next week, you'll have a new experience to add to that impressive list."

"Hank mentioned heli-skiing." Lane leaned forward eagerly. "I've always wanted to try it. Fill me in."

Before Arthur could respond, there was the sound of a key turning in the lock, and the apartment door swung open.

"Hi, it's me." A woman's voice, one that presumably belonged to Morgan Winter, drifted in from the hall, followed by the muffled sounds of her shrugging off her coat and hanging it up. "I hope I didn't hold things up."

"Nope," Jill called back. "I just made more juice, and Mom put out the food. We're about to hear what wild adventures Dad has planned for next week. So come on in and join us."

"Coming." The *click-click* of heels on the tile floor, and then a pause as she reached the entrance to the living room. "Here I am."

Lane wasn't quite sure what he was expecting, but it wasn't the fine-boned brunette who walked in. Shoulder-length hair. Pale green eyes. Fine features and delicate build that conveyed fragility. But with a take-charge self-assurance that completely contradicted the vulnerable image. No, actually it enhanced it. Sensitivity and strength, composure and fire, with a depth and expressiveness in her eyes that spoke of compassion and pain.

"Hauntingly beautiful" was the term that sprang to mind.

Rising to his feet, Lane watched her approach him.

"Hi. Morgan Winter," she introduced herself. She extended her hand, shook his in a firm, businesslike handshake.

"Nice to meet you," he replied. "Lane Montgomery."

"I see the resemblance to your father."

"Really?" One brow rose. "Tall, dark, and handsome, or scary, overbearing, and fashion-impaired?"

"Hmm." Morgan's lips twitched. "Tough choice. How about tall, dark, and dynamic?"

"Safe. Where do the other adjectives factor in?"

Her gaze skimmed over him, taking in his dark blue sweater and khaki slacks. "Scary—no. Overbearing—possibly. Handsome—in the eyes of the beholder. Fashion-impaired? Definitely not." She raised her chin, met his gaze. "How was that?"

"Honest. Straightforward but tactful." He glanced from her to Jill and back. "Two beautiful, intelligent women—one, charming and intuitive, the other vivacious and enthusiastic. It's a pretty unbeatable combination. I can see why clients flock to your agency."

"Maybe you should be one of them," Jill suggested. "You're single. Unless you already have a significant other, why don't you make an appointment and find out just how good Winshore is?"

Morgan bit back her laughter at the reaction Lane didn't have time to disguise. "Now *that's* an expression I've seen a dozen times before. And it's been wrong every single time."

"What expression?"

"The one that says, 'Who me? Superstud? I don't need a social agency. I'm doing just fine on my own.'"

"Well, now that you mention it . . ."

"Now that I mention it, you have no lack of success with women and no self-esteem problems?" Morgan's lips curved. "That's obvious. And, for what it's worth, I agree with you. For the kind of relationships you have in mind, you're better off on your own. Someday, when you're looking for a meaningful relationship, one that requires a true partner, give us a call."

Lane felt like he'd been issued two challenges in the past five minutes. One from Congressman Shore, and the other from Morgan Winter. He wasn't sure which was more of an adrenaline rush.

This evening was turning out to be a lot more stimulating than he'd expected.

"Fair enough." He tipped his glass of vegetable juice to Morgan and to Jill. "I'll keep that offer in mind. Be sure to give me a business card before I leave."

"I'll do that." Morgan's gaze shifted to Elyse, who'd filled a plate with fruit and cheese and was handing it to her. "Thank you." She looked like she wanted to refuse the snack, but saw how anxious Elyse was, and took it. "This looks great."

"It should," Arthur commented drily. "It's probably the first thing you've put in your mouth since that muffin you ate at noon."

Morgan gave a guilty shrug. "It's been one of those days. Crazy busy."

"Then you shouldn't have stopped to run an errand on the way here," Elyse scolded. "You're exhausted. It could have waited."

"No, actually it couldn't have." Morgan sank down onto the sofa and nibbled at a slice of pineapple. "I stopped by the Manhattan D.A.'s office. I wanted them to have copies of those newspaper clippings. I gave the originals to Detective Montgomery." She sent a curious glance in Lane's direction. "Did Arthur tell you I hired your father?"

Lane could feel the congressman's probing stare, a reminder not to get into anything too heavy.

"He mentioned it, yes." Lane kept his answer short and sweet. "Although I'm sorry it's necessary." He resettled himself on the sofa, accepting the plate of fruit Elyse offered him with a murmur of thanks. "In any case, let me assure you, you're in very capable hands. Nothing gets by Monty. Believe me, I know from personal experience. I didn't get away with squat, not as a kid or as a teenager. He was always one step ahead of me."

"Something tells me you've made up for that since then," Morgan commented wryly.

"Maybe. But we still do our share of butting heads."

"He's your father," Jill summed up. "That comes with the territory."

"Especially when the two of you are a lot alike." Morgan studied Lane thoughtfully. "Which I get the feeling is the case with you and Detective Montgomery."

"You're right. It is." Lane arched a teasing, quizzical brow at Morgan. "Did I just help or hurt my image?"

Morgan didn't respond with lighthearted banter. She didn't even smile. Instead, she stared down at her plate, a strained expression tightening her features. "I can't say enough about your father. Once upon a time he was a lifeline for me. I'm praying he will be again."

Lane wanted to kick himself for triggering her reaction. "He will be," he stated flatly. "Monty won't walk away until he's restored your peace of mind. Count on it."

"I am." Morgan's chin came up, and the strained look receded—with an effort. "You have no idea how much."

"I have an idea," Elyse cut in. "Jill, Morgan, and I have a few final details to go over for Winshore's holiday party. Why don't we go into the den and do that while you gentlemen go over whatever reckless adventures you're planning for next week." She shuddered. "Just listening to the itinerary makes my insides twist. I'm better off making myself scarce."

"Good idea." Arthur agreed right away. "You ladies do your thing. We'll do ours. Then afterward, Lane can take a few family shots, and we'll call it an evening. I've still got a dozen phone calls to return, and a late dinner meeting to attend."

"A dinner meeting?" Elyse looked startled. "When did that happen? I thought you were eating with us."

"I'd planned to. But your father called a couple of hours ago. He set up this meeting, and not easily. He had to accommodate the schedules of four busy CEOs. This was the one night they could all free up. So tonight it is."

"CEOs," Lane repeated thoughtfully. "Of banks?"

A measured look. "Banks and corporations. Why?"

"Because I don't envy you." The news correspondent in Lane was blunt. "The financial industry has been key to your political success. Now you have to persuade them to swallow a bill that's going to cost them big bucks. This is bound to be a tough meeting."

"Probably." Rather than being put off, Arthur gave an accepting shrug. "But I believe strongly in my legislation. I believe it'll benefit everyone in the long run. It's my job to get that point across."

"I wish you luck."

"I also have Daniel Kellerman in my corner. I won't pretend to minimize what a strong ally he is."

"In other words, he'll have laid the groundwork."

"Exactly. So, all in all, I expect the dinner to be a success."

"Speaking of Grandpa, send him my love." Jill edged a quick glance at her mother, who was still clearly upset about her husband's unexpected vanishing act. "This is Mom's, Morgan's, and my chance to try that new Thai restaurant. We'll order takeout and finish up whatever party planning we don't get to now."

"This holiday party sounds like it's going to be quite an event," Lane commented.

"It will be." Jill gave him a broad grin. "Why don't you come? It's the nineteenth, at seven P.M., at Mom's gym. It just so happens I have a few extra invitations in my purse." She rummaged through her Coach bag and produced a tastefully calligraphied invitation. "Here you go." She handed it to him. "It'll be good for you. You can see what you're missing by not registering with Winshore."

Lane glanced down at the gold lettering. Normally, he hated these kind of parties. They were frivolous and shallow, filled with phony people and bullshit conversation.

He was still on the fence when he happened to glance up and see Morgan watching him from the opposite end of the sofa. Gone was the vulnerability she'd exuded a few minutes ago. Now her arms were folded across her breasts, and there was a knowing gleam in her eye.

"You were about to refuse?" she supplied helpfully.

"Was I?"

"Mm-hmm."

"And you were about to convince me otherwise?"

Her lips twitched. "Absolutely. Why not go for it? It's a weekday evening, too late for cocktails and a quickie, too early for nightcaps and bed. The food will be incredible, the eggnog homemade, and if the people are as vapid as you're anticipating, you can always use the time to do a total body workout. It is, after all, a gym—with the finest fitness equipment in all of Manhattan."

Lane couldn't help but chuckle. "You drive a hard bargain."

"No bargain. The only one who stands to win, or lose, is you."

Okay, that did it. This was a different kind of adrenaline rush—one he was no sooner walking away from than he did any other.

"You're right," he conceded, tucking the invitation into his pants pocket. She'd left the ball in his court. He was playing it. "It sounds great. Thank you for the invite. I'll be there."

EIGHT

Karly Fontaine was truly enjoying herself. The food at La Grenouille was superb, the man across the table from her was a good-looking, successful attorney, and the conversation was stimulating.

Once again, Morgan had chosen well. That young woman really knew her stuff. Her matchmaking instincts were uncanny.

"More wine?" Charlie Denton was asking.

"That would be lovely, thank you." Karly smiled as her date poured another half glass of Cab into her goblet. He'd been attentive all evening, an excellent listener and good conversationalist. She did get the sense that he was tired and somewhat stressed, but she didn't hold that against him. She herself was pretty wiped out, and managing models paled in comparison to prosecuting criminals. She didn't even want to envision some of the grisly cases he must have on his plate.

It quickly became clear that he didn't want to discuss his work. Whether that was because of confidentiality issues or simply because he wanted to escape, she took the hint and let the subject drop. Her line of work was much more conducive to casual chitchat, so she wasn't surprised when he veered the conversation in that direction. She told him about the Lairman Modeling Agency, and about how she went from model to manager at their L.A. headquarters, then relocated here three months ago to manage their newly expanded Manhattan branch.

Charlie seemed fascinated. He interlaced his fingers and leaned forward to listen. Well into the discussion, his gaze began to stray to a point over Karly's left shoulder, then rapidly returned to focus on her. At first, she thought he might be seeking out the waiter to inquire about dessert and coffee. But when no waiter appeared and Charlie's distraction became increasingly evident, Karly began to feel curious, and yes, insecure.

If it was some ex-girlfriend or a random acquaintance, that was one thing. But if a younger, prettier woman had caught his eye, that would bother her—a lot. Beauty was her business. She'd devoted her life to it. She prided herself on her face and figure, not to mention her exceptional flair for fashion. Whether or not she ended up wanting Charlie Denton was irrelevant. It would be ego deflating to think he was eyeing another woman during their date.

"Charlie?" She gave him a bright smile, easing back her chair. "Would you mind ordering some coffee? I'm going to find the ladies' room."

"Of course." He rose quickly to his feet and went around to pull her chair back the rest of the way.

"Thank you." Her smile still intact, she scooped up her purse and rose, all long legs and shimmering red-gold hair. She turned around, glancing in the direction Charlie's gaze had been straying.

She didn't see what she'd expected to. Not by a long shot.

The restaurant was fairly quiet, since the hour had gotten late. The only occupied table in that section was a large round one, nestled in the corner. Not one of the six occupants was female. They were all older men, probably in their late fifties or early sixties. Based upon the way the maître d' was hovering around their table and the conservative, expensive suits they wore, they were obviously VIPs. So it was a power dinner. Nothing unusual about that.

She was about to avert her gaze, when it settled on the man who was doing the talking at the moment, and recognition struck. She might have been in New York only since September, but that particular man had been making headlines a lot longer than that. She'd just seen his photo in the *Enquirer,* along with a sordid story about him and some twenty-four-year-old woman who'd come and gone from his staff with the speed of lightning, after they'd allegedly been spotted together in a lip-lock behind some Washington hotel.

Her brows rose, and she continued on her way to the ladies' room. But halfway there, she glanced back over her shoulder.

Charlie Denton's stare was aimed directly at Congressman Shore.

ACROSS THE ROOM and unaware he was being scrutinized, Arthur sliced his duck á l'orange, listening as his father-in-law made a few strong points about his proposed legislation to the four dubious businessmen who were their guests.

"Let's not play semantics, gentlemen." Daniel Kellerman put down his glass of wine as he spoke. "The way I see it, you'll all be thanking Arthur for writing a bill that considers the impact on your industries. So we'll be expecting your support."

The four CEOs exchanged glances. "Okay, we get it."

"I thought you would."

ELYSE WAS LYING in bed, staring at the ceiling, when she heard the front door open, then quietly shut. She glanced at the illuminated numbers on her alarm clock: 1:15. Way too late for La Grenouille to be open on a weeknight.

From out in the hall, the familiar late-night sounds echoed—Arthur hanging up his coat, shutting the closet door, and locking up for the night. Then his footsteps. He didn't come straight to the bedroom, but stopped off in the den, no doubt to make his usual late-night phone calls.

Elyse rolled onto her side, feeling none of the pain she once had, only emptiness and resignation. When had that transition occurred? she wondered. When had caring become weariness, and then just a hollow void?

Sometime between then and now.

So much had happened. So much that had complicated everything, sapped away her emotional reserve. It had been hard enough in the beginning, but the facade had taken its toll. The lie she was living was starting to suck the life out of her.

Idly, she thought back to college, to the days when Lara was alive and the two of them had the bold dreams of youth. Both of them were going to restore and revitalize humanity—Lara, emotionally and psychologically; she, physically and nutritionally. Somewhere along the way, Jack and Arthur had entered the picture. But they'd only augmented the dreams, made them bigger. Never detracting, only enhancing.

That had been a lifetime ago.

Bonds had been forged, vows taken. Careers took off. Then, just three months apart, Jill and Morgan were born. It was a time of joy. The dreams of the Winters and the Shores should have continued to grow.

They didn't.

Priorities shifted. Everything started crumbling. Elyse had clung to denial as long as she could. Eventually, that stopped working. So she'd moved on to keeping up appearances.

Tragedy struck, and the world unraveled.

Pressing her lips together, Elyse rolled onto her other side, just as the bedroom door opened a crack and Arthur slipped in. He moved around the room quietly, changing into the gym shorts he wore to bed, then disappearing into the bathroom to wash up.

Ten minutes later, he came to bed. He eased between the sheets with as little motion as possible.

As usual, he didn't want to awaken her.

Most of the time, she pretended he hadn't.

Tonight was different.

"I'm up." Elyse spoke in a low monotone, watching her husband's profile. Even in the dark, she could see his jaw tighten.

"I didn't mean to disturb you," he told her.

"Of course not. Who was she this time?"

Arthur blew out an impatient breath. "You know where I was, Elyse. I was with your father."

"Dinner till one? La Grenouille must have extended their hours."

"No, dinner till eleven. Then a drink and a meeting recap with your father."

"Who'll, no doubt, vouch for you." A bitter smile. "After all, what's more important, his daughter or the political favors he gets from his high-ranking son-in-law?"

With an exasperated grunt, Arthur slid down until he was supine, his arms folded beneath his head. "I'm not having this conversation again, Elyse. It's getting old. Besides, I'm wiped. It's late."

"*Very* late," Elyse agreed, meaning a lot more than the hour.

"Then let's call it a night. I've been 'on' for hours."

"And you're drained and exhausted. Well, so am I." Elyse paused, struggling for control. "More so than you can imagine." Despite her efforts, her voice quavered, tears underscoring her words.

Arthur wasn't unaffected. He twisted around, propping himself on his elbow and gazing down at his wife. "Don't cry, Lyssie," he murmured, his knuckles caressing her cheek. "We've got so much going on. Let's not compound the tension by bickering over nonsense." He bent down, pressed his lips to her shoulder. "We have to be there for Morgan. She's going through hell. So are we. There's a lot at stake. Let's turn toward each other, not away."

Two tears slid down Elyse's cheeks, and she choked back a sob. "I want that. You know I do."

"Well, so do I." Arthur drew her into his arms, tipping up her chin and giving her that intimate look that still melted her insides and reminded her how things between them had once been.

How they sometimes still were.

"Come here," he murmured, as if reading her mind. His hands glided under her nightgown and over the curves of her body. "Let me make it better."

Elyse was already responding, tugging off her nightgown as Arthur worked free of his shorts, then pulled her under him. She closed her eyes and let the pleasure swamp her, blotting out the pain of what had been, what would be.

She didn't lie to herself. This wasn't just sexual. Not for her. Emotionally detached as she'd learned to be, she still loved her husband fiercely. She would—and had—done anything for him.

Arthur made love to her as only he could, with an expertise, passion, and intensity that made her feel like she was the only woman in the world.

And for those moments, that night, she was.

MONTY PUNCHED ANOTHER pillow until it was plumped up just the way he liked it. Then he shoved it behind his head, wedging it between himself and the headboard. With a grunt of frustration, he continued scribbling down names and notes, all stemming from the pile of newspaper clippings Morgan had given him earlier that day. He'd made a shitload of phone calls after she left, called in some favors, and gotten piles of information.

Currently, he was delving into Carl Angelo and all his slimy contacts, past and present. Angelo was a high-stakes drugs and weapons dealer, a scumbag who'd been indirectly responsible for the deaths of countless people, and whom Jack Winter had put away two months before he and Lara were murdered.

There was an interesting tie-in here. One that had surprised him. Tomorrow morning he'd follow up on it, peel back every layer to see if there was something solid at the core. If it materialized into a real lead, he'd mention it in the update he'd be delivering to Congressman Shore on Monday.

"Hey." Sally sat up in bed, blinking as she reached over to rub Monty's arm. "Aren't you ever planning on turning off that light and getting some sleep?"

He angled his head toward her, and his features softened at the sight of her, all wrapped up in the down comforter with just her bare shoulders peeking out. Tenderly, he rumpled her already-tousled hair, brushing it around to the nape of her neck. Her skin was warm from sleep, and she looked sated and drowsy from their earlier lovemaking.

"You dozed off, so I was getting a little work done. I'll turn in." He shoved the papers into the file and put it on his night table. Then he clicked off the lamp, sliding down in the bed and settling Sally against him, her head on his chest.

"It's the Winter case," she stated. "It's hitting you harder than even you expected."

"Yeah." Frowning, Monty stared up at the ceiling. "And not just because of the compassion I feel for Morgan Winter, or the guilt I'm dealing with knowing I screwed up and let the real killer get away. It's more selfish and personal than that. This investigation is taking me back to the lowest point in my life—a point I try hard to forget."

"I know," Sally acknowledged softly. "But life doesn't always work that way. Sometimes it just drags us back to the past whether or not we want to go."

"That much I get. What I don't get is why I let our family fall apart."

"Our family didn't fall apart, Pete. *We* did. And neither of us *let* it happen. We made a decision. At that time, we each needed such different things. Our priorities were diametrically opposed. Our relationship was a mess. Ending the marriage was the only answer at the time. But we all survived. You and I even found our way back to each other."

"That part I'm grateful as hell for." He blew out a breath. "As for the rest, don't let me off the hook so easily. It wasn't quite that simple. Those different priorities existed because I was an idiot. I really believed I could give my all to the force and still be what you and the kids needed. Even after the split, I told myself I could compartmentalize my life and make it all work. It didn't. And the kids took the major hit."

"Kids always get hurt the most in a divorce," Sally agreed. "On the other hand, they also get hurt living in an atmosphere of constant stress and arguing."

"That's what the textbooks say." Monty's retort was dry. "Who knows if they're right. In the meantime, I bought the idea that I could be a visiting father and still keep that same tight bond the kids and I always shared. Talk about a farce. Lane couldn't wait to leave for college. Then he moved to the other side of the country and jumped headfirst into a thrill-a-minute, no-personal-ties career. He's too goddamned much like me, and I can't do a thing about it."

"Pete . . ."

"Then there's Devon. She ping-ponged back and forth between you and me, torn with guilt over where her love and her loyalties belonged. And Merry? She hadn't even started kindergarten. She understood zip about why I left. In her mind, her daddy had abandoned her. She reacted by shutting me out. It's only now that she's starting to come around. The whole situation sucked."

"You're right. It did," Sally surprised him by saying. "But not just for the kids. For you. I watched your face every time you brought them home. Living apart from them was killing you."

Monty swallowed. "I never knew you could miss anyone like that; like a piece of you had been ripped out. I became more of a machine than a human being. I worked, I drank, and I made myself emotionally numb."

"No, you didn't." Sally twisted around to gaze up at him. "First of all, stop making it sound like you abandoned the kids. You didn't. Your door—and your heart—were always open, whether or not you realized it. As for desensitizing yourself of all feeling, that's bull. Why do you think you were able to give so much to Morgan Winter? You channeled all that emotional energy you claim not to have had into empathy for her. Look at the good that came out of it. Because of the way you identified with her sense of isolation and loss, she pulled through a tragedy that might otherwise have destroyed her."

With a disbelieving shake of his head, Monty studied his wife. "How do you do it? After all these years, all we've been through, you still manage to find a silver lining in every situation. The way you view life, with such upbeat idealism—it never ceases to amaze me."

Sally's eyes twinkled. "That's why you fell in love with me, remember? You always said I was the perfect counterpart for a cynical cop."

"Damn straight. I was right. And, at times like these, I need all the idealism I can get."

All teasing vanished. "You'll solve the case, Pete. I know you will. Just invest your energy into making that happen. Making peace with the past will come naturally, and in its own time."

"In other words, fix what's in my power to fix and leave the rest alone."

"Don't leave it, learn from it. Savor what you have, and what you've rediscovered." She bent down, pressed her lips gently to his. "Start by telling me you love me. Then let that overactive mind of yours get some sleep so you can tackle the world in the morning. Think you can manage that?"

He gave her a hard squeeze, then pressed her closer to his side. "Yeah," he murmured, burying his lips in her hair. "Piece of cake."

NINE

The problem with the weekend was that it gave Morgan too much time to think.

Saturday morning was spoken for. She had a 9 A.M. session with Dr. Bloom. Then she arrived home to find several messages from her friends, suggesting they get together. But she wasn't in the mood. Even Jill couldn't coax her out.

Instead, Morgan spent most of Saturday going through her parents' things again. She realized she was grasping at straws, but she couldn't get past the hope that she might stumble on some sort of clue, something that could point them in the right direction.

All she succeeded in doing was driving herself crazy, and triggering waves of nostalgia by poring over old photos.

She finally settled on something positive—her mother's journal. Reading through it gave her a sense of connection. It also provided insight into the branch of Winshore she was dedicating to her mother's memory.

A great number of Lara's entries referred to Healthy Healing, a women's counseling center not far from the Brooklyn shelter Lara had run. Barbara Stevens, Healthy Healing's main psychologist and a close colleague of Lara's, was a name that came up again and again—no surprise, given how closely and often they had worked together.

A lump forming in her throat, Morgan studied her mother's handwriting—the flowing letters, the achingly familiar use of circles to dot her *i*'s. There was so much she remembered, yet so much she'd never learn. She'd give anything to know her mother now that she herself was an adult, mature enough to build a friendship with a woman capable of bringing so much richness to life.

Her gaze settled on Barbara's name, and on impulse, Morgan picked up the phone, punching in Healthy Healing's phone number. It was Saturday. She'd probably get voice mail, in which case she'd request a weekday appointment.

To her surprise, the receptionist answered and told her that Barbara was in. She asked for Morgan's name, then offered to put the call through.

Morgan jumped at the opportunity. She repeated her name to the receptionist and asked if Barbara had a few minutes to see her today. She might not be able to solve her parents' homicides, but she could do something to feel closer to them. And maybe, in the process, she'd pick up a scrap of information that would help the investigation. Maybe her mother had mentioned something to Barbara in those final days, something seemingly innocuous that referred to one of her father's current cases, or a previous case in which a convicted felon had resurfaced and was harassing him.

It was worth a shot. And, even if it yielded nothing, it would give her a chance to meet a woman who'd meant a great deal to her mother, and to hear personal stories about Lara.

Barbara had time to see her, and a half hour later Morgan buttoned her coat and left her brownstone, Metrocard in hand.

SEVEN BLOCKS AWAY, Monty settled himself on Lane's living room sofa, plopping the Winter file down beside him. He wanted to hear all about Lane's meeting last night with Arthur Shore. But first things first.

Taking a belt of the coffee his son had brewed, he leaned over the rect-

angular cherrywood coffee table and laid out the twenty crime-scene photos, arranging them directly in front of his son. "I called Puzzle Palace
about the negatives," he informed Lane. "They're working on digging them
out."

The term "Puzzle Palace" needed no further explanation. There wasn't
an insider in the department who didn't use that nickname for the NYPD's
headquarters at One Police Plaza in lower Manhattan.

"Any time frame?" Lane asked.

"With enough pressure, I'll have them for you on Monday. In the
meantime, take a look at these." He pointed.

Lane perched on the edge of the sofa and hunched forward, studying
the shots. "Not bad," he muttered. "A few photos of the gunshot wounds
are a little overexposed. Probably too much flash. Nothing I can't compen-
sate for." He continued his scrutiny. "Okay, talk to me about what you
found when you arrived at the scene. Describe everything I'm looking at.
Later, we'll get to what I'm looking *for*."

The question was standard—business as usual when Lane and Monty
worked together.

"The crime took place in the basement of a shitty building on Williams
Avenue in Brooklyn," Monty began. "You can see for yourself—broken cement floor, chipped walls; your basic dump. The row of photos closest to
you was taken first, before anything was touched or either of the bodies
moved." Monty pointed to the ten photographs in question. "There were
three shell casings from a Walther PPK found, which ballistics matched up
with the two bullets in Jack Winter and the one bullet in his wife. Jack was
shot execution style—facedown, two bullets to the back of his head. There
are obvious signs of a struggle; overturned chairs, a scattered stack of two-
by-fours, construction buckets knocked around. Lara Winter was shot once
in the side."

"That's why there's so much blood and organ damage." Lane was studying the close-up photos of Lara's body and the scaled photo of her bullet
wound.

"Yeah, the perp did a good job of blowing out her insides. Judging from
her position—twisted to the right with that two-by-four next to her
body—she tried to defend herself. He shot her while she was swinging."

Monty indicated the wood board lying a few feet away from Lara's crumpled body. "Her fingerprints were on the two-by-four. My guess is she grabbed the board either to try stopping the guy from waling on her husband, or to fend him off when he turned the gun on her. The bullet struck her from about ten feet away. Jack was shot at a much closer range."

Lane pursed his lips, glancing from the initial photos to the others, taken after the bodies had been shifted and photographed from other angles. "A struggle? I'd say there was more of a knock-down, drag-out fight. Jack Winter's face is a mess."

"That's misleading. I'm sure he and the perp exchanged punches, but most of the gashes and gouged-out holes you see on his face came from his impact with the floor. Like I said, the place was a dump—broken chunks of cement, stones, pieces of wood, you name it. The M.E. found a contusion on the left side of Jack's head; the imprint was from the Walther PPK. So Jack must have lunged at the perp, catching him off guard. The perp would instinctively take his first swing while he was still clutching the gun, so it clipped Jack's head, then went flying. They fought. At some point Jack either fell or was shoved down on his face. The perp pinned him down, recovered the gun, and shot him."

"Execution style—that's why you thought this was personal," Lane mused.

"It usually is, with that scenario. On the other hand, could it have been coincidental? A robbery gone bad? Sure." Monty gave a grunt of disgust. "What else can I tell you? Judging by the angle and shape of the contusion and the fact that it was on the left side of Jack's head, we know the perp was right-handed—just like ninety percent of the rest of the world."

"And sometime during this struggle, Lara tried to save her husband and/or herself by grabbing the two-by-four and swinging at the assailant."

"Getting herself shot to death in the process."

"What about the gun? Was it ever recovered?"

"Nope. Of course, Schiller claimed to have dumped it in the river. But since his confession was bogus, so was his story about the murder weapon. So where the gun is now is anyone's guess."

Lane acknowledged that with a nod. "Moving on, we have blood splatter and blood on the victims' clothing. Jewelry and wallets missing. What about fingerprints? Did you find any that were distinguishable?"

"Just the victims'. And even those were smudged, other than the ones on the two-by-four, which were definitely Lara's. There were a bunch of footprints, most too blurry to make out. Remember, it was cold and snowy that December. The shelter was heated. Which meant we found lots of melted snow puddles, and lots of rats. Not exactly the best conditions for pulling physical evidence. The few footprints we could make out—not counting the victims'—belonged to a size-ten men's Dunham Waffle Stomper. A popular men's shoe size, and a popular hiking boot. Plus no guarantee it belonged to the perp." Monty grimaced. "What better, more ironic proof than the fact that Nate Schiller owned a pair."

"Talk about being screwed," Lane muttered. "There you were, dead in the water again."

"Huh?" Monty arched a quizzical brow.

Lane inclined his head, regarding his father with that wise, probing look. "You just couldn't catch a break. No wonder you were so pissed off."

"I'm not following."

"I was sixteen, Monty. I remember. You were never on board with the theory that Schiller did it. Not really. I heard you on the phone—with your precinct, with the D.A., with everyone involved with the case. I remember you kept repeating that the pieces just didn't fit. Something felt off. I didn't get the whole picture; not then. But now, hearing the lack of tangible evidence, I can imagine how frustrated you felt. The D.A. had nothing but Schiller's confession and pressure to solve the case. You had a gut feeling that contradicted both. Too bad they didn't listen."

Monty leaned back against the sofa cushion, folding his arms across his chest, his forehead creased in surprise. "I never realized you were so plugged into my work."

It was Lane's turn to look surprised. "You've got to be kidding. You knew how much I looked up to you."

"Yeah, but like you said, you were sixteen. We barely saw each other, even on our scheduled weekends. You were either on a ski trip or with a girl. I didn't have the slightest idea you listened to my phone calls, or paid attention to my caseload."

"Paid attention?" A corner of Lane's mouth lifted. "I hung on every word. You were one hell of a role model."

"I was a jackass." Monty jumped on the chance to speak his piece. "It took me half a lifetime to realize what was important. Don't emulate me, not in those ways."

"It's a little late, Monty." Lane gave an offhand shrug. "I am who I am. But don't be so hard on yourself. You were a great father. You still are. Pig-headed as hell, but great. How about taking some advice from your adult son? Stop viewing things in such a binary fashion. If I've learned any-thing from my career, it's that very little is black-and-white. Images, photographs—it's all about shades of gray. And since life imitates art . . . well, you get the drift."

"Yeah." Monty felt a tremendous surge of pride at the man his son had become. "I get the drift. I'll try to bear it in mind." He cleared his throat, reverting to the original topic. "So, is that everything you need to know about the crime-scene photos?"

"For now. I've got lots to work with. The bodies. The blood splatters. The basement. The exterior of the building. Once I get the negatives, I'll scan them all into my computer. Then I'll bust my ass until I find some-thing to show you. Something that'll help you put the real killer away."

"That's what I want to hear. And not just for my sake."

"Right." Lane lowered his gaze, staring at the rug. "I met Morgan Winter last night. I see why you feel for her. It's obvious she's going through hell."

"Did you tell her you're working with me?"

"No. Before she showed up, Congressman Shore specifically asked me to steer clear of the subject. As it is, Morgan's pretty obsessed with this in-vestigation. The reason she was late getting to the Shores was that she stopped by the D.A.'s office to drop off copies of some newspapers clippings. But you already know that. She said she'd given you the originals."

A nod. "They're articles about her father's more noteworthy arrests. I've dug up some pretty interesting facts from them—some of which I'll need to clarify with Congressman Shore at Monday's meeting."

"Okay, now you've aroused my curiosity. Anything you can run by me now?"

Monty got that intense homicide-detective look. "Jack Winter put away a big-time drug and weapons dealer named Carl Angelo a few months before the murders. Angelo had quite an entourage on his payroll over the years. I did some research, going way back. Thirty years ago, Angelo hired a twenty-six-year-old piece of street scum to transport hot guns for him. The guy was caught in the act and arrested. The charges were dropped. The file is sealed."

"Someone cut a deal."

"Sure looks that way. And this scum and Jack Winter must have built a long-term relationship, one that included testifying against Angelo at his trial."

"Okay, so you're figuring the guy was a confidential informer."

"Had to be. If he wasn't a CI, why would they drop the charges and seal the file? And why would he be testifying against Angelo thirteen years later? I plan on getting hold of the accusatory instrument read at Angelo's arraignment. Plus, if this CI really *was* a CI, and Winter needed him for Angelo's arrest, then there's a master file somewhere with his forms and registration number. I plan on getting my hands on that, too."

"Matching a name with a CI registration number is a tall order. Especially in the D.A.'s office."

"Not to worry. Even though those control officers are determined to protect their informers' identities, I've got my contacts. I've also got Congressman Shore's leverage. In the meantime, I'll start out the easy way. I'll call the Central Clerk's Office and have them dig the Angelo case file out of storage. That's a matter of public record. I'll go over the trial transcript with a fine-tooth comb. When I find the witness testimony I'm looking for, that's when I'll call in my favors from the D.A. I'll get a copy of this CI's documents, or at least a couple of forms with his registration number, some basic info, and some dates on them. I'll compare the details there with the details of his testimony. Believe me, I'll be able to figure out if it's the same guy."

"You're going to a lot of trouble to follow up on this angle. Who is this guy?"

"His name is George Hayek. He's an international arms dealer." Monty studied his son's expression, saw no visible recognition. "I guess you didn't cross paths with him in your overseas assignments. He lives in Europe;

Belgium, I think. He's made a fortune, selling weapons to foreign governments. Whether or not those deals are legit, I don't know."

"Is there evidence to say otherwise?"

"No."

"Then I don't get it. Why are you focusing on him in connection with the Winters' homicides? What's the tie-in?"

"Hayek's arrest record. Not the sealed one. He had a previous conviction before the gunrunning incident. Nothing major, just an attempted car boosting. He got off with a couple of months' time and community service. I got hold of that online booking sheet. Hayek made one phone call—to Lenny Shore."

Lane did a double take. "Lenny? What's Hayek's connection to him?"

"Good question. But there definitely was one. Lenny posted Hayek's bail. Which gives us an interesting link. Lenny is Arthur's father. Seventeen years ago, Arthur was a state assemblyman *and* Jack Winter's closest friend. And Jack Winter was prosecuting Carl Angelo, who I suspect Hayek was informing on for years and who testified against Angelo in court."

"So the Winters' homicides could have been an act of revenge."

"It's a distinct possibility. Or maybe Hayek ratted on Angelo to move up in the gun-trafficking world. It's still all supposition. I need the D.A.'s records and the court transcripts. Most of all, I need to learn about what makes Hayek tick. I'm hoping I can learn that from Lenny Shore. I'm glad we're eating at his place on Monday."

"Me, too. This is starting to sound more exciting than my heli-skiing trip with the congressman later in the week."

"Speaking of which, what happened the other night at the Shores' ?"

"The evening was short, and pretty benign. Some vegetable drinks, some casual family photos, and a discussion of next week's itinerary. Oh, and an invitation to Winshore's holiday party. Apparently, Jill Shore thinks I need a life partner."

Monty's lips twitched. "Doesn't sound like a bad idea. Although I'm sure you turned down the invitation."

"Actually, I accepted. Not to find a life partner, just to have a few kicks. Or, to be more honest, because I was provoked into it."

"By who—Jill?"

"Nope. Morgan." Lane chuckled, remembering. "She might be emotionally raw, but she's also quite a ball-breaker."

"Now *that's* a side of her I've never seen." Monty reached for his coffee and took a belt. "What made her choose your balls to break?"

"She read my facial expression, or my body language, or both. I'm sure I looked less than enthused about attending a Christmas party of beautiful people talking about insipid crap."

"And she pushed you into changing your mind?"

"More like challenged me into changing my mind. Let's see." Lane drummed his fingers on his knee. "I think her exact words were: 'Why not go for it? It's a weeknight. Too late for cocktails and a quickie, too early for nightcaps and bed.'"

Laughter rumbled in Monty's chest. "Sounds like she sized you up pretty well."

"Uh-huh. And she dared me to prove her wrong. She didn't use that phrase, but it was out there. So I took the dare."

"Interesting." Monty eyed his son. "She's a very pretty woman. Some might call her beautiful."

"No arguments there." Lane paused, brows drawn in concentration. "But 'beautiful' is too generic. 'Haunting.' 'Riveting.' 'Complex and fascinating.' Those seem to better apply. Something about her draws you in."

"It obviously drew you in."

"You're right. It did. Not only is she a knockout, she's sharp and direct. I see the same vulnerability you do, and I understand why you're worried about her. But I also see another side—a confident, self-assured woman. Don't underestimate Morgan Winter. She's got a quiet inner strength. It'll see her through this crisis—and anything else life throws her way." A corner of Lane's mouth lifted. "Plus she's quick. One hell of a sparring partner."

"She made quite an impression on you."

"Enough to make me go to Winshore's holiday party." Lane shot his father a look. "And now that we've agreed that Morgan is smart, assertive, and sexy, we're dropping this conversation."

"Sexy? I don't remember that adjective coming up."

"Monty." That was Lane's warning voice. "We're done here. You have nothing more to ask and I have nothing more to say."

"You're wrong. *I* have something more to say." Monty finished off his coffee and set down the cup with a thud. "Normally, I stay out of your personal life. Not this time. That girl's been through hell. I saw it firsthand. Now she's being forced to relive it. Don't do anything to mess with her emotionally."

"Monty . . ."

"I mean it, Lane. Don't."

TEN

Morgan took the C train to Euclid Avenue in Brooklyn's East New York section. From there, she walked to the Cypress Hills housing project where the Healthy Healing Center was located. Today was colder than yesterday, and the wind cut through her camel-hair overcoat as she hurried by construction sites and old, run-down buildings toward her destination. The apartments were sprinkled with Christmas decorations, and from somewhere on Fountain Avenue a Salvation Army Santa rang his bell. The sights and sounds of the holiday season carried a bittersweet quality, registering a certain incongruity in this area of the city still plagued by poverty and crime.

Morgan paused for a moment, looking back over her shoulder in the direction of Williams Avenue, where her mother's shelter had been. She knew the building was still standing, although it was now a thrift store. Swamped by nostalgia, she was half tempted to turn around and . . .

No. She couldn't. No matter how strong the pull was. She'd never be able to handle it. The effect of walking in there, confronting the scene of the nightmare, the effect would be devastating. Maybe someday. But not now. And not alone.

She forced herself to continue on her way, not pausing until she reached the Cypress Hills housing project. Sucking in a breath of frosty air, she walked into the low-rise brick building adjacent to it.

The receptionist at the desk finished her phone conversation and rose, flashing Morgan a warm, cordial smile. "Ms. Winter?" At Morgan's nod, she continued. "I'm Jeanine. We spoke earlier. Barbara's expecting you. I'll let her know you're here."

"Thank you."

A minute later, Morgan was shown into an inner office—a ten-by-twelve paneled room with the same color scheme and modest decoration as the reception area, only homier, thanks to a window ledge filled with thriving plants. A big old walnut desk dominated the floor space, its surface piled high with paperwork, file folders, and a steel nameplate that read BARBARA STEVENS, COUNSELOR. Behind the desk sat an attractive, middle-aged African-American woman in a lemon-yellow turtleneck sweater and toast-colored slacks, whose entire demeanor emanated warmth and comfort.

As Ms. Stevens rose and extended her hand, Morgan had a flash of recall: this same woman—younger, with a more trendy hairstyle, but with the same soothing presence—walking up to the front of the chapel and squeezing a traumatized ten-year-old's arm.

Yes, Barbara Stevens had been at the funeral. Morgan remembered.

That twinge of sorrow that never quite went away darted through her.

"Morgan . . ." Barbara was greeting her, sentiment warming her gaze. "I would have known you even if you'd come in unannounced. You look so much like your mother."

"I hear that quite a bit." Morgan met the older woman's handshake. "But no matter how often I do, I take it as a compliment."

"You should. Lara was a beautiful and special person, inside and out. She was also the most psychologically intuitive woman I've ever met." A painful pause. "I read about the wrongful conviction that was just discovered by the D.A. It's appalling. I can't imagine what you're going through. I'm so terribly sorry."

"Thank you." As she heard the glowing description of her mother, Morgan's twinge was replaced by pride. It was amazing how many lives Lara had touched—through her work in social services, fund-raising for charitable causes, and most of all, through starting up and running the women's abuse center. She'd become an emotional lifeline to dozens of women. Morgan had been peripherally aware of it as a child. But now, as an adult, she truly understood it. Lara had offered these women not only security but a foundation for a renewed sense of self-worth.

Barbara Stevens had been an integral connection to that.

"Are you all right?" she asked Morgan gently.

"Yes. And, with regard to what you said, my mother thought just as highly of you. I've discovered that more and more over the past weeks. I found her last working journals, and I've been reading through them. Your name is mentioned constantly."

Barbara acknowledged that with a soft smile, indicating the armchair across from her desk. "Please. Have a seat. Can I offer you a cup of coffee? I just made a fresh pot." As if to verify her words, the drip coffeemaker on the end table gave a few sputters of finality.

"I'll grab a cup. Thanks." Morgan scooted over and helped herself, then sat down and crossed her legs. "I appreciate your time."

"I'm glad you called. Given what's happened, I'm sure you need to talk."

"Yes." Morgan felt a wave of relief that Barbara understood her need to feel closer to her mother. But where to begin?

"Your parents were killed on Christmas Eve," Barbara said with quiet insight. "The holidays must be very difficult for you, even on a regular basis, much less this year."

"They are. The odd thing is that this year was particularly bad, even before I knew about the wrongful conviction. I felt so unsettled, and I had an eerie sense of foreboding. And now—I have this strong need to feel connected to my parents. I've been going through their things every night, searching for clues, for closure. It's like I need to personally solve this case, or at least have a major hand in doing so. I know it's not logical. But it's real."

"I don't doubt it. Plus, you mentioned finding your mother's last journals. That must be both a comfort and a torment."

"It is. I keep poring over them. Sharing her inner thoughts is tearing me up inside. But I can't seem to stop."

"And you have questions."

Morgan leaned forward. "Did you see her a lot those last weeks before she died? Personally or professionally?"

Barbara didn't dance around the point. "You want to know if she did or said anything that could point you toward the real killer. Believe me, I've asked myself that question a dozen times this week. I've relived our visits and our conversations over and over in my mind, racked my brain for a clue. The truth is, there wasn't one. Mostly, we discussed the women we were counseling or offering sanctuary to. As far as personal news, I remember her telling me you'd won a spelling bee at school that week, and how proud she and your father were."

A soft chuckle escaped Barbara's lips. "Lara said that Jack had literally raced out of Supreme Court during a recess so he could be at the school to see the principal give you your certificate. She said he hadn't left work that quickly since the day she went into labor."

Morgan swallowed. "Anything else about my father's career—general or specific?"

"She expressed concern for his safety. But that wasn't unusual or surprising. You father prosecuted some dangerous criminals."

"I know." Morgan jumped on that. "During those last weeks or months, did my mother bring up any specific names? Of the criminals themselves or any of their associates? Did she mention my father receiving any threats? Phone calls? Even an unpleasant altercation?"

Barbara gave a rueful shake of her head. "I wish I had something solid to offer you. But the truth is, Lara and I were so absorbed in figuring out ways to help the women who came to us, there was little or no time for small talk."

"I understand." Morgan's shoulders sagged. It had been a long shot and she knew it. Still, it didn't ease the frustration.

"I'm sorry, Morgan—truly. If I think of anything, anything at all, you know I'll call you."

"I know." Morgan nodded, wishing that restless feeling in her gut would subside.

It didn't.

So she dealt with it by switching gears, moving from the professional to the personal. "Barbara, I have tons of memories of my mother. But they're all childhood memories. I never got the opportunity to know her as a woman—and she was obviously a remarkable one. Elyse talks about her sometimes, but not easily. They were like sisters, and the pain of losing her still obscures the joy of remembering her. So, please share some anecdotes with me. They don't have to be life-altering, just moments that would make her come alive, make my memories of her fuller, more multi-dimensional."

"With pleasure." Another nostalgic smile. "Lara loved Milky Way bars. So did I. We used to call them our greatest weakness. One night, after a particularly stressful week, Lara showed up here with four giant-size bags. She challenged me to a Milky Way eating contest. We ate ourselves sick. I would have happily called it a draw. But Lara insisted on counting the wrappers to see who'd won. It turned out I had, by two. She had those two wrappers framed for my birthday that year." Barbara leaned across her desk, picked up a five-by-seven frame, and handed it to Morgan. "As you can see, I still cherish it."

Morgan looked at the delicate, filigreed gold frame, inside of which were two neatly trimmed and flattened wrappers, placed one above the other on a parchment background. A gold crown had been drawn in the upper left-hand corner of the parchment, beside which was penned: *To the Queen of the Milky Way* in her mother's familiar script.

Tears burned behind Morgan's eyes. "My dad and I were big Snickers fans. But I remember how much my mom loved Milky Ways. No matter how stuffed with food our freezer was, we always had a bag of Milky Ways crammed inside."

"Eating them frozen was the best. It was definitely Lara's favorite. But not for binges. We found that out the hard way. We tried it. Three candy bars later, Lara could barely move her jaw and I had chipped a tooth. So we gave in, settled for the soft, squishy version. It was a small price to pay."

The two women's gazes met and they laughed—a genuine, heartfelt laugh. Morgan was amazed how good it felt.

"Most of the time we got together, we forgot to eat altogether," Barbara admitted. "We were so immersed in our work. Without Lenny's sandwiches, we probably would have starved."

"I know *that* feeling." Morgan gave a commiserating nod. "Sometimes I think half of Brooklyn and Manhattan would starve without Lenny. He never forgets a meal, or a customer. As for me, I'm really lucky. He sends Jonah all the way up to my office just so Jill and I won't starve."

"You're family. Both of you." Barbara studied Morgan's face. "You do feel that way, don't you?"

"Absolutely." Morgan didn't hesitate in her reply. "All the Shores are wonderful. Elyse and Arthur have treated me like their own since the day they took me in. They're fine people."

"But they're not your parents," Barbara concluded simply. She leaned forward, took Morgan's hand. "No one ever will be. That privilege belonged to Lara and Jack."

"I know that." Morgan gave an unsteady nod, and handed Barbara the picture frame. "Tell me more about her."

"Everyone thought of Lara as soft-spoken and softhearted. And she was—most of the time. But if someone pushed one of her buttons, look out."

"What were some of her buttons?"

"You, your father, her friends—she'd defend you like a lioness. The same applied to her principles and the women she helped. Some more than others. She was the champion of the underdog. She threw herself into cases involving victims with the least strength, ability, or resources to defend themselves. Children who were abused along with their mothers. Young girls who were abandoned when they were barely more than children themselves and who fell pray to men who dominated them and stripped them of their self-worth. Situations like those infuriated her.

And she instinctively took the victims under her wing. That was your mother."

"I'm seeing that firsthand in the journal entries I'm reading," Morgan murmured. "The situations were heartbreaking. Especially little four-year-old Hailey and her mother Olivia."

"Those were their file names. We never used their real names, other than on their original registration forms."

"You were protecting their confidentiality."

Barbara nodded. "It doesn't surprise me that Lara did the same in her journals. Like I said, she was fiercely protective of those she helped."

"It still horrifies me to think about what Olivia's violent, alcoholic live-in boyfriend did. Locking Hailey in a dark closet for hours, leaving that poor child in there to listen while he beat and tormented her mother. I can't imagine how traumatized she must have been."

"*Deeply* traumatized," Barbara confirmed. "Lara wasn't giving up until she got them out of that environment for good. She did it, too."

"Since then—have things worked out?" Morgan asked.

"It was a long, hard road, but yes, they have. Before she died, Lara found Olivia and Hailey an affordable apartment and government funding to give them the jump start they needed. But Olivia did the real work. She had the courage and the determination to start over."

"How wonderful."

"Read more of Lara's journal entries. Nothing will make you feel closer to her than those."

"You're right. I just started reading a new entry about a teenage girl, Janice, who ran away from home after being sexually assaulted by her stepfather."

"Yes." Barbara blew out a breath. "That was another heartbreaker. Unfortunately, it didn't end nearly as happily as the previous one."

"I gathered as much. I've only just started reading, but my mother's outrage is palpable."

"Her reasons were valid. Janice's sexual abuse left lasting scars. She couldn't get past them. She continually sought relationships that victimized her. It became a vicious cycle. With each choice she became more careless and self-destructive. The culmination—" Barbara broke off. "Let's just say your mother took it very much to heart. And, yes, she was angry. *Very* angry. It's hard to excuse sick men like Janice's stepfather."

"That's because there *is* no excuse for them."

Another of Barbara's gentle smiles. "You've got a lot of your mother in you." She paused, her smile fading and her expression becoming intense. "I don't want you to get the wrong idea. While Lara expressed her indignation privately, publicly she was all encouragement. She exuded positive thinking and action, and was convinced that laughter and camaraderie healed far better than anger."

Morgan reflected on what Barabara had said. Suddenly her head came up. "Oh, that reminds me—when my mother referred to the lighter moments, she kept mentioning 'cardathons.' Was that an inside joke?"

"Cardathons." Barbara began to laugh. "I'd almost forgotten. No, no joke. One of Lara's pet programs. She was a crackerjack cardplayer. When it came to gin rummy, almost no one could beat her. She taught the women in the shelter how to play. Two Saturday nights a month, she held all-night marathons, which she playfully called cardathons. She gave out prizes—a spa day at Elizabeth Arden, a shopping spree at Bloomingdale's, a complete makeover with a professional hairstylist and makeup artist—things the women at the shelter never imagined in their wildest dreams. It did wonders. In some cases, jobs and career paths materialized. Most of all, it generated hours of fun, friendship, and laughter."

At that moment, the intercom on Barbara's desk buzzed. "Yes, Jeanine?" She glanced at her watch. "Goodness, I had no idea it was three o'clock already. Please tell her I'll be with her in a minute." She hung up. "Morgan, forgive me, but I have a counseling appointment."

"I'm the one who's sorry." Morgan was already on her feet. "I came to chat for a few minutes. Instead, I've taken up an hour and a half of your time. I really apologize."

"Don't. I've loved every minute of this. Meeting you after all these years. I was hoping you would seek me out when you were ready to learn about your mother." She squeezed Morgan's hand. "Stay strong, just like your mother. The police will find your parents' killer. And if I think of anything that could help, I'll call you. I promise. In return, if you need to talk, don't hesitate to pick up the phone. I mean it."

"I know you do." Impulsively, Morgan leaned forward and hugged the older woman. "Thank you. Thank you for everything."

ELEVEN

L ane was unusually restless.

He'd spent hours scrutinizing the photos Monty had given him, until there was nothing more he could do without the negatives. He then began prepping for next week's assignment with Congressman Shore.

By eight o'clock, he was stiff, cranky, and getting cabin fever.

He changed into a black cable-knit sweater and khakis, grabbed his shearling-lined leather jacket, and left his brownstone a little after eight, with no particular destination in mind. He headed over to Central Park, then down Fifth Avenue, where the Christmas decorations had a magical quality. Somewhere between his place and the park, it started to flurry. It got colder, too, although not unpleasantly so. It felt good, invigorating, another testimonial to the upcoming holidays. The sidewalks were packed with shoppers, the streets were jammed with taxis, and Lane just drank it all in, shoving his hands in his pockets and watching his breath emerge in frosty puffs.

For some unknown reason, he cut over to Madison Avenue and found himself standing in front of the Carlyle Hotel. Bemelmans Bar was just inside. He hadn't been there in ages. It wasn't his usual haunt—too old-money-ish. But the decor, with that black granite bar and amazing mural, was striking, the piano bar was a real draw, and the Black Angus burger was ground to order and delicious. In fact, the more he thought about it, an Angus burger, a spectacular cocktail or two followed by a cognac, and an hour of good music sounded damned good, especially since he hadn't eaten a thing since breakfast. So he found himself walking in.

He was just settling himself at a table not far from the piano, which was temporarily deserted, when he spotted a familiar face seated at a table down the way. She was sitting alone, either for the moment or for the evening, staring intently into her glass and twirling the swizzle stick around in her drink.

He gestured for the waiter to hold off taking his order, then walked over to her table. "Morgan?"

Her head came up, and those extraordinary eyes widened in surprise. She was wearing a lime-green cashmere sweater, her dark hair loose, tumbling around her shoulders. She looked fantastic. She also looked solemn, preoccupied, and very worn out. "Lane. Hi. What brings you here?"

"Actually, my feet." A corner of his mouth lifted. "I needed air. I took a walk. Next thing I knew I was outside the Carlyle. It's been a while, but the thought of a good drink and some mellow piano jazz hit the spot. So here I am."

"Funny. Sounds identical to my story."

"So maybe it wasn't just my feet. Maybe it was fate." Lane glanced around politely. "Are you alone?"

"Very."

Her pointed tone hit its mark. "Meaning you'd prefer to keep it that way?"

She tucked her hair behind her ear, giving a long-drawn-out sigh. "The truth? No. I'd rather have company. Would you like to join me?" Her sense of humor intervened, and her eyes twinkled. "Unless you have one of your numerous no-strings-attached dates waiting for you."

"Nope. I'm all by my lonesome. And I'd love to join you." He was already signaling to the waiter, alerting him to his plans. "Have you eaten?"

Morgan's forehead creased in thought. "Now that you mention it, not since breakfast."

"Good. Me, either. And I hate eating alone. The Angus burgers are great. So are the marinated lamb chops. We'll order both."

"Sounds perfect."

"What are you drinking?"

"A Dreamy Dorini Smoking Martini." Morgan's lips twitched as she spoke. "It's vodka and some kind of smoky single-malt scotch. It's actually pretty fantastic. You're adventurous. Try one."

"Done. And I'll get you another." Lane gave their order to the waiter, then turned back to Morgan. "This could just end up being the highlight of my day."

Her brows arched slightly. "I'm not sure that's a compliment. You sound like you've had a pretty tedious day."

"Not tedious. Intense. I was working. But running into you would be a pleasure no matter what."

"Very smooth." Morgan took a sip of her drink. "You're quite the charmer. No wonder your batting average is so high."

Laughter rumbled in Lane's chest. "My batting average? You either have a very high or a very low opinion of me."

"Just an accurate one. No judgment intended."

"Okay then, as long as we're being honest, I don't keep score. As for what I said about running into you being a pleasure, I meant it." He paused, eyeing her speculatively. "Although you look like you've had a pretty rough day yourself."

"I have."

"Work?"

"Trying to figure out who killed my parents."

Lane lowered his gaze, contemplating the obvious segue he'd just been offered. She'd been blunt. Time for him to be the same.

"Morgan, with regard to the murder investigation—the other night I didn't get the chance to tell you something. There wasn't an opportunity and Congressman Shore asked me to avoid upsetting you by bringing up the subject."

"Tell me what?"

"You asked me if my father had mentioned you'd hired him."

"And you said he had."

"Right. What I *didn't* say is that he didn't just mention it in passing. He called me specifically to discuss it, and to arrange a meeting. We had that meeting today. In fact, we spent a good couple of hours together, reviewing the crime-scene photos. There's nothing yet, but I'll have the negatives on Monday. Hopefully, they'll yield more clues."

Morgan blinked. "I don't understand. You're a photojournalist. Why would you get involved in a criminal investigation?"

"Because I'm also a specialist in photo image enhancement." Seeing the noncomprehension on her face, he explained. "I find visual clues using sophisticated digital technology. The field was relatively obscure seventeen years ago, mostly the domain of the military, NASA, and a few academics. All that's changed now."

"I see." Morgan fiddled with her napkin. "So you've got experience and equipment that could help spot evidence that was originally missed."

"Exactly. And Monty wanted me to let you know my role in this case, since you're his client." Lane tried to lighten the mood. "So, hey, you hired Monty, but you got two Montgomerys for the price of one."

"That doesn't please me," Morgan returned in a short, clipped tone.

Lane started. He hadn't expected her resistance. "Why? I'm more than trustworthy and, not to sound immodest, I'm damned good at what I do."

"I'm sure you are. Neither of those things are the issue."

"Then what is?"

"I appreciate your time and your skill. But I insist on paying for them. Your father wouldn't accept a dime. Which means that any compensation you're getting is coming out of his pocket. So tell me your rates, and I'll write you a check."

"Take it easy." Lane reached over and stopped her as she opened her purse to extract her checkbook. "First of all, I had no idea what your financial arrangement with Monty was. And second, he's not paying me a dime, either. So we're even." He eyed her dubious expression, waiting to continue until after their waiter had placed their drinks on the table.

"I'm not lying," he leaned forward to assure her. "Monty and I don't work that way. We don't bill each other. We just like working together. It's our form of recreation. Think of it as a challenging father-son project, you know, like building the tree house we put together when I was twelve."

"A tree house?" The image caught Morgan off guard, and her tension eased, a smile tugging at her lips. "That's quite an analogy. Although knowing you and your father, I'm sure building a tree house together was as challenging and competitive as doing detective work together. I can just visualize it: the two of you fighting over who was in charge, who was quicker, who was more thorough, and who produced the best results. All that testosterone in one tree—it boggles the mind. I shudder to think how the poor tree survived."

By this time Lane was chuckling. "Point well taken. And you're right; it was a battle of alpha males. But the result was one solid, serious tree house. When Monty and I take on a project together, success is a given." He raised his voice a bit as the piano player returned, resumed playing some soulful background music. "So have I convinced you what an unbeatable team my father and I are?"

"I never needed convincing."

"Fine, then have we settled this monetary nonsense? Are you okay with me analyzing the photos?"

"More than okay," Morgan admitted, lowering her wall of pride. "I'm grateful."

"Don't be. Not until I find something. Which I will."

"You sound just like your father. I hope you're both as confident as you seem, and not putting on a brave front for me."

"We don't do brave fronts. We do solutions."

"Good." Her hand slightly unsteady, Morgan raised her glass, took another sip of her drink, then regarded the glass for a long, thoughtful moment. "I guess you're used to seeing homicide photos. But I'm not. And these particular photos . . ." She drew a long breath. "I'm just not sure how I'll react when I see them."

"Do you have to see them?"

"Yes. Not to challenge myself or to prove a point. But to get at the truth. I can't leave a single stone unturned. I have to do anything, *everything*, that might lead us to the killer." She shut her eyes for a second. "That means reliving that night, and all the months that led up to it, trying to see if I have information locked away in my mind I don't realize is there or I'm unaware is significant. It means scrutinizing those photos, one by one, focusing on every detail to see if it triggers a memory. I have to. But I'm terrified. Staring at those pictures, when the nightmares are still so horrifyingly vivid—I'm just not sure how I'll hold it together." Her lashes lifted and she met Lane's gaze. "I don't know how much your father told you. But I'm the one who discovered the bodies."

"He didn't have to tell me." Lane saw no point in being evasive. "I already knew."

Her brows drew together. "How?"

"Let's just say that seventeen years ago was a dicey period for my family. The time my sisters and I spent with Monty was broken into chunks. That made it hard for him to draw his usual definitive line between us and his work. Devon and Merry were young—eleven and five. Their focus was on Monty as their dad, not as a homicide detective. But I was sixteen—and on the reckless side. I thought the danger and excitement of my father's career was cool. I hung around him a lot, even when he didn't know I was there. I listened to his phone calls, watched him reviewing evidence. This case drove him crazy. He couldn't let it go. It's not something I forgot."

"Neither did he," Morgan surprised him by saying. "And not just because the end result didn't sit right with him. It's because he personalized the investigation. He'd just moved out. I was about the same age as your sister Devon. Losing my parents reminded him how much he missed his kids."

Lane's jaw practically dropped. "He *told* you that?"

"Not in so many words. Your father's not exactly the type to spill his guts."

"That's the understatement of the year."

"What he told me was that no separation could break or weaken the bond between parent and child. He mentioned your names, saying that he wasn't living in the same house as you anymore, but that he loved you just as much as he had then. He was obviously hurting. The hurt was raw, which meant the separation was new. I was too young to fully understand it. But I understand it now. I've had many years to reflect on the things he said to me that night, and to recognize the paternal way he comforted me.

So it doesn't surprise me that he was preoccupied with the case. He needed to make it right—for many reasons."

Lane took a hefty swallow of his drink. "You got all that from one conversation?"

"It wasn't just what he said. It was the pain in his eyes. The way he didn't push me away when I glued myself to his side. The way he brought me to the precinct. The way he sat with me when I sobbed. The way he found a cot for me to sleep on, and left a light on so I wouldn't be afraid. The way he ran interference until I was ready to leave and face the other people who loved my parents." A sad smile touched Morgan's lips. "Every one of those things is what a father does to protect his child. I know, because I remember my own father."

With each passing moment, Lane was gaining new insight into why Morgan felt such fierce admiration for and gratitude to Monty. "I didn't realize Monty had factored so heavily into helping you cope with your loss."

"He helped me survive that first night. I was in shock. I was also in denial." A faraway look came into her eyes. "That basement was horrible. It was dark and creepy, and there was a sickening smell in the air—decay and blood and death. My parents didn't belong down there, lying on that broken filthy floor. I had to get to them. But no one would let me. They kept holding me back. But they couldn't make me look away. All I could do was stare at their bodies. There was blood everywhere: under my father's head, in a pool around my mother, in splotches on the floor. I almost stepped in one, I was so frantic to break away and run to my parents' sides. I kept screaming their names, begging them to wake up—even though I knew that wasn't going to happen. No one could get through to me, not even the grief counselor. The entire scene was surreal, like disjointed flashes of a nightmare."

Morgan wet her lips and continued. "Your father stepped in. He didn't try to make it go away. He knew he couldn't. He just told me to let the police and the ambulance workers do their jobs. He wrapped a blanket around me and led me away. He was nonjudgmental, kind, and honest. He told me the truth. But he also told me my parents weren't in pain, and I wasn't alone. He made me feel safe. And he was real, human. The grief counselor was so professional; it was like relating to a caring textbook. Elyse and Arthur were the opposite—way too personally involved. Not that I blamed them. They were my parents' closest friends. They were emotional basket cases. I needed someone who understood, but didn't intrude. That was your father. He simply took care of me. You and your sisters are lucky; I'm sure he did—and does—the same for you."

An immediate nod. "You're right. He does. That's Monty's MO—taking care of the people he loves, and the people he feels responsible for."

"Well, the night my parents were killed, I certainly fell into the latter category. Actually, I still do because, in your father's mind, he never fulfilled his responsibility to me. Not really. Not when the real murderer is still walking the streets."

Lane folded his arms across his chest, eyeing Morgan with undisguised admiration. "No wonder you're so good at what you do. You've got quite a handle on human nature."

"Hey, that's what a master's degree in human behavior will do for you."

"Maybe the master's degree helped. But what I'm describing isn't acquired in a lecture hall. It's innate. You really get what makes people tick. And what you lived through obviously enhanced that ability."

"What I lived through is something I was hoping to relegate to the past. So much for that idea." Morgan massaged her forehead, visibly affected by reliving that night.

"You've been through hell," Lane observed quietly.

"Yes," she agreed. "And it looks like I'm back there again."

It was with great restraint that Lane didn't reach over and take her hand. But instinct told him she wouldn't welcome the physical contact.

He was about to suggest they change the subject, when the waiter solved the problem by choosing that moment to arrive with their food.

A look of sheer relief flashed across Morgan's face. "This looks fabulous." She smiled her thanks at the waiter, then turned her attention to her burger, picking it up and taking a big, juicy bite. "Yum."

Lane followed her lead, falling silent as he prepared his own food, took a few appreciative bites. "Don't forget the lamb chops," he reminded her a few minutes later. "We're splitting those." He indicated the two plates.

"Don't worry. I won't. In fact, I'm so hungry that if I were you, I'd protect my half."

He chuckled. "Feel free. I'll order more, if necessary."

Morgan took another bite, chewed slowly, then swallowed, watching Lane as she did. She put down her burger and tucked her hair behind her ear. "We've discussed the hell out of me. Let's talk about you for a change."

He made a wide sweep with his arm. "I'm an open book. What do you want to know?"

"What got you interested in photography?"

"Life did. Life and my personality. I always found it fascinating to capture the essence of an entire story in one shot. There's a great deal of truth to the expression 'a picture's worth a thousand words'—if it's the right picture, of the right story, taken by the right photographer."

"Which, in your case, it is."

"Usually. Hopefully. Added to that was my fascination with photographic technology. F-stops and photo-lab chemistry were cool enough. Then came the modern age—digital cameras and computer image enhancement. I'm in my glory."

"Not to mention traveling all over the world, and inserting yourself right in the middle of high-risk situations like civil wars and natural disasters, and participating in thrill-seeking adventures like the ones you and Arthur are about to embark on."

Lane grinned. "Yeah, that, too. I admit there's a lot of daredevil in me."

"How long have you been photographing professionally?"

"Since college."

Morgan whistled. "That's impressive."

"Not when you hear how I made my money back then. I was full of myself, my skills, and my immortality. I wanted a fast life and a fast buck. So job number one was as a paparazzo." A corner of his mouth lifted as he saw Morgan's reaction. "Pretty skanky, huh? Following the rich and famous in the hopes of catching them doing something newsworthy, or gossip-worthy, that no one else has snapped them doing before?"

"It's not a career I would aspire to. That doesn't mean I don't understand why you did it."

Now *that* comment irked him. He wasn't sure why. Yeah, actually he was. The way she said it, so clinically, as if she were figuring him out so she could properly place him—it made him feel like one of her clients. Which was the *last* thing he wanted to be.

"This should be interesting," he noted drily. "I can't wait to hear your analysis of what drives me."

Her brows rose. "Testy, aren't we?"

"Just skeptical."

"In other words, I'm good at what I do so long as I don't do it to you."

Dead-on again. "That's not what I meant." He wasn't giving up without a fight. "It's just that, given how differently we approach life, I can't imagine you understanding my motivations."

"Why not? Because I don't enjoy pushing the boundaries of my own mortality? That's not because I don't understand. It's because I know how fragile life is."

He'd walked right into that one. And he felt like a bastard. "Morgan, I . . ."

"Don't. I'm not offended." Morgan dismissed his upcoming apology. Interlacing her fingers, she rested her hands on the table and regarded him intently. "I'm not going to analyze you. I don't know you well enough. Plus, I'm not a therapist. But I go to one often enough to understand the fundamentals of human behavior. So here's my take on your paparazzo stint. You were sixteen when your parents split up. Your foundation was rocked. Risk became more palatable, since there was less you could count on. Anticipation was infinitely more appealing than complacency. So you went with it. The adrenaline rush felt great, growing in intensity after each assignment. So you kept on going, pushing the boundaries more each time, to up the ante and heighten the rush. It worked. It still does, even though you've changed the direction your assignments take. It's still exciting, still dangerous, still a major adrenaline rush. Am I warm?"

"Hot." Lane propped his elbow on the table and rested his chin on his hand, which, of its own accord, tightened into a fist. He could feel his blood pumping, the same way it had the other night at the Shores'. There was something about this woman that made all his senses come alive. She went from disarming him and making him want to comfort her, to challenging him and pissing him off, to exciting him and making him want to bury himself inside her until neither of them could breathe.

The last part was what was driving him crazy right now.

"Thrill seeking is like sex," he muttered, his voice barely audible above the piano. "Pushing the boundaries, upping the ante—it all heightens the rush, and intensifies the pleasure."

She got his meaning, loud and clear. Color stained her cheekbones, but she didn't avert her gaze. "The rush. The pleasure. What about the risk?"

"It's worth it."

"Maybe. If the experience is as incredible as you claim." A heated glint lit her eyes. "Still, I'm a pretty grounded woman. I like to have a clear picture of my odds before I plunge in."

"And how do you manage to get that clear picture?"

"This, coming from a master photographer?"

"Yes. This, coming from a master photographer."

There wasn't an iota of teasing in his tone. He was dead serious.

She answered in kind, responding to his fervor with her own. "By taking my time. By letting the excitement build. If thrill seeking is like sex, then anticipation is like foreplay. It has its own rewards. It's also an adrenaline rush unto itself. Plus, waiting has other merits, like reaching a modicum of certainty."

"Ah. Looking for something stable and secure."

"No, just something that feels right. Life is tenuous. Who knows what's stable? And security—that's never a guarantee. But feeling good mentally is just as important as feeling good physically. And when you feel both at the same time, well, it doesn't get any better than that."

"I'll take your word for it."

"Do that. In fact, try it. You might reach new levels of pleasure that surprise even you."

She let her words hang in the air for a moment, until the tension was drawn so tight, it felt like it might snap.

Exhaling on a wispy sigh, Morgan reached forward, picking up the serving fork and spearing the lamb chops, placing a few on each of their plates. "Let's eat these before they get cold," she murmured.

"Right." Lane was still staring at her heatedly, making no attempt to disguise what he wanted. And it wasn't the lamb chops.

"There you go." As she felt his scrutiny, Morgan's hand trembled ever so slightly as she handed him a plate. "Equal portions." She sat back, her lashes lifting so she could meet his gaze head-on.

"Enjoy," she urged softly. "Savor every bite. Oh, and never let it be said I didn't meet you halfway."

TWELVE

The early lunch crowd was already congregating at Lenny's when Monty crossed Delancey Street, strode down to the middle of the block, and pushed open the glass door.

He was greeted by the enticing smell of hot pastrami and potato knishes, and the familiar shouts of orders being called across the counter and the whoosh of razor-sharp knives slicing repeatedly through deli meat that was then placed on platters or between slices of Jewish rye.

There were still some things in life you could count on. Lenny's deli was one of them.

Monty shrugged out of his parka and glanced around the restaurant, glad they'd set up this meeting for noon. By twelve-thirty, the place would be a madhouse. He wouldn't be able to hear himself think, much less up-date Arthur Shore on the murder investigation.

"Hey, Monty!" Lenny bellowed his name, waving and gesturing for him to wait a minute. Without missing a beat, he continued entering numbers into the cash register while handing over a hefty shopping bag bulging with food to one of his customers. Simultaneously, he beckoned at Anya, his stout, buxom, lightning-quick waitress who'd come over from Russia, settled in the Brighton Beach section of Brooklyn, and worked the past twenty years at his deli.

"Anya," Lenny instructed. "Set up a table. In the back. For three . . . no, four. I want enough space so I can pull up a chair and join them."

"Okay, okay." Anya held up the tray she was carrying, which was filled to the brim with ready-to-be-served platters. "Right after I deliver these." She headed over to table three, distributed the entire order, then sashayed off to do her boss's bidding.

"You're early," Lenny informed Monty. "Neither of our boys is here yet."

"That's because they're both old and we're young. We move faster."

Lenny threw back his head and laughed. The guy was amazing. Seventy-eight years old and still going strong. Quick as a whip, steady-handed, and seemingly tireless, Lenny still ran his deli almost full-time. His wife, Rhoda, kept the books, paid the staff, and made the coffee, the matzo-ball soup, and the chopped liver from scratch every day. The two of them had opened the deli over forty-five years ago, and taken the place from a small-time sandwich shop to a New York landmark. Some of that success was due to the food, some to the personable warmth of the owners, and some to the political fame of their congressional son.

Whatever the reason, it didn't matter. The space and the clientele might have grown along with the profits, but Lenny Shore hadn't changed a bit. Quite simply, he loved what he did. He liked his customers and they liked him.

"How's Sally?" Lenny walked over to Monty, wiping his hands on his apron before reaching out to shake Monty's hand.

"Great—but jealous. I told her where I was eating. She said not to come home without a pastrami sandwich and a pound of Rhoda's chopped liver."

"I'll give you two pounds. Save some for when the kids come over. Let's sit down. Tell me about the family." He led Monty to the rear of the restaurant, which was slightly quieter than the rest of the place. "I already know how Lane is. Busy. Half the countries he's been to, I've never even heard of. But he's doing well, and he's happy. So that's all that matters. Tell me about those beautiful daughters of yours."

"Grown up." Monty scowled. "Time passes too damned fast. Merry's a senior at SUNY Albany already. She's graduating this spring, and going on to get her master's in education."

"A teacher like her mom."

"Yeah, she's a lot like Sally—softhearted and superattuned to kids. And she's got a law school boyfriend, but let's not go there." Monty grunted. "As for Devon, her veterinary clinic is thriving. It's been written up in more publications than I can name. Oh, and she and Blake just bought a big house in Armonk. They're hoping to become homebodies, and actually see each other once in a while. He spends too many hours running Pierson & Company. They need some downtime."

"A house?" That perked Lenny up. "With lots of bedrooms? Sounds to me like that town house of theirs is getting too small. And you know what *that* means. Any day now they'll be calling you and Sally up with the happy news that—"

"Not yet." Monty cut him off with a grin. "At least not right away. But it wouldn't surprise me if they decided to make me a grandpa in a few years."

"That would be wonderful! Especially since, given Lane's lifestyle and the number of women he's dated, I wouldn't hold my breath in the hopes that he'll do you that honor first."

"Believe me, I'm not."

"There's nothing like grandchildren. They fill your life with joy." A pained look crossed Lenny's face. "My poor Morgan. It makes my insides twist when I think of what she's going through. I know she's not mine by blood. But I love her the same way I do Jill."

"I know you do." Monty blew out a breath. "This whole screwup sucks."

"You're helping Arthur, though, right? He said you're launching a whole new investigation."

"That's a little overstated. Morgan hired me, Arthur's throwing his support behind me, and yeah, I'm reinvestigating the Winters' double homicide. But I'm a PI now, not a cop. So I'm not launching anything—at least nothing official."

"I know you, Monty. If you're in it, you're on top of it. So what did you find out?"

"Bits and pieces." Monty had intended to wait until Arthur arrived before addressing the issue that had been bugging him all weekend. But given Lenny's interest, he decided the hell with it. "Listen, Lenny. I have a question for you."

"Shoot."

"What do you know about George Hayek?"

Lenny's gray brows arched. "George? Wow, talk about a blast from the past. He worked as my delivery boy when he was a kid, right after he and his mother fled from Lebanon and came to the U.S. It must have been thirty-eight, maybe thirty-nine years ago, a handful of years after we opened. Why?"

"Because I was sifting through some paperwork and I found his arrest record," Monty answered evasively. "He listed you and your deli in the phone-call section of his booking sheet. It was the only name he specified."

"That's not a surprise. His mother didn't speak English. And he had nowhere else to turn." Lenny's forehead creased as he thought back all those years. "George was basically a good kid. But his father was killed in Lebanon, and he came over here a pretty angry teenager. He had no role model, so, yeah, he became a little wild. He acted out, fell into a rowdy crowd. They boosted a car, and he got caught. It was stupid, and he knew it. He needed a break, someone to give him a little support. So I filled that role. I showed up on his behalf, and I posted his bail. Why? How did George or his arrest record come up in your investigation?"

"It didn't. Not directly. I had the Central Clerk's Office in Manhattan dig up some old case files for me—all the ones Jack Winter successfully prosecuted during the last year of his life. One of those cases involved a guy named Carl Angelo, a big-time drug and weapons dealer. Jack Winter got him convicted a few months before the murders. Angelo had a long list of scumbags on his payroll. A couple of those scumbags used to run in the same crowd as George Hayek. Like you said, they were a pretty sketchy bunch."

"That was when they were teenagers. Who knows what they grew up to be? They could be murderers. They could be priests." Lenny turned his palms up in an it's-anybody's-guess gesture. "As for George, he didn't deal in drugs or guns. He stole a car. And that was twenty years before that Angelo guy was arrested."

"True." Monty nodded. "Are you and Hayek still in touch?"

"Nah." Lenny shook his head. "The deli was just a starting point for George. Once he got enough cash under his belt, he left. Wanted to start his own business, help some of his family back home. And he wasn't exactly the letter-writing type. The last I heard, he'd moved out to L.A., then to somewhere in Florida. I don't know where he settled."

"But he left here on good terms."

"Hell, yeah. Like I said, George was a good kid. Worked for me for almost a year, and never stole a nickel."

"He put in a lot of overtime?"

"More than a lot. He busted his ass to support his mother."

"So he spent long hours at the deli. Did he know Arthur?"

"Did who know Arthur?" Congressman Shore strode over, hanging his overcoat on the hook beside the table.

"Monty's asking about George Hayek. I think he's worried that George had some kind of grudge against us."

"Why?" Arthur looked startled.

"Why was I asking about him, or why was I worried that he might have a grudge against you?"

"Both." Still visibly perplexed, Arthur pulled back a chair and sat down. "George Hayek—I haven't heard his name in years."

"I'll fill you in." Monty repeated the story.

"I see." Arthur frowned. "Do you have any evidence that George was on Angelo's payroll?"

"Nope. It was a long shot," Monty replied. "But I had to run down the lead. I'm running down *every* lead. And when I saw Lenny's name on Hayek's booking sheet, I saw a potential motive."

"What motive?" Lenny demanded. "I'm still not following."

"I am." Arthur pursed his lips, nodding as he contemplated Monty's reasoning. "You're asking about George and me because you're wondering if we got along. We did. Not that we saw much of each other. I was away at college and he was here, working for my father. But I saw him whenever I came home for vacations. I even went with him and my father to the movies a few times." Arthur gave Lenny's shoulder a squeeze. "Dad had a soft spot for George, given how much he'd lost. He figured we could include him in some of our father-son time. George appreciated it. He wasn't much of a talker. But it was obvious how much he respected us. Especially Dad. He never forgot the breaks my father gave him. George's loyalty ran deep."

"Well, that shoots that theory to hell." Monty sat back in his seat.

"You figured that if George had it in for me, even after twenty years, he'd go after my closest friend?"

"It's not a new motive. Hatred. Vengeance. It's been used before. You were a state assemblyman, an influential man who was on the political fast track. Plus, it didn't have to be you he was after. *If* he'd stayed in New York, kept hanging out with that gang of his, and ended up running guns for Angelo, you might not even have factored into the equation. Angelo was convicted. It was only a matter of time before his flunkies went down, too. One of them might have decided to take care of Jack before Jack could take care of him."

Again, Arthur nodded. "Good point. Sobering, too. Even though George didn't fall into that category, there must have been dozens of criminals who did."

"Yeah, very few of whom were investigated last time. Schiller's confession took care of that."

"Hi, all. Sorry I'm late." Lane wound his way over to the table, putting down his camera bag and eyeing the clock on the wall. "Actually, I'm not late. I'm two minutes early. What time did this meeting get started?"

"It didn't," Lenny assured him. "How could it? There's no food on the table. I'll fix that." He stood up, pointing at each of them in turn. "Lane— pastrami, lean, potato knish, and coleslaw. Monty—brisket-and-corned-beef combo and a bowl of matzo-ball soup. Arthur—a hot open turkey platter, a bowl of sour pickles, and a piece of your mother's noodle pudding, if you know what's good for you."

His son grinned. "I'm not dumb. I'll eat every bite, then call her later and tell her how good it was."

"Smart boy." Lenny patted him on the back. "I'll take care of the order myself. You boys talk." His gaze settled on Monty. "Thank you for helping Morgan. She's been through hell and back."

"I remember." Monty gave a terse nod. "Don't worry. I'll chase down every lead till I find the right one."

"I know you will." Lenny turned toward the kitchen, his customarily upbeat mood restored. "And I'll make sure Sally's order is ready when you go. Rhoda's chopped liver beats a dozen roses any day."

"No argument." Monty watched Lenny cut through the crowd and disappear through the swinging door. "He's something else."

"He sure is," Lane agreed. "He's got more energy than I do, his memory's better than mine, and he's always chipper and happy. I don't envy you, Congressman. He's a tough act to follow."

"You're right. And, please, call me Arthur. I already feel older than my father, and you call him by his first name."

"Good point." Lane chuckled. "Fine—Arthur." He sent a sideways look at Monty, then glanced quizzically at Arthur. "I'm not sure how you want to handle this meeting. My role here is a little nebulous, at least as I see it. My editor explained that having Monty and I meet with you together will optimize your time efficiency. That's fine. But you're going to have to define my limitations."

Lane summarized the specifics, counting off on his fingers. "Tell me when we're on the record and when we're off; when I'm taking the lead in this interview and when I'm taking a backseat; and when you want me to make myself scarce so the two of you can talk privately. Officially, I'm here to take whatever photos and corresponding text you want readers to see regarding the homicide investigations. At the same time I want to give maximum exposure to your proposed legislation. I already have photos of you with your family. I'll want some of you among your constituents. The order and the structure of how things get done is up to you. I'm at your disposal."

Arthur steepled his fingers in front of him, tapping them together as he spoke. "Let's start by cutting through the BS. You and I are flying out to

Colorado tomorrow, and driving up to the Poconos a couple of days later. We'll be together for the better part of a week while you chronicle our adventures for *Time*. There'll be plenty of time to talk. Believe me, I'll chew your ear off about my bill. In between trips, we'll find more than enough photo ops. But today's meeting is about who really killed Jack and Lara. I know your involvement in this investigation is more in-depth than the photo essay you're doing for *Time*. So tell me, where do things stand with the crime-scene photos?"

Lane was ready for the question. It confirmed what he'd already suspected—that this was the real reason Arthur had wanted this collaborative meeting. He was aware of Lane's expertise, realized Monty had tapped into that expertise, and wanted to amass the information cumulatively.

"Everything I've done is preliminary," Lane informed him. "I expect that to change in about two hours. That's when the negatives are being delivered to my town house. Once I scan those negatives into my computer, I'll be able to enhance every detail. If there's something there, I'll find it."

Arthur turned to Monty. "Is there any correlation between what you've asked Lane to focus on, and the path you were pursuing with my father and me a few minutes ago? Is Lane searching for something visual that would connect the Winters' murders to one of the criminals Jack put away right before he died?"

"No," Monty stated flatly. "It would be stupid to narrow our scope. Not without a shred of proof. Lane's got an expert eye. The best thing he can do is view those photos without any preconceived ideas; only facts. That way he won't overlook anything. In the meantime, I'll keep pounding away at my investigation. Anything I uncover that impacts his analysis, he'll hear about ASAP. We want to keep this as open-minded an investigation as possible, until we're damned sure we're heading in the right direction. No more screwups. Not this time."

"Amen," Arthur muttered. "I still can't believe no one saw through Schiller's bogus confession."

"If by 'no one' you mean you, don't be so hard on yourself," Monty replied. "Schiller's a thief and a murderer. It wasn't a reach to think the Winters were two more names on his victims list."

"Right." Arthur's tone was rife with self-censure. It was evident he still hadn't forgiven himself. "Anyway, what else have you got?"

"I've got the rest of Jack Winter's caseload to go through. I've got leads on everyone from perps he prosecuted, were convicted, and who were either released or paroled right before he was killed, to relatives, friends, or associates of perps still serving time, to none of the above."

"What's none of the above?"

"You name it. Unrelated perps with histories of breaking and entering or theft who were in Brooklyn in December 1989. Also, guys with police records and histories of violence whose wives frequented Lara Winter's shelter. It's possible that one of those husbands flipped out that night and came to the shelter to teach his wife a lesson. Lara and Jack could have been casualties of that visit. And that's just the tip of the 'none of the above' iceberg."

"God, there's so much ground to cover." Arthur rubbed his forehead in a weary, frustrated gesture.

"Yup. The good news is, I work fast." A pensive look crossed Monty's face. "How's Morgan? Is she holding up okay?"

Arthur's shrug was ambivalent. "She spent most of the weekend alone. Jill tried to coax her out, but no luck. This investigation is eating away at her. So 'okay' is a relative term. Elyse and I are really worried."

"She's hanging in there," Lane supplied quietly. "It's not easy, but she's a strong woman."

Both men looked at Lane in surprise.

"You spoke to her?" Arthur asked.

"Actually, I ran into her. Saturday night. We both wandered into the Carlyle for a drink. We ended up having dinner together. She was definitely more relaxed when I walked her home."

"Good." Arthur sighed with relief. "I'm glad she got out. And that she had a little fun. Thank you, Lane."

"No thanks necessary. I had a great time. Truthfully, I was wound pretty tight myself. So the evening did as much for me as it did for Morgan."

Monty opened his mouth to say something, but was interrupted by the arrival of their lunch.

"Here you go." Anya whisked over and began unloading plates of food onto the table. "I'll be right back with your drinks. Lenny's on his way out; he's putting together Jonah's next big delivery order."

"Thanks, Anya." Arthur gave her a broad smile. "This looks great."

"Save the compliments for your mother," she advised him with wry humor. "Eat all that noodle pudding." She pointed at the side plate, which could barely hold the enormous square of steaming noodle pudding that was hanging over the edges.

"Yes, ma'am." Arthur snapped off a mock salute.

Anya had just left, when Jonah shuffled over to the table, looking awkward and uncomfortable. "Hey, Lane? Sorry to bother you, but you said to let you know when that package from the Central Clerk's Office was delivered. It showed up at your place just as I was leaving."

Lane exchanged a surprised glance with Monty.

"Earlier than expected," Monty murmured. "That's a first."

"Yeah." Lane turned back to his assistant. "Thanks, Jonah."

"No problem." The lanky teenager was visibly relieved that his good news had been well enough received to eclipse the inconvenience of his intrusion. Hoping he was on a roll, he angled his head in Lane's direction. "Is it okay if I put in a few extra hours later today? I could use the cash. Or do you need the lab to yourself now that that package arrived?"

"Unfortunately, I need the whole lab. I'll be spread out all over the place." Lane paused as a spur-of-the-moment idea struck him. "But I might have a way for you to put in those extra hours and earn that cash." A questioning glance at Arthur. "I assume you have afternoon meetings?"

"I do," Arthur confirmed.

"In Manhattan?"

A nod.

"Why don't you pick a time and place that works. Jonah can be there and take some preliminary shots of you among your constituents. I want to get him involved in this photo-essay project of ours, anyway. He has the skill. We need the help. And there's no time like the present."

Arthur got the message. Lane was taking care of the vital, confidential aspect of things, and Jonah could handle the more mundane.

"Sounds good. How about outside my office around three o'clock?"

Arthur suggested to Jonah. "I'll be checking in with my staff around then anyway. And it'll give you more than enough time to do your lunch runs for my father, and pick up whatever camera equipment you need from Lane's lab."

"Great. Thanks." Jonah's eyes were huge, like he'd been handed a grand prize. "Your office is over on Lex. I'll be there at three sharp."

"Fine."

"Jonah, there you are." Lenny bustled out, two large insulated Styrofoam boxes clutched in his arms. "Here's the first part of the order. It's for Monty's old haunt—East New York. And there's more." He winced a little as he shifted the heavy boxes from his grasp to Jonah's. "I've got another two of these being packed. So stick those in the truck, then come back in and wait."

He watched Jonah head off, then glanced down at his right hand and scowled. "Damn," he muttered. He reached over to an adjacent table, whipped out two napkins, and wiped off the gold initial ring Rhoda had bought him for their twenty-fifth anniversary. Then he grabbed a few more napkins and wrapped them around his bleeding forefinger.

"What happened?" Arthur asked.

"Nothing. I'm just a klutz. I was slicing some sour pickles, and I cut myself."

"Go tape it up," Monty advised him as a little blood soaked through. "It looks like you did quite a number on it."

"Nah, I was just doing too many things at once. I'll slap on a Band-Aid after the lunch crowd slows down."

"Did you have your blood tested this month?" Arthur demanded, frowning as his father grabbed another napkin, wrapped it around the others.

Lenny shot him a look. "No, and don't start. I'll go next week. It's been too hectic here for me to break away."

"Not *that* hectic. Forget next week. Go tomorrow, or I'll tell Mom."

A grimace. "You would. Fine, I'll go tomorrow. Now let me get the rest of Jonah's order."

Arthur rolled his eyes as Lenny hurried back to the kitchen to get the rest of Jonah's delivery order. "Stubborn as an ox. He's on blood-thinning medication. He's supposed to get his levels checked every month. It's just routine, but it's doctor's orders. Try telling that to him. He thinks he's immortal."

"He is," Lane replied.

"He's also territorial about the deli," Monty added. "It's his life's work. He doesn't trust anyone else to run it." A pause. "I can relate."

"Yes," Arthur agreed, nodding as Monty's analogy sank in. "I'm sure you can. You two are a lot alike. Neither of you believes anyone can do your job as well as you. The irony of it is, you're right. No one can."

"Which is why I'm going to be the one to solve this case." Monty's jaw set. Abandoning conversation, he grabbed his soup spoon, downed a healthy portion of matzo-ball soup, then dove into his combo sandwich, chewing it with gusto. "Enough chitchat. Let's eat. I've got an investigation to get back to."

THIRTEEN

The agency was hopping. Phones were ringing off the hook, clients were setting up appointments, and referrals were pouring in by the droves.

Never had Morgan been more grateful to be busy.

She'd dashed down to the office early for a new-client consult. Then came two existing-client follow-up meetings. After a quick microwaved cup of soup, she'd taken off for three back-to-back outside appointments.

The first of those appointments was with Charlie Denton, a fact that pleased her on several levels. Professionally, she wanted to expand Charlie's chances of finding the right mate. She wanted to hear everything about his weekend—he'd taken out both Karly Fontaine and Rachel Ogden. Both women would be strong complements to Charlie, each in different ways.

And, yes, she had a personal motive in wanting to see him, too. She was anxious to know if Charlie had had any success in prying information out of *anyone* in the Manhattan D.A.'s office.

They met at a Cosi in midtown, halfway between the agency's Upper

East Side location and the D.A.'s downtown office. Over a light lunch and a cup of coffee, they talked.

"You look tired," Charlie began, studying Morgan's face.

"I guess I am. Life is hectic on all fronts, and I'm not sleeping well." She pulled out the file she'd brought with Charlie's name printed on it, ready to jot down notes. "I'm dying to hear about your dates with Rachel and Karly." A weighty pause. "But first, I have to ask, has anyone in the D.A.'s office come through for you? Did you learn anything new?"

Charlie lowered his gaze, concentrating on stirring his coffee. "Nothing I can discuss."

Morgan went very still. "What does that mean?"

He sighed. "Look, Morgan, I'm pushing as hard as I can. But this is a delicate situation. It requires a fair amount of diplomacy—and I *don't* mean because I'm covering my own butt. Like it or not, my sources have to feel certain that I'll keep whatever I'm told in confidence."

"In other words, *they're* protecting *their* butts."

"In some cases, yes. In some cases, they're not working with facts, only supposition and hearsay. And in some cases, I'm easing my way through a chain of command in order to find the right person to supply my answers— if those answers exist."

"Does that mean you don't know anything yet, or you know something but aren't authorized to share it with me?'"

"It means you have to give me a little time. I'm operating on instinct and bread crumbs of information I'm picking up along the way. When I have something concrete under my belt, I'll speed-dial your number. I promise."

Reluctantly, Morgan accepted his explanation and his assurance. "I appreciate that. I realize you're putting yourself through this primarily because of the pressure Arthur is exerting."

"You're wrong," he interrupted. "My office's motive is one thing. Mine's another." He leaned forward, staring at her intently. "It's true that Congressman Shore has a lot of influence. And, yes, the D.A. is eager to offer his cooperation. But I'm not doing this for the congressman. I'm doing it for your father—and for you."

Morgan's cup paused halfway to her lips. There was an intensity about

Charlie's tone, and his words, that caught her off guard. She'd known he admired her father, maybe even hero-worshipped him a little. But what he'd just said sounded like more than that. It sounded personal.

She sipped at her coffee, trying to figure out how to approach this. Ultimately, she decided that direct was best. "Charlie, is there something you're not telling me? Something you had firsthand knowledge of seventeen years ago that's driving you now?"

Clearly, the question startled him. His eyes narrowed. "Where are you going with this?"

"I'm not sure. It's just the way you said that, about doing this for my father and me, you sounded . . . I don't know, invested."

"I am invested," he replied flatly. "I thought the world of your father. I think the world of you. Anything I can do to set things right, I will."

"I don't doubt that." Morgan wasn't ready to back down. The feeling she had wasn't going away. And her instincts were rarely without basis. "I'm not questioning your motives. I'm questioning your suspicions. You were working for the D.A. when my father was killed. Were you privy to something that didn't seem right, but that you dismissed as unrelated at the time?"

Charlie's gaze hardened. "Don't pump me, Morgan. I'm a prosecutor. I manipulate information out of people, not the other way around."

"Right. And you work for the D.A. Your allegiance has to encompass more than just my father and me."

"It has to. That doesn't mean it does."

"What are you—" Morgan bit off her question. She was dying to push this. But something in Charlie's expression made her back down. She'd have to bide her time. Otherwise, she'd blow one of the few inside connections she had.

"Okay," she said carefully. "Let's drop this for now. Whatever it is, you'll tell me . . . when you're ready."

A flash of irony flickered in his eyes. "Count on it." He resumed eating his sandwich.

Taking a deep breath, Morgan changed the subject. "Let's talk about the weekend. How did things go with your dates?"

"Very well." Charlie's words seemed forced, complimentary or not. "Rachel might be young, but she's a real go-getter. I admire her ambition. Hell,

I see it in myself. Anyway, we went to dinner, saw a show, then had drinks and debated the death penalty until three A.M. As for Karly, she's great-looking, charming, and intuitive. My energy level was low the night we got together. She picked up on that right away, and kept things mellow. We had a leisurely dinner at La Grenouille. Actually, we saw Congressman Shore there. He was with Daniel Kellerman and several other business-men. I would have said hello, but they seemed to be in the middle of a heavy discussion."

A shrug. "Probably about the bill Arthur's sponsoring. He has dozens of meetings between now and January, when Congress reconvenes." Morgan dismissed the subject with a wave of her hand. "So back to Karly and Ra-chel. Any sparks? Any desire to see either of them again? Because it sounds to me more like you're delivering a keynote address than reporting on dates with two incredible women."

Charlie's lips curved slightly. "Does it? I didn't mean for it to. They were both lovely. Maybe it's just my state of mind right now. Maybe I'm just distracted."

"Then I'm not doing my job well enough," Morgan declared. "Because I'm supposed to help you find someone who'll overcome that distraction." She eased her plate aside and flipped open the file to a clean sheet of paper. "Let's talk specifics. I'm hell-bent on finding you the woman of your dreams."

Charlie raised his coffee cup. "Then here's to specifics. May they hold the key to my happiness."

RACHEL OGDEN AND Karly Fontaine had never met.

So they had no way of knowing they crossed paths on Madison Ave-nue at one-forty that afternoon.

Rachel was on her way to the St. Regis hotel for the consult she'd sched-uled with Morgan. She'd just finished up a half-day meeting with a major advertising firm she was working with on acquisition candidates. Her mind was in a million places at once, and she was striding through the city on autopilot.

She should be getting back to the office. She really didn't have another hour to devote to her love life. But Morgan had a way of inspiring confidence. Her approach promised results. And with the way Rachel's career was skyrocketing, the long hours she was putting in, she wouldn't have a minute to personally seek out fascinating men. So why not have Winshore do it for her? They were pros, and besides, she'd done a lousy job of managing her love life on her own. Her track record stunk. The men she found were either totally self-involved, unwilling to compromise or commit, or married.

No more of that. Time to level the playing field.

Rachel reached the corner of Fifty-third and Madison, and was waiting for the traffic light to change. That's when Karly Fontaine approached, coming from the opposite direction.

Karly's day had been equally hectic. Botched photo sessions. Massaging delicate egos. Soothing irate magazine publishers. Her modeling agency had been like the set of a bad soap opera since 8 A.M. Now she was headed for the subway station to catch the E train downtown, in the hopes of putting out yet another fire.

The two women never saw each other. The corner was jammed with pedestrians elbowing to gain advantage. Rachel edged her way between two people and stepped into the street the minute the light turned green. Karly was half a step behind her.

It happened in an instant. A beat-up white van screeched around the corner and struck Rachel head-on, sending her flying through the air and then crashing to the street, where she rolled to the curb. Several bystanders screamed. Cars swerved to avoid her. Even taxis slammed on their brakes.

The van never stopped.

Without glancing back, the driver weaved through traffic, racing up Madison Avenue until the van was swallowed up and gone.

FOURTEEN

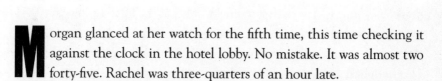

organ glanced at her watch for the fifth time, this time checking it against the clock in the hotel lobby. No mistake. It was almost two forty-five. Rachel was three-quarters of an hour late.

At first she'd attributed it to whatever accident was causing the past hour's traffic tie-up. Sirens had wailed by in rapid succession. Morgan's concern had prompted her to step outside. She'd spotted the flashing red lights down the street, and hoped it was nothing serious. But she'd also noted that the road was partially blocked off, so maybe Rachel had had to take a detour to get to the St. Regis.

On the other hand, she hadn't called. That seemed odd, given Rachel's type-A personality.

Flipping open her cell phone, Morgan pressed send to redial Rachel's number, since she'd called it three times already. The number rang and rang, then went to voice mail.

Morgan left a brief message, then punched off. She couldn't wait here much longer. She had a thousand things to do, plus an appointment with

Karly Fontaine in less than an hour. Frowning, she fished in her purse and pulled out her PDA, searching until she found Rachel's office number. She'd call her there. If nothing else, maybe her assistant could explain what the holdup was, and reschedule their appointment.

The direct line rang twice. Then a young female voice answered, her tone distraught and nearly drowned out by a commotion in the background. "Rachel Ogden's office."

"Hi, this is Morgan Winter. Rachel and I had an appointment slotted for two o'clock at the St. Regis. I'm still waiting, but—"

"Oh, Ms. Winter, I'm so sorry," the young woman interrupted. "This is Nadine, Rachel's assistant. I meant to call you, but the office is in chaos. Forgive me. I'm just so freaked out and in shock."

"In shock? Why? What happened?"

"Rachel was taken to emergency. She was mowed down by a hit-and-run driver on her way to the St. Regis."

"Dear Lord." Morgan raked a hand through her hair and sank down into a lobby chair. "Is she all right?"

"I don't know. From what the police told us, she's alive, but in pretty bad shape. Fortunately, a woman standing near her at the intersection called 911 immediately. The paramedics took her to New York–Presbyterian. She's either still in the emergency room, unconscious, or she's in surgery. That's all I know right now."

Morgan was having a hard time processing all this. "You said it was a hit-and-run—someone must have seen the car."

The background noise was getting louder, and Nadine was clearly distracted. "It was a white van. I'm sorry, Ms. Winter, but I've got to hang up now. The police want to speak to me."

"Of course." Morgan cut the conversation short. "I'll let you go. Please keep me posted. I'll say a prayer for Rachel."

"Thank you." Nadine's voice broke. "She needs all the prayers she can get."

THE MINUTE HE got home, Lane snatched up the package the Central Clerk's Office had messengered over. He unlocked the door to his digital photo lab, flipped on the light, and deactivated the alarm system. With almost a quarter of a million dollars of equipment and highly sensitive information inside these four walls, his photo lab was a secure lockbox, off-limits to everyone except him.

The windowless room looked similar to most offices with computer workstations, except on a larger and grander scale. The equipment was state-of-the-art—way beyond most budgets. Then again, most budgets weren't partially subsidized by the U.S. government, since most photographers didn't take on covert assignments for the CIA.

Lane wasn't most photographers.

And his lab wasn't most labs.

The IBM T221 LCD monitor alone cost $10,000, and Lane had two of them. With twice the resolution of other high-quality displays, the monitor made it possible to see minute details in digital images—details other monitors wouldn't even show. And that was only a small portion of the elaborate digital darkroom.

Lane walked over and turned on the air-conditioning unit. Even in wintertime, with all the equipment running, the room would quickly become an oven. One by one, he powered on each piece of equipment in sequence, and as they hummed to life, he turned and opened a drawer underneath the work surface, removing the necessary equipment and supplies to transform the film into digital images.

His mind was racing faster than his hands, reflecting on the conversation that had been taking place at Lenny's when he arrived.

He'd been ten feet from his father's table for a good five minutes before announcing himself. He'd perched behind the coat stand, leaning over his camera bag, his back to the table so as not to be spotted. Having heard the name George Hayek, he'd decided to eavesdrop.

He'd been bugged by the George Hayek link to Lenny all weekend. He'd been stunned, and baffled. Given what he knew through his CIA connections, he couldn't figure out where Hayek fit into the picture. Monty, of course, wasn't privy to the same information he was. So, like the pro he was, Monty was pursuing the angle like a dog with a bone. But nothing in the conversation Lane had overheard had triggered any warning bells. Still, given what Hayek was currently involved in, he planned to keep a close eye on things, and act on them, if necessary.

Turning back to the work at hand, Lane completed his preparation. Then he opened the envelope, extracting the negative carrier and carefully removing the first negative strip from the sleeve. Taking his ionizer gun, he eliminated the accumulated dust with blasts of electrically charged air. That done, he held the strip up to the light, pleased to see there were very few fingerprints on the film. He carefully placed it inside the SlickMount drum and, using a pipette, carefully added a few drops of oil between the film and the inside surface of the drum. Then he inserted the drum into the scanner and closed the cover. Returning to his workstation, he fired up the ScanXact software and the scanner came to life.

He was eager as hell to get started. For Monty's sake. For justice's sake.

And, yeah, for Morgan's sake.

She was getting under his skin, that was for sure. There was something powerful happening between them, something downright riveting. And it wasn't just sexual tension, although that crackled like a live wire. But there was more, something that was entirely new and extraordinarily intriguing.

In the midst of all this, she was hurting, fighting a nightmare she'd never escaped and was now being forced to confront again.

He was determined to help her.

JONAH STOOD IN the reception area of Congressman Shore's office, fiddling with the F-stop on his camera as he waited for the congressman to finish up. Jonah was nervous. This was the first solo assignment Lane had given him; and it was a big one. He was responsible for capturing just the right photos of the congressman—shots that depicted him as the charismatic, committed representative of the people of New York that he was.

Right now, he was chatting with one of his local aides, a perky young woman who emanated good looks and wide-eyed admiration. She was gazing up at the congressman as if he were a superhero, and he was answering her question with warmth and intensity, his body language conveying a keen interest in what she was saying. He was leaning toward her, his head cocked slightly to one side, his forehead creased in concentration as he listened, nodding every minute or two, alternately listening and talking.

Impulsively, Jonah raised his camera and snapped a couple of shots. It would round out the photo essay to show the congressman interacting with his staff as well as interacting with his constituents.

"Don't bother." It was a woman's pained monotone, coming from just behind Jonah's shoulder. "There are enough of those shots in the *Enquirer*."

Startled, Jonah turned. He recognized the petite, attractive middle-aged woman immediately. "Mrs. Shore," he managed, feeling self-conscious at the strain on her face, in her voice. "I didn't mean to . . . I'm just assisting Lane Montgomery in his . . ."

"I realize that." The look in her eyes was hollow, like she'd been through something bad and was desperately trying to come to grips with it.

She stared directly at her husband, swallowing hard as she did. "You're just doing your job. You want to capture the congressman doing what he does best. Which you are. But trust me, this isn't what *Time* wants. If anything, it's what they want to avoid." She turned away. "So do I."

MORGAN CALLED THE hospital to check on Rachel while she waited for Karly at the Greenwich Village café where they'd arranged to meet.

Karly walked in just as Morgan was finishing up. She snapped her phone shut, feeling moderately encouraged by what she'd been told. The doctors had operated on Rachel. Her prognosis was good, although she'd need a fair amount of physical therapy to come back to herself. Fortunately, she was young and strong. But she'd suffered internal injuries, including a ruptured spleen and several broken ribs. There'd been internal bleeding, and a pelvic fracture, so the prediction of pain was almost guaranteed to be true.

Karly slid into her chair, looking as depleted as Morgan felt, although she forced herself to smile. "Hi. I appreciate your going so far out of your way to meet me. My last appointment was way downtown. It was pressing or, frankly, I would have bagged it and just gone home. This day has been . . ." She shook her head. "Anyway, after we talk, I'm heading home. I can't even think of going back to the office."

"I hear you," Morgan murmured. "It's been a hellish day—obviously for both of us."

"Amen." Karly massaged her temples. "But no business crisis seems to matter—not after what I witnessed a few hours ago. I was on my way to catch the subway at Madison and Fifty-third, and I saw a young woman get struck by a hit-and-run driver. It was horrible. I can't get the image out of my mind. The creepy part is, I was right behind her. Five seconds later, and it could have been me. That van flew out of nowhere. The whole thing happened in an instant. I didn't even have a chance to react, much less to prevent it. One second she was brushing by me, and the next she was lying in the street bleeding. I could scarcely keep myself together long enough to call 911."

Morgan's eyes widened. "Are you talking about Rachel Ogden?"

"Yes, that was her name." It was Karly's turn to look surprised. "Do you know her?"

"She's a client. She was on her way to the St. Regis to meet me when the accident happened."

Karly exhaled sharply, interlacing her fingers. "I had no idea. What a horrible coincidence." A tentative, questioning look. "Do you know how she's doing? I called the hospital, but they wouldn't release any information to me."

"I just hung up with them. Rachel's assistant was kind enough to get my name put on the list of family and friends." Morgan gave a weak smile. "She'll be okay—eventually." Briefly, she filled Karly in on the update she'd just received.

"That poor girl." Karly's throat worked as she visibly battled emotion. "Life is so random. Like I said, seconds later, and it might have been me lying in that hospital. On the one hand, I feel lucky and relieved. At the same time I feel guilty for feeling that way. Most of all, I feel responsible. If only I could have grabbed her."

"Well, you couldn't, and you're not." Morgan reached across the table and squeezed Karly's arm. "If anything, you should feel good about yourself. According to Rachel's assistant, you saved her life by calling 911 so fast. A few more minutes and she might not have pulled through."

"I'm glad. To be honest, I barely remember using my cell. The whole thing was a blur. I know I made the call, but I was frozen in place when I did. Everything felt surreal. I remember the sirens and the flashing lights.

I remember the paramedics doing their jobs. I talked to the cops. I told them what I saw, which wasn't much. I didn't get a license plate, didn't get a make or model, didn't even see the driver. He was hunched over the steering wheel. I guess he realized what he'd done and was trying to escape without being seen. The bastard. Why didn't he stop?"

"Because he was a coward," Morgan supplied. "He knew he'd be arrested for reckless driving, or maybe even drunk driving."

Karly nodded. "The way he tore around that corner, he could very well have been drunk. And after he hit Rachel, he floored the gas. He was weaving in and out of traffic like a lunatic."

"The police will trace the van. They'll find out who did this. And they'll toss his butt in jail." Morgan sighed. "Now let's just pray Rachel makes a full and speedy recovery."

"Amen." Karly glanced at the file in Morgan's hand. "Would you mind if we rescheduled this follow-up? I don't have the presence of mind to discuss my social life right now."

"I'm not at my peak, either," Morgan admitted. "Why don't we do a telephone follow-up later this week? Or you could come by my office instead. You've never seen the place, and now is the ideal time. It's got more holiday spirit than Santa's workshop. Jill's converted it into a holiday extravaganza—Christmas, Hanukkah, Kwanzaa, and the winter solstice all rolled into one. She's an equal-opportunity celebrator."

"Jill?" Karly's brows drew together in question.

"My partner. That's right, you've never met her. Well, we'll have to rectify that."

Karly blew out a breath. "That meeting might have to wait. Ditto for the visit. I'll have to take you up on your offer to do our follow-up on the phone. I'm crazed between now and Christmas. But I'd love to meet your partner. Maybe after New Year's. Or do the decorations come down right away?"

"Are you kidding? At Winshore, the holidays last until mid-January. That's when Jill starts working on Valentine's Day."

For the first time, Karly chuckled. "This partner of yours sounds like quite a dynamo."

"She is." Morgan smiled back. "You'll see for yourself. Even if you can't break away long enough to come to our office, you will be at our holiday party, right?"

"I have the date in my PDA. A week from Tuesday. Seven P.M. I wouldn't miss it."

"Excellent. Then you'll be meeting Jill then. She planned the party, so it's bound to be an affair to remember."

"I'll wear my new Chanel dress. It'll be perfect. And who knows? Maybe that's the night I'll meet Mr. Right."

"Speaking of which . . ." Morgan leaned forward, curious to hear if Karly's take on the evening was the same as Charlie's. "What did you think of Charlie Denton?"

A shrug. "Nice guy. A little on the introspective side, but very charming. A great listener. Intelligent, too, and intense." Karly wrinkled her nose. "I wish he'd directed a little more of his intensity at me, and not at the businessmen at the next table."

Morgan knew exactly who Karly was referring to, since Charlie had mentioned Arthur's powwow. "Charlie said something about a high-powered meeting going on at a nearby table. But he didn't dwell on it. He just mentioned it in passing."

"Well, he was definitely distracted. So much so that, at first, I thought he was staring at another woman. Which didn't do much for my ego, given I was his date. But then I saw it was some businessmen and politicians he was focused on. So I assumed his interest must have been work-related. Still, it did put a damper on the evening, having only half his attention."

"I'm sure it wasn't personal. As a prosecutor, Charlie must have a lot on his plate."

"True, but the crowd at the next table wasn't on that plate. At least not while he was out with me." Karly broke off with a rueful expression. "Sorry. I don't mean to sound bitchy. I'm just not a very good sharer. When I'm out with a man, I expect his undivided attention. Call it self-centered, or call it insecurity." A shrug. "In any case, I don't hold it against him. We had a lovely dinner. As I said, he's a nice guy. A really nice guy."

"Just not *the* guy," Morgan concluded.

"No—at least not for me."

"Enough said." Morgan filed away the nuances—those she'd picked up from Charlie, and those she'd just had reinforced by Karly. "Let's see what we can do about zeroing in on *the* guy."

HOURS HAD PASSED. Lane was exhausted but satisfied with the results. He had coaxed every bit of resolution out of the original crime-scene negatives. He was in the middle of backing up the files to DVDs when his doorbell rang.

Right on cue.

He tore himself away from his work long enough to leave the lab and let his father into the brownstone. "Hey, Monty," he greeted wryly. "What took you so long?"

"Cut the chitchat." His father marched inside. "What did you find? And what were you doing skulking around Lenny's like Secret Agent Man, hiding behind a coatrack?"

Lane exhaled sharply. He should have known. Nothing got by Monty. "I was getting a feel for the turf, figuring out what aspect of the investigation you guys were talking about."

"In other words, this is about Hayek. Fine. You'll tell me when you're ready. Just make it soon." Monty didn't miss a beat. "Back to my question— what did you find out?"

"Give me a break, Serpico," Lane retorted, rolling his eyes. "I just finished turning your precious negatives into digital gold nuggets. I haven't had time to do anything beyond making sure that the scans were high quality."

That response was greeted with a scowl. "How much longer before we get our answers?"

"This isn't like shooting Polaroids, Monty. They don't develop in three minutes."

"Fine. I'll give you five minutes."

"Gee, thanks. Tell you what. Instead of harassing me, why don't you make yourself useful? Go out and pick us up some dinner. And buy us three jumbo cups of coffee each. It's going to be a long night."

"Great." Another scowl, this one surlier than the last. "I'd better call your mother and tell her I won't be coming home. She's going to be pissed and it's your fault. I'll be sure to tell her that, too."

"She'll forgive me." Lane looked unconcerned. "I'm her favorite son."

"You're her *only* son."

"True. You, on the other hand, might not be so lucky."

"Why? I'm her only husband."

"Yeah, but if she doesn't get her pastrami sandwich and Rhoda's chopped liver, you'll be sleeping on the couch for a week."

"Not to worry. I'm safe. I drove home after lunch and delivered Lenny's food. Your mother will find it in the fridge when she gets home."

"Ah. Then there's hope for you yet." Lane jerked his thumb in the direction of the front door. "Enough banter. You get dinner and coffee. I'll get back to work. We have a lot of ground to cover. The sooner I start, the sooner we'll have our answers."

MORGAN WAS JUST popping a Lean Cuisine into the microwave when her phone rang. She scooped up the telephone as the microwave whirred into action. "Hello?"

"Morgan?"

"Yes, who's this?"

"Charlie Denton. I wanted to make sure you were all right."

She paused in the process of reaching for a pot holder. "Why wouldn't I be?"

"That hit-and-run on Madison. I'm sure you heard about it on the evening news. The victim was Rachel Ogden. I requested a copy of the police report, which I just got. It turns out that Karly Fontaine was the person who called it in."

"Yes, I know. The whole situation's tragic. Rachel had to go through surgery, and it'll be months before she's herself. And Karly—she's a mess. I spoke with her. She's pretty traumatized."

"I'm sure she is. But what about you?"

"Me?"

"Morgan, you're the common denominator here. It worries me. Think about it. Two of your clients, both in the exact same spot at the exact same time. Not only that, but it happens to be the exact instant that some maniac driver comes barreling around the corner and plows one of them down."

"It's a horrible coincidence, I agree. But—"

"Coincidences like that don't happen."

Morgan sank down into a chair. "Where are you going with this? You think this was personal?"

"Maybe. Maybe it was a warning."

"A warning?" Morgan was trying to assimilate what Charlie was telling her. "How would hurting one of my clients be a warning to me? Why would I even make the connection you're alluding to?"

"Who was Rachel on her way to meet?"

A tense pause. "Me."

"Right. Which means you'd find out about the so-called accident quickly. As for Karly being at the scene, that tells me someone went to a lot of trouble to familiarize himself with both women's schedules. His goal was to send you a message. Twice the number of clients meant twice the likelihood you'd realize the message was for you."

"And what was this message?"

"To back off. To have *me* back off. I don't have a concrete answer for you. But the timing, the women involved, the fact that I just spent virtually back-to-back evenings with those women, and the fact that I'm poking around the D.A.'s office, asking sensitive questions, maybe getting close enough to push someone's hot button—doesn't that strike you as too much of a coincidence? Because it sure as hell does me. It tells me someone doesn't like the direction we're heading in, or what we're on the verge of finding."

Morgan was starting to tremble. "So you think this was planned. Someone was sitting in a van, waiting for Rachel to show up so he could hit her. If that's the case, why choose my client? Why not go for the gold and run me down instead?"

"Because he's smart. Smart criminals aren't obvious. They're subtle. They do something personal enough to make their point, not explicit enough to get the cops interested. In this case, with your parents' case reopened, running you down would be like waving a red flag in a bull's face."

"You really think . . . ?" Behind Morgan, the microwave started a rhythmic beeping, announcing it had finished cooking her Lean Cuisine. She scarcely heard it. "Charlie, you're scaring me."

"That wasn't my intent. But I'm a prosecutor. Unlikely coincidences jump out at me. And if there's a chance I'm right, if someone is trying to scare you off, I had to let you know. To make sure you were okay, and to advise you to be careful."

"Thanks—I think."

"Just lock your door and put on your alarm. In the meantime, I'll keep working this angle. I'll see what else I can find out, and call you tomorrow. Okay?"

"Okay."

Charlie heard the apprehension in her tone, and responded to it. "Hey, Morgan? Hang in there."

"I'll try."

FIFTEEN

Lane and Monty were in the kitchen, finishing their take-out burritos and polishing off their first giant cups of coffee, when Monty's cell phone rang.

He glanced at his watch: 10:15. Late enough for the call to be important; not so late that it meant something was wrong.

He punched on the phone. "Montgomery."

"Detective . . . hi. It's Morgan Winter." She sounded surprised to hear him, live and talking to her. Clearly, she'd been expecting voice mail.

She also sounded rattled.

"I hope I'm not calling too late."

"Nope. Perfect timing," he assured her. "For the past three hours, I've been sitting on my ass . . . sorry—my butt. It's numb."

"Sitting. Then you must be hanging out, relaxing with your wife. Please apologize to her for me. I didn't mean to interrupt your evening."

"Not to worry. I'm not home. I'm at Lane's. He and I are going through the scans—or, rather, he is. I'm just watching from the sidelines, waiting for something that looks out of place."

"Lane's? Isn't his town house near mine?"

"Not far."

"Too far to ask you to drop over?"

"Now?"

"If that's possible."

Monty's eyes narrowed. "Is everything okay?"

A jittery pause. "I'm not sure. I could be overreacting. But I'd feel better if I ran this by you and got your opinion. And as long as you haven't left the city yet . . ." Another pause. "This is ridiculous. It's late. You and Lane are working—on my case no less. Forget I called. We'll pick this up tomorrow—"

"I'm grabbing my coat," Monty interrupted to inform her. "I could use some air. And Lane will be thrilled to have me off his back for a while. I'll be there soon." He punched off, lifting his head to meet Lane's gaze. His son had swiveled around on the kitchen stool and was eyeing him quizzically—and with more than a touch of concern.

"What's going on?"

"No clue. But whatever it is, it's got Morgan pretty freaked out. I'm going to run over there and see what's up."

"I'll go with you."

"No, you won't. You'll go back into your lab and scrutinize those scans until you have something to tell me."

Lane was about to protest, when his doorbell rang.

"Damn," he muttered, coming to his feet. "It's a moot point. I can't leave. That's Jonah. I completely forgot he was dropping by."

"It's a little late for a mentoring session, isn't it?" Monty sounded annoyed. "Besides, much as I like the kid, I don't want him distracting you from these scans."

"He won't. This will be quick. He finished developing the photos he took today of Arthur Shore, and he's eager for me to look at them." A pensive frown. "I also got the feeling something threw him for a loop, and he wants to talk to me about it."

"Then I'm outta here." Monty was headed toward the door. He strode through the hall, snatched his jacket off the hook, and was shrugging into it when Lane opened the door for Jonah.

"Hey," Lane greeted him. "Come on in."

Jonah hovered in the doorway, glancing from Lane to Monty. "Hi, Detective Montgomery." He shifted awkwardly. "If this is a bad time, I can come back."

"Not a bad time at all," Monty assured him. "I've got an errand to run. I'll be gone an hour or so. That'll give you and Lane some time to talk before I drag him back to work."

"Thanks."

Monty zipped up his jacket, then shot Lane a purposeful look. "I won't be long. Get back to those photos as soon as you can."

"Will do." Lane shut the door behind his father.

"Sorry." Jonah kicked snow off his boot. "I hope your dad's not pissed."

A corner of Lane's mouth lifted. "That wasn't his pissed voice. That was his Dick Tracy voice. He's in his get-it-solved mode. Don't take it personally." Lane extended his arm. "Give me your coat, and grab a seat anywhere—just not in the lab. It's a zoo."

"And off-limits. I get it." Jonah handed over his parka, simultaneously whipping out an envelope and offering it to Lane. "Here are the photos. I got shots of the congressman at his meetings, among his constituents, and even in his office. I think a bunch of them work. But I want your opinion."

"No problem," Lane replied, taking the envelope. "Although I'm sure you did a great job. Now let's get to what's bugging you. I got the feeling there was something on your mind other than getting my professional opinion on your photographic assignment."

A nod, as Jonah dropped onto the sofa. "I had kind of a weird experience at Congressman Shore's office today. I need some advice. Maybe some perspective. Maybe some reassurance."

"Go on." Lane leaned against the wall, folding his arms across his chest.

"Like I said, I took some shots of the congressman in his office. Mostly they were candids of him with his staff. I zoomed in on one aide in particular—Heidi Garber. She's about twenty-three, really photogenic, and she's got a great rapport with the congressman. They were talking, going over his agenda. The interaction captured a side of him that worked. Warm. Tight with his staff. So I snapped six or seven shots in rapid succession. In the middle of it, Mrs. Shore walked in. She got ticked off, told me to pick another angle to focus on. I'm not dumb. I get where it's coming from. I'm just not sure how to handle it. This is my first big assignment. I don't want to blow it. Do you think I did?"

Lane felt a wave of compassion for Jonah. The uncertain look in his eyes, the nervous pumping of his leg—they only served to remind Lane that his assistant was just an insecure teenager trying to prove himself. And finding himself in the middle of all the personal drama surrounding Arthur Shore couldn't be easy.

"You didn't blow anything," he assured Jonah. "Elyse Shore might be sensitive about certain issues surrounding her husband, but she's a nice lady. She's actually pretty laid-back and upbeat. She's not going to throw a monkey wrench in your work or at you—not unless you outright insulted her. Did you?"

"Uh-uh." Jonah shook his head. "I didn't even answer her. I was too tongue-tied. I just stood there. The good part is, I don't think she noticed. She turned and walked out right after she saw her husband hanging out with Heidi."

"Then I'd say you're safe."

"I hope so." Jonah shuffled in his seat. "It's hard to imagine Mrs. Shore as laid-back. She was pretty uptight when she told me to change perspectives. And the way she looked when she left was anything but upbeat. She looked beaten up. I don't mean physically—"

"I know what you mean," Lane interrupted. "And you did the right thing by staying out of it. Here's some advice, for both work and play: never get in the middle of a relationship. *You're* the one who'll end up beaten up."

"I hear you." Jonah looked relieved. "Anyway, I shifted gears after that. Just some random shots of the congressman at work. They have less eye appeal, but they're a lot safer."

Lane chuckled. "Let me take a look." He opened the envelope, slid out the prints Jonah had made. The kid had definite talent. In a couple of rolls, he'd captured the essence of "Congressman Shore wins his district's faith, support, and hearts."

"These are exceptional," Lane informed his assistant. "You've got real talent, Jonah. Don't let anyone tell you otherwise."

"Thanks." Jonah released the breath he'd been holding, pride and pleasure lighting his eyes. "Coming from you, that means a lot."

"It also means you'll be doing more on this project—if you want to."

"If I *want* to? Are you kidding? Just tell me what you need and it's done."

"I like your enthusiasm. Plus, I think it would be good for you to spread your wings. Photography's a big field. I'd be remiss if I didn't point that out to you. There's a ton of different career paths you can take. Photojournalism's just one, especially given the other talents you bring to the table. Your technical aptitudes are off the charts, not only behind the lens but on the computer, in the lab. Explore every avenue."

Rather than puffing up at the compliment, Jonah grimaced. "You're not talking about taking more courses, are you?"

"No," Lane answered thoughtfully. "I wasn't thinking of more classroom training. You're on the right track in that area. But speaking of school, what's your schedule this week? Brooklyn Tech is on break for the holidays, isn't it?" He waited for Jonah's nod. "Good. Because that matters for what I have in mind. How'd you feel about joining me on the road, as they say? Or in this case, in the air—to Colorado and the Poconos?"

Jonah nearly leaped to his feet. "Say when and I'm packed."

"Tomorrow. Of course, I'll need permission from your folks. It'll only be for a couple of days, and you'll be under my supervision at all times. And before you ask, no, you don't get to jump out of planes or go heli-skiing. You just get to take ground and aerial shots of the congressman and me doing that."

"I can live with that." Jonah paused, his excitement suspended as a thought struck. "I hope my parents will be okay with this. We've got some heavy stuff going on at home right now."

"Really." Lane's brows rose. It was the first time Jonah had offered up anything personal about his home life. Lane knew that the Vaughns lived in the Sheepshead Bay section of Brooklyn, that Jonah's father worked as a mechanic and his mother as a hospital aide. He'd never met either of them, except by phone, and that was a perfunctory call when Jonah started working for him. They'd seemed like a normal, caring set of parents, asking questions and expressing pride in their son.

Clearly, whatever "stuff" was going on was bugging Jonah. Lane didn't want to pry, but he didn't want to give Jonah the impression he didn't care, either.

"Anything you want to talk about?" he asked carefully.

Rather than shutting down, Jonah seemed torn, like he wanted to open up but wasn't quite ready to. "Maybe later." His response confirmed Lane's assessment. "Right now, I'm still trying to sort it out." Abruptly, his head came up. "I'm not in any trouble, if that's what's worrying you."

"It's not. If you want the truth, what's worrying me is that it might be financial. If so, I'd like to help."

"Thanks, Lane, that's really cool of you. But, no, it's not about money. It's about me, who I am. I've got issues to come to terms with. So do my parents." He rubbed the back of his neck. "But, man, I really want to go on these trips with you. And a couple of days won't change anything anyway."

Lane processed that, studying his assistant. Whatever identity crisis Jonah was going through, he needed something solid and real to lean on. And in his case, photography was it.

"How about if I call your folks?" Lane suggested. "I'll tell them about the opportunity, and the fact that a credit in *Time* could clinch a scholarship for you. Do you think that would help?"

"Yeah." Jonah blew out a relieved breath. "Yeah, I think that would help a lot. In fact, I'm pretty sure it would give me the green light."

"Consider it done, then." Lane glanced at his watch. "Damn. It's eleven o'clock. You've got to get home, and I've got to get back to work. I've got a mound of work to accomplish before I take off for Colorado. So I'll call your parents first thing in the morning."

"My dad goes into the shop at seven," Jonah quickly supplied. "My mom's at the hospital by eight. The whole house is awake at six."

"Got it. I'll call at six-thirty. That'll give your parents time to open their eyes. And it'll give you plenty of time to pack. We're not leaving till ten."

"Great." Jonah got up and snatched his jacket. "So we'll talk in the morning?"

"Yup. And pack warm clothes. It'll be freezing in the San Juans."

MORGAN HEARD THE knock at her front door. She walked quickly down the hall, although she had no intention of even touching the lock until she knew who was on the other side of the door.

Detective Montgomery saved her the trouble of asking. "It's Pete Montgomery," he called.

Gratefully, she unlocked the door and let him in. "Thank you so much for coming. I feel like an idiot bothering you at this time of night."

"It wasn't a bother, not if you've got some coffee." He'd already yanked off his parka.

"Already brewed." Morgan managed a smile, hanging up Monty's jacket and leading him toward the staircase. "Let's go to the second-floor sitting room. It's more comfortable, and right next to the kitchen—which means it's near the Impressa."

"The what?"

Her smile curved into something real rather than strained. "The Impressa. My über-elite coffee center. It brews everything from espresso to cappuccino to latte." She preceded Monty up the staircase, tossing a reassuring look over her shoulder. "Don't worry. I sensed you weren't a latte kind of guy. So I brewed a pot of regular."

"Good." He marched upstairs behind her, already wired and willing to become more so. "Caffeine's good for cops and PIs. It keeps our minds and bodies working overtime."

"I doubt you need it. That seems to come naturally to you." Morgan showed Monty into the sitting room and left long enough to bring him a steaming mug. "Here you go."

"Thanks." Perched at the edge of the settee, Monty took an appreciative gulp. "Strong and leaded, the way I like it." He raised his chin, fixing Morgan with a probing stare. "Now, tell me what happened to freak you out so much."

"A couple of things." Morgan sank down across from him and crossed her legs. "Did you hear about today's hit-and-run on Madison?"

"Yeah. On the radio." Monty made a face. "When those happen in East New York, the stories barely make the eleven o'clock news. When it's in a classy section of midtown, it's on every local channel at five. Go figure." His eyes narrowed. "Why? Did you know the woman?"

"She's one of my clients. So is the woman who called in the accident."

"Interesting." Monty's facial expression didn't change. "Go on."

Morgan detailed the entire scenario for him. "Rachel's going to be okay. Initially, that's all I focused on. Meaningful coincidences never entered my mind. Then I got this cryptic phone call from Charlie Denton."

"Denton?" This time Monty's brows rose. "Where does he factor into this?"

"I matched him up with both Karly and Rachel. He saw each of them this past weekend. The fact that they were the women involved in this hit-and-run, combined with the fact that he's digging around for me—he thinks it could be some kind of message telling me to back off."

"Or telling *him* to back off."

"In this case, isn't that the same thing?"

"Not necessarily." Monty shook his head. "Denton's a prosecutor. He's got enemies, just like your father did. Maybe one of them's been following him around and decided to go after the women he's seeing. I wonder why his mind didn't go in *that* direction—unless he has reason for it not to."

Morgan jumped on that one pronto. "You think he knows something he's not ready to share." She didn't wait for an answer. "So do I. In fact, he all but admitted it. He just shuts down whenever I press him, asks me to be patient and give him time and space."

"Then give him the time and space he's asking for. Keep your relationship with him strong and positive. Let me be the bad guy. Or Congressman Shore—*if* it comes to that. I hope it won't. A direct confrontation should be our last resort. We're much better off soft-pedaling it. Pressure would only piss Denton off or scare him off, and we need him in our corner."

"But if he's withholding inside information . . ."

"Then he might have a good reason for doing so," Monty finished for her. "Remember, he's wading through mounds of red tape, and avoiding land mines along the way. That's a rough job. As far as we know, he's loyal to you and your father—unless he proves otherwise." A pensive pause. "Let's see if I can get some answers from a different source."

"Such as?"

"Such as, you let me worry about that." Monty's head came up and he peered around curiously, as if becoming aware that something was missing. "Speaking of Jill, where is she? I thought you said she was home."

Morgan nodded. "She is. It's her yoga time. She's upstairs, centering herself." A sigh. "Jill's amazing at finding ways to unwind. I wish they worked for me. I'm not too good at finding inner peace."

"I hear you. My wife keeps trying to reform me. She's not the yoga type, but she's into the great outdoors. She finds herself when she's hiking, camping, or horseback riding. Since I moved back in, she's got me taking long walks with her. She says they're energy-restoring, physically and mentally."

"And?"

"And I like them. They get my blood pumping, and give me a chance to tromp around in the snow with Sally. But as for being restored, the only part of me that works for is my body. My mind is running on a treadmill of its own."

Morgan smiled, leaning forward and propping her chin on her palm. "Lane's a lot like you, isn't he?"

"Afraid so."

"He's got two sides to him," Morgan continued, speaking as much to herself as to Monty. "One side's warm, insightful, and charismatic."

"And the other's a stubborn, independent, reckless pain in the ass."

"Exactly." Realizing how brusque that sounded, Morgan gave him a rueful look. "Sorry. That came out pretty insulting."

"Nope. Just true." Monty shrugged. "Lane's a complex guy. He'll get there. He just needs to understand why."

Before Morgan could question that cryptic remark, Monty's cell phone rang.

"I'm a popular guy tonight," he noted, glancing at the caller ID. "Ah, speak of the devil." He punched the send button. "Lane? Did you find something?" His eyes narrowed. "Huh. No, no major surprise. The better question is, does it show us anything meaningful? Fine, keep enhancing. I'll be back soon." A pause. "Yes, she's fine. Just spooked by some fluke-ish events. Sure, hang on." He handed the cell to Morgan. "He wants to talk to you."

Morgan took the phone and put it next to her ear. "Hi. I take it you're still enhancing."

"Like a demon. I'm just checking in. You okay?"

"Fine. Your father's got my minidrama under control."

"Nothing serious?"

"Just more puzzle pieces."

"Monty will solve them."

"I know. With your help."

"Count on it." Lane blew out a breath. "Listen, you know I'm going to Colorado with Arthur tomorrow."

"Jill reminded me, yes."

"Well, I'll be back on Wednesday. Are you free for dinner?"

Morgan's lips curved. "I'll be a boring aftermath to heli-skiing."

"I disagree. You'll be a major source of inspiration."

There was that charisma, sucking her in. Lane Montgomery at his best was near impossible to resist. "In that case, yes, I'm free."

"Not anymore. You're taken for the evening."

"Ah, and you're the taker? So this is an order, not a request?"

His chuckle brushed her ear. "Point made. I'll rephrase. Would you please join me for dinner on Wednesday night? I'd like nothing more. I'll even make it your choice of cuisine."

"Nice incentive. I'd be delighted to."

"Excellent. Is it all right if I call you with an exact time? I'll have a better idea of what's what on Wednesday, before we take off for home. Then you can tell me where you want to eat, and I'll make the reservation."

"Works for me. We'll talk then. Have fun." She gazed quizzically at Monty. "Do you want to talk to your dad?" she asked Lane.

"Have him call me on his way back to my place. We'll talk as he walks."

"Is there something to talk about?"

"I'm not sure. I'll let Monty explain." A pause. "Good night. Take care of yourself."

"I'll try." Morgan punched END and handed the phone back to Monty. "He said you should call him while you're walking back to his town house."

"Will do."

"He also said you'd tell me what he was calling you about."

One dark brow rose. "*Me?* Funny, I got the feeling he was calling *you.*"

Morgan refused to take the bait, although she did feel her cheeks flush. "What did Lane find?"

"An extra negative," Monty replied, sobering. "Whether or not that turns out to be significant remains to be seen."

"I don't understand." She turned up her palms in noncomprehension. "What do you mean an extra negative? Where did it come from?"

A shrug. "Could be we never saw a print of it because it wasn't clear enough to use seventeen years ago, and now technology's changed that. Could be it resembled another negative closely enough to be overlooked as a duplicate. Could be a print was made but it got lost in another file, or was swiped by a cop who wanted it for his collection. It sounds nuts, but it happens. What's more important is what Lane can get off of it, if anything."

Morgan's gaze remained steady. "Is it a picture of my parents' bodies?"

"Yes."

Her nod was tight, but resolved. "I need to see those photos. Let's do it tomorrow, while Lane is away and won't need access to them."

"You're sure?"

"Positive. It's time you and I had that in-depth conversation you suggested. We'll do it all at once. The photos, the entire case file, and your probing into my childhood memories. If I have information I don't realize I have, it's time we found out."

Monty's mouth thinned into a grim line. "Did you talk to your shrink about this? Does he think it's a good idea? That you're ready?"

"He agrees it's necessary." A humorless smile. "He'll be on standby, in case I go to pieces. But I won't."

"No, I don't think you will. Fine. We'll make time tomorrow."

"I'm at your disposal. Morning or afternoon?"

"Let's go for afternoon. I'll use the morning to look into that hit-and-run." Monty paused. "Speaking of evening, I take it you're seeing Lane on Wednesday."

"We're having dinner. But don't worry. I promise to send him right back to the photo lab."

"That's not why I asked." Another pause, as Monty studied her. "There's an interesting chemistry going on between you and my son."

That startled her. "I . . ." The flush was back on her cheeks. "Is that a problem?"

"Not for me. Not in the way you mean." Monty waved away her embarrassment. "Sorry. My observation came out wrong. I don't screen Lane's dates. I stopped doing that ages ago. He's thirty-three, way past the point where I butt into his personal life." A wry grin. "Actually, this is a strange, ironic position for me to be in."

"I'm not following."

"I'm very protective of my daughters; overly so, they'd both tell you. Their mother would agree. You should have seen what I put my son-in-law through before I gave his relationship with Devon my stamp of approval. And my other daughter, Meredith—she's got a boyfriend, but I'm not happy. She's just turning twenty-two, way too young to be involved with a guy."

"Let me guess." Morgan's lips twitched. "You've had a double standard where it comes to your son."

"Sort of. My values were the same. But I worried less. Till now."

"You're worried about Lane—because he's seeing me?"

"Nope. It's the other way around. Lane's not the one I'm worried about. You are. I don't want you getting hurt. I told that to Lane, too—in no uncertain terms." A wry grin. "I told you the situation was ironic."

Morgan felt oddly touched. She and Detective Montgomery had just grazed each other's lives—once, seventeen years ago, and again now—and yet there'd been a paternal quality to his behavior toward her from day one. And the funny thing was, she not only understood it, she reciprocated in kind. The bond they'd forged the night her parents had been killed, the way she trusted and respected him, the way she turned to him when she needed help—Pete Montgomery was definitely a father figure to her. Not in the same way as Arthur was; he'd raised her since she was ten. But in a distinct and different way that was hard to describe.

"I understand," she said simply. Contemplating the rest of what he'd said, she asked, "So did you manage to scare Lane off?"

One dark brow lifted in pointed response. "You talked to him—did it sound to you like I did?"

"I guess not."

"And I guess you're glad." Monty went on, evidently deciding a reply wasn't necessary. "Okay, I get it. I'm relieved to know that whatever vibes I'm picking up on are mutual. So, I'm out of this." A pause. "Almost. First some advice. Stay grounded. You've got a good, level head. You've also got a quick mind and a sharp tongue. They'll keep my son in his place."

"Check," Morgan quipped. "Anything else?"

"No, that about covers it."

"Then you're safe. I'm not the type to be swept off my feet. Not even by a charmer like your son." Morgan sobered. "To be honest, I think Wednesday night will be good for me. Lane has a way of distracting me, keeping me from obsessing over my darkest moments. And given the afternoon you and I have planned for tomorrow, what we'll be delving into, a distraction won't be just welcome. It'll be crucial."

Lines creased Monty's forehead. "You can still change your mind about going through the crime-scene photos."

"No." An adamant shake of her head. "We both know that without digging into the past, we won't get the answers we need. And that thought is more terrifying to me than anything I'll have to face tomorrow."

"I can't argue that point." Monty polished off his coffee and rose. "I have to get back to Lane's. We've got a long night ahead of us."

"Detective . . ." She stopped him from leaving without some tangible reassurance. "You'll call me if you find anything significant?"

"Yes, but don't expect any overnight miracles. Lane's lectured me repeatedly that what he does is a precise, detailed, and lengthy process. So you and I are going to have to conjure up some patience. If anything does turn up sooner rather than later, you'll hear from me. Also, I'll call you in the morning if I learn something about the hit-and-run." He turned, gave her a questioning look. "As for our afternoon get-together, do you want to meet here? Or would it be easier to do this on more neutral turf?"

"More neutral and less harried," Morgan murmured, folding her arms across her breasts. "Why don't I come to your office?"

"If you can break away, that would make more sense."

"I'll be there."

Nodding, Monty headed for the staircase. "Get some sleep," he instructed over his shoulder. "And start eating, or I'll rat you out to Lenny. In which case, he and Rhoda will send over a U-Haul of cold cuts and noodle pudding."

"Too late." Morgan followed him downstairs, plucking his parka off the coatrack and handing it to him. "Arthur already blabbed. My fridge is so full, it groans when I open it."

"Then empty it by eating." Monty gave her a long, stern look. "You've got to stay strong. Not just emotionally, but physically."

"I realize that, Detective. I promise to do my best."

"Do that. By the way, now that I've stuck my nose in your personal life and nagged you about your health, can we cut the formalities? Call me Monty."

She shifted a bit. "That's going to be hard. You're a police detective. I met you as a child. You were bigger than life. You still are."

"Interesting. You were raised by a famous politician. Do you call him Congressman Shore?"

Morgan's lips twitched. "I see your point. Okay, you win. I'll try— Monty."

"See how easy that was?" Monty shrugged into his parka. "Now lock up behind me. Read a book. Put on a CD. Or go upstairs and join Jill. Get into frog position, or whatever the hell it's called. See you tomorrow."

OUTSIDE THE BROWNSTONE, Monty didn't waste a minute. He punched up Lane's number as he started on the brisk walk back.

"Hey," his son greeted him. "Are you on your way?"

"As we speak. Tell me about that extra negative."

"Like I said, it's a shot of Lara and Jack Winter's bodies. The good news is it's pretty clear, it's centrally focused on both bodies, and crime scene took it before they touched or shifted anything or anyone. Which means we've got a fair chance of finding something here. If I had to choose one overlooked negative, this would be it."

"It shouldn't have been overlooked in the first place," Monty muttered. "It was careless and stupid. Everything was just chucked in a box and filed away once Schiller confessed. That should never have happened."

"Don't go down this path, Monty. It's total BS, and a waste of energy. Even if you'd kept digging, you wouldn't have made any progress. The technology didn't exist back then to enhance these images. Now it does. The case has been reopened for less than a week, and you're all over it like white on rice. Stop rethinking the past. You're fixing it. We'll finish what you started."

"Seventeen years too late. After permanent scars have formed."

A hint of a pause. Then Lane cleared his throat. "Is Morgan okay? What was this minidrama she was referring to?"

"A coincidence and a manipulation." Monty filled Lane in on the details. "The hit-and-run I can easily get the specs on, and figure out if it really was just a coincidence. As for Charlie Denton, he knows something. Whatever it is, he's keeping it close to the vest. That bothers me, but not as much as why he's doing it. Obviously, he's protecting his job. For that, I don't blame him. But the rest falls into the gray zone. Is he really in our corner? Is all this secrecy just to minimize the fallout? Or is it a whole lot more personal, and uglier, than that?"

"Meaning?"

"Meaning he was working in the Manhattan D.A.'s office when the Winters were killed. Does whatever he's hiding tie directly back to him? Is it his job he's fighting to save, or his ass?" Abruptly, Monty changed the subject. "Speaking of Morgan's well-being, I heard you ask her out. So I took the liberty of giving her a few tips about you. Now it's a level playing field. So I feel better."

Lane groaned. "What did you tell her?"

"To stay one step ahead of you. To keep the ball in her court. Not to let you get away with anything. The basics."

"Are you *trying* to sabotage this relationship?"

"Nope. I'm trying to make sure Morgan knows what she's letting herself in for. Apparently, she does." A chuckle. "You, on the other hand, are in for a few surprises. Kiss your ego good-bye."

"Thanks for the tip. But make it the last one. Butt out."

"Done." Monty rounded the corner. "I'm almost at your place. Which reminds me, I'm assuming you're alone."

"Yeah. Jonah left a while ago. He was pretty upset. Apparently, Elyse Shore walked into Arthur's office this afternoon while Jonah was taking shots of the congressman hovering over a young, pretty staff member, and she didn't react too well. She ripped Jonah a new one. The severity of her reaction kind of surprised me."

"Why? It can't be pleasant to watch your husband constantly coming on to other women, most of whom are young enough to be your daughter."

"Agreed. But Elyse knows who she's married to. Plus, I've met her enough times to get a feel for what she's like. She's free-spirited like her daughter. She's also composed and easygoing. Barking at Jonah seems out of character."

"What'd he say in response?"

"Nothing. She turned around and walked out. Which is weird, too. He said she looked emotionally beaten up."

"First hostile, then depleted. Sounds like she needs some Prozac." As he spoke, a far-fetched idea formed in Monty's head. "What time did Jonah take those office photos?"

"I don't know. Three-thirty, four o'clock. Why?"

"Just asking."

SIXTEEN

Getting the police report on the hit-and-run was the easiest part of Monty's day. By the time Lane and Jonah had joined Arthur Shore on the private jet he'd secured, Monty had assimilated all the facts.

Running down those facts proved very interesting.

It turned out that the white van that struck Rachel Ogden was a delivery vehicle for a florist located near Union Square. The delivery guy had foolishly double-parked it—still running and with the keys in the ignition—long enough to dash into an office building and leave a holiday poinsettia at the front desk. He'd exited two and a half minutes later, to find the van gone.

At the time, the cops had treated it like a straightforward car theft. They'd interviewed a few people who'd been in the area, none of whom had noticed much. They'd all assumed that whoever drove away with the van was the same guy who'd arrived in it—at least until he'd rushed to the curb shouting that his van had been stolen. Two local construction workers had come up with a less-than-exciting description of the thief: he'd been wearing a hooded parka and army boots, and was slight of build and quick on his feet.

Which, to Monty, meant a punk kid who was either a run-of-the-mill car thief, *or*—if the incident had been related to the Winter cases—a hired hand.

The van itself had provided no answers. It had turned up, dumped and stripped, in a seedy area of the Bronx. The cops had dusted it for prints; no matches turned up.

That left Monty with several paths he could take.

He could interview Karly Fontaine and Rachel Ogden, assuming Rachel's doctor would let him speak with her. He could lean on his contacts and start the ball rolling on what the real scoop was with Charlie Denton—assuming there was one. Or he could stop by and chat with Elyse Shore, see if his long-shot theory about her odd behavior had any merit.

He planned to do all three. The question was, which first. He had four hours before Morgan showed up at his office. The more information he could give her, the better. Therefore, the best use of his time would be to spend it on areas he could make rapid progress on.

Karly Fontaine and Rachel Ogden could wait. Ditto for Charlie Denton. The women were better deferred until Morgan had provided him with both their full backgrounds and profiles. And digging up dirt on Charlie Denton would require caution and stealth. It would also take a lot more time, and involve peeling back a lot more layers.

But Elyse Shore—now that was intriguing.

Agenda set, he made a few calls to start the ball rolling on Charlie Denton, then headed over to Third Avenue and Elyse Shore's gym.

The bell over the front door tinkled when Monty stepped inside. Not that anyone heard it. There was too much noise coming from the revving Lifecycles and whirring treadmills, plus the adrenaline-pumping background music thumping out the rapid pace of an aerobic class being held in a glass-enclosed exercise room.

Monty glanced around the place and blinked. He felt like he'd stepped into a resort spa. A cluster of exercise areas—all filled with jumping, spinning, or kickboxing people—filled the back wall. There was a whirlpool center, a yoga room, a complete smoothie bar, and enough heart-rate-increasing and weight-lifting equipment to train an Olympic team. The entire gym was accented in white marble and water colors, with seashell white, aerobic-friendly carpet, sand-hued yoga mats, and soothing aqua walls.

The clientele looked like they'd been plucked out of a fashion magazine. The women were slim and toned, the men were muscled with six-pack abs, and the instructors and trainers were walking fitness advertisements.

Monty found himself thinking he was glad he'd kept in shape and that he still ran through his daily exercise regimen. A guy with a gut would probably be shot on sight.

He scanned the room, spotted Elyse Shore standing beside the sweeping curved front desk, chatting with a member. She was wearing black yoga pants and a matching Lycra bodysuit, a damp towel draped around her neck. Clearly, she'd just finished giving a class. Good. Monty's timing was perfect.

She didn't notice him right away, which gave him a minute or two to scrutinize her.

Jonah wasn't wrong. She did look wired. And wrung out, too, lines of sleeplessness etched beneath her skillfully applied makeup. It wasn't only fatigue. It was something more, even if it was well hidden. Pain. Resignation. If Monty had to guess, he'd say she'd been crying. Her eyes were a little too bright and the area around them was slightly puffy.

She must have sensed his scrutiny, because she turned her head in his direction and blinked in surprise. Instantly, the facade snapped back into place—although she still looked taut and anxious. Excusing herself, she walked over.

Her first question told Monty the cause of her anxiety.

"Detective—why are you here? Is everything all right with Morgan?"

Motherly concern. That was only natural under the circumstances.

Maybe more so, depending on how extreme the circumstances were.

"She's fine," he assured her. "I was just hoping to have a quick word with you. Is that possible?"

"Of course." Elyse didn't hesitate. She pointed toward the spacious front office—a marble-and-chrome eye-catcher, then headed toward it, gesturing for him to follow. "We can talk in my office."

Once inside, Elyse shut the door. "Water?" she asked, opening a small fridge and pulling out two bottles.

"That would be great." Monty took the proffered bottle, twisted off the cap, and took a gulp.

Elyse did the same, then perched at the edge of the desk. "What can I do for you?"

"You can answer a question." Monty's stare and delivery were direct. "Since the reopening of the Winter homicides, have you experienced anything out of the ordinary? Letters? Phone calls? Threats to your family?"

All the color drained from Elyse's face, and Monty had his answer.

"Why do you ask?"

"Because I understand you weren't yourself yesterday afternoon. And the timing of your uncharacteristic behavior coincided with a hit-and-run accident that took place near the St. Regis. I'm sure you heard about it. The thing is, there's a common denominator between the victim and an eyewitness of that crime: Morgan. So, if something was going on with you at the same time that Rachel Ogden was mowed down—like if you or your family were being threatened—then that 'accident' might not have been an accident at all."

"Oh God." Elyse sank down behind her desk, gulping some water as if it were a lifeline. "I kept telling myself I was being paranoid, that my nerves were shot. But based on what you're saying, and what happened yesterday, I'm deluding myself. It's all been planned and deliberate."

"What has?"

Elyse ran both hands through her hair, visibly trying to calm down. "I've been getting telephone hang-ups. Here. Home. My cell."

"Give me specifics." Monty had whipped out a pad and was scribbling down the information. "Is there a pattern to the calls? Does the caller say or do anything before hanging up? Can you tell if it's a male or a female? What display shows up on your caller ID? Take me through it from beginning to end."

"It's a man. The only reason I know that much is that when he calls the gym, he asks whoever answers the phone for me. When I take the call, he hangs up. No words. Just deep, even breathing. He makes sure to do that long enough so I know it's him; almost like he's issuing a wordless threat. As for my cell, he only calls when I'm alone, walking or driving. The same with my home—the calls only come when I'm by myself. It's like he knows my schedule. Caller ID is useless; it always reads 'private.'"

"How long has this been going on?"

A heartbeat of a pause. "Since the day after Morgan hired you."

Monty stopped writing and looked up. "And you've said nothing? Not even to your husband?"

"What could I say?" Elyse leaned her head back against the chair cushion. "I couldn't even be sure it meant something. Arthur's a congressman. It's not the first time some weirdo's harassed him. He's gotten phone calls, e-mails, you name it. And now, with him sponsoring a major piece of legislation, it could just as easily have been related to that."

"Except that he's not the one being harassed. You are."

"I know." Elyse pressed her lips together. "But my family's under so much pressure right now. You know that better than anyone. To announce that I was getting creepy hang-up calls would only make things worse. And without any real proof that the caller was anything but a crank . . . I thought it was best to keep quiet."

"Until yesterday. You mentioned something happening then."

A nod. "I took a walk down Fifth Avenue at lunchtime. I was hoping the cold air and some window-shopping would calm my nerves. From the minute I left the gym, I had the oddest feeling I was being followed. I turned around a half-dozen times, but no one was there. Truthfully, I was beginning to think I was losing it from the stress. I headed back to the gym. As I got there, I felt someone staring at me. The feeling was so strong that I swerved around to scan the area. I saw a man standing diagonally across the street, leaning casually against a van, watching me. When he realized I'd spotted him, he abandoned the whole casual act. He averted his head, fumbled with the car door, then jumped in and drove away."

"A van?" Monty repeated, his gaze narrowed on Elyse's face. "What kind of van?"

She shrugged. "I don't know. Worn. Nondescript. Like every other van in Manhattan."

"Was it white?"

"Yes." An apprehensive look. "Is that important?"

"Could be. The car that ran down Rachel Ogden was a white van. What did the man look like?"

"I couldn't make out his features. He was wearing a hooded parka and jeans. But he was slight, and not too tall."

"Do you remember what time this was?"

Elyse thought for a moment. "Around one-fifteen, give or take a few minutes."

Monty's mouth thinned into a grim line. "Rachel Ogden's hit-and-run occurred at one-forty, on the corner of Fifty-third and Madison."

"It must have been the same car." Elyse's voice was practically a whisper. "Which means both incidents were intentional. But what's the motive?"

"To scare the hell out of you. To get Morgan to back off this case." Monty swung his pad shut. "The tactics are extreme. Then again, I doubt the guy meant to hurt Rachel Ogden so badly. He was probably hired to knock her off balance, maybe cause some cuts and bruises. Either to Rachel or to Karly Fontaine."

Elyse turned up her palms, still dazed and confused. "I'm not following. Are you saying Rachel wasn't the intended victim?"

"I'm saying either one of them would do, if the goal was to give Morgan a warning. Whoever planned this did his homework. He knew both women's schedules. He must have cross-checked them. It's not a reach that they'd each routinely cross that intersection—it's right in the heart of midtown, and so are they. He just found a time interval when the odds were good they'd both be nearing that corner—which maximized the chance that his hired hand would clip one of them. One thing's for sure. This is more than enough proof in my book to confirm that the Winters' double homicide was no random robbery gone bad. It was murder, pure and simple. And whoever killed them is still out there, determined not to get caught."

THE FOUR-AND-A-HALF-HOUR flight from Teterboro to Telluride was uneventful.

Arthur worked nonstop, alternately reviewing paperwork and calling influential people to garner support for his legislation. Once or twice, he got up to stretch his legs, to swallow a glass of springwater, and to check in with the pilot.

Lane slept for the first couple of hours, having stayed up all night working for Monty. He woke up in time for a fabulous brunch of fresh-squeezed orange juice, warm croissants, and a sautéed crabmeat, grilled asparagus, and provolone omelet. After that, he unpacked his Canon EOS 5D, peered out the window of the Gulf Stream V jet, and took several awesome shots. He also took a few shots of Arthur, forehead creased in concentration, talking intently on the phone, then leaning back in the plush leather seat to review his notes.

There was a lot to be said for traveling with the rich and powerful.

Instead of being shuffled around like pieces of cargo, Lane and Jonah had been escorted by limo to Teterboro airport. They'd swung by the Marriott Glenpointe to pick up the congressman, since he'd attended a dinner there and spent the night. Minutes later, they arrived at Teterboro.

The private jet had been waiting on standby. No arriving hours early. No pain-in-the-ass baggage checking. No enduring long lines at check-in and then security. No being squashed in a narrow seat between a screaming infant and an offensive-smelling passenger who removed his shoes five minutes into the flight. No endless delays and running for connecting flights to reach an area of Colorado as remote as the San Juan Mountains.

Yup, Lane could definitely get used to this.

Glancing across the aisle at Jonah, he had to grin. The kid had been awestruck during the entire limo ride. His jaw had dropped when they boarded the private jet provided by one of Daniel Kellerman's business associates. And it had remained that way as he marveled at the lush interior, smooth ride, high speed, and sumptuous brunch that accompanied their flight.

Right now, he was glued to the window, staring out at the view.

And what a view it was.

Catching his first glimpse of the peaks below, Lane could see why people referred to this as God's country. The San Juans were breathtaking, a cluster of white peaks piercing a bluebird sky.

"Wow," Jonah breathed, grabbing his camera. "Talk about awesome."

"No argument," Lane murmured. "It doesn't get any closer to heaven than this."

Nature at its most miraculous unfurled before them. She'd worked in their favor, since autumn in Colorado had been particularly snowy, leaving the alpine zones awash in powder. That had prompted consideration of an early season opening. Congressman Shore's influence and the fact that his adventures were being featured in *Time* magazine clinched it. The heli-skiing company caved easily, and agreed to open even earlier than contemplated. Hell, they couldn't buy that kind of publicity for any amount of money.

"Are we heli-skiing today?" Jonah asked.

"*We?*" Lane arched a brow.

A sheepish grin. "I heard my mother's end of your conversation today. I know she told you what a good skier I am, how many years I've been at it. I started with my youth group when I was eight. I've been skiing the black diamond trails since I was twelve."

"Quit while you're ahead." Lane cut him off with a wave of his hand. "I got the whole rundown from your mom. And since you were eavesdropping, I'm sure you know I agreed to let you take part in the heli-skiing. As long as you listen to our guide and don't try anything dumb."

"I will. And I won't." Jonah's whole face lit up. "Think of the cool shots I can get when I'm up close, cutting through that heavy powder, zooming down the mountain with you and the congressman."

Arthur had just finished up a phone call and caught the tail end of the conversation. "Sounds like he's got the bug, Lane." He chuckled. "Another powder hound in the making." He turned to Jonah. "I don't blame you. When I was seventeen, you couldn't have dragged me away from an adventure like this."

"Thank you, sir." Jonah looked from one of them to the other. "Do we go right away?"

"Nope." Arthur shook his head. "There's not enough daylight left. Safety and the heli-skiing company say we wait till morning. Don't look so crestfallen," he added, seeing Jonah's expression. "We've got something cool on tap for today, too. The company's giving us an aerial tour of the mountains we'll be skiing tomorrow. That means a helicopter ride and a preview of what's to come."

"And lots of photo ops," Jonah added, his upbeat mood restored. He peered out the window, his forehead crinkled as he intently scrutinized his field of view. "*Time* is going to be blown away by what we give them."

SEVENTEEN

Morgan was a nervous wreck when she showed up on Monty's doorstep at two-thirty.

She'd spent the morning trying to prepare herself for what lay ahead. She'd gone through the motions of her day, called the hospital to check on Rachel's condition—which, thankfully, was improved—and forced down a sandwich in the office kitchen with Jill and Beth.

The fact that Monty hadn't called meant no new information had surfaced, which put extra pressure on the session they were about to have. More and more she was starting to believe that she and her memories were going to be central to solving her parents' murders.

Monty gave her an encouraging look when he opened the door. Morgan didn't delude herself into thinking it signified anything but emotional support. She gave him her coat, straightened her shoulders, and marched into his office like a prisoner facing a firing squad.

"Hey, relax. We'll get through this." Monty shoved a mug into her hands. "Here's something to help. My famous hot chocolate. Whipped cream and all. I perfected the formula when my kids were young. And trust me. You don't want my coffee. Sally says it tastes like driveway sealer. Besides, you're wired enough. This'll soothe you. Guaranteed."

"Thank you—Monty." This time the name came easier. "Not just for the hot chocolate, but for trying to calm me down. Although I admit that chocolate's my weakness; it's the ultimate comfort food." Morgan took a sip, then gave him a thumbs-up. "Yum. Definitely worthy of its reputation."

"Told you." He gestured toward his well-worn office sofa. "Have a seat."

Nodding, Morgan crossed over and sank down on the tweed cushion. "I take it nothing turned up this morning."

"Actually, yeah, something did." Monty dropped into the easy chair across from her, the files they were about to peruse spread out on the rectangular table between them. "But not what you were expecting."

The mug paused halfway to Morgan's lips. "What then?" Her eyes widened as she listened to the details Elyse had filled Monty in on. "I had no idea about any of this."

"No one did. Apparently, Elyse kept it to herself."

"Poor thing. She's the ultimate nurturer; always trying to protect her family. But now that she knows that the hang-ups and the harassment were part of a bigger agenda, she must be thrown."

"She seemed pretty shaken, yeah."

A hard swallow. "And that agenda is me. Charlie was right. Everything, right down to Rachel's accident, were warning messages for me."

"Let's talk about Rachel," Monty suggested, propping his elbow on the chair arm. "Tell me what you can about her background, her interests, even her taste in men. Then do the same with Karly Fontaine."

"Why?"

"Because I want to figure out if they were randomly selected from the people you know, or if one or both of them was specifically targeted."

"I see where you're going with this. But it's a sticky question. My client interviews are confidential."

"Yeah, and your parents' killer is out there." Monty wasn't mincing words. And he wasn't letting Morgan's ethics get in his way. "Look, I'm not asking because I want to pry into these women's love lives. I need this information before interviewing them. Just give me some basic facts."

"Fine. They're both attractive. Rachel's on the petite side, dark-haired, and in her midtwenties. She's probably the youngest management consultant in her firm. That's because she's superintelligent and aggressive. She prefers older men. Young ones can't deal with her strength or success. The older ones who measure up to her are usually married. My job's to find one who isn't. Karly's tall and willowy, thirty-four, with red-gold hair. She started her career in L.A. as a model—magazine and runway. She's now the managing director of the New York branch of the Lairman Modeling Agency."

"Okay." Monty was writing. "And I take it both women are looking for long-term relationships?"

"Not just long-term. They want men with substance and character, a variety of interests, and a high level of ambition. That's why I arranged dates for each of them with Charlie Denton. There were strong correlations in their profiles. Plus, my instincts told me the fits were good."

"Does Elyse know either Rachel or Karly?"

The question caught Morgan by surprise. "I don't think so. Why? Is that important?"

"Only if it takes us in the right direction. I'm trying to see if there's an overlap between Elyse's clientele and yours."

"Absolutely. She's given us great word of mouth, which is invaluable in both our businesses. As for Winshore, referrals are the mainstay of our business. We have several hundred clients at this point. Frankly, I'd need some time to recall who referred each of them." Morgan's smile was rueful. "Half the time, Jill and I don't even meet each other's clients for months. Once a rapport is established with a new client, whoever that client's initial contact was tries to build a level of trust. It helps not to shove an entire staff in their face. Besides, most—though not all—client meetings take place outside the office—in restaurants, hotel lounges, even a client's office, if they live and work in the suburbs. We try to make it as convenient as possible."

"Interesting." Monty was still scribbling. "Are you okay with my chatting with Rachel and Karly?"

"I have no problem with it. I can't speak for Rachel's doctor; you'll have to check with him. I'll give you his contact information, and Karly's cell number."

"Good." He set down his notebook. "How's your hot chocolate?"

"Gone." Morgan placed her empty cup neatly on a coaster. "Now let's get to the main purpose of our meeting while I'm still clinging to my bravado." She shifted to the edge of the sofa cushion, her back ramrod straight, and pointed at the photograph envelope on the table. "Are those the original or the enhanced shots?"

"The originals. Lane's still working on the enhancements. He was at it till dawn."

"And now he's heli-skiing?"

A corner of Monty's mouth lifted. "He's used to a no-sleep, high-performance lifestyle. He's had to be, in his line of work. But don't worry. Not only is he resilient, he's adaptable. He probably slept on the plane." Monty reached for the envelope of photos, all humor vanishing. "I'm going to lay these out in a specific order. It's not to protect you; it's to get maximum recall out of you."

"I understand." A weighted pause. "I'm ready."

Monty studied her for another brief moment. Then he took out the photos and laid two before her. They were glaringly devoid of human beings. "Do you remember the room itself?"

"Yes." The familiar tightness gripped her chest, but she tamped down on it, pushing past the panic that started to coil inside her. "The basement where it happened. I was upstairs, putting glitter on some holiday decorations. We were waiting for the food to be delivered. My parents went down to get the paper goods. The guests were scheduled to arrive soon." She could see it as clearly as if it were happening again, right in front of her. "My mother had put music on; 'A Holly, Jolly Christmas.' That was why I didn't hear any of the sounds . . . the gunshots . . ."

"Right. What made you go downstairs?"

"They were gone so long. I got scared. And, for what it's worth, I never saw the room from either of these angles you're showing me. I walked down these stairs." She indicated the far left corner of the photos. "And when I got to the bottom, all I saw were their bodies. I couldn't look away. So why don't you show me those photos. They're more apt to jog any memories I might have repressed."

"I plan to." Monty pulled out a few more shots and glanced at them. Morgan could tell by his expression that this was it.

He placed the photos on the table in front of her. "These were taken from the foot of the stairs. It's the angle you walked in on." His tone was steady, but his gaze was fixed on Morgan.

Her parents' bodies. Bleeding. Lifeless.

For a long moment she stared, unable to look away. She was dragged back into the living nightmare, not in the surreal way she'd expected, but in a palpable way. She was there again, standing at the foot of the steps, staring at the unthinkable, gripped by terror and denial. Basement sounds—a clanging pipe, a hissing boiler—drowned out her first cry. And the smell—that awful stench of blood and body waste—it made her gag. She kept gagging as she ran over to them. She tripped a couple of times, once on a bucket, once on a wooden board.

She reached her mother first. She was crumpled in a heap on her side, her white dress soaked with blood, pieces of her insides not where they should be. Her arms were spread out, her face turned away, her eyes open but unseeing.

Morgan called out to her, over and over. *Mommy, Mommy* . . . But there was no response. She was afraid to touch her, afraid she'd make it worse. And there was so much blood. A pool of it around her, growing, spreading. Morgan couldn't fix it. Only one person could.

Daddy. She crawled over to her father. He was lying flat, prone, face-down. His hair was matted with blood, which was still oozing out from two holes in back of his head. His body looked okay, so she shook him. But he felt weird, stiff, and he didn't move or wake up.

Somehow she knew he wouldn't.

She crept away, cutting her knees on broken chips of cement, then scrambling to her feet, bumping into an overturned chair, skidding on a stone and nearly landing in a pool of blood. And there were splatters every-where . . . and her mother's purse, contents dumped on the floor, her compact red and sticky . . .

She started screaming then, screaming their names, screaming for help.

The rest was a blur.

"Morgan." She was back in Monty's office, and he was wrapping a fleece blanket around her. He looked worried, as if he wanted to comfort her and didn't know how. "Are you okay?"

Her face was wet. She tasted the tears, but she didn't remember starting to cry. And she was trembling, violently. The fleece felt warm, soft, and secure as it absorbed her inner chill.

"Morgan?"

She gave a shaky nod. "I'm fine. I just . . . I knew it would hit me hard. I expected it. God knows, I've relived it a thousand times. But this was different. Staring at those photos—it was like being transported back to the scene, like it was happening right now. I'm sorry. I didn't mean to fall apart."

His jaw tightened. "You didn't fall apart. You revisited hell. Do you want to stop?"

"No." Her tone was adamant. "We've come this far. Let's keep going."

"Okay." Monty sucked in a breath. "While it's fresh in your mind, describe to me exactly what you just relived."

Insides clenched, she did.

"You said that when you first crossed the room, you tripped over a bucket and then a wooden board."

"Yes. I assume the bucket and the chair were overturned during the fight between my father and the killer, and the wooden board was the two-by-four my mother swung at the killer to try to save my father."

"That's my assumption, too. Do you remember if any of the objects you struck—the bucket, the chair, or the two-by-four—moved when you tripped on them?"

She considered that. "I don't think so. They were pretty solid. I remember feeling the sting in my leg and my foot when I collided with them. I was a slight, skinny kid. If anything, those objects moved me, not the other way around." She paused, and when she spoke again, her voice was an unsteady whisper. "That smell I'm remembering. It was death, wasn't it?"

"Yeah." Monty pulled out a few more photos, handing them to Morgan. "You said you walked around your parents' bodies when you tried to wake them. See if anything in these triggers a memory." He kept talking, focusing her and bolstering her at the same time. "I know the pools of blood look big, and they must have seemed even bigger to you at the time. But they're only about two feet in diameter. As for the blood splatter you described, it was used to determine the distance of the shootings. The shots were fired at close range. Death came quickly."

"And without much pain—that's what you're telling me."

"Exactly."

"My father was killed execution style, at point-blank range. My mother was shot from what—several feet away?"

"At most. The object you skidded on was a shell casing. We recovered all three of them."

"Two for my father, one for my mother. I remember the two holes in back of his head." Morgan swallowed hard. "What about the weapon?"

"It was a Walther PPK. Never found."

"Another dead end. And obviously, there were no fingerprints at the crime scene."

"Just your parents'. Primarily your mother's, on the two-by-four."

"What about DNA?" Morgan asked, unable to tear her gaze off the photos. "My mother's purse was rifled. My father fought with the killer, so he had to have prints on his clothes."

"None clear enough to lift. And nothing that matched our database. Believe me, I've already called my old precinct and told them to rerun your parents' personal belongings for new DNA evidence. They're tearing through red tape to get what they need."

"Red tape." Morgan's tone was bitter. "Manhattan and Brooklyn will still be embroiled in a turf war and you'll have solved the case."

"That's the plan. Let them fight it out. It'll keep them busy and off my back."

"You don't think the DNA testing will show us much."

Monty shrugged. "I wouldn't rule anything out, but DNA testing wasn't nearly as sophisticated in the eighties as it is now. Not to mention, the turnaround time sucked. So did the number of facilities capable of doing it. Talk about a hassle—the evidence had to be driven up to a lab in Massachusetts, and it took two weeks to get our answers. Now everything's different."

"So . . ."

"So it all depends on what we have to work with."

The vagueness of his response wasn't lost on Morgan. "In other words, we'd have to exhume the bodies to find anything concrete. Even then, we're grasping at straws. My mother probably never touched him. And my father might have punched him out, but that doesn't mean we'd find skin cells or hair, especially not after seventeen years."

"You've been watching forensics shows on TV." Monty tried for some dry humor.

"Just reading up on a subject that's integral to my life."

"Well, you're right. So, no, I don't think our answers are as likely to lie there as with the file and the photo negatives. Mostly with the negatives, and Lane's expert analysis." Monty watched her studying the photos. "And with you."

Morgan extended her hand, palm up. "In that case, let me see the rest of the photos."

"No."

The adamancy of Monty's refusal startled Morgan, and her head came up.

The look on his face left no room for argument.

"Why not?"

"Because there's no need for it. It wouldn't add anything to the investigation. You'd been escorted from the room when crime scene took the photos. There's nothing positive that can come out of your looking at them now."

"Tell me what you're not letting me see."

"Not necessary."

"It is to me."

Monty's stare was piercing—and uncompromising. "There's not a single thing in these photos that's as gruesome as what you saw when you walked into that basement. You have my word on that. But you've done your homework; you know how crime-scene photos work. After the initial shots, the bodies are shifted around so different angles can be photographed."

"And? Was my father brutalized during the fistfight? Was something more done to my mother than I know?"

"No and no." Monty blew out a breath, ran a hand over his face. "Look, Morgan, what goes on during the crime-scene procedure appears very dehumanizing, especially to someone who loved the victims as much as you loved your parents. It's no secret that we're all dust in the wind. But there's no need to shove that in our faces. Remember your parents as they were—caring, vital human beings."

"As opposed to objects, bodies without souls." Morgan lowered her gaze, staring at the carpet as she tried to cope with the indescribable pain lancing through her. "You made your point. In which case, I'm not sure how much more help I can be. I described everything as I saw it. After that, I fuzzed out. You probably remember more of what came next than I do."

"What about before?"

"Before?"

"Before the party preparations. Before that night. Any memories come to mind? Think about it." Monty rose, went into the kitchen, and returned with a bottle of springwater. "Here you go."

"Thanks." Morgan took the bottle with a tight smile. "Are you sure you're not a therapist? Mine asks the same kind of questions. He even gets me water when he wants me to have quiet time to think."

"Did it work—not with your therapist, with me?"

A long, silent moment. "That night was Christmas Eve. It was all about the holiday party my mother had arranged for the abuse center. She and I spent the day shopping for decorations and little gifts to put under the tree—enough for all the women who'd be attending. We made eggnog and Christmas cookies. We would have cooked, but Lenny donated all the food."

"Did your father stay home to shop and bake with you?"

"No, he had to go to work. But he came home early; I don't remember what time. I do know the party was set for eight-thirty. My parents and I got there two hours early so we could set up. Our only detour was to the Kellermans' penthouse; they were hosting a holiday party in Arthur's honor. We didn't stay long. I remember feeling bad about that, because I wanted to play with Jill, since we hadn't seen each other in a while. But it wasn't the night for it. My mother was itching to get to the abuse center. She, my father, and I headed over there straight from the Kellermans'. It would have been a magical night for those women. And not just because of the things we bought. Because of my mother."

Morgan raised her head and met Monty's gaze, tears glistening in her eyes. "I wish you'd known her. She was so amazingly empathetic. Even in her journal entries, you can feel her personal involvement with the women who came to her. I feel as if I knew them. When one of them turned her life around, my mother's life turned around, too. And when one of them gave up, felt trapped and incapable of escaping her own hell, my mother refused to walk away. She stayed by their sides until she found a solution. Near the end, she helped one woman and her daughter make a fresh start. She also stood by a teenage girl who was sexually abused as a child, messed up her whole life, and found herself pregnant and abandoned."

"Your mother was quite a human being," Monty replied. He sat back in his chair. "Tell me, how did your father react to this? Having a wife whose heart is in so many places must take its toll."

More memories. Conversations at the dinner table. Loving debates about who was more married to their work.

"He was proud of her," Morgan murmured, remembering as she spoke. "Sometimes he got upset. He thought she was being taken advantage of. He worried about her. In retrospect, I realize he was obviously more cynical than she was. He was a prosecutor. She was an idealist."

"During the weeks before the murders, were there any situations in particular that concerned him?"

Morgan forced herself to think. Flickers of recall. Some closed-door conversations. Passionate more than heated.

"My mother was grappling with how to handle something. I think she and my father had different ideas about the best way to do it. They didn't have a big shouting match. But they were on edge. Neither of them was sleeping. I'm not sure why. It could have pertained to my mother's work. Or it could have pertained to one of my father's cases. My mother always agonized over the more dangerous ones he took on. That's why I gave you those newspaper clippings. My father prosecuted some scary, high-profile criminals. Maybe he was prosecuting one of them when he died. I just don't know. As for the tension in the house, I'm not sure if it was caused by my father's current caseload. In her journals, my mother talks about a teenager at the shelter she was trying to help. Maybe it was that. Or maybe it was something unrelated I knew nothing about. I've been sitting in my den reading my mother's journals all week. I can sense the urgency in her tone. On the other hand, my father—"

Morgan broke off, dropping her head in her hands. "I'm going around in circles. I don't know what I'm saying anymore. Maybe none of my babbling means anything. I was ten years old. I didn't understand what pressures existed in my parents' marriage. Nor was I invited to try. When it came to private discussions, they talked alone, in their bedroom, at night. What I'm recalling now are fragments. And what I'm trying to do is resurrect childhood memories and interpret them with an adult mind. I'm not sure that's possible."

"Hey, you did great." Monty squeezed her arm. "Look, we've covered more than enough for one day. Let me cogitate on what I've heard. Plus, I need to set up appointments with Rachel Ogden and Karly Fontaine. You take tonight off. Hang out with Jill, watch some TV. And get a good night's sleep. You've got dinner plans tomorrow night. And my son's a night owl."

EIGHTEEN

With its rustic beamed ceilings and warm, low lighting, the great room at the Inn at Lost Creek was the perfect place to unwind and enjoy après-ski cocktails after a long day.

It was five o'clock, and Arthur, Lane, and Jonah were sitting around the large crackling stone fireplace. Holding his old-fashioned filled with the area's best single-malt scotch, Arthur settled himself more comfortably on the plush brown velvet sofa. His cell phone, for the moment, was blissfully silent, and he took advantage of the time just to lean back, savor his drink, and relax in front of the fire.

Across the way, sprawled in one of the room's matching club chairs, Jonah vegged, sipping his Coke and checking out the beautiful people strolling into the lounge.

And on the opposite sofa, Lane nursed his own scotch, rolling the old-fashioned between his palms and thinking how pumped he felt physically, how psyched he was about hitting the slopes tomorrow—and how antsy he was about what was going on back in New York.

The latter was a first for him.

Home never accompanied him on these thrill-seeking ventures. His bouts with nature were all about living in the moment, with the rest of his life tucked away on the back burner. Consequently, nothing—and no one—permeated his cerebral high.

But this time was different. And that difference had a name.

Morgan Winter.

He was definitely involved with her. Partly because of the role he was playing in the reinvestigation of her parents' homicides. And partly because of Morgan herself.

Yup, he was surprisingly involved with her. More surprisingly, he wanted to deepen that involvement.

He glanced at his watch. Seven o'clock eastern time.

He pulled out his cell phone and punched in the home number she'd given him.

The line rang twice, then she picked up. "Hello?"

"Hey, it's Lane."

"Hi." She sounded surprised, and emotionally drained. "I didn't expect to hear from you until tomorrow. Is there a change in plans? Do you have to postpone our dinner?"

"Not a chance." He was startled by the fervor of his reply. But he didn't retract it. "I'm waiting with bated breath."

A hint of laughter. "Now *that* I doubt. Not with the rush of those majestic snow-covered mountains just waiting to be conquered."

"I'm psyched about the heli-skiing. I'm just as psyched about tomorrow's dinner. I want to see you."

She was quiet for a moment. "I know. I want to see you, too."

Her admission elicited a surge of pleasure. "It looks like we'll be finishing up on the slopes around four. After that, it's homeward bound. My guess is I'll be landing in Teterboro between nine and ten eastern time. I know it's late, but—"

"I like late dinners."

"Good. I'll call you when we're airborne. But that's not the reason I'm calling now. You've been on my mind. You—and your meeting with Monty today. It must have been tough. I wanted to check on you, make sure you were okay." He paused, abruptly changing gears. "I also wanted to hear your voice. It's sexy."

This time her laughter came naturally. "You know every right thing to say."

"Maybe. But I mean every word."

"I . . ." She cleared her throat. "Thank you. And thank you for checking up on me. It was a very sensitive thing to do. As for the meeting, you're right. Looking at those photos, reliving it all—it was even more brutal than I expected. I remembered all kinds of things I'd buried away. But your father was amazing. He walked me through it. And he made it bearable."

"I'm glad." Lane leaned back, took a sip of scotch. "You'll fill me in tomorrow. But tonight, I don't want you to think about it. I want you to put it away—the meeting with Monty, the memories—all of it. Relax. Pour yourself a glass of wine. Curl up in bed with a good book or a movie. Think of me. Not in that order, of course."

"Of course." He could hear her smile. "Actually, Jill and I are having a girls' night. We just ordered a million calories of comfort food. As for the wine, we opened a bottle of Chianti twenty minutes ago. I'm halfway done with my first glass. And we rented two different chick flicks, so the movies are covered." She paused, lowering her voice a tad. "For the record, I've already been thinking of you. But I promise to keep doing so."

Lane's entire body reacted. "Do that. And don't stop until I get off the plane. I'll take it from there."

"I'm counting on it."

ACROSS THE WAY, Arthur's solitude was shattered by the buzzing of his phone against his side. He'd put it on vibrate, and shoved it in his pocket, but that still didn't make it go away.

Grimacing, he pulled it out and glanced at it, hoping against hope it was someone he could ignore.

He saw the caller's name. Definitely not someone to ignore.

He punched on the phone. "Hi, hon."

"Hi." Elyse's tone was dry. "Are you sure you know which 'hon' you're talking to?"

Clearly, he had his work cut out for him. "Come on, Lyssie. I only have one hon, and that's you. So, yes, I know exactly who I'm talking to."

"Good start. Let's move on. Who did you spend last night with?"

"You know the answer to that. I had dinner with Larry Cullen to secure his support for my bill. I met him in Jersey because his office is near Teterboro. I spent the night at the Marriott, and was on the plane heading out here by ten A.M. What's the problem?"

"The problem is the missing hours; you know, the ones between dinner and flight time. Who was she this time, one of your regulars or a new one?"

"I was alone, Elyse. Please let's not do this. I love you. And I miss you. *Only* you."

She blew out a resigned breath and Arthur realized, with some degree of relief, that this round was over. Still, it wasn't like Elyse to be so openly confrontational. Something was wrong.

"Elyse?"

"I didn't mean to jump at you like that," she replied. "It just hasn't been a stellar day. Or a stellar week, for that matter."

The glass of scotch paused halfway to Arthur lips. "Why? What happened?"

"Detective Montgomery showed up at the gym today. He thinks that hit-and-run accident near the St. Regis yesterday was a blatant warning to Morgan to back off this investigation. Especially after I told him about the things that've been happening to me this week."

Arthur tensed. "You'd better explain."

She did.

Arthur's jaw set as he listened to his wife's recounting of the week's incidents and the subsequent conversation she'd had with Monty. "Dammit, Elyse. It's *my* ear you should be chewing, not Montgomery's. Why didn't you talk to me first?"

"First? In other words, so you could put the right spin on my story? What would you have suggested I tell him?"

"Certainly not details that would shove us even further into the limelight. I'm trying to control what leaks out on the investigation. That's why I'm dodging questions on the subject, and spearheading the effort to keep

Montgomery's investigation on track and under the radar. I want to keep a low profile on this, keep the focus on my bill. There's enough smut about me in the tabloids as it is. I don't need another personal exposé to cloud my agenda."

"A personal exposé? This is about threats to Morgan, and possibly to us. That's criminal activity, not social scandal."

"Exactly. Which increases the likelihood of it getting out. I've been keeping a lid on my public statements regarding the reopening of the double-homicide investigation. The whole country knows that Jack and Lara were our closest friends. If I make any kind of impassioned statement, it will piss off either the cops or the D.A.'s office. I can't risk that. Primarily for Morgan's sake. It'll send the media flocking in her direction. Plus, it'll throw all kinds of monkey wrenches into this investigation—an investigation I want wrapped up fast and without any additional personal or political uproar."

"Primarily for Morgan's sake?" Elyse's words were tinged with more than a trace of cynicism.

"Yes, dammit. I don't want her harassed. And I don't want her suffering any more than she already has. But if you're asking if it's for my sake, too, the answer's yes. I don't need the controversy at this time in my political life. The press are like a flock of vultures. Keeping a lid on this has already been like holding back a dam with my bare hands. So if this new information leaks out—"

"Then people will know we're human, vulnerable. Maybe that'll generate positive press. Or are the details of that positive press the real source of your concern? Tell me, Arthur, are you more worried about word of the threats getting out, or about the profile of the hit-and-run victim getting out? From what I heard, she was young, beautiful, and drawn to older, successful men. Anything you want to tell me?"

Arthur swallowed the rest of his drink. "You're being ridiculous, Elyse. There's no link between me and that woman. I never met her. I don't even know her name. And I sure as hell don't know who ran her down."

"Her name is Rachel Ogden. The name of the eyewitness who saw her get hit is Karly Fontaine. Both of them are Winshore clients. And, like I said, Rachel is definitely your type."

"Thanks for the news flash. But I'm not sleeping with her. Like I said, I don't even know her. Or the other one—Karly Fontaine."

"That's good. Because Detective Montgomery is interviewing them both tomorrow."

"Shit." Arthur dragged a palm over his face. "Why is he letting this sidetrack him? Those women are not going to help him solve the case, not if Morgan's the common link here. All he's going to succeed in doing is to escalate the hype."

"I doubt it. He's discreet. But he's also thorough. That's why Morgan hired him."

"I know." Arthur's wheels were turning. "I just hope he treads carefully. One thing Pete Montgomery is *not* known for is his political correctness."

"He is known for his street smarts. He realizes you're a public figure. I'm sure he'll act accordingly." Elyse paused for a second. "Arthur, if there's anything I should know about Rachel Ogden, tell me now. I can protect you better if I'm armed with all the facts."

"I told you, there's nothing to know," he snapped, careful to keep his voice down. "If you don't believe me, ask one of your high-paid detectives. You know, the ones who've been following me around for the past three decades, keeping track of my whereabouts."

Elyse made a sound that was half laugh, half snort of disgust. "I hate to disappoint you, but I discontinued their services years ago. Partly because the rag magazines did such a thorough job of keeping tabs on you, no PIs were needed. And partly because I was emotionally sapped. I love you, Arthur. More than anything. But I'm worn out, resigned. You are who you are. Relentless PIs and revealing snapshots are never going to change that."

He was quiet for a moment. "I'm not perfect, Lyssie. But I'm also not lying. Not this time. I have no connection to that hit-and-run victim. I never met her. And I'm not sleeping with her." A caustic note crept into his tone. "Neither of which is going to stop the *Enquirer* from saying otherwise."

"That's true. But for what it's worth, I believe you."

"It's worth a lot." Another pause. "How's Morgan taking this?"

"Not well. She and Jill are spending tonight eating pizza and watching movies. Hopefully, it will be good for her. But she's not giving up. Threats or not, she'll be right back at it tomorrow, digging up every lead until she and Detective Montgomery find Lara and Jack's killer."

Arthur exhaled sharply. "That's the worst thing she could do. Between the memories and the press, this could push her over the edge. And if the threats are real, she could be in danger. So could you. The hang-ups, the person following you, the white van . . . I'm not happy. I'm going to call Montgomery, hire some extra security, for you and for Morgan. Jill, too, for that matter."

"Thank you." There was genuine relief in Elyse's voice—relief and a touch of nostalgia. "When you're like this . . . let's just say that this is the man I fell in love with."

"Then keep that picture in your mind. I'll take care of you. I'll take care of everything. Starting now. You sit tight. I'll set things in motion. And I'll be home before you know it."

ARTHUR STARED AT his cell for a long moment after hanging up, his mind racing. He glanced across the great room, checking to see what Lane and Jonah were doing. They were standing by the fire, deep in conversation. Judging from the motions Lane was making with his arms and his body, he was clearly demonstrating some powder-skiing moves to Jonah.

Capitalizing on this narrow window of privacy, Arthur walked off to a quiet alcove. He lowered himself into one of the lounge's corner chairs, nursing his drink and waiting to make sure no one was approaching him. Bad enough he'd argued with Elyse while sitting in the middle of the room—albeit quietly and with very few guests in the vicinity. But it was crucial that these next conversations be conducted with no chance of being overheard.

This whole situation was a disaster in the making. He was worried. And he was pissed. He had to protect his family. And he had to protect his career.

Time to put the screws into Detective Montgomery. And then, time to call in a marker.

———

MORGAN SIPPED HER Chianti, letting its soothing effects swirl through her system.

"Is that some semblance of a smile?" Jill teased, crossing the kitchen and helping herself to another slice of pizza. "Hmm—could it have something to do with that call from Lane Montgomery?"

"Good guess." Morgan put down her glass and sank back in her chair. "It's ironic. I see right through him. You know the package—effortless self-assurance, natural sex appeal, and enough magnetism to move a steel I-beam."

"You forgot a few things," Jill supplied helpfully. "Great body, exciting career, and that independent male aura that draws women like flies."

"I stand corrected. But the scary part is that I've warned dozens of clients to stay away from his type. So what am I doing? I'm walking directly into the line of fire. I see all his flaws, anticipate every technique he's using to draw me in—and yet . . ."

"And yet they're all working."

"I wish I knew why. All I know is that somehow it's different. *He's* different."

"Maybe there's more to Lane Montgomery than you're willing to admit, even to yourself."

"Or maybe I'm just so attracted to him that I can't think straight."

"There's no denying there's chemistry between you."

"Too much chemistry." Morgan sighed. "I just hope there's something besides that."

"Relationships aren't a science, Morg. We know that better than most."

"We also know that lasting relationships require something more than physical attraction and great sex. Lane and I are total opposites. I'm super-cautious. He's a daredevil and a player. I must be crazy."

"There's only one way to find out." Jill refilled both their glasses. "You're having dinner with him tomorrow night?"

"More like midnight supper. Arthur's plane won't be landing until around tenish."

"Okay, so a late dinner." Jill took a sip of wine, slanting a casual look in Morgan's direction. "Any chance that late dinner will extend into breakfast?"

Morgan's brows arched. "Aren't you subtle?"

"Nope. Never have been. Never will be. Now answer the question."

"Maybe. Probably not. It depends." Morgan took a healthy swallow of Chianti. "I don't have the slightest idea."

"Decisive. I like that."

Morgan rose. "There's just one thing I *am* sure of right now. I need some Ben & Jerry's ice cream. Want some?" She headed for the freezer.

"Don't waste time and dishes," Jill advised. "This conversation calls for two pints, two spoons, and no regrets."

Five minutes later, they were alternating between sips of Chianti and spoonfuls of ice cream.

"I reviewed the crime-scene photos today," Morgan blurted out.

Jill's spoon paused halfway to her mouth. "So that's why you were at Detective Montgomery's for so long. Why didn't you tell me? I would have gone with you."

"Believe me, you wouldn't have wanted to see these."

"At least I could have offered you moral support."

"Thanks. But this was one of those things I had to do alone." Morgan stared into her ice-cream carton. "I thought I was prepared. I wasn't. It was like being sucked into a black hole."

"I'm so sorry. It must have been agonizing for you." Jill gripped her spoon, stabbing at the ice cream.

"It's okay. I'm hanging in." Morgan leaned forward, squeezed her friend's arm. Jill's kind, loving nature was just like Elyse's.

That made Morgan feel doubly guilty for the subject she had to broach now. "Did you and your mom touch base today?"

Jill looked surprised. "A little while ago, yes. But only for about ten seconds. She was on her way over to my grandparents' to spend the night. That seemed kind of weird. I hope she's not reacting to one of my dad's indiscretions."

"Not this time."

Morgan's solemn tone struck home, and Jill's head came up. "Clearly, you know what's going on. What did Mom tell you?"

"Nothing. What I heard, I heard from Detective Montgomery." With a heavy heart, Morgan relayed the entire scenario to Jill.

"This has been going on all week?" Jill's features tightened with concern. "She didn't say a word."

"Not to anyone. Not even your father. Although now that she's aware of the link between Rachel's hit-and-run and her own creepy episodes, she'll want to fill Arthur in."

"And he'll be all over it," Jill said, taking comfort in her own words. "There's no way the two vans weren't the same. Which means whoever did this drove all the way from Union Square to the Upper East Side then back to midtown, just to make a point."

"Not a point. A message. Delivered to me. Via my family."

Anxiously, Jill searched Morgan's face. "He didn't try to hurt Mom? You're sure of that?"

"Positive. This was a scare tactic. Nothing more. If it was . . ." Morgan met Jill's gaze, raw tears glittering in her eyes. "After losing my parents the way I did, I could never—*ever*—put Elyse, or any of you, in danger."

"I know that. Does Detective Montgomery have a theory?"

"Yes. Besides scaring your mom, he also thinks the van driver hurt Rachel a lot more seriously than he was instructed to. He believes the order was to sideswipe her, knock her off balance. But hired hands are amateurs, and amateurs screw up. So Rachel was an innocent casualty." Morgan's lips thinned into a grim line. "There's only one person this sicko wants to get to—me. He's trying to frighten me into backing off. That's not about to happen. Especially now. He's just confirmed what Detective Montgomery and I already felt in our bones. He's no random burglar. He killed my parents in cold blood. And he's still out there."

NINETEEN

Wednesday morning couldn't come fast enough for Monty.

He was up at dawn, out the door by seven, and making arrangements on his cell phone during the entire two-hour drive from his Dutchess County home to New York–Presbyterian Hospital.

By the time he arrived for the fifteen-minute interview Rachel Ogden's doctor had grudgingly permitted, he'd lined up enough full-time security to keep an eye on Jill, Elyse, and Morgan.

Last night's phone call from Arthur Shore had brought back memories of the riled-up man who'd ridden Monty's ass after the double homicide seventeen years ago. This time, the congressman had raved about the vulnerability of his "girls," and given Monty carte blanche about whom he hired and how much he paid them to watch Elyse, Jill, and Morgan round-the-clock.

There was no denying that Arthur cared about his family. That much, Monty could relate to. So he'd made the requisite arrangements, set the security team in place.

Now he had two interviews to conduct: first, Rachel Ogden; then, Karly Fontaine.

He didn't expect either meeting to yield any earth-shattering revelations. After a fair amount of background digging, he still believed the two women were arbitrary pawns.

Still, a few curious pieces of information had come up, one pertaining to each woman. Neither was a glaring red flag. But both were interesting enough to address.

Karly Fontaine's real name was Carol Fenton. She'd glamorized it when she moved from New York to L.A. and became a model. Nothing unusual there. It was the timing of it that captured Monty's attention. Sixteen-plus years ago, just six months after the Winters' homicides. Worth bringing up in conversation.

As for Rachel Ogden, she was the living embodiment of what Arthur Shore liked in his mistresses, right down to the fact that she gravitated toward successful, married men. In addition, her appointment book—which her assistant had agreeably shared with Monty—included a dozen recent client meetings, all generically listed sans names or numbers, and all conducted in hotel restaurants. Ironically, all the hotels in question were located within a several-block radius of Arthur Shore's Lexington Avenue office, and all the meetings occurred on dates when Arthur Shore was in New York—reportedly in and out of his office all day.

There was no actual evidence that the two of them were sleeping together. That didn't mean it wasn't happening. And that, of course, piqued Monty's interest, especially in light of the story Elyse Shore had told him yesterday.

His first impression had been that Elyse was being straight up with him. Still, there were a couple of points still bugging him.

The first was the timing of the accident.

The punk who'd mowed down Rachel Ogden had taken a huge risk. He'd ripped off the van on Tenth Street, driven to the Upper East Side to harass Elyse Shore, then shot over to midtown to hit Rachel, finally dumping the van in the Bronx. Talk about time and territory. He'd pushed the limits of both. Whoever hired him had to know that the longer the van went missing, the greater the chance it had of being spotted by the cops.

It was quite a risk to take, just to upset Elyse and put the fear of God in Morgan.

Then there was the news coverage.

The local media stations had broadcast word of the hit-and-run on the evening and the eleven o'clock news—complete with Rachel's and Karly's names. Yet, based on her surprise this morning, Elyse was clueless about the identities of the victim and the eyewitness, and equally clueless about the fact that they were both Winshore clients. For a savvy woman with a high-powered political husband, it seemed odd that she'd be so out of touch with the day's current events.

So could Elyse be lying? Possibly. But why?

Monty could think of just one reason for her to devise such an intricate fabrication—and that is if she were the culprit, not the victim.

It was a long shot. But it had to be considered, especially in light of what he'd learned about Rachel Ogden. After all, how did that saying go? Hell hath no fury like a woman scorned. Jonah had said that Elyse was in a foul mood when she'd shown up at her husband's office. Well, orchestrating a scare tactic for your rival—one that went way further than planned—would do that.

If—and Monty still considered it a huge if—Elyse had invented the story she'd told him to mesh with the timing of the hit-and-run, it would explain why she seemed totally oblivious to the identity of the women involved, and it would scrap the uptown leg of the van's trip, making the timing and the route more plausible.

On the other hand, if Elyse was telling the truth, there was another, more unnerving fact to consider—one he had refrained from mentioning to Morgan. And that was that, on paper, Rachel Ogden's description matched Morgan's to a tee. Slight build. Corporate dress. Shoulder-length dark hair. Green eyes. Expected in the area of the St. Regis at hit-and-run time.

Following that logic, it was a very real prospect that the error made by the punk who'd stolen that van hadn't been that he'd hurt Rachel Ogden too badly, but that he'd run down the wrong woman. And if *that* was the case, his orders might very well have been to kill, not injure, Morgan.

Lots of theories. An equal number of outstanding answers, some grimmer than others.

Monty pulled into the hospital parking area. He was impatient to have this chat with Rachel Ogden.

JILL HAD JUST organized some files on her desk when her cell phone rang. She glanced at the caller ID and punched it on with lightning-quick speed.

"Dad—hi. I've been waiting for sunrise in the Rockies so I could call. Glad you beat me to it."

"Why the urgency?" Her father's tension was palpable, even through the phone.

"Everyone's fine. But last night, Morgan told me what's been going on with Mom. I called her at Grandma and Grandpa's right before I turned in, and she still sounded drained, but less stressed out. Talking to you obviously helped. Whatever you said calmed her down."

"It did. And now it should calm you down, too. I just got off the phone with Detective Montgomery. He's arranged for round-the-clock security to keep an eye on your mother, on Morgan, and on you. No one's going to come near you—*any* of you."

Even though she could have predicted her father's reaction, Jill felt a surge of relief. "That's great. Thanks, Dad. If nothing else, it will grant us peace of mind." A forced laugh. "Not to mention that it will rescue Mom from spending another night with her parents. I know Grandpa's your staunchest ally, but he drives Mom crazy. Her conversation with Detective Montgomery must have *really* freaked her out for her to decide to sleep over there."

"I'm sure she had her reasons."

"I invited her to stay with Morgan and me."

"And?"

Jill sighed. "Morgan and I had scheduled a girls' night. And you know Mom. Much as I told her she was one of the girls, she decided we needed our privacy to talk about personal stuff like guys. Particularly the guy you're about to go skiing with."

"Lane?"

"Yup. Did he tell you he's taking Morgan out the minute your plane lands tonight? Of course not." Jill supplied her own answer. "Men never communicate about anything. So I'll fill you in. There are some definite sparks between those two. They have late dinner plans tonight."

"No great eye-opener there." Arthur's reply was tinged with dry humor. "Despite your belief that we men are clueless, I did pick up on the vibes between Morgan and Lane. Last night in the lounge, I saw him talking on his cell, and it didn't look like a business call. So I'm not surprised they have plans."

"It'll be good for her." Jill chewed her lip. "Morgan's even more wound up now than she was when she first hired Detective Montgomery. Things were bad enough when she was dealing with her initial shock and pain over the reopened investigation. But now she's dealing with the fact that people she loves are being directly affected. Instead of scaring her, it's infuriating her. Forget the idea of her taking a passive role. If she has her way, she's going to be right there, center stage, solving this case alongside Detective Montgomery."

"That's the worst thing she can do to herself," Arthur said fervently. "She's already on emotional overdrive. If she becomes any more obsessed with this investigation, she'll make herself ill."

"That's why Lane couldn't have come into her life at a better time. I hope they have a fabulous time tonight. At the very least, he'll be a great distraction. But I have a hunch it'll be more, maybe even explode into a full-blown romance. Either way, I'd be thrilled. Anything to divert her focus."

"I agree." A thoughtful pause. "Maybe you should spend tonight at our place. Extra security or not, I'm not thrilled with the idea of you or your mother being alone. I won't be home until late, which means Morgan will be out with Lane until all hours. I'd feel better on all fronts if you stayed with us. Morgan, too, for that matter. I don't want her walking into an empty house. I'll talk to Lane, tell him to drop her off after their date."

"Uh—I'd hold off on that," Jill advised.

"Why?"

"Dad, do I have to paint you a picture? It's possible that their *date* might last longer than expected. Your instructing Lane about where to drop Morgan off would definitely throw ice water on any romantic plans he might have."

Arthur cleared his throat. "I see your point. How do you suggest I handle it, then?"

"Don't handle it at all. I'll tell Morgan where I'll be, and that she's welcome to join us if her dinner ends before sunrise. Either way, she won't be alone."

RACHEL OGDEN WAS propped up in her hospital bed, looking pale and definitely weary, when Monty walked in. Still, there was more than a trace of curiosity in her wide green eyes as she asked him to sit down.

"Thanks for seeing me," Monty began. "I'm sorry about your accident."

"I look worse than I feel," she replied with a faint smile. "I just finished my morning physical therapy session. I'm convinced their goal is to divert my attention from my injuries to the pain they inflict." She took a sip of water. "My doctor said you're a PI. I don't get meeting requests from many of those."

"I'm sure you don't." Monty sized her up as he settled himself in the armchair across from her bed. Even banged up and having undergone surgery, she was clearly great-looking. Devoid of makeup, she looked young, but Monty could tell that she had a presence that would make her seem older, more sophisticated. He'd be willing to bet that when she was at her corporate best, Rachel Ogden was a ball-breaker.

"Morgan hired you to investigate the accident?" she was asking. "Why? Is there something more than the police have told me?"

It was Monty's turn to smile. "There's always more than what the police tell you. I should know. I was one of them for thirty years." He flipped open his pad. "You're aware that both you and Karly Fontaine, the woman who called in the accident, are clients of Winshore?"

She nodded. "My assistant told me. I asked her to send Karly flowers as a thank-you. We never met before, but she was apparently right behind me on that street corner." A rueful grimace. "Two New Yorkers, rushing to their appointments with their minds rushing elsewhere. Typical."

Monty grunted his understanding. "Let me begin with the obvious. To your knowledge, is there anyone who'd want to hurt you?"

"In business? There are a handful of people who'd do anything if it meant beating me up the corporate ladder. In reality? No one I can think of."

"That's pretty harsh."

A shrug. "I'm a management consultant, Detective. The youngest in a brilliant and cutthroat company. My colleagues aren't known for their big hearts. That doesn't mean they'd run me down."

"What about outside of work? People you've had falling-outs with? Ex-lovers?"

"Or their wives?" Rachel shot him an astute look. "I'm sure you've done your homework. You know I'm not a Girl Scout. That's one of the reasons I went to Winshore, to change the profile of the guys I got involved with. As for the married men in my past, trust me, they were either estranged from their wives, or forgetful about mentioning they had one."

"Is one of those men a major political figure?"

For a moment, Rachel looked blank. Then her brows shot up. "Are you referring to Congressman Shore?"

"You said it, not me."

"Probably because you'd either get sued or get your ass handed to you if you did. But I'm willing to answer the question, since I'm very fond of Morgan. No, Detective, I'm not sleeping with Arthur Shore. I may be less than stellar about my choice of partners, but I'm not stupid. Why? Is one of his mistresses a suspect?"

Monty liked this girl. She told it like it was, accepted her flaws, yet made no apologies for them. "There *are* no suspects. As things stand, this was an accident caused by a cowardly idiot. I'm just covering all the bases." He jotted down a few notes. "In your opinion, was the fact that you were the victim just a random event? Could it just as easily have been Karly Fontaine who was hit?"

"Sure. If she'd been in a little more of a hurry and gotten by me before I darted ahead, she'd have beaten me into the street. That's why I doubt this was some premeditated plot. It was too iffy."

"I see your point." Monty wrote down a few more words, then rose. "I don't want to overtax you. As it is, your doctor wasn't too thrilled about my visiting so soon after your surgery."

"I won't lie." She winced. "It hurts like hell. But I'm a fighter. My assistant's on her way over here with my BlackBerry. I'll be caught up by noon. So if you have any more questions and my doctor gives you a hard time, just e-mail me. I'll get right back to you."

"Thanks. You take care of yourself. The world of corporate barracudas awaits."

TWENTY

The Manhattan branch of the Lairman Modeling Agency—a classy office suite located in a high-rise in the heart of midtown—was a tribute to its success stories. Minimally furnished, it drew a visitor's eye right to the glossy white walls, which were covered with photos and magazine spreads of all the beautiful people it represented.

Karly Fontaine was the ideal candidate to manage the place.

In her midthirties, with red-gold hair, a willowy build, and sculpted features, she was clearly an ex-model herself, probably one of the agency's most highly touted success stories. Model to manager. It didn't take a brain trust to figure out why.

Monty was clued into this, not only from his first impressions, but from his research. Karly Fontaine had started out a virtual nobody, waitressing to pay for modeling school. When she'd heard that a major shampoo manufacturer was looking for a newcomer to represent the all-natural hair-care line they were rolling out, she'd walked in cold and auditioned for the job.

She got it.

After that, the Lairman Agency was more than happy to snatch her up as a client. The new hair-care line took off, leading to all sorts of catalog and magazine opportunities. Within a year, Karly Fontaine had become an in-demand model with a thriving career. The rest, as they say, was history.

Now she walked forward, extending her hand and smiling as she shook Monty's. "Detective Montgomery. I'm Karly Fontaine." She glanced around, noted that the chair behind the front desk was empty. "May I get you something—coffee? Tea?"

"Actually, your receptionist is already doing that. She was nice enough to put up a fresh pot. I'm not a connoisseur, but I am an addict. A somewhat fussy one. I like my coffee strong and without bottom-of-the-pot sludge."

"I hear you." This time the smile was less practiced, more spontaneous. "Why don't we have a seat in my office? Cindy will bring in the coffee when it's ready."

Monty followed Karly into the power corner office down the hall from the reception area. Cream leather chairs. Scandinavian wood. Art Deco area rug. Very eclectic.

"Thanks for taking the time to see me," he began.

"Not at all." She gestured for him to take a seat, then lowered herself into the cushy chair behind her desk just as Cindy knocked, brought in two cups of hot, great-smelling coffee. Karly nodded her thanks, waiting till the receptionist left, shutting the door behind her, before she turned back to Monty.

"Are you a caffeine freak, or just a coffee junkie?"

"Both. Don't know many cops or PIs who aren't." Monty took an appreciative swallow.

"That applies to all workaholics," Karly amended with a rueful smile. "This is my second cup today, not counting the Diet Pepsi I gulped down between phone calls, and it's barely lunchtime."

"I win. No Pepsi. But four cups of coffee, one of which was monster size." A corner of Monty's mouth lifted. "If I were in your line of work, I'd need double that. Charm and tact? Not my strengths. I'd need all the help I could get."

Hearing her chuckle, seeing the tension in her body ease, Monty was comfortable that he'd done enough icebreaking to get down to business.

He flipped open his pad. "I won't take more than ten or fifteen minutes of your time. I just have a few questions about Rachel Ogden's accident."

Karly nodded. "You mentioned that Morgan hired you. I hope she's not worried about something absurd like a lawsuit. She isn't responsible if her clients happen to be standing at an intersection when some lunatic roars by."

"No, nothing like that. Although Morgan does feel terrible. She's clearly fond of both you and Rachel. And she wants to make sure this hit-and-run was strictly random." Monty studied her, rolling his pen between his fingers. "You're a successful woman. You were a visible, sought-after model. You sailed up the corporate ladder in a backstabbing business. Now you're managing an entire regional office. Any chance there's someone out there with an ax to grind?"

"Wow." Karly blew out her breath. "You really are direct." She interlaced her fingers in front of her. "I won't deny this is a dog-eat-dog business. I'm sure lots of girls resented me. I know I resented the hell out of modeling success stories when I was the one living hand to mouth. But that was ages ago. I haven't modeled in six or seven years. As for the management track, I didn't sail. I climbed—rung by rung. And, no, I didn't make the kind of enemies who'd hate me enough to run me over."

"What about men? Any harasser types? You know, wack jobs who'd feel like you had some sort of connection? Maybe one who'd follow you here from L.A.?"

Rather than looking worried, Karly looked amused—and somewhat pleased. "I'm flattered that you find me young and desirable enough to warrant a stalker. But I haven't had one of those die-hard fans since I was twenty. And even then, it wasn't like something out of *Fatal Attraction*. No psychos."

"What about the regular men in your life? Guys you're dating, or have dated?"

"That's a lean list. I spend most of my hours working. That's why I signed on with Winshore as soon as I moved back east. At this point, that's where all my dates originate. And I'm sure Morgan is very thorough about weeding out the nutcases."

"I'm sure she is." Monty scribbled down a reminder to himself. "Your real name is Carol Fenton?"

She nodded. "I changed it when I got to L.A. At seventeen, I wanted a more exciting name—one that screamed stardom. Carol Fenton seemed too ordinary for the fabulous modeling career I was determined to have."

"Makes sense. What about your family? Do they call you Carol or Karly?"

Sadness flashed across her face. "I don't have any family. My parents died when I was in my teens. And I'm an only child."

"Is that why you originally left New York and moved to L.A.?"

"Partly, yes. There was nothing tying me to New York, nothing but pain and loss. I wanted to make a fresh start. So I did."

"You said partly. What's the other part of why you left?"

"To jump-start my modeling career."

"Huh. I understand the need for a fresh start. But isn't the modeling industry centered in New York?"

"Some aspects of it, yes." It was obvious that Monty's interrogating style was starting to upset her, maybe bringing back raw memories. "New York is where the fashion magazines are based. But L.A. has the film industry, TV advertising, and the modeling school I wanted to attend." She took a sip of coffee, and Monty noted that her hand was trembling. "Forgive me, Detective. But I was a pretty messed-up kid back then. I'd lost everyone I loved. I acted on impulse. It was a ridiculously drastic move. Still, as it turns out, I'm not sorry. I wound up with a pretty amazing life."

"Yes, you did." Monty shut his notepad. "I'm sorry. I didn't mean to stir up painful memories."

"I realize that. You're just doing your job." Karly took another sip of coffee. This time her hand was steady. "May I ask you a question?"

"Shoot."

"Is this really just caution talking? Or is there some reason Morgan believes this accident was intentional, and that it was aimed at one of her clients?"

"There's no evidence to support the claim that this was anything but a random accident. If you're asking if I believe someone targeted you in particular, the answer is no. I meant what I said—Morgan hired me to check into the coincidence of you and Rachel being in the same place at the same time as this hit-and-run because she cares about her clients. Also, to be blunt, I pushed for the investigation. Anytime you have a high-profile family, especially a political one, everything—and everyone—should be checked out."

Karly spread her hands quizzically. "I'm not following. Is Morgan's family in politics?"

"You didn't know?" Monty's brows arched in surprise. "No, I guess maybe you wouldn't. You've only been back in New York for three months. And Morgan and Jill don't exactly publicize their family's congressional connections. In fact, from what I've seen, they draw a distinct and separate line between their agency and their personal lives. That having been said, it's no secret that Jill's last name is Shore. So I'm sure most of their clients know who she is. And with her father's bill being front-page news every day—like I said, you can't be too careful."

Karly's eyes had widened in astonishment. "Shore? Jill's father is Congressman Arthur Shore?"

"One and the same. And Morgan's lived with the Shores since her parents were killed seventeen years ago. The Shores and the Winters were very close."

"I had no idea." Karly processed that for a minute. "That sheds new light on why you're here. Given what I've read in the tabloids, the congressman's notoriety extends beyond his role in the House of Representatives."

Monty gave an offhand shrug. "I don't read the tabloids. And I don't pay attention to rumors."

"I've learned over the years that where there's smoke, there's often fire." Karly leaned her head back against the chair cushion, eyeing Monty pensively. "Let me ask you something, Detective. I asked you before if you'd been hired to ward off lawsuits. You implied that Morgan's mind wouldn't work that way, and I agree. But would the congressman's? Is that what this is about? Is Arthur Shore the real reason we're having this meeting— because he wants to put a lid on any ugly publicity this hit-and-run might generate?"

Karly Fontaine might not have Rachel Ogden's education, but she sure as hell matched her in street smarts.

Monty kept his answer short and sweet. "Congressman Shore didn't initiate this meeting. He also didn't hire me. Morgan Winter did. My being here isn't about damage control. It's about making sure that Rachel's accident *was* an accident. Question answered?"

"Most succinctly." Karly's tone was dry, but she looked more than a little taken aback. "You don't pull any punches, do you, Detective?"

"Nope. I'm a no-BS kind of guy."

"So I see."

Reminding himself that Karly Fontaine was used to more genteel interactions, Monty purposely softened his approach. "Look, I didn't mean to come off like a Brooklyn cop. Old habits die hard. Your question was a legitimate one. So, for the record, yeah, the congressman is dedicated to his career. But he's more dedicated to his family. Any concerns he has about Rachel's hit-and-run are grounded in issues of security, not politics. Okay?"

"Okay." Karly's tone had lost its edge. But her face was drawn tight.

"I've taken enough of your time." Monty shut his notepad and rose. He reached into his jacket pocket and whipped out a business card, passing it across the desk to Karly. "If you think of anything we didn't touch on, give me a holler."

KARLY POPPED A Valium the minute Monty left. This hit-and-run had suddenly taken on a whole new meaning, one with her in its crosshairs. Especially in light of the confidential meeting she'd had on Monday.

The New York relocation was beginning to feel like a huge mistake.

AS SOON AS he left the Lairman Modeling Agency, Monty acted on the reminder he'd jotted down for himself when Karly pointed out that Morgan restricted who did and did not become a Winshore client.

The reminder was Charlie Denton.

He was the third component of Monty's immediate action plan. He was also most definitely a Winshore client, a very relevant one. Not only was he the common denominator between the two women Monty had just interviewed, he was also a factor in both Morgan's life and Jack Winter's life—a factor Monty couldn't quite wrap his mind around.

The guy was an enigma. He was a kick-ass prosecutor, who definitely had his eye on the prize—climbing the advancement ladder in the D.A.'s office. Monty got the fact that making waves didn't jibe with Denton's plan. So it made sense that the A.D.A. was less than thrilled about the digging around he was being pushed to do, even if it was unofficially sanctioned by his boss.

Still, there was another side to him. And that side definitely had a personal interest in the Winters' case. What Monty couldn't shake was the feeling that Denton's interest was rooted in something more substantial than scoring points with Morgan or securing justice for Jack.

Monty was impatient for answers. He'd put out the necessary feelers yesterday morning, and his contacts were the best.

Time to start calling in the results.

He flipped open his cell and started the process as he walked to his car. By the time he paid the parking attendant and pulled out of the lot, he had enough information.

AT TWO-THIRTY, MONTY was in his office, poring over specific aspects of the old case files he'd requisitioned, when the doorbell rang.

Good. Right on time.

He tossed down the notes he'd been reviewing—and was about to put to use—rose from his chair, and headed to the front door.

In one smooth motion, he pulled it open, his expression unreadable. "Denton," he greeted. "Come on in."

The A.D.A. was planted on the front stoop, hands shoved in his coat pockets, looking harried and pissed off. He gave one guarded look around, then complied, striding into the office with a definite air of irritation.

"I'm not thrilled about meeting here," he began, shrugging out of his coat and tossing it on a chair. "My involvement in this case is being kept pretty well under wraps. If I'm seen, I'm screwed. But you made it sound important."

"It is. As for being seen, none of my neighbors would know who the hell you are if they fell on you. And, believe me, you'd rather have this conversation here than in the D.A.'s office. The walls there have ears. Plus, you're not here because I made it sound important. You're here because you want to gauge how much I know. Have a seat." Monty pointed toward the cluttered sitting area.

Charlie remained in place for a moment, studying Monty with a wary expression. Then he crossed over, perching at the edge of the settee. "Okay, your shock and awe worked. I'm all ears. Get to the point. What's the goal here, to interrogate me into spilling my guts the way you do some two-bit criminal? I'm a prosecutor, Montgomery. A good one. Don't try to play me. Just tell me what you want to know, and why."

"Fair enough." Monty spread his hands in an affable gesture. "Let's start by talking about your professional loyalty to Morgan's father. It's pretty strong, considering the man's been dead for seventeen years."

"That's not exactly a news flash. You've known from day one how much I admired and respected Jack Winter. He was a hell of a role model. I learned the ropes from him when I was a rookie, right out of law school. He took me under his wing, just like he did everyone on his team."

"But in your case, he also took you into his confidence."

Something glittered in Charlie's eyes. "Every case that comes into the D.A.'s office is confidential."

"Some more than others."

A hardened look. "I'm not playing cat and mouse with you, Montgomery. If you've got something to ask me, ask."

Monty jerked his thumb in the direction of the thick file sprawled across his desk. "That's the Angelo case file. The Central Clerk's Office did me the favor of digging it out of storage. I've been going through it, document by document—from initial arrests to prosecution and conviction. I paid special attention to the trial transcript, analyzing it with a fine-tooth comb. I'm sure you remember the trial; it concluded just a few months before Jack and Lara Winter were killed."

"I remember it. I also remember it was one of the cases Morgan suggested we revisit to find her parents' killer. Clearly, you're zeroing in on it for a reason."

"Yup." Monty rose, strolled over to the desk, and flipped through the file contents. "Angelo had clusters of gunrunning, drug-trafficking scumbags on his payroll all over the country. A bunch of them are still out there; high-level ones, too, who are still taking orders from their incarcerated boss. One of them could easily have arranged for a hired hand to steal that van and run down Jack Winter's daughter—especially if she was getting close to fig-uring out that Angelo had something to do with her father's murder."

Clearly, that wasn't what Charlie was expecting to hear, and it got his attention big-time. "You think that hit-and-run was meant for Morgan?"

"It's possible. The specs of her physical description are identical to Ra-chel Ogden's. And she was headed for the St. Regis that day, just like Rachel was."

"Jesus." Charlie ran a palm over his jaw. "I figured the incident was meant as a scare, not a hit." He shot Monty a quizzical look. "Even if you're right, what makes you think it was Angelo who was behind it? Jack put away a lot of well-connected criminals."

"True. But this case has a hook to it the others don't. One of the wit-nesses who testified against Angelo was a confidential informer for the D.A.'s office. A *long-term* CI, one who played a key role in helping Jack Win-ter put Angelo away." Monty waved a piece of paper in the air. "Here's a transcript of his witness testimony. According to him, Angelo hired him when he was twenty-six—that would be thirty years ago and thirteen years before the trial—to transport hot guns for him. The perp was caught in the act and arrested. Funny thing was, the charges were dropped and the file was sealed, even though he wasn't a juvie."

"So? The D.A. cut a deal. The guy got off and became an informer."

"For Jack."

"Fine, for Jack. What's the red flag?"

"You tell me. I want to know this CI's name."

Charlie's jaw hardened. "If you're suggesting I get that information for you, forget it. I don't have access to the master files linking CIs' names with their registration numbers, and you know it. The control officers guard that information like Fort Knox."

"Take it easy. I don't expect you to break into restricted files. Like I said, I've got a transcript of this CI's testimony right here, complete with his reg-istration number. Now all I need is paperwork that'll help me put a name to the number. That paperwork is accessible in Jack Winter's files. Documents. Forms. Records of basic interactions between Jack and this guy, along with the dates of those meetings. Anything you can find with the same CI number on it. Make copies of the documents and get them to me. By comparing what I see, I'll be able to figure out if it's the guy I think it is."

"And who's that?"

"I'll let you know afterward—if I'm right." Monty leveled a steady gaze at Charlie. "You didn't happen to work with Jack Winter on the witness list for that case, did you?"

"No. Nor did I know the identities of any of his informers." Charlie bristled. "I don't know where you're going with this, but if it's to put the screws into me because you think I know something, don't bother. I don't know anything. I was a newbie. There's not a chance I'd be privy to such high-level restricted info."

"But you stuck close to Jack Winter. He thought a lot of you. You were his protégé."

"So?"

Monty leaned forward. "So you're hiding something. My guess is it's either something personal about Jack, or something that's a potential political nightmare. Which is it?"

Charlie stood up. "This conversation's over. Whatever it is you think you have on me, run with it. You'll only come up empty."

"If you're so sure of that, why did you take the bait on my shock and awe? Why'd you show up?"

No reply.

"Sit down, Denton," Monty stated flatly. He walked around to the fridge, pulled out two bottles of water, and tossed one to Charlie. Twisting open his own bottle, he took a long, deep swallow, then regarded Charlie intently.

"First, I'm not accusing you of anything except maybe a misplaced sense of loyalty, at least where it comes to the powers that be." A shrug. "Then again, who am I to judge? I thumbed my nose at the powers that be, and they had a party the day I retired. So drink some water and relax."

With obvious ambivalence, Charlie lowered himself back into the chair. "You're right. I walk the straight and narrow. That doesn't mean my loyalties are as black-and-white as you're implying."

"I hear you." Another gulp of water. "Okay then, here it is. I'm not a cop anymore. I'm not part of a pissing match between the NYPD and the D.A.'s office. I'm also not trying to screw you out of a promotion or nail you for something you didn't do. Like I said, my sources say you're honest. So do my instincts. My agenda's simple: I just want to figure out who killed Morgan's parents. I think you want the same thing. You're obviously wrestling with something. I think it's about Jack Winter, not his office. Tell me what you know so I can help."

Charlie stared at his unopened bottle for a moment. Then he twisted off the cap, sinking back into the chair as he drank. "I don't *know* anything," he declared after a few reviving gulps. "But I don't believe in coincidences."

"Neither do I."

Another prolonged silence. "I've played this back in my head a hundred times. There's nothing there but circumstantial events and supposition."

"Go on."

"You're right. It's about Jack. He wasn't himself those last few weeks. He was moody and short-fused. Something was obviously eating at him."

"One of his cases?"

"Uh-uh." Charlie shook his head. "He was a bulldozer about nailing the accused, but he wasn't the type to transfer that sharp edge to the junior staff. Besides, this wasn't about work. I know, because I heard him on the phone—not once, but several times. He was behind closed doors, but my cubicle was near his office. I could make out his tone, and I picked up a word here and there. The conversations weren't pleasant. They were deep, heated—and personal. He was upset when he hung up. I could hear him pacing, flinging files around. When he came out, he looked like hell."

"Do you know who he was arguing with?"

"His wife."

That was one Monty hadn't expected. "Lara? You're sure?"

"Yes. He said her name enough times. Plus, the last argument was in person. She came to the office. She looked as upset as he sounded. Again, I didn't hear specifics; Jack shut the door. But judging from their tones, it was serious. Lara was crying when she left. And I heard Jack tell her something about principles having to trump personal feelings, no matter how deep those feelings ran."

"Interesting." Monty pursed his lips thoughtfully. "Do you think they were having marital problems?"

"It's possible. I'm just not sure. All I can say for certain is that there was definite friction between them, and that they were coming from different places about the way something should be handled. It was a major issue. Whether it was their marriage, or something else, I have no idea."

"But whatever it was, it was something they felt passionately about. Which means that if it wasn't personal, it was something professional with a personal impact."

"Like?"

"Like a high-risk case that made Lara afraid for her husband."

The bottle of water paused halfway to Charlie's mouth. "You're talking about the Angelo case again."

"My gut still says so. Which means I need you to get me those CI documents. I'll give you the guy's registration number. Take it. Pull any papers with a matching number. Photocopy all communications between him and Jack. Do it fast. If this guy is who I think he is, we might have found a solid revenge motive. One that would explain a lot. Because it extends beyond the courtroom, to the closest people in Jack and Lara Winter's lives."

TWENTY-ONE

I t was just after one-thirty when Lane, Arthur, Jonah, and their guide, Rob, put on their fat skis in the thigh-deep snow and checked their safety equipment in anticipation of their last run of the day.

Lane gazed around him, experiencing a sensory high. He was transfixed by the beauty of the snow-covered mountains—powerful, defiant, and free from man's interference, except for the insignificant lines carved by their skis in the huge expanse of white that rose all around them. Even those would be gone in a day or so, and all traces of their presence would be wiped out, buried under a new fall of snow.

Maybe that was nature's way of cleansing herself from intruders.

Eager to preserve the image, Lane shot some stills, then twisted around and focused on Arthur, who was giving Jonah a few pointers. The scene looked so natural and appealing. A middle-aged man and a high school teen standing side by side, their postures alike, their minds in sync, as one taught, the other learned. From an artistic and a human standpoint, it was inspiring. And from a pragmatic standpoint, it made Congressman Shore come across as that much more human, seeing him share his knowledge and experience with a budding young man.

This spread for *Time* was going to knock their readers' socks off.

JONAH'S SKIING HAD gotten progressively better, particularly with Arthur's periodic coaching. His inexperience was transforming into confidence. Until now, he'd restrained himself from letting loose with his newfound skill. But now . . . the day was almost over. His chance of reveling in the full experience was nearing an end, despite the soreness and fatigue he was starting to feel.

For the last run, they'd agreed to let him lead.

Time to show off his recently acquired prowess.

Adrenaline thrumming through his veins, Jonah headed down the hill. Using his poles, he pushed off.

At first, his rhythm matched the grade perfectly. He was able to ignore the twinges and weakness in his muscles. But as time passed and his descent continued, the weakness intensified. His legs began feeling rubbery and nonresponsive.

Unwilling to give in, he started into the next turn. His mind issued instructions, but his body wouldn't—couldn't—comply.

The grade sharply increased. So did Jonah's speed.

He lost the battle.

Pitching forward, his momentum sent him careening down the mountain, tumbling through the deep snow until his fall was broken by a small tree. He struck it and bounced off. Stunned, his lungs gasping for air and his body throbbing, he lay there, buried in the snow, clutching his side and moaning in pain.

The others quickly caught up to him.

"Jonah, are you all right?" Lane was kneeling beside him.

"I . . . I think so," he managed.

"Are you able to stand?" Arthur demanded.

They all watched as Jonah tried to comply, and failed, wincing as he did.

Rob, their guide, who was also a trained EMT, sprang into action. He partially unzipped Jonah's shell so he could feel for any bleeding. Jonah groaned when his left side was touched.

"Let's get him checked out," Rob determined.

"I'm fine." Jonah was struggling to get up, visibly upset and embarrassed by his fall and the scene it had caused.

"Probably," Lane agreed, helping him to his feet. "But we're not taking any chances. And, by the way, we all take spills. That was a tough section. Not your best skiing of the day, but you held your own for most of it."

"Pretty agilely at that," Arthur added, manning Jonah's other side as Rob radioed the chopper pilot and directed him to their location. "I've got to tell you, Jonah, I'm impressed. You've got a natural stance and aptitude for this. That was some pretty impressive heli-skiing for a first-timer."

"Thanks, sir." Jonah's breathing and color were returning to normal.

"Don't let it go to your head," Lane retorted. "What you did was still reckless."

"And we both would have done the same thing," Arthur amended drily. "Right, Lane?"

Lane shot him a look. "You're not helping, Congressman."

"I know." Arthur grinned. "Then again, I can afford to be honest. I'm not the one who has to face his parents."

By this time, the sound of the chopper reached their ears.

"Let's go," Rob instructed.

They removed their skis, and Rob motioned to Arthur to help him with Jonah. Slowly, they carried him down the mountain, Lane following just behind with their equipment.

After what seemed like forever, they reached a flatter section of terrain and headed over to where the helicopter had perched. Lane scrambled aboard and with Arthur and Rob's help from the ground, he lifted Jonah and guided him into the nearest seat. Then Arthur climbed aboard while Rob quickly loaded their gear and joined them in the chopper for the descent down the mountain. Once they were safely aloft, the pilot radioed ahead for an ambulance.

"I feel so stupid," Jonah muttered. "I'm just a little banged up, and we're making such a big deal out of it. Plus, we cut the whole day short."

"We were finishing up anyway," Lane assured him. "The afternoon shadows were about to move in. And we're not making a big deal. This is standard procedure. You'll get checked out and we'll be on our way home."

THE DOCTOR AT Telluride Medical Center examined Jonah thoroughly. As expected, his left side was bruised and tender to the touch. But the acute pain had subsided—a positive sign that seemed to rule out internal injuries. When Arthur informed the doctor that he had a private jet at Telluride Regional Airport waiting to fly them home, the doctor gave the green light for Jonah to travel—on the condition that should he exhibit any worsening symptoms, he would immediately check into a New York hospital and have a CT scan performed to ensure there were no internal injuries. Lane and Arthur assured him there'd be no arguments on that score.

They were on their way within the hour. Arthur had called ahead to have the jet's sofa made up into a bed. Jonah was lifted out of the car, placed on his back on the bed, and secured with a seat belt.

The doctor had given Jonah a dose of oxycodone, so that by the time the plane took off, he was fast asleep. Once they were airborne, Lane called Jonah's parents and gave them a calm but thorough heads-up. He also told them that Arthur had already arranged for a car service to pick them up at home and drive them to Teterboro to meet their plane so they could see for themselves that Jonah was fine, after which he could ride home with them. Initially, they were upset, but Lane succeeded in putting their minds at ease. They were also very grateful to the congressman for his generous assistance.

With everything under control and all the necessary preparations made, Lane settled himself in one of the plush leather seats and made the personal phone call he'd been itching to make.

MORGAN AND JILL had just finished working out the night's logistics. They'd made alternate provisions based upon differing scenarios, the variable being how Morgan's date turned out. Now Jill was upstairs, packing an overnight bag before settling into her yoga ritual, and Morgan was shutting down her desktop computer for the night.

She was interrupted by the ringing of her cell phone.

Watching the computer screen to ensure it went into shut-down mode, she groped for her cell, punched it on, and tucked it in the cradle of her shoulder. "Hello?"

"Hey," Lane greeted her. "Ready for our dinner?"

A smile curved Morgan's lips and she perched at the edge of her desk so she could talk. "Not yet. It's only seven-twenty here. I've got lots of time to get ready." She paused as it dawned on her that the humming sound in the background was the jet engine. "Don't I?"

"That depends on what you define as lots. I'd say you have a little over two hours. We've been airborne for a while. The winds are with us, so we should be landing by around nine-thirty."

"That's earlier than I expected."

"Yeah, well, we cut the day a little short. Jonah took a fall on the last run. The doctor says he's fine, but we wanted to get him home so he can take it easy."

Morgan's brows drew together. "You said he's all right—nothing's broken, I hope."

"Fortunately, not. He just bruised his side. A little rest and he'll be as good as new." A pause. "I'll be riding home separately with Arthur. His driver can drop me off at my place, or I can come straight to yours. Your choice."

"Actually it's not. It's Arthur's choice. He wants Jill and me at his and Elyse's apartment in an hour, accompanied by our newly assigned, nondescript bodyguards."

"Bodyguards—why?" Lane's entire demeanor changed, tension lacing his tone. "What happened since Monday night that I don't know about?"

She sighed. "I thought maybe Arthur would mention it. I guess not. He asked your father to hire security for Jill, Elyse, and me. Evidently, the guy who hit Rachel with that stolen van was tailing Elyse before he headed down to midtown. She spotted him across the street from her gym. On top of that, she's been getting crank calls, actually just hang-ups. And she has the sense that she's being followed."

"Arthur didn't say a word." Lane's wheels were clearly turning. "There's no longer any question that you're the link here. What did Monty have to say? Does he think the hit-and-run was intentional?"

"He thinks it was a scare tactic that got out of hand. He's all over this, even without Arthur's pressure. But Arthur felt better with the added security."

"I don't blame him." Another pause, this one heavy with reluctance. "Would you rather postpone our date?"

"No," Morgan replied bluntly. "I've been looking forward to it all day. I need to get my mind off things. Would you feel really uncomfortable picking me up at Elyse and Arthur's place?"

"Not a bit. The only thing is, I won't have a chance to change. Did you have your heart set on a jackets-required dinner?"

"The truth? I'm dying for a Greek salad and a slice of cheesecake at Gracie's Corner. It's close, it's delicious, and it's open all night. It's also casual enough so you can stay in whatever you're wearing, and I can change into jeans and a sweater." She sighed. "It sounds better the more I think about it."

"Gracie's Corner." Lane smacked his lips. "Now you're talking. I can wolf down a twin cheeseburger platter and a hunk of chocolate layer cake. I've been skiing all day, and I'm starved."

Morgan laughed. "I guess you liked my idea."

"You guess right. I'll swing by Arthur's place and get you. How's the weather?"

"Cold, but clear."

"Good. We can walk. So dress warm."

MORGAN WENT UPSTAIRS and took a hot shower, letting the water ease the tension of the day from her muscles. She'd meant what she said to Lane—she needed this evening away from the insanity of the past week. She'd also meant what she said to Jill—she had no idea where this evening would lead. But she was eager to find out.

She pulled on a pair of Citizens jeans and a lavender cashmere V-neck sweater—low enough to be alluring, not so low as to be obvious. She kept her makeup simple, and her hair loose, brushed off her face and down to her shoulders. For now, she padded around in a pair of warm socks. Her Ugg Fluff Mamas were in the hall closet along with her lightweight down jacket—she'd jump into both on her way out.

She yanked out her weekender tote, packing a change of clothes and some toiletries. Even though Arthur's insistence that she and Jill spend the night there seemed a bit excessive, she had to admit that the thought of being here all alone at this particular time made her antsy.

Morgan glanced at the clock. A little after eight. The pan-flute music that had been drifting out from Jill's room had been replaced by cheerful whistling and the sounds of clothes being stuffed in a bag.

"Hey, Morg, you ready?" she called out a minute later.

"All set," Morgan called back. She grabbed her totebag and purse and left her room.

Reflexively, she glanced at the den. It would be the first night in weeks she hadn't spent poring through journals or scrutinizing photographs. The thought of that was a relief. At the same time she felt as if she were leaving a crucial part of herself behind.

Before she could analyze it further, she'd walked in, gathered up the piles of mementos, and tucked them in her totebag. Like a child with its stuffed animal, she thought, mentally rolling her eyes. She needed them close by, a grown woman with a grown-up security blanket.

There'd be a time when she'd have to let them go—when she'd be *able* to let them go.

But now wasn't that time.

FORTUNATELY, THE TAILWINDS were strong and Arthur had asked the pilot to do whatever was necessary to get home quickly. He'd also instructed the flight attendant to dispense with the usual amenities and instead devote all her attention to Jonah's comfort.

The plane landed at 9:27 P.M.

The car service was there with Jonah's parents, who eagerly embraced their still-groggy son, helped him into the town car, then thanked both Arthur and Lane and climbed in. Minutes later, they were on their way back to Brooklyn.

Arthur's limo was waiting. By the time the town car's taillights disappeared around the bend, Arthur's driver had the congressman and Lane settled in the limo, and he was behind the wheel, pulling away from the curb.

Lane glanced over at Arthur. "I spoke to Morgan. She told me what's been going on with Elyse."

"Did she?" Arthur didn't sound surprised. "I assumed she would, if not today then tonight, while you had dinner. Truthfully, I would have told you myself, but I didn't want to spoil those few euphoric hours on the slopes." A weary sigh. "Blocking out the world for a while becomes essential for survival. Because after that, reality has a way of catching up and biting you in the ass."

"Don't I know it," Lane agreed grimly. "I'm glad you hired more security. Obviously, this hit-and-run was personal. Someone's delivering a message to Morgan—loud and clear."

"I want someone with her at all times." A sideways look. "Tonight, that someone is you. I don't know if she told you, but she and Jill went over to my apartment to hang out with Elyse until I get home."

"She told me. That's where I'm picking her up."

"And dropping her off. Unless . . ." Arthur cleared his throat self-consciously. "Look, Lane, I don't want you to think I'm one of those overbearing father types who inserts himself where he doesn't belong. Morgan's personal life is her own business. It's just that, under the circumstances, I'm a little concerned. So suffice it to say, if the two of you are together, that's fine. But if the evening should happen to wind down . . ."

"I'll see her safely to your door," Lane assured him. "And I won't leave until Morgan is inside with the dead bolt thrown."

"Thanks." Arthur's brows arched in question. "When are you and your father reviewing the photographs you're enhancing?"

"Tomorrow. I'll be working exclusively with Monty the rest of this week, except when I'm photographing you at various appearances and, of course, on Friday, when you and I are heading up to the Poconos to go skydiving." Lane frowned. "I hope Jonah will be up to joining us. The poor kid's been living for these chances to contribute to the *Time* photo essay."

"Yeah, I can see that." A nostalgic smile. "I really enjoy watching Jonah's sense of excitement and discovery. Maybe it sounds melodramatic, but it feels like yesterday that I was his age. It's gratifying to live vicariously through him, and to remember when things were new and unspoiled."

Lane was surprised by the raw emotion in the congressman's tone. "Don't relegate yourself to a rocking chair just yet," he informed him. "You're in the best physical shape I've ever seen."

"I wasn't talking about skiing. I was talking about life." Abruptly, Arthur slid down, leaned his head back. "Enough philosophizing. Let's grab a forty-five-minute nap. We both need it. Especially you. Trust me, you won't earn points by falling asleep in your entrée."

FALLING ASLEEP WAS the furthest thing from Lane's mind as he sat across the table from Morgan.

She looked strained, there was no doubt about it. Her features were drawn, and there were dark circles under her eyes that no amount of concealer could hide. Facts were facts. The events of the past week had taken their toll on her.

Still, she looked gorgeous, emanating that sexy combination of soft femininity and cut-to-the-chase dynamo that he'd found a major turn-on from day one. Her body was the kind that made heads turn, and the way her sweater V'd just to the top of her cleavage made it almost impossible for him to tear his eyes off her. On the other hand, she solved the problem for him just by being herself. Because if he didn't keep his mind on their conversation and off her breasts, he'd never be a worthy sparring partner. Her pointed quips and personal insights were razor sharp and dead on. She kept him on his toes, challenged him at every turn—and he felt as pumped as he had on the ski slopes.

Maybe more.

Besides the excitement, there was an easy banter here, one he found unique and refreshing. And he respected her lack of pretense, the passion of her conviction, and the heartfelt sensitivity that underscored their more serious discussions.

Plus, he wanted her more than he could ever remember wanting a woman.

"So," Morgan commented, abandoning her Greek salad and leaning forward, fingers interlaced, to regard Lane with great curiosity and interest. "From the brief overview you gave me, it sounds like you and Arthur blazed new trails in the San Juan Mountains."

"We did." Lane put down the cheeseburger he'd been chomping on, his eyes glittering with excitement as he attempted to recount the experience for her. "It's hard to describe the feeling. The scenery was breathtaking. There wasn't a mark on the snow, that's how pristine it was. And the sharp drops, the speed, the skill it took to master the experience—it was awesome."

Morgan absorbed every nuance of his reaction. "You really love it, don't you? The adrenaline rush, the risk—all of it."

"Yeah. I do."

"Don't you ever get frightened? Feel vulnerable, mortal?"

"I suppose I would, if I let my mind go there. But I don't. In fact, I don't think at all. I just live in the moment."

"It must be amazing to have that ability. I don't."

"I know. Then again, you have your reasons."

"We've certainly led very different lives," she agreed. "Your parents divorced. That's never easy. But they were still alive, in your life. Plus, you were sixteen, old enough to understand, and to cope. With me, I was a child. I was totally alone. I've never really gotten over that feeling. So, yes, in my case, security trumps all."

"You're very aware of who you are. That's a huge plus in life."

A grimace. "You'd be surprised what seventeen years of therapy will do for you."

"Now it's time to learn all you can be."

Morgan's brows arched. "Are *you* psychologically assessing *me?*"

Lane gave her a lopsided grin. "Hey, you're not the only one who's good at reading people. We just do it in different ways. Mine's through a camera lens."

Visibly intrigued, Morgan contemplated that analogy. "I never thought of it that way. But you're right. A photographer has to be able to read people. And one who's as sought after as you, a veritable expert in his field, has to have really fine-tuned instincts."

"See? We're not so different after all." A very pointed pause. "Except in the ways that matter—the *good* ways."

"We're different in *lots* of ways," Morgan amended, but the color tingeing her cheeks and the sparkle in her eyes told Lane that they were coming from the same place. "Some of those ways are setting off loud warning bells in my head, telling me to run in the opposite direction."

"And is your head listening?"

"No." More of that arousing candor. "Those *good* ways you're talking about have it hands down."

"I'm glad." Lane reached across the table, took her hand. "Cards on the table," he said quietly, his thumb tracing her palm. "You think I'm a player. Maybe by your definition I am. But, Morgan . . ." He paused, feeling the tiny quiver that ran through her hand and sent white-heat shooting through him. "I'm not playing this time."

"I know." Her fingers slid between his, interlacing their hands in a way that was wildly erotic. "*You're* not playing. And *I'm* not playing it safe. Sounds like a plan."

Lane's entire body tensed. Where they were, who they were, what they were talking about—all of it ceased to matter. Now there was just now.

"I'll have them wrap the food," he said in a low, urgent tone. "We'll take it with us."

She nodded, already reaching for her jacket. "Don't forget my cheesecake," she managed.

"I won't. Or my chocolate layer cake. I have a feeling we'll both need the energy boost."

He'd signaled the waiter and was halfway out of the booth, when Morgan stopped him, capturing his forearm. "Lane?"

Turning, he shot her a questioning look. Questioning? More like imploring. He felt like a horny teenager who was praying his date hadn't gotten cold feet.

Morgan smiled, reading his expression. "Not a chance," she assured him softly. "My jacket will be zipped and I'll be at the door by the time you get our doggy bags. It's just that . . ." She wet her lips with the tip of her tongue, pushing out her next words with an effort. "I realize my place is only four blocks away. It's close. It's empty. It's the logical choice. But . . ."

"But you don't want to go back there tonight."

"No, I don't. I want to shut out everything. I want to think about only tonight. Better yet, I don't want to think at all."

"Then don't. My place is only seven or eight blocks farther. We'll make up the time by grabbing a taxi instead of walking." He snatched up his own jacket, yanking it on as he spoke to the waiter.

In a minute flat, he'd ordered their dessert to go and whipped out the money to pay their check. While the waiter totaled everything up, Lane angled his head in Morgan's direction, gave her an intimate wink. "Meet you at the door in five."

"Nope," she countered, zipping up her jacket and plucking her purse off the seat. "Meet me outside. I'll have a cab ready and waiting."

TWENTY-TWO

Fifteen minutes later they were inside Lane's apartment.

Morgan got a fleeting glimpse of the first floor, bathed in the entranceway light, as Lane threw the dead bolt behind them.

The place was very relaxed, very homey, very male. A living room with caramel leather sofas and chairs, a hearth and fireplace, and, off of that, a media room with a big-screen TV and lots of high-tech audio equipment. Beyond that, she could see a room with a ceramic-tile floor and stainless-steel appliances—obviously the kitchen. In the opposite corner was a dead-bolted door that had to lead to Lane's digital photo lab. It was probably very impressive, as was the rest of the place, but Morgan didn't—couldn't—concentrate on asking for a tour. Not now.

"The second floor's my home gym," Lane said in a low, husky voice, pulling off her jacket and his and tossing them aside. "Want to see it?"

"I want to see the whole apartment—later." Morgan shook a few snowflakes off her hair, her mind and body wired. "Unless you're dying to show it to me now."

"Uh-uh." Lane walked over to her, rubbing his palms up and down the cashmere sleeves of her sweater. "What I'm dying to show you now is my bedroom."

She tipped back her head, gazed up at him with undisguised desire glittering in her eyes. "My thoughts exactly."

"The problem is, it's on the third floor, two flights up." His fingers glided through her hair, tucking it behind her ear. "Both bedrooms are." He lowered his head, his lips grazing the side of her neck.

"So far away," she whispered, her voice and body trembling.

"I've got a perfect solution." His lips shifted to the hollow at the base of her throat. "I spend hours in my photo lab." He kissed his way up to her jaw. "I crash in the media room. It's got a cushioned air mattress—king-size. We could—"

"Yes."

He lifted her arms around his neck, nibbling at the corner of her mouth as he backed her toward the media room. "I'm being a lousy host," he murmured. "Can I offer you something—a drink? A glass of wine?"

"A kiss," she replied, turning her head until her lips brushed his. "I've fantasized about that all week."

"So have I . . . and a lot more." He stopped in his tracks, his hand sliding under her hair, anchoring her for what was to come. "Let's start with this."

His mouth opened on hers. Hers opened under his. The kiss was hot, penetrating, openly carnal. Their lips fused, parted, then fused again, his tongue pressing deep, rubbing against hers in a blatant overture of what was to come.

Morgan whimpered—an aroused, impatient sound—and pressed closer, molding her body to his. Even through their layers of clothes, the contact was electrifying.

Lifting Morgan's feet off the floor, Lane half carried her the rest of the way to the media room, covering the remaining distance in long, uncompromising strides.

Together, they dropped down on the air mattress, the fleece blanket that covered it a warm, soft nest beneath them. They tugged at each other's clothes, pulling sweaters over heads, unsnapping and unzipping jeans, and struggling with socks and boots. Lane unclasped her bra, and Morgan shrugged out of it, her progress slowed by Lane hooking his arm under her back, arching her up to his mouth to give him free access to her breasts. His lips closed around each taut nipple, tugging with his lips, lashing with his tongue, until Morgan cried out in frustration. She shoved at his shoulders until he released her. Then she wriggled free of the impeding bra, tossed it to the floor.

Lane's hot gaze burned over her, through her, and he drew a rough breath, reaching down to make quick work of her thong. His fingers lingered for a moment, caressing her thighs, between her thighs, slipping up and inside her.

It was good—too damned good.

Neither of them could stand it another minute.

Lane dragged himself away just long enough to shed his briefs and kick them aside. Then he leaned down, lifted Morgan slightly so he could peel back the blanket, place her on the flannel sheet beneath it.

Then he was on her, covering her, his body pressing hers into the mattress.

The world stopped at the first contact of their naked skin.

Morgan made an inarticulate sound of pleasure, instinctively lifting herself closer, rubbing her breasts against his chest, creating exquisite friction as his crisp hair rasped across her nipples.

Lane went rigid, a hard tremor vibrating through him, and he forced out his words in a rough, unsteady voice. "Keep that up and this is going to be over way too fast."

Her fingertips traced his spine. "I can't wait for slow."

"Morgan." He caught her head between his hands, his mouth plundering hers in a scalding kiss. He kept kissing her, but his hands shifted, slid over the curves of her body until they reached her thighs. His fingers curled around them, and his fingertips trailed lightly over the sensitive skin of her inner thighs, absorbing the tiny quivers he created.

Restlessly, she squirmed, parting her thighs wider, and his erection slid lower, pulsing against her core, finding the opening of her body and probing.

She arched to accommodate him. He hooked his arms under her knees, angling her for the deepest penetration possible. He tore his mouth from hers, and their gazes met, fiery and urgent.

"Now," she breathed.

"Now's not soon enough." He was already pushing into her, stretching her as he did, creating a friction that was so complete, so utterly perfect, that she moaned, her head tossing on the pillow.

Lane paused, the muscles in his arms trembling with the effort of holding back. "Is it too much?"

"No. God . . . no." She pushed at the base of his spine.

"You're tight," he ground out.

"I'm dying," she gasped back. "Lane . . ." Her inner muscles clenching around him.

"Damn." He gave it up. "I've got to get inside you." In one inexorable push, he was all the way there.

They both sucked in their breath.

Then Lane began to move, ignoring the screaming dictates of his body. He was determined to prolong the experience, to make every sensation last, and he paced himself, thrusting into her in deep, slow strokes.

Morgan understood, and her body met and matched his rhythm. Everything inside her was clamoring for release, but she tamped down on her own urgency, equally intent on sustaining this incredible feeling for as long as possible.

It built, escalated, until restraint was no longer an option.

Lane let it go, giving in to what he needed, what they both needed. He said her name, first in a guttural whisper, then in a shout as he pounded into her, felt the clenching spasms of her climax begin, heightening as he pushed deeper, farther inside her.

She cried out—a wild, shocked cry of completion—and totally unraveled, her inner muscles contracting again and again. Lane poured into her, coming in hard spasms that shook him to the core, drained every drop of him.

Utterly spent, he collapsed on top of her, his breath coming in shallow rasps, his body drenched in sweat. He was fairly sure he'd never move again. Beneath him, Morgan went limp, her arms and legs going slack, sliding to the mattress. She was still quivering with tiny aftershocks, and her heart was racing as she dragged air into her lungs.

Lane knew he was too heavy for her, that he should shift his weight, but his body just wouldn't comply.

"I'm hurting you," he managed hoarsely, his lips in her hair.

"No." The word was barely a whisper, but she punctuated it with a slight shake of her head so Lane knew he hadn't imagined it.

The assurance was good enough.

Giving in to his exhaustion, Lane turned his face against her neck, inhaled her scent, and shut his eyes. His last thought before drifting off was that he couldn't remember any adrenaline drop being as good as the rush that preceded it—until now.

Morgan lay awake for a long time after Lane's even breathing told her he was asleep. She was physically spent, her muscles weak and watery, and her entire body cried out for rest. But her mind, her emotions—those were on raging overload.

Something told her she'd just made a huge mistake.

She'd known that getting involved with Lane Montgomery was a risk. Even so, she'd gone into it with her eyes wide open. But what she'd expected was, at worst, a very hot, very satisfying one-night stand, and at best, a torrid affair of some unknown duration that would offer her welcome relief from the turmoil she was going through.

Talk about a miscalculation.

She'd never anticipated the magnitude of what had just happened between them.

It wasn't just the sex, although that had surpassed even her most erotic fantasies.

It was more. It was deep, it was complex, and it was undeniable.

It was also the last thing she needed right now. Her emotions, her state of mind, her life were on total overdrive. She needed something simple, something uncomplicated, not another emotional avalanche.

God help her, she was in trouble.

———

THE WIRY MAN ambled down East Eighty-second Street until he reached the address he was looking for. He climbed the steps of the brownstone, glancing around as he hovered at the front door.

It was 3 A.M., pitch-dark, and deserted. He was dressed in black so he blended in with the night. And he was traveling light.

He opened the leather case containing his picks and started on the top lock. He inserted the tension wrench and applied pressure in a counter-clockwise direction. The lock was a Schlage. No problem. He selected the particular pick that experience had taught him would be most effective, expertly working each pin until the wrench turned in his hand and the bolt retracted into the door.

One down, one to go.

He repeated the process on the bottom lock.

Mission accomplished.

The front doorknob turned in his gloved hand. He was in.

WARM LIPS BRUSHED Morgan's shoulder, and gentle fingers threaded through her hair, moved it aside so those same lips could find the curve of her neck.

Her lashes fluttered, then lifted, and for a moment she couldn't get her bearings. It was nighttime. The room was dark, other than a pale, flickering glow. And the bed was low to the ground and unfamiliar.

She twisted around toward the source of the kisses—and abruptly her memory returned.

Lane was propped on one elbow, watching her from beneath hooded lids. There were a couple of lit candles on the nearby end table, which explained the soft glow filtering the room. On the floor beside the air mattress, there was a tray containing two glasses of wine, two slices of cheesecake, and two hunks of chocolate layer cake.

A slow, intimate smile curved Lane's lips. "Hungry?"

"Starved." Morgan squirmed into a sitting position, tucking the blanket around her. Candles, dessert, and wine. It might be clichéd, but it still did the trick. "What a lovely surprise," she murmured. "Especially since gestures like this are usually part of the seduction dance. And since that dance has already reached a roaring crescendo . . ." Her eyes twinkled. "I think this could be described as superfluous."

"Funny, I'd describe it as sustenance." Lane's knuckles grazed her cheek, his intimate gaze still enveloping her. "The dessert—*and* the dance."

Morgan swallowed. There was no denying his effect on her. The scary part was that she was having a hard time convincing herself that it was all part of his standard MO. The words rang too true—assuming she had enough objectivity to assess them. "When did you do all this?" she asked.

"A few minutes ago. After I got my fill of watching you sleep."

"Now *that* sounds like an enthralling pastime." She raked a hand through her tousled hair.

"It was."

"I hope I didn't snore."

"You didn't. In fact, except for an occasional murmur, you were out cold." Lane's humor vanished. "I got the feeling it was the first decent sleep you've had in weeks."

"It was." Morgan saw his concern, recognized its basis, and nipped it in the bud. "Lane, please, let's not go there—not tonight. For tonight . . ."

"For tonight, there's just indulgence, spontaneity, and pleasure."

"Is that okay?"

"It's better than okay. It's essential." Lane brought a lock of her hair to his lips.

"Speaking of tonight . . ." Morgan peered around, looking for a clock and not spotting one. "There's not much of it left, is there?"

"No. But we'll make the most of what there is."

"Do you happen to know what time it is?"

"More or less. I glanced at the kitchen clock when I left with our dessert. It was just after three. It must be three-thirty by now. Perfect time for our next indulgence." Lane rolled to his opposite side, reaching over and plucking the two goblets of wine off the tray. He handed one to Morgan, following it with her plate of cheesecake and a fork. "Dig in."

She did, savoring the creamy mouthfuls and smiling as she watched

Lane scarf down his first hunk of chocolate cake. "You really *were* hungry."

"I worked up an appetite."

"Enough for two hunks of that cake?"

"Nope. Just one." He used his thumb to wipe a bit of cheesecake off her lower lip. "But I'm hoping for an encore workout session—one that's just as consuming as the last, but even more creative."

"Are you now?" Grinning, Morgan licked her fork. "I'm impressed. You either have enormous stamina or a hugely overinflated ego."

"I'll let you be the judge. But first, let's finish our dessert." He raised his goblet. "Shall I make the toast?"

"Please do."

He tipped the glass in her direction. "Here's to similarities and differences. Here's to exploring every adventure life has to offer. And here's to being all we can be."

"I'll drink to that."

They clinked glasses, and Morgan took a slow, appreciative sip. Sauvignon Blanc—the perfect complement to cheesecake.

She glanced from the half-eaten cake to the rapidly disappearing wine to the heated gleam in Lane's eyes.

Dessert was nearing an end. The sparks between them were already crackling to life.

She could say no, get out while she still had a fighting chance.

Problem was, she didn't want to.

CONFIDENT THAT THE street was deserted, the intruder stepped outside the brownstone, the necessary implements clutched in his gloved hands.

Things had gone like clockwork. He'd followed orders, and even added a few touches of his own. The fact that the place had no burglar-alarm system had afforded him the time and the freedom to do that. No sirens, silent or otherwise, to alert the cops. No motion detectors to pick him off.

He inserted his wrench in the lock and twisted clockwise. Then he manipulated the pick until all the pins were in place, and with a twist of his wrist, the bolt reengaged into the jamb.

Job done. Everything was as it had been when he arrived.

Or so it seemed from the outside.

AN ICY DAWN was about to make its presence known when Morgan fished out her keys and scurried up to her front door.

"Hurry," Lane urged, coming up behind her and wrapping his arms around her down-clad waist. "It's freezing out here. The temperature must have dropped ten degrees since last night."

"You don't fool me," Morgan retorted, sliding the key into the top lock. "You just want a cup of latte from my Impressa. Well, forget it. That baby's for clients only."

Lane chuckled, nuzzling her hair as she moved on to the bottom lock. "I'm an espresso man myself. And you're damned right. In fact, if you refuse, I'll be forced to tell Congressman Shore where you spent the night."

Morgan tossed a grin over her shoulder. "I have a feeling he knows."

"I'm sure he does."

"Besides, if I wanted to keep Arthur in the dark about my sex life, I'd have cut the night short by an hour, and asked you to take me over to his and Elyse's place. Everyone would have been asleep. I could have slipped into the guest room unnoticed."

"True. But think what you'd have missed out on—what we'd *both* have missed out on." Lane's voice was husky, his lips warm against her ear. "Remember what we were doing an hour ago? Would respectability really have been worth sacrificing that?"

"No." Morgan swallowed, her memories of what Lane was referring to vividly alive. *Too* alive.

She was about to respond with some lighthearted quip, when a gust of wind kicked up, swirling fine particles of snow around them and sending a torn sheet of paper tucked beneath the corner of her doormat flying directly at her.

Instinctively, Morgan's hand came up, her gloved fingers closing around the tattered page. She pulled it away and glanced down at it, her brows knitting as she saw what it was. "Where did this come from?"

"What is it?" Lane peered over her shoulder.

"A photo of Arthur and Elyse. An old one. Elyse hasn't worn her hair like that in years." She pointed. "See? It's dated November tenth, 1998."

"Yeah, but it was printed yesterday. The date's down here." Lane indicated the lower-right-hand corner, which had survived the diagonal tear that had eliminated half the page. "Who printed this and why is it on your doorstep?"

"I have no idea." Morgan turned the knob and pushed open the door, flipping on the light so Lane could see his way in. "Maybe Jill's compiling a scrapbook of Arthur's postelection . . ." Her words died in her throat as she gazed around. "What the . . . ?" Her eyes widened with shock. "Oh my God."

TWENTY-THREE

The office was trashed.

Papers were strewn everywhere. File cabinets were overturned, the folders in them dumped with their documents tossed around helter-skelter. Morgan's desk was a disaster area, drawers pulled out and turned upside down, everything that had been in them scattered on the carpet. Ditto for the desktop, which had been swept clean.

Newspapers and magazines were tossed randomly about, pages ripped out, some shredded, some just strewn around the ground floor like confetti.

"Shit." Lane got a glimpse of the damage. He grabbed Morgan's arm, stopping her from continuing into the building. "Don't."

"What?" She looked and sounded as dazed as she felt.

"Don't go in there."

"Why? Do you think someone's still inside?"

"I doubt it. But you're not going to be the one to find out. Plus, it's a crime scene. You don't want to contaminate it. Come on." He pulled her outside.

Morgan's teeth started chattering, whether from the cold or shock, she wasn't sure. "Who would . . . ? How could this . . . ?"

Lane had already whipped out his cell and was punching in a number on speed dial. He plunged in without preliminaries. "Monty, someone broke into Morgan's place and wrecked it. The ground floor, at the very least. No, I don't know about the rest of the place. I didn't let Morgan get that far. No, she wasn't inside. She was with me. Yeah, all night. We arrived together, just now. Uh-uh, no one was home. Jill was at her parents'. She still is." A pause. "Not yet. I called you first. Yeah, okay."

He punched the off button on the phone. "As usual, one of my father's gut feelings paid off. He spent the night in his office. So he's in Queens, not upstate. He'll be here in fifteen minutes. Let's give him a ten-minute head start. Then we'll call the cops."

Morgan's brain was starting to function again. "He wants to be here when they go inside to check things out."

"Right." Lane frowned at the hollow look in Morgan's eyes, the fierce chattering of her teeth. "Come here." He wrapped his arms around her, pressing her face against him and rubbing his gloved hands up and down her back, in a gesture meant to comfort as much as to warm.

"I guess down jackets aren't what they used to be," she mumbled into his coat, a feeble attempt at humor.

"They're meant to withstand cold, not the trauma of seeing your home violated."

"My home." Morgan tilted back her head, gazed up at Lane. "God knows what they did to it. All we've seen so far is part of the office." Her jaw set. "I can't just stand here doing nothing. Not even for ten minutes."

Lane studied her determined expression. She wasn't budging in her resolve. Then again, neither was he. "You're not going in there. So if you want to do something productive, start putting together a mental list of your valuables. Jewelry. Antiques. Electronic equipment. That way, the cops can get a quick handle on what's missing."

"You're placating me," Morgan countered. "Don't. We both know this wasn't a robbery. Winshore is doing well, but Jill and I are pouring all our profits back into the business. The Impressa is the most expensive purchase we've got in the place, other than our computers and our server. As for personal property, I collect self-help books and Jill collects yoga CDs. There's not much resale value in those. No. This break-in is tied to the murder investigations. That's why that photo was shoved under my doormat. Whoever did this must have planted it there."

"Okay, fine, I agree." Lane's restless gaze swept the brownstone, and Morgan realized he was as impatient for answers as she was. "So let's move on to the next question. Was this just another scare tactic? Or was the intruder actually after something? If so, what? And did he get it?"

At Lane's final question, Morgan's hand instinctively went to her tote bag. "Probably not. Not unless I have something of my parents that I'm not thinking of. Because the most obvious tie to them would be these." She pulled out a packet of snapshots and newspaper clippings. "These and all the other personal items—journals, mementos—that I've spent every night poring over these past few months."

Lane's brows rose. "You packed everything for one night?"

A nod. "I know it sounds strange. But as I was walking out of my bedroom last night, I got this weird feeling about leaving it behind. So, at the last minute, I crammed everything into my tote bag."

"Good impulse."

"Maybe." Morgan blew out her breath in a frosty puff. "*If* any of this is what they were after. Assuming they were after anything at all." An edgy pause. "Or any*one* at all."

Lane glanced at his watch. "Let's stop speculating. Time to call the cops."

TWO PATROL CARS from the Nineteenth Precinct pulled up to Morgan's brownstone about three minutes before Monty's Corolla roared up to join them. He hopped out of his car, nodding at Al O'Hara—the PI he'd hired to be Morgan's bodyguard—who was dashing over at the first sign of police activity.

"Chill, O'Hara," Monty advised, gesturing for him to wait a discreet distance from the building. "Ms. Winter is fine. No one was hurt, or home. I'll call you if I need you."

"Okay." The PI posted himself near the curb, lighting up a cigarette.

Monty strode up the stairs to where Morgan and Lane were starting to brief the cops. There were four in all, two darting into the brownstone, hands on weapons, the other two interviewing Morgan.

"Impressive," Monty noted as he reached them. "Four officers for a simple B and E. Must be your congressional connections, Morgan." He winked at her.

She managed a thin smile in return, realizing that despite his casual air and wry humor, Monty was scrutinizing her, trying to assess her state of mind.

"You okay?" he asked bluntly.

"More or less."

"Hey, Montgomery." One of the cops—a middle-aged guy with a balding head and a solid build—greeted him, his tone and demeanor a tad aloof. "I'm not surprised to see you. I heard you were hired to work this case. But you sure got here fast."

"*Help* work this case," Monty corrected him. "As in: assist, facilitate, do what I can. Don't worry, Stockton. I have no intention of stepping on your toes. We want the same thing."

Stockton's thick salt-and-pepper brows rose. "Yeah, you gave me that same BS the last time we worked a case together. It was a bit of a stretch."

"That was different. I was a cop back then. I had the same pressure on me you did. Both our precincts wanted to take credit for the arrest of that three-borough rapist. This time, you can take full credit. All I want is for the perp to be caught."

"And you want in when we search this place."

"Damned straight. And now, when you talk to my client. It'll save her the trouble of repeating herself."

"Fine." Stockton gave the okay nod to his partner, then turned back to Morgan. "You said that you and your boyfriend here—" A quizzical look at Lane as he scribbled down notes. "What's your name?"

"Lane Montgomery."

Stockton's pen paused, and his head came up. "I don't suppose you're any relation to Monty here."

"He's my father."

A grimace. "Of course he is. That explains his quick arrival." Stockton waved away Lane's forthcoming explanation. "Forget it. Let's keep going." He angled his head back toward Morgan, his pen poised to resume writing. "You said the front door was double-locked when you got here."

"Yes." Morgan was shivering again. "I used both my keys to open it."

Stockton glanced around the outside of the building. "You have a door around back?"

"Leading to the terrace, yes. But it's dead-bolted from the inside. That's the only way it's accessible, not from the street."

"So it's doubtful the perp got in that way. Same with these lower-level windows. They're all barred. Which suggests he broke in either through an upstairs window, or through the front door by picking the locks. Do you have a security system?"

Morgan shook her head. "It was on our when-we-have-money list. But, frankly, this neighborhood is very safe, so we didn't have a sense of urgency. Plus, Jill and I were trying to hold off for a while, not incur any more huge expenses."

"By Jill—you mean, Jill Shore?"

"Yes."

"The front door locks were picked," Monty announced. He'd squatted down and was examining the keyhole area. "There are scratch marks here—" He pointed. "And here. Whoever did this is a pro. A confident SOB, too. He took the time to reengage the bolts into the jambs before he took off. You'd think he'd run like hell the minute he finished robbing the place. He didn't."

"Yeah," Stockton agreed. "You'd think. So maybe that torn page wasn't planted. Maybe he dropped it."

"What torn page?" Monty demanded.

Wordlessly, Morgan produced the ripped page containing a laser-printed photo of Elyse and Arthur.

"It flew out from underneath Morgan's doormat," Lane explained.

At that moment, the other two cops emerged. "All clear," one pronounced. "Wrecked and with a pretty pointed message left behind, but the perp's gone."

Morgan made a raw sound.

"In that case, would it be possible for us to continue this inside . . ." Lane shot a quick glance at Stockton's badge to ascertain his rank. ". . . Sergeant Stockton? It's freezing out here, and Ms. Winter looks like she's about to collapse."

"Of course." A brusque nod. "Just don't touch anything."

"I know the drill." Lane wrapped an arm around Morgan's shoulders and escorted her inside, closely followed by Monty and the four officers.

"I've got to call Jill." Morgan halted in her tracks as the realization struck. "She's at her parents' apartment. She needs to know about this."

Stockton's green-around-the-gills coloring was a vivid indication that he recognized the ramifications of that statement. Congressman Shore was about to become involved, and there wasn't a damned thing he could do about it.

"Go ahead and call," he said, trying to keep the edge out of his voice. "We'll start a thorough search of the place." He cleared his throat. "Tell Ms. Shore that we'll wait till she gets here to examine her room."

"Thank you. I'm sure she'll appreciate that." Morgan made the phone call, bile in her throat.

Elyse answered, a gasp of shock escaping her when she heard what had happened. Three times, she asked Morgan if she was okay. When she was convinced of that, and of the fact that Lane, Monty, and four policemen were all with her, she regained control and announced that she, Arthur, and Jill would be right over.

Morgan could hear Arthur and Jill firing questions in the background as she ended the call.

IF TELLING THE Shores was bad, viewing the apartment was worse.

The damage could be fixed. It required only the investment of time and hard work. The cost would be negligible since, as Morgan suspected, nothing had been stolen.

But the anguish, the sense of violation, that was something else.

The invasion of her personal space—her night table and dresser drawers having been rifled through, her intimate apparel having been touched by a stranger, an intruder—that alone made her skin crawl.

It didn't come close to the wrenching of her insides when she saw the chilling message the police officer had referred to. It was more graphic and more devastating than Morgan had ever imagined.

A series of visual horrors had been carefully arranged on Morgan's bed.

There were newspaper photos of Arthur and Elyse, some from clippings, others pulled off the Internet and printed. Most of the photos included Jill, some included her. All of them were slashed multiple times, red paint dribbled on their faces and bodies. To add to the gruesome effect, there were holes punched in the center of their foreheads—clearly simulating bullet holes.

The macabre centerpiece to this display was a sheet of paper stuck to her pillow with a chef's knife taken from Morgan and Jill's kitchen. The knife had been plunged through the pillow and buried deeply in the mattress below. The laser-printed note, set in a large font and boldface type, read: *Stop digging into the past or this will be the future. One family down. One to go.*

Morgan stared at the words, her hands flying to her face, a strangled cry lodging in her throat.

"That explains the carefully dissected newspapers all over the place," Monty muttered. "And the torn Internet photo shoved under the doormat. The bastard took the time to construct a collage."

"With his own personal touches," Stockton agreed.

"Talk about being prepared, our perp was a regular Boy Scout." Monty's forehead creased as he scrutinized the scene. "He came equipped with everything, right down to his own arts-and-crafts supplies." A quick glance at Stockton. "Humor me and let me know if something turns up when you dust for prints. I'm sure van Gogh wore gloves—but you never know. Maybe he took them off for the finer strokes."

"What happened? What have you found?" Arthur shoved his way past his wife and daughter and into the room. Behind him, Jill hovered in the doorway, her face sheet white as she peered into the room. She looked lost and in shock. So did Elyse, who gave her daughter's shoulders a protective squeeze before going straight to Morgan.

"Morgan?" Elyse gripped her hands. "Are you sure you're not hurt?"

A mechanical nod. "I wasn't here when it happened. I only got home a little while ago."

"And walked in on this." Elyse sounded ill, her gaze growing more and more grim as it swept the room.

"I asked what you found," Arthur repeated, his hard stare flickering over Stockton and coming to rest on Monty.

It was clear which one of them he was addressing.

Stockton didn't look offended. He looked relieved to be off the hook.

"What we found is pretty much what you're looking at." Monty took the congressman's authoritative air right in stride. "The front door locks were picked. The whole place was rifled. But the heavy-duty ransacking was done to Morgan's things—her desk, her files, and obviously her bedroom." A quick glance at Jill. "Your room's not bad. Messy, but not too wrecked. Once the cops are finished doing their thing, it should take no time to straighten up."

"Thank you," Jill replied. She was clearly fighting back tears.

Monty saw that, and his tone gentled. "Your desk and work space were barely touched. Just a few knickknacks tossed around for effect. Your biggest job will be rearranging your holiday decorations. But they're all salvageable."

Jill swallowed hard. "It's not me I'm worried about."

"Maybe you should be," Stockton interjected. "The threat being issued here doesn't just single out Ms. Winter. It includes your whole family."

"Let's not overreact." Monty sounded like he wanted to choke Stockton. "It's property, not people."

"That's not the tune you were singing a half hour ago," Stockton retorted. "You were all over this."

"I still am. But *I* can afford to step on toes. *You* can't. This case has already pushed hot buttons at the Manhattan D.A.'s, the Brooklyn D.A.'s, and the Seventy-fifth. The D.A.s want the case solved. The Seventy-fifth wants it to go away. I doubt the Nineteenth wants to be dragged into this mess because of an unrelated B and E."

"*If* it's an unrelated B and E."

"Find out. Check out the evidence. If there's a link, by all means jump in with both feet. In the meantime, tread carefully. We've got nothing but a vandalized house and some creative artwork. Nothing was taken. No one was hurt. The perp waited till no one was home to do his thing. Clearly, physical assault wasn't part of his plan."

"Not this time. But—"

"But nothing." Monty was done letting Stockton follow through with this line of speculation. It was only intensifying the fear and tension already pervading the room. "Either this is some wack job's idea of fun, or it's a warped stunt meant to scare the hell out of Morgan."

"That's what we're here to find out." Stockton wasn't pleased about being managed in front of the congressman. "So let's finish our search. We've still got that spare bedroom to go through."

Monty knew what bedroom Stockton was referring to. It was where Morgan kept her parents' memorabilia. And he didn't want that stuff confiscated.

"The spare room can wait," he declared. "This bedroom was the primary target. Besides, we already did a once-over on that room and—"

"Go ahead, Sergeant." Lane's agreement drowned out Monty's preemptive strike. "It's your case. You do the search. Monty and I will talk to the Shores—*and* stay out of your way." A wry grin at Stockton. "Don't fault him. He's the best in the business. But taking a backseat's not his strength. Not to worry—I'll sit on him so you can do your job."

"Thanks." Stockton was pumped up again, looking smug and pleased by the vote of confidence from Monty's son.

Monty shot a quick look at Lane, and a current of silent communication ran between them.

"Fine," Monty said, changing gears. "I'll stay in here and keep looking around."

"Don't touch anything," Stockton cautioned.

"Yeah, Stockton. I went to the Police Academy, too."

With a blistering glare, Stockton walked out, gesturing for his partner to follow him.

They'd barely rounded the corner into the hall, when Monty planted himself in front of his son, arms folded across his chest.

"Morgan has it—*all* of it." Tersely, Lane answered his father's unspoken question. "In there." He jerked his chin in the direction of the tote bag. "No need to remove evidence from the crime scene."

"You're sure?"

"As sure as I am that I just saved your ass."

A corner of Monty's mouth lifted. "Thanks."

"Don't mention it."

From across the room, Morgan took in the exchange. No one else was paying attention.

"What was that inane crap you just spouted about overreacting?" Arthur asked Monty, pausing from his agitated pacing by the windows. "Was that your attempt to manage us?"

"No," Monty countered. "It was my way of downplaying a personal crisis you're trying to keep from becoming front-page news. Besides, there's no cause for panic. I've got men assigned to watch every member of your family."

"That doesn't appease me anymore," Arthur shot back. "These scare tactics are escalating. What if whoever's responsible takes the next step? What if he goes after—"

"Dad . . . stop." Jill waved away his words. Leaning forward, she gave Morgan a fierce hug. "I'm so sorry."

"*You're* sorry?" Morgan was trembling, and her lashes were damp with tears as she hugged her friend. "None of this would be happening if it wasn't for me. I feel like some kind of pariah. The truth is, Arthur's right. We don't know if this is an idle threat or a real one. And I refuse to play Russian roulette with your lives."

"Morgan." Quietly, Lane commanded her attention, waiting until she met his gaze. "Don't do this to yourself. More important, don't give up. See this through. If you don't, you're letting this son of a bitch win."

"Maybe," she admitted, her tone equally soft. "But I don't care." A hard swallow. "As I told you, to me, security trumps all." She averted her head, emotionally compelled to rescrutinize the violent display on the bed. "When it was just my life I was gambling with, it was one thing. But I'm putting the people I love at risk. How can I live with that?"

"You can't," Monty supplied in a hard voice. "And you won't."

He didn't have a chance to elaborate. Approaching footsteps told them the cops were returning.

"The closet in the spare room was ransacked," Stockton announced as he reentered the bedroom. "That's about it." A questioning look at Morgan and Jill. "Anything of significance in that closet?"

"Just guest linens and storage boxes," Morgan supplied. "I'll go through it with you and account for everything."

They were gone and back in five minutes.

"Nothing was taken," Stockton announced.

"I didn't think it would be," Monty returned drily.

"We've covered every room now except Jill's," Morgan said. "And—" She broke off, weaving on her feet.

"That's it." Monty reached over, caught Morgan's arms. "Lane, get her out of here. Buy her breakfast and tuck her in. She's had enough for one day."

"Done." Lane was already there, looping an arm around Morgan's waist and leading her out of the room.

"I have more questions for Ms. Winter," Stockton protested.

"They'll wait." Monty blocked the path between Morgan and Stockton. "Ms. Winter will be reachable by cell. I'll give you the number."

Stockton frowned. He glanced uneasily at Jill. "Are you feeling up to going through your room with us for verification purposes?"

With a shaky nod, Jill agreed. "Sure."

"Ten minutes, Sergeant," Arthur instructed. "Then we're calling it a morning. My family's been traumatized. And Detective Montgomery's right—you've got your work cut out for you. Stay here as long as you like. Bag evidence. Dust for fingerprints. Fill out your report. Then figure out who did this. We're leaving." He pulled out a pad, scribbled something down, and ripped off the sheet of paper. "Here's my home phone and my cell phone. You can reach me any hour of the day or night."

"Okay." Stockton nodded, taking the paper. "That'll work—for now. But, with all due respect, sir, I will need to follow up with your daughter and Ms. Winter. This is their home."

"Yes. And they'll be staying at mine." Arthur's tone left no room for argument. "Thank you for your sensitivity."

TWENTY-FOUR

'm fine," Morgan told Lane as soon as they were outside the brownstone.

"Right." His grip around her waist didn't loosen. "You almost fainted."

"I didn't almost faint," she retorted. "I never faint. But I'm glad I was convincing. If you believed me, hopefully so did Sergeant Stockton."

"Huh?" Lane shot her a puzzled look.

"The sooner I got out of there with this"—she held up her tote bag—"the better. Stockton hadn't gotten around to asking me if I had taken anything with me, and I wasn't waiting around to give him the chance." A smile curved her lips. "You might have saved your father from being charged with interfering with a police investigation, but I was wide open for obstruction of justice."

Lane stared at her for a moment, then began to laugh. "Very clever. You certainly had me going. Here I thought I was rescuing you."

"You were." Morgan zipped her jacket way up to her chin. She was still shivering from the shock of the past hour. And the frigid temperatures weren't helping. "I don't think I could have stayed in there another minute without coming apart. The sense of violation is bad enough. But that horrifying display on my bed . . . I'll never get that image out of my mind."

"Yeah. It was pretty gruesome." Lane tucked her close to his side, picking up their walking pace. "Let's give the subject a rest. You may not be about to faint, but you are on major overload. We'll head back to my place. I cook a mean plate of bacon and eggs."

"I'm not hungry."

"I know. But you've got to eat. Monty's orders, remember? Food and rest. Besides, I have a feeling he'll be showing up as soon as he's finished with Stockton. That'll give him, you, and me a chance to get on the same page."

"True." Morgan considered that concept, and nodded. "Although I'm not sure he's going to like what I have to say."

MORGAN WAS RIGHT. Monty didn't like what she had to say. But he wasn't surprised by it, either.

He arrived at Lane's place about forty minutes after they did, stalking through the door and into the kitchen just as they were finishing breakfast.

"I used my key," he announced. "Hope you don't mind."

"If I minded, I would have thrown the dead bolt. We've been expecting you." Lane rose and went over to the fridge. "There's extra bacon. I'll crack open a few more eggs. I assume you're starved."

"I am." Monty pulled up a chair and straddled it, giving a terse nod of approval as he glanced at Morgan's near-empty plate. "You're eating. Good."

A weary smile touched her lips. "Are you kidding? I wouldn't dare disobey your orders."

"Smart girl." Monty took a gulp of the coffee Lane had poured for him. "Speaking of which, nice touch back at your place, that whole swooning routine. Next time give me a sign. If I didn't have the reflexes of a cat, you'd have been splat on the floor."

Morgan stopped chewing, and her head came up, her brows knit with concern. "Did Stockton guess?"

"That you were conspiring to get out of there? Nah. He was way too busy placating Arthur. It went right over his head. Besides, he's not as sharp as I am."

"Or as modest," Lane commented drily as he scrambled eggs on his cooktop.

"You're just pissed because you didn't pick up on Morgan's act, either." A smug look. "Then again, I didn't expect you to. You can't be the White Knight and Columbo at the same time."

"Cute." Using the spatula, Lane scooped the batch of eggs onto a plate, placing four strips of bacon beside them. "Here." He handed it to Monty. "Give the wisecracks a rest and eat."

"Good move keeping your parents' personal belongings to yourself," Monty told Morgan.

"They'd get lost at the police precinct. Either intentionally or unintentionally."

"No argument. The Seventy-fifth wants the double homicide—and the D.A.—to go away. The Nineteenth wants to close out today's incident as a B and E. The precincts won't play nicely together and neither wants to devote time and resources to a complex case that's a political nightmare waiting to happen. So keeping your stuff to ourselves and out of the cops' hands will keep both precincts like mushrooms—in the dark and bathed in fertilizer—*and* out of my hair."

"Are Jill and Elyse okay?" Morgan asked abruptly.

"They're fine." All banter vanished, and Monty folded his hands on the table in front of him, regarding her intently. "Nothing was taken from Jill's room, not even the diamond studs sitting in clear view on her dresser. The cops waited while she and Elyse packed suitcases—enough to last each of you a couple of days. Arthur took Elyse and Jill home. He canceled his morning appointments. He's expecting me to deliver you to his apartment in a couple of hours—after you've had a chance to rest."

"I'm not tired." Morgan raked both hands through her hair. "Monty, look. You know how I feel. I'm haunted by the fact that whoever killed my parents is still out there. I was willing to risk anything—including my own life—to catch him and put him behind bars. But it's not just my life he's threatening anymore. It's the Shores'. He stalked Elyse on the day of the hit-and-run. And now? In order to pull off that sick break-in, he had to be watching both Jill and me, to know when we'd be out. That means he's following Jill, too. As for Arthur, his schedule's an open book, which makes him a walking target. And with that grotesque warning we found on my bed—"

Morgan broke off, struggled for composure. "The threat is clear. Either I back off, or the Shores will die. I can't let that happen. If I were the sole target . . . but I'm not." A hard swallow. "Please understand. They're the only family I've got left. I can't lose them. I'm dropping the investigation."

"And then what?" Throughout Morgan's speech, Monty had sat calmly, his face devoid of reaction. Now it was his turn. He leaned forward, met and held Morgan's gaze. "Do you think that will make this bastard go away? If so, you're deluding yourself. He'd pop up again—in your life, in someone else's life. He's like a cancer. He needs to be cut out and destroyed. It's the only way everyone's going to be safe—and that includes the Shores."

"But—"

"I need you to trust me." Monty never changed his tone or averted his gaze. "He's scared. He knows we're getting close. That's why he took the risk of breaking into your house and leaving that crap on your bed. And it was quite a risk. Before now, law enforcement was leaning toward the theory that some two-bit punk killed your parents during a robbery, and that he might very well be dead by now. But last night changed all that. Our guy exposed his hand. He told us he's out there. He told us he's a pro. Most of all, he told us he's feeling cornered. He took that risk because he's counting on you to walk away. So don't."

Tears gathered in Morgan's eyes. "I'm afraid," she whispered. "What if he hurts Jill or—"

"He won't. I won't let him," Monty interrupted. "You have my word. Morgan, I was there the first time. I know what he stole from you. I'd never let you go through that again. I'll get him. I promise. Just trust me."

"I do. I . . ." Indecision warred on Morgan's face. Finally, she nodded. "Okay. We'll see this through."

"Yeah. We will." Monty resumed eating his eggs. "Did Lane feed you enough?"

A watery smile. "More than enough."

"Then go lie down. Recoup your strength."

"Good idea." This time Morgan didn't argue. She rose, turning to Lane with a self-conscious expression. "May I use your couch? Or a spare bedroom?"

Monty snorted. "No need to stand on ceremony. Not for my sake. I may be middle-aged, but I'm not dead. Use Lane's room. As you know, it's got that comfortable, king-size bed."

"Actually, I—" Morgan broke off, color staining her cheeks as she met Lane's gaze.

"I'll take Morgan up and get her settled." Once again, Lane came to her rescue—this time in an entirely different way. "Finish eating," he advised Monty. "When I come down, we can get back to the scanned photos."

Monty paused over his bacon. "Speaking of scanned photos, Morgan, while you're resting, would you mind if I took a look at your photos and the rest of your parents' mementos?"

"Of course not." She went over to her tote bag and pulled out all the material Monty had requested. "Here. I'm not really comfortable carrying this around with me anymore, anyway. I feel like any minute it's going to be snatched—either by the cops or the killer."

"How about if I store it here for you?" Lane suggested. "I'll put it where I keep my negatives—in a fire-resistant safe that's secured with a high-tech alarm system. We'll be the only ones with access to it."

"That would do a lot toward giving me peace of mind."

"Then it's settled," Monty announced. "Now sleep tight."

LANE WALKED BACK down to the kitchen a few minutes later. Monty had organized Morgan's memorabilia into piles, and was studying the personal photos.

"Morgan was asleep before her head hit the pillow," Lane notified him.

"I'm not surprised." Monty's head came up. "Given the morning she's just been through, following a hectic all-nighter—" A pointed look. "I take it you two never even made it upstairs."

"Butt out, Monty."

"No wonder she's wiped."

"Monty . . ."

"I'm not prying, Lane. Just reminding you that she's in a fragile state."

"I know." Lane recognized where his father was going with this. He'd already gone there himself. And what he'd come up with was a hefty punch in the gut. It would require a lot more thought, a couple of deep conversations, and some major getting used to.

"Something on your mind?" Monty inquired.

"Nothing I'm ready to discuss with you yet," Lane returned bluntly. "Just know that what's happening between Morgan and me is good. For now, let's leave it at that. Let's put our energies into our work, not my relationship."

"You got it." Monty's eyes twinkled as he returned to the snapshots. "Looks like you'll be bringing someone up to the farm for Christmas after all. Your mother will be thrilled."

"I don't doubt it." Lane was leaning over Monty's shoulder, scrutinizing the photos. "Who took these?"

"Mostly, the Winters and the Shores, with an occasional stand-in behind the lens when it's a group shot. They're family vacations, parties, major events in their lives." Monty grinned, holding up a photo of two bright-faced little girls in Halloween costumes—one Sleeping Beauty, one Cinderella. The snapshot was labelled: *Jill and Morgan, Halloween, 1987.* "Look at those smiles. No wonder their parents took this one. You've got to admit, Morgan made an adorable Cinderella. Hope you're up to the role of Prince Charming."

A corner of Lane's mouth lifted. "Yeah, she had that rare, delicate beauty, even then." He sobered, reaching over to sift through the pictures. "Are these in chronological order?"

"No, but I pulled out the ones taken the night of the Kellermans' Christmas Eve party. They're the last pictures of Lara and Jack Winter taken before they died."

Nodding, Lane picked up the shots, scrutinizing them one at a time.

They were typical party pictures, some with the host and hostess, some with the guest of honor, some with his family and friends. Morgan and Jill were in a few of the pictures, although they were clearly more interested in running around among the guests than they were in being photographed.

Lane came to a photo of Arthur and Elyse, standing with Jack and Lara. Something about it caught his eye, and he paused, studying them with a frown. Their body language. It was tense. The same tension that was mirrored on their faces.

He continued examining the party shots, only this time more slowly and carefully. He found himself organizing the evening into two segments: pre- and post-inebriation, giving him a sense of the order of events. In the post-inebriation shots, everyone was much more relaxed and uninhibited. The ruddy cheeks and glazed eyes said it all.

Lane spotted a photo of Arthur and his father-in-law, clearly taken when the festivities were well under way. There were champagne flutes in their hands and they were making a mutual toast, facing the camera in a staged—if slightly off-balance—pose. Lane concentrated on each and every detail. Then he looked back at a previous shot of Arthur, taken much earlier in the evening. His gaze narrowed as he compared the two.

"What is it?" Monty asked, seeing the intent expression on his son's face.

"Maybe nothing. Maybe a lot. Give me some time to find out." Lane snatched up the two photos and headed toward his lab.

"How much time?" Monty called after him.

"Twenty minutes. A half hour, tops."

"Great. And you're not going to give me a hint about what you're looking for?"

"Be patient. If I'm right, it'll be worth the wait."

NORMALLY, MONTY WOULD be pissed off about being held at bay when so much was at stake. But the truth was, he had plenty to keep him busy for the next thirty minutes.

Something about that damned B&E wasn't sitting right with him. The timing had been just a little too convenient, the technique too professional. Plus, whoever hired the perp had brains. He'd arranged for his guy to have all the necessary newspaper clippings and Internet printouts before going to Morgan and Jill's place. Quite a painstaking task, considering some of those archived news stories dated back months and had to be researched to find.

The whole incident was like a well-rehearsed play, one whose acts had been coordinated by someone who knew the story and the characters intimately.

This wasn't just a pro. This was an inside pro.

Pensively, Monty refilled his coffee mug. His instincts told him it was time to reexamine some vital loose ends.

HE WAS JUST reading through a fax, when Lane emerged from his lab.

"I was right," Lane announced, holding up two eight-and-a-half-by-eleven color prints. "Now we just need to figure out what this means."

Monty shoved aside his fax. "Show me."

Lane laid out the original photos, then placed his color prints beneath them, side by side. The prints were zoomed images of Arthur from chin to chest, with his neck, shirt, and tie center stage.

"What am I looking for?" Monty asked.

"The shirt."

"A white dress shirt—hardly original."

"Right. They all pretty much look alike. Which is probably why Arthur made the mistake." Lane pointed at the photo taken earlier in the evening. "Look at the collar. It's a standard three-point spread." His finger shifted to the other print. "Now check out the collar here."

"It's narrower." Monty picked up the two prints, scrutinized them closely. "These are two different shirts."

"Yup. Which means Arthur changed while the party was going on." Lane's tone took on a skeptical note. "He could have spilled a drink on himself."

"Drink, my ass. If that were the case, he would have mentioned it during one of the dozens of conversations we had about the night of the murders. More likely, he slipped out to boff one of his 'Angels.'" Monty ran a palm over his face. "Another red flag with Arthur Shore's name on it."

"Meaning?"

"Meaning I just got a fax from my contact who ran a couple of background checks for me. One was on Charlie Denton. Seems that as a kid in law school, he worked on Congressman Shore's—then State Assemblyman Shore's—campaign. Their parting was abrupt and, evidently, not amicable. I'm coming up dry on the specifics. But Denton never mentioned it."

Monty picked up the fax, skimmed through the pages. "Then there's the other link to the Shores. George Hayek. I can't shake the feeling that he's involved in this. He goes way back with the Shores. If I'm right, he was a CI for Jack Winter. His file is sealed, so I have no idea where things stood between him and Jack, or him and Arthur, when he moved to Belgium. But my sources tell me that he's been a busy little beaver these days, raking in money from everywhere. Could be legitimate weapons trading. Could be illegal and unsanctioned. Plus, my contact says that Hayek's got a slew of markers he could call in from 'associates' with diplomatic immunity in the U.S.—'associates' sophisticated enough to have pulled off the trashing of Morgan's place. No surprise—a few of those bastards are always hanging around the U.N., their consulate, or running up parking tickets all over the city and never paying."

Lane didn't reply.

"Make the phone call and check it out, Lane," Monty stated flatly, his head coming up so he could meet his son's gaze. "I know it's classified. I'm not asking for details. Just find out if Hayek's status has changed, or if the CIA is pulling his strings in any new and interesting ways." A hard pause. "If you won't do it for me, do it for Morgan."

"I've got to run back to the lab for a minute." Lane's expression never changed.

"You do that."

INSIDE THE LAB, Lane shut the door.

He made the call on his secure line. It was answered on the second ring. He quickly got a vehement denial—along with a not-too-friendly warning to leave this one alone.

Backtracking to the kitchen, he reported tersely, "No status change. It's a dead end—at least for me."

"In other words, they're not telling you squat," Monty muttered. "Well, like I always say, if you want something done right, you've got to do it yourself."

"Tread carefully, Monty."

"Don't worry about me. You just find something in those high-tech scans. Bust your ass. Tomorrow's a lost day; you have your next boys-with-toys adventure with Arthur. Oh, and stick those color prints you just made in your safe. Now, before Morgan wakes up. There's no reason for her to see them—yet. I need time to cogitate, to talk to a couple of people, and to make sense out of all these loose ends. When there's something to say, we'll tell her."

"Agreed." Lane glanced toward the staircase. "But that 'when' better be soon."

Monty's forehead was creased in thought. "It will be."

AT CIA HEADQUARTERS in Virginia, Lane's operative punched in the number to a secure telephone in Belgium.

A man's voice answered in French. "*Vas-y! Parles!*"

"Hayek?" The response came in clear, irrefutable English. "What the fuck are you doing?"

TWENTY-FIVE

Morgan had definitely regained her strength, and her resolve, by the time Monty delivered her to the Shores' apartment.

She grilled him the entire way. First, because she was sure he and Lane had discussed something of importance while she was asleep—something they were keeping her in the dark about. Second, because she was determined to conduct a regular business afternoon, depleted or not. And third, because she wanted to conduct that business at Winshore.

The last argument was the easiest one for Monty to win.

"Your brownstone is a crime scene," he said, nodding at the Shores' doorman, who buzzed upstairs to announce their arrival. "It'll be taped off and off-limits all day so the cops can do their jobs. If you insist on working, it'll have to be out of the Shores' apartment. Which shouldn't be a problem; Jill's here, too."

"It's seeing clients that'll be the problem," Morgan explained. "We sometimes meet with them at Winshore, but normally at a mutually convenient location—which won't be happening, since Arthur will never let Jill and me out of the apartment today. Not that I blame him; he's worried about our safety. Plus, there'll be a media fest waiting to pounce on us."

"I can't control the media part, although I did convince Arthur not to give them any added ammunition. We spoke while you were sleeping. He agreed to head up to the Poconos tomorrow as planned. As for his family's safety, it'll be taken care of. He was on his way over to the Nineteenth Precinct to fill in whatever information they need to file their report."

"I'm surprised he left Elyse and Jill alone."

"He didn't. Two of my men are with them. After I drop you off, I'll swing by Arthur's office. I'm arranging extra security to ease his mind."

"Great. So it'll be just Jill, Elyse, and me—and the 'Secret Service.' I guess asking clients to drop by here is out."

"Good. Then maybe you'll take it easy for a day."

Morgan slanted him a look. "Would you?"

A chuckle. "You got me there." Monty pressed the up button on the elevator.

"The truth is, if I don't keep busy, I'll lose my mind."

"Understood. So do business via telephone and e-mail. It's only for a few days. Your clients will cope just fine. And so will you."

"Why do I feel placated?" Morgan asked as the elevator doors let them out on the twenty-fifth floor. "If you and Lane saw something, or found out something, I have the right to know."

"Yeah, you do. But we didn't. All we did was explore what-ifs. None of them went anywhere—yet. I won't hide facts from you, Morgan. But I also won't take you on wild-goose chases. It's counterproductive and upsetting. You're just going to have to continue to trust me."

"I do and I will."

Monty knew how much this was costing her. He also knew there was just one way to fix it.

The Shores' apartment was just ahead.

"Before I go meet Arthur, I'd like to talk to Elyse again, review some of the details she gave me the other day. I need her calm and focused. Can you and Jill make yourselves scarce?"

"Of course." Morgan nodded. "Just please go easy on her. She's taking this hard."

"By 'this,' do you mean the threat to your family?"

Morgan's features tightened. "You mean as opposed to the threat to her privacy and her marriage? Yes, that's what I mean. Believe me, she's used to the 'Arthur's Angels' stories splashed across the front page of the *Enquirer*. It's been years. She's pretty immune."

"To the stories or the infidelity?"

"The stories. Infidelity's not something you ever get used to." Morgan's brows knit quizzically. "Why this line of questioning? It's not like you to go for someone's Achilles' heel, at least not a personal one."

"I'll go for anything that helps find our killer. Otherwise, you're right; I don't believe in invasion of privacy and I couldn't give a damn who sleeps with who. I'm just getting a handle on Elyse's state of mind. The fact that she's in bad shape over the threat to her family doesn't surprise me. She's obviously the maternal type."

"Yes. She is."

They reached the Shores' apartment and stopped. Monty waited while Morgan fished out her keys.

"It's me," she called out as she pushed open the door.

"Hi." Jill was waiting in the foyer, dressed in comfortable sweats, her hair pulled back in a scrunchie. She looked pale and drawn as she walked over and gave Morgan a hug. "I'm glad you're home. Did you get some sleep?"

"A little. What about you?"

"Same." Jill turned to Monty. "Detective, can I get you something?"

"Not a thing," he assured her. "I'll be taking off soon."

"Where's Elyse?" Morgan asked, scanning the area.

The two security guys nodded at her. They were posted at separate corners of the living room. Between the two of them, they had a full view of the hallway leading from the front door to the rest of the apartment. Comprehensive, but nonintrusive. They were drinking coffee and munching on slices of Jill's all-natural banana bread.

"Mom's getting dressed. I got her to take a nap and a shower. She should be out any minute."

On cue, the master-bedroom door opened and Elyse walked out. Monty couldn't help but feel sorry for the woman; she looked like she had the weight of the world on her shoulders. Drawn, white-faced, and with a bleak, defeated look in her eyes.

"Hello, Detective," she greeted him. "Thank you for bringing Morgan here safely." She went over, gave Morgan a short, hard hug. "I made you some chicken soup. It's on the stove, whenever you want it. Also, I picked up a bag of Snickers. I thought you deserved a little comfort food."

Morgan smiled. "Thanks. I might polish off the whole bag this afternoon."

"Any breakthroughs?" Elyse was looking at Monty again.

"Not yet. But there will be." Monty glanced at his watch. "I'm meeting your husband in a little while to discuss added security. Before I go, do you have a few minutes? I'd like to review the details of our conversation the other day."

"I'm not sure what else I can tell you. But if you think it will help, of course we can talk."

"Use the kitchen," Morgan inserted quickly, before Jill could offer to stay with Elyse for support. "Jill and I will head off to my old room. I need a shower. And since I'm not crazy about being alone right now, she can hang out in my room and talk to me through the bathroom door."

"That's fine." Elyse nodded, gesturing for Monty to follow her. "Have a seat at the table, Detective. I just made a fresh pot of coffee for our security team. You can warm up with a mug of that, and we can talk."

"And you're welcome to my banana bread, too," Jill added. "I baked three loaves since we got home. Nervous energy."

"Thanks." Monty waited until Jill and Morgan had disappeared from view, then he followed Elyse into the kitchen.

Over coffee and banana bread, he calmly reiterated his questions about the crank calls Elyse had received, her feeling of being followed, and the driver of the white van she'd spotted outside the gym.

Her answers were the same. But her nerves had definitely frayed.

"Have you received any calls since Tuesday when we spoke?" he asked.

"No." Elyse poured herself a cup of coffee, clutching the mug with unsteady hands. "I guess the caller moved on to bigger and better things—running down women and trashing apartments."

"Speaking of the hit-and-run, I had a chance to interview both Karly Fontaine and Rachel Ogden."

Elyse definitely tensed. "Did either of them provide information on who was driving the vehicle?"

"Nope. The incident happened too fast. They both offered to help in any way they could. Even Rachel, who'd just come through surgery. She's one strong young woman. They both are." Monty's brows drew together quizzically. "Do you know either of them?"

"No. Why would you ask?"

A shrug. "Morgan mentioned that sometimes you and Winshore refer clients to each other. I thought maybe this was one of those times."

"It wasn't." Elyse took a swallow of coffee.

"In that case, you should meet these two. They'd fit right in with your clientele. Karly's a former model who's now an executive in her modeling agency, so I don't have to tell you the amount of time she spends working out and the kind of physical shape she's in. And Rachel's a knockout—a lot younger than Karly, and super-high-powered. She's some kind of management consultant. It's hard to believe that someone in her midtwenties could be so accomplished."

"I'm sure you're right." Elyse was staring into her mug. "Youth is a big plus in this superficial world of ours."

Monty broke off a piece of banana bread, watching Elyse as he chewed. "You're right. This is a youth-oriented society. Especially for women, when it comes to looks. It's a shame men can't see past their . . . well, you get the drift."

"Yes, I do." Elyse's head came up. "What I don't get is why we're discussing this. Is there something about this Rachel Ogden I should know?"

"Such as?"

"You tell me. You're certainly dwelling on her enough."

Monty pursed his lips, pushing the envelope a tad farther. "Maybe that's because there's a possible tie-in here that worries me."

A flash of emotion—anxiety mixed with hurt and insult—crossed Elyse's face. It didn't take a rocket scientist to figure out what she assumed the tie-in was.

"If this relates to some gossip about Arthur . . ."

"Arthur?" Monty's brows rose. "No. It relates to the fact that, on paper, Rachel's physical description matches Morgan's. Add last night's break-in to the mix, and I'm starting to worry that whoever trashed Morgan and Jill's house and left that ugly warning on Morgan's bed is going after her more aggressively than I originally thought."

"Oh." Elyse blinked in surprise. She quickly recovered, surprise transforming to fright. "By more aggressively . . . are you saying you think he means to kill her?"

"If he's the one who killed her parents, he's certainly capable of it."

"Oh God." Elyse sank down in a chair, her coffee mug striking the table with a thud. "What do we do?"

"For one thing, we don't tell her. She's at the breaking point as it is. But the extra security your husband wants employed is a good idea. It'll be taken care of today."

"What about dropping the investigation? Wouldn't that make the most sense?" Elyse blurted out. Seeing the startled disbelief on Monty's face, she rushed on. "I realize how callous that sounds. Maybe I'm being horribly selfish. But I love my family. I need them safe. I loved Lara and Jack, too; they were my dearest friends. And, yes, it sickens me that their murders have to go unpunished. But they're dead, Detective. Morgan's alive. Isn't it our responsibility to make sure she stays that way? Risking her life won't bring Jack and Lara back. But it could endanger her—and the rest of us, for that matter."

"Not nearly as much as leaving whoever murdered Lara and Jack out there, free to kill Morgan or someone else." Monty shook his head. "No. Dropping this investigation's not an option. I'm finding this killer." He eyed Elyse speculatively. "To find him, I need to find his motive. Which means digging around where I'm not wanted."

Elyse went very still as Monty reached into his jacket pocket and pulled out the extra set of color prints Lane had made him.

"Take a look at these. They're from the party your parents threw for Arthur on Christmas Eve, seventeen years ago."

She glanced down, first uneasily, then with great puzzlement. "I don't understand. That's Arthur, or rather, a portion of Arthur."

"His neck," Monty supplied. "So tell me, why did your husband change shirts during the party?"

Elyse's jaw tightened, but she kept it together. "I don't know what you're talking about."

"Look again. Regular collar. Narrow collar. Same party. Different shirts. Why?"

"I have no idea. Maybe he spilled something on himself."

"Ah, so he was in the habit of bringing along a spare shirt for just those types of emergencies?"

"No, of course not." Elyse's voice had gone up, and her pulse had accelerated. Monty could see it fluttering at her throat.

"In my experience, this is a classic indicator of a man having an affair," he stated flatly. "Wouldn't you agree?"

Silence.

"Let's try this again. Do you remember your husband leaving the party at some point during the evening? If so, what time and for how long?"

Tears gathered in Elyse's eyes. "Why are you doing this?" she managed. "Is it giving you some perverse enjoyment, like it does the media?"

"Not in the least. What I'm trying to figure out is why, during the numerous conversations we had after the Winters' homicides, the congressman never mentioned to me that he left your parents' party. Why is that?"

"Probably because it had nothing to do with your investigation."

"Or maybe it slipped his mind. A flash in the pan. Still, I'd appreciate her name. I need to interview every person who interacted—even peripherally—with any of the Winters' friends, colleagues, or loved ones on the night of the murders."

"Friends? Loved ones?" Elyse was slowly unraveling. "Shouldn't you be concentrating on enemies?"

"I'd say a murderer qualifies as an enemy." A probing, inquisitive look. "Her name—do you recall it?"

Abruptly, Elyse came to her feet. "I'm not going to dignify that with an answer. Now if you'll excuse me, Detective, I need to make some phone calls. And you need to meet with my husband about hiring additional security. Please show yourself out."

———————

KARLY FONTAINE GLANCED at her watch, and grimaced.

Time to call Morgan, to keep her appointment for their follow-up. The problem was, she had no time, no energy, and no ability to pretend the past few days had never happened.

Summoning her inner reserve, she dialed Winshore.

A strange man's voice answered. "Hello?"

Karly paused. "I'm sorry. I must have the wrong number. I was calling Winshore LLC."

"You've got the right number. Who's calling?"

The man's tone was blunt and unnerving. Plus, Karly wasn't in the habit of giving out her name to strangers. "Who am I speaking with?" she asked.

"This is Officer Parino, Nineteenth Precinct."

"Officer . . ." Every muscle in Karly's body tensed. "Why are the police at Winshore? Has something happened?"

"I'm not at liberty to discuss this, Ms. . . . ?"

"Fontaine. Karly Fontaine. I have a twelve-thirty conference call with Morgan Winter."

"I'd suggest you reach her on her cell. You have the number?"

"Yes. I have it. I'll call her now."

She couldn't disconnect the call fast enough. Her fingers shook as she punched in Morgan's cell-phone number.

Morgan answered right away, sounding tired but calm. "Hi, Karly," she greeted, recognizing the caller-ID display.

"Is everything all right?" Karly asked anxiously. "I just called your office and a policeman answered the phone. He wouldn't give me any information, just that I should reach you on your cell."

"Yes, well, we had a little excitement at our brownstone last night." Briefly, Morgan told Karly about the break-in and the way the intruder had ransacked the place. As Monty and the authorities had instructed, she carefully omitted any mention of the defaced newspaper clippings or the threatening note.

"Morgan, how horrible," Karly responded with genuine distress. "Were you home when he broke in?"

"Fortunately not. Neither Jill nor I was there. We're very lucky."

"*Very* lucky. What did he take?"

A brief hesitation. "Actually, nothing was stolen."

"I don't understand."

Morgan blew out a breath. "Karly, you've only been in town a few months. So there's a lot you might not know, unless you're an avid newspaper reader. My parents were murdered seventeen years ago. It's just come to light that the police convicted the wrong guy—another violent criminal, just not the one who killed my parents. My partner, Jill—the one I mentioned to you—her parents are Congressman Arthur Shore and his wife, Elyse. They were my parents' best friends. I've been sort of their adopted daughter since I was orphaned. So we're all pretty much in the public eye. This could have been some sick prank, or a way to get in the newspapers. I don't know. That's what the police are investigating now."

"I don't know what to say." Karly was staring at her computer screen as she spoke, rereading the articles she'd pulled this morning, after two sleepless nights. "I'm sorry this happened. If there's anything I can do . . ."

"Not a thing. Jill and I are staying at Arthur and Elyse's place, so we're in good hands. Just understand that Winshore is operating at less than maximum efficiency. It'll only be a day or two. By Monday, we'll be back to business as usual. Would you mind if we postponed your follow-up session until then?"

"Of course not. I'll call you next week and set something up. I'm just grateful you're okay—you *and* Jill."

"Me, too."

KARLY SAT AT her desk for a long time after hanging up, a sick knot forming at the pit of her stomach. Then she reached for her purse, pulling out the envelope she'd unearthed from her box of personal odds and ends, recently unpacked from her cross-country move. She glanced inside the envelope. The note and business card were intact.

She knew what she had to do.

Penning a quick message on a Post-it, she peeled it off and stuck it to the outside of the envelope. Then she slipped the whole thing into a Tyvek envelope and sealed it.

She reached for the phone book, flipping through the yellow pages. It didn't take long to find what she was looking for. A messenger service that was off the beaten path.

She pulled on her black wool coat, flipping up the hood so it covered her head and hair. Next, she slipped on a pair of sunglasses.

No credit cards, she reminded herself.

Rifling through her wallet, she found a hundred-dollar bill, and stuffed it into her coat pocket. Then she returned the wallet to her purse, which she locked in her bottom desk drawer. She couldn't present ID she didn't have. She'd simply say she left her purse at home. Cash was a wonderful motivator.

Five minutes later, she left her office and the building.

She was taking an enormous risk.

But she owed an enormous debt.

TWENTY-SIX

The Friday-morning sky was clear. The Poconos made a great backdrop. Lane's jump had been spectacular.

Too bad Jonah felt like shit.

He'd been tired and light-headed since they got there, and the equipment setup and constant movement had made the dizziness and fatigue worse. He'd tried downing a muffin and some Gatorade, but neither helped.

Fighting his body's discomfort, he struggled with the unwieldy camera, made heavy by the telephoto lens and motor drive. He had only one chance to capture the congressman on film. As it was, the pressure was on. They'd practically had to tear the congressman away from home, convince him that the publicity was necessary enough for him to leave his family—even for an abbreviated day. This shoot would be short and sweet, then home.

With Lane taking aerial shots from the plane, the ground shots were Jonah's responsibility.

Normally, he'd be totally psyched and in his element.

But his hands were sweaty and his muscles were weak. He felt feverish, like he was coming down with something. Just his luck. He'd made an asshole of himself with that stupid skiing accident the other day and now he was getting the flu.

No way. The flu was just going to have to wait until after he got home tonight.

Turning his attention back to the task at hand, he pointed the camera skyward and followed Arthur's smooth descent, the motor drive snapping each frame in rapid succession.

He was pretty sure he'd pulled it off—and pulled it off well.

But he still felt like shit.

AS AGREED, MONTY arrived at Charlie Denton's office at twelve-fifteen. He walked in right on time, and with the agreed-upon pastrami sandwiches, chicken soup, and Dr. Brown's cherry soda from Lenny's for a "lunch-and-learn meeting."

Monty wasn't walking out without answers to two open questions: Were his suspicions right about who the CI in Angelo's file was, and what was the basis for Charlie's beef with Arthur Shore? His bargaining chip was giving Charlie George Hayek's name, which he was more than willing to do—*if* he got what he wanted.

His gut told him that Denton would be a strong ally at this point, especially after Wednesday night's break-in at Morgan's place. The threats against her were escalating, which would prod Denton into action, given his loyalty to Morgan and to Jack. Plus, he was familiar with the criminal mind, saw the patterns in their actions. Like Monty, he'd realize that the perp's escalating threats meant he was feeling vulnerable. And *that* meant they were closing in on him.

"The entire office is probably buzzing with the news that the lead detective on Jack's murder case is visiting me," Charlie complained in greeting, shutting the door behind Monty with a firm click. "I'll be fielding questions all afternoon."

"And you'll handle them just fine. Say I was here to clarify details of the criminal cases Jack was prosecuting before he died. Your colleagues will like the fact that the angle I'm pursuing will further the image of Jack Winter as a hero."

"He *was* a hero," Charlie corrected him, sitting down behind his cluttered desk and pulling out a thick manila folder that he put in front of him. "Too much so. It probably got him killed."

"We don't know what got him killed. But we're going to find out." Eyeing the folder like a kid in a candy store, Monty forced himself to be patient. There was no point in jumping all over Denton. Better to put him in the mood to exchange confidences. And, if all else failed—well, that's what Rhoda's matzo-ball soup was for.

Calmly, he passed a sandwich, a tall container of soup, and a can of soda across the desk to Charlie, then plopped down in the opposite chair. "Lenny's finest," he announced.

"Bribery?" A corner of Charlie's mouth lifted.

"Camaraderie." There was no point in trying to snow the guy. He was a seasoned prosecutor. He'd see through BS in a minute. "The way I see it, we're on the same team, especially now. I think Morgan's life depends on it."

Charlie's smile faded. "How is she?"

"Holding up. Frightened. Ambivalent. After what she walked in on Thursday morning, she was ready to drop the case."

"The D.A. won't let that happen."

Monty shrugged. "He can pressure whoever he wants, but without the right person digging in the right places, he'll come up empty."

Unwrapping his sandwich, Charlie shook his head in disbelief. "And you, of course, are that right person." A humorless laugh. "Your arrogance is staggering. Somehow, the NYPD survived before you joined and they seem to be surviving just fine since you left."

"This has nothing to do with my leaving the force. Frankly, they're better off without me. I suck at following the rules, and red tape and paperwork were beginning to make my blood pressure go up. This has to do with my familiarity with the case, my gut feeling that we're on the verge of solving it, and the fact that I'm not going away until that happens—rules or no rules." Monty took a bite of his sandwich and a healthy tablespoon of soup. "Damn if Rhoda's matzo-ball soup isn't the best there is. You're lucky she likes me. You and I each got a large container instead of a small."

"Yeah, well, thanks for that. It's freezing outside. Chicken soup is just what I need." Charlie ate some of the soup, then leaned forward, folding his hands on the desk. "I agree with you about Morgan being at risk. These threats are too aggressive. And they're coming too close together. Someone's scared."

"The question is, who?"

One of Charlie's brows rose. "I guess it's show-and-tell time."

Monty put down his lunch. "What have you got for me?"

"The CI you were asking about—you were right that he and Jack went back a long time." Charlie opened the file, flipped through some photocopied pages. "I've got a log and some written reports I dug out of Jack's old files, spanning at least a decade. The entries all have the same CI number on it."

"The one I gave you—the one belonging to the inside witness who testified at Angelo's trial."

"Right."

"Is there any personal data on this guy?"

"Nope. Only summaries of his meetings with Jack. These documents will give you the dates and times you asked for, plus details of each encounter. But all biographical info, photos, registration form, anything with the CI's name on it, are in his restricted master file."

"Did you go to the control officer who has it, try to persuade him to share?"

Charlie's jaw tightened. "There's just so far I'll go for you, Montgomery. I've already gone out on a major limb. But what you're suggesting smacks of blackmail and borders on career suicide. Now, do you want the copies of the reports I made for you, or not?"

"Damn straight I want them."

"Good." Charlie opened his manila folder and passed a chunk of pages across the desk. "Don't read them here. Just stick them in Lenny's take-out bag and take them with you when you leave. I don't want anyone spotting you walking out of my office with pages that have our letterhead on them."

"Got it." Monty took the documents. He couldn't wait to pore over them. In the meantime, he couldn't help but notice that they were just a percentage of what Denton had in that folder. Clearly, the rest weren't for sharing.

That had to be remedied.

"Who's the CI you have in mind?" Charlie demanded.

"Let me read through this stuff first," Monty replied. "If it matches up with the background check of the guy I suspect, you'll hear from me."

"That sounds like a stall tactic."

"It's not. I'll call you by the end of the business day. You have my word."

"I'll hold you to it."

"Do that. If this is who I think it is, the lead is all yours. Run with it. Earn yourself a commendation and a fat promotion."

With a grimace, Charlie resumed eating his soup. "I'm not holding my breath on either of those. Solving this case will serve justice. That doesn't mean it'll serve everybody else."

Monty shrugged, munching on his sandwich. "Toes get stepped on. People get over it."

"Maybe in your world. Not mine. The D.A.'s office is a political one, in case you haven't noticed."

"I noticed."

"Yeah, well, between you and me, politics sucks."

"I noticed that, too." Monty studied Charlie's expression. His lids were hooded and he was focusing on his lunch. But his wheels were definitely turning. He was wrestling with something.

"Anything you want to tell me?" Monty inquired.

Charlie's chin came up. "Just a question. An off-the-record question."

"Shoot."

"I know who pulls my strings. On this investigation, who's pulling yours—Morgan, or Arthur Shore?"

"First of all, no one pulls my strings—ever. That's why I left the system. But if you're asking who I'm working for, it's Morgan. The congressman's added leverage in getting things done. Why?"

"Is he privy to everything you and I discuss?"

"Not if I don't want him to be. At least not from my end. I can't vouch for what your boss tells him."

"Yeah. He and the D.A. are tight. That's part of why I'm walking on eggshells."

Evidently, Monty's other agenda had found him. "You don't trust Arthur?"

Charlie rubbed his forehead. "Politically? I think he's a hell of a congressman. He's done great things for New York."

"You helped get him elected. My rundown indicated that you worked on his political campaign."

"For state assembly, yes." Charlie polished off his soup. "We didn't part on the best of terms. Then again, I'm sure your rundown mentioned that, too."

"Yup." Monty waited, biding his time.

"Our differences weren't professional. They were personal. I have a kid sister. It was the summer before her freshman year in college when I worked for the Shore campaign. I was heading into my final year at law school. I convinced Trish to pitch in. It didn't take long for her to start idolizing Arthur Shore. She and every other campaign groupie in the place. Trish began working late, stuffing envelopes for mailings. One night I showed up early to pick her up. She was in Shore's office with him, alone and half-naked."

Charlie blew out an angry breath. "The guy was in his thirties, married, with a kid. Trish was eighteen, barely out of high school, and impressionable."

Monty was disgusted, but far from surprised. This was classic Arthur Shore. "You must have been ripping mad. What did you do?"

"To Shore? Nothing. If I started throwing around phrases like 'sexual harassment,' I'd be pumping gas instead of prosecuting criminals. I was a law school student. He was an assemblyman. He was also corporate counsel to a powerful real estate development company—one run by his father-in-law—with enough resources to squash me. So I did what I could. I wrapped Trish's coat around her and dragged her out of there. We never went back."

"And now?"

"Now nothing. Shore's a congressman; I'm an A.D.A. Our paths don't cross. He called me when the Winter cases were reopened and asked me to use my influence to get you what you needed. I agreed. I certainly didn't bring up Trish, and he didn't ask about her."

"Did you ever fill Jack in on this incident? It still had to be pretty fresh in your mind when you came to work here. And Jack and Arthur were good friends."

"Lara and Elyse were good friends," Charlie corrected. "Jack and Arthur socialized by default. I won't say Jack didn't respect Arthur's abilities; he did. But their morals were day and night. I didn't need to fill Jack in on my story. There were many others like it." A long pause. "Sometimes I think that's what Jack and Lara were arguing about. I could be all wet, but I think Jack felt Elyse should be told what her husband was doing. Lara disagreed."

"You heard her say that?"

"I heard her say Elyse knew everything she needed to. That could have applied to Arthur's infidelity, or to something completely unrelated."

"You didn't mention any of this to me the other day."

"I chose not to. It's pure speculation on my part, and it could bite me in the ass big-time."

"*If* I opened my mouth," Monty surmised aloud. "Well, I won't. This conversation remains between us. I am glad you told me, though. It explains a few things." A thoughtful silence. "Denton, you can punch me out if you want to, but is there any chance your sister changed her mind and had that fling with Arthur? Maybe not then, but a few years later?"

"No." A one-word, clipped reply.

"How do you know?"

"Because for the weeks following that incident, I didn't let her out of my sight. After that, she left for Michigan. She lined up a part-time waitressing job there, got settled, and started class at U Mich in August. She came home for holidays, but by Thanksgiving she had a boyfriend—a *normal* boyfriend, one her own age. There were lots of other boyfriends over the years. But she never mentioned Shore again. Why?"

"Here's the part where you're going to pound me. Where was Trish on Christmas Eve, 1989?"

You could have heard a pin drop in the room.

"The night of the murders?" Charlie finally responded. "You're kidding."

"I'm dead serious. Do you know where she was?"

"In Spain. Junior year abroad. And I'm restraining myself from punching your lights out—but only because you're doing your job and because

I'm itching to know your reasoning. Arthur Shore wasn't out scoring with an intern that night. He was at a Christmas Eve party with his wife. At her parents' place."

"True. But I have cause to believe he found time for a quickie. It would help to know what time and with whom."

"You think the 'with whom' in question had something to do with the murders?"

"I think she's a new player we didn't know about seventeen years ago. I also think we have to determine if Congressman Shore needs to supply an alibi—which he would, if he were missing from his in-laws' party between the hours of, say, seven o'clock and eight-thirty."

Charlie let out a low whistle. "You're stirring up a hornet's nest."

A shrug. "Worse comes to worst, I'll lose my VIP status at Lenny's."

"No, worse comes to worst, you'll lose your license. Who knows how pissed off Shore will get, or what favors he'll call in if word leaks out that you asked him to provide an alibi for the night of the homicides. Any way you slice it, you're asking him to prove he isn't a killer."

"I'm asking him to do the same thing everyone else who knew the Winters did. No more, no less. This is a murder investigation. If Shore's innocent, he'll be offended, maybe even royally pissed, but he'll cooperate. He's the one who rode my ass when the double homicide first occurred, until Schiller confessed. And he's been just as aggressive this time around. I'll handle him calmly, privately, and unemotionally. But no matter how he reacts, I'm getting what I need."

"Plus a whole lot of what you *don't* need," Charlie muttered.

"That's my problem. And Denton?" Monty pinned Charlie with a meaningful stare. "Shore won't be getting any heads-up on why I want to see him. Just like what you told me about your sister, this is confidential and off-the-record."

"Don't worry." Charlie waved away Monty's pointed message. "I'm steering way clear of this one. Any involvement on my part would be career suicide. But I've got to give you credit, Montgomery. You've got balls."

"And proud of it," Monty returned drily.

"Speaking of balls . . ." Charlie shifted uncomfortably in his seat. "That quart of soup and can of soda just hit my bladder. I'll be back in a minute."

"No problem."

A grin tugged at Monty's lips as Charlie dashed around his desk and took off for the men's room. Bless Rhoda's soup. It had done the trick.

He waited ten seconds. Then he leaned forward, plucked the manila folder off Charlie's desk, and quickly flipped through it.

Lots of extraneous crap. Paperwork. More paperwork. Interoffice memos. Legal documents building Jack's case against Angelo. Intermittent mention of his meetings with the CI in question. One bunch of xeroxed pages clipped together.

Those, Monty rapidly scanned. They referenced the original paperwork on the CI's arrest, with all names and specifics blacked out, and only the CI number substituted.

The last few pages of the packet had the NYPD logo on them.

Those had potential.

With lightning speed, Monty ran through them. He knew these forms like the back of his hand. The final page was a poor-quality photocopy of the online booking sheet the arresting officer had supplied.

Monty held the sheet up to the light, frowning when he couldn't see through the black marker. Damn.

His time was running out. Denton would be back any minute. There had to be something.

Bingo.

Way at the bottom of the sheet, was the perp's contact info, blacked out just like the rest of the data. Only here the marker had grown faint near the end of the line. Monty could make out the last four digits of the phone number: 0400.

Finally. Something to go on.

Monty replaced all the documents and laid the file neatly on Charlie's desk.

THERE WAS NO time to waste in driving back to Queens, so Monty went directly to Lane's apartment, flipped on the computer, and started his search. He punched in the 212 area code—the only one that existed in NYC thirty years ago—and tried every conceivable exchange. He knew damned well he could be royally screwed; if the phone number had been disconnected or transferred to another party decades ago, finding out who it belonged to back then would be a bitch.

Luck was on his side, because thirty minutes later, he hit pay dirt.

The number 212-555-0400 was still very much in existence. It belonged to a mega-successful real estate development company that had been thriving for many years—the same company Charlie Denton had mentioned before.

Kellerman Development, Inc. The company where, thirty years ago, Daniel Kellerman's brand-new son-in-law, Arthur, had been corporate counsel.

Another solid indicator that the CI in question was George Hayek.

The timing of all this fit with Monty's theory. Hayek had made the call after his gunrunning arrest. That explained how he'd become an informer for the D.A. Arthur must have contacted Jack, and they'd struck a deal. Jack got a great inside informer, and Arthur got Hayek off the hook—probably for Lenny's sake.

Interesting. Arthur had lied to Monty about never having spoken to Hayek since he left Lenny's.

That made two distortions on the congressman's part: his unexplained shirt change at the Kellermans' Christmas Eve party, and the phone call from Hayek and subsequent deal cut with Jack.

What else had he lied about?

Monty had all Denton's paperwork to pore over; details, dates and times to match up. And after that, he and Congressman Shore were going to have a nice, long chat.

Hours passed.

Monty was deep into reading and note taking, when his cell phone rang.

Annoyed, he glanced down at the caller ID. He had no intention of answering, until he saw that it was Morgan.

He punched on his phone. "Hey. Everything okay?"

"I'm not sure." Morgan sounded more emotional than scared. "I just got a very unnerving package."

"A package?" Monty was on instant alert. "What kind of package? And what do you mean by unnerving?"

"It's a Tyvek envelope. And I don't mean dangerous, so don't panic. There are no twisted threats. It's only a card, a note, and a Post-it. It's just that—" Morgan's voice broke, then she resumed. "It's not something I can get into on the phone. I'll only cry, and that'll waste time. I spoke to Arthur's doorman. He said the Tyvek arrived by delivery service, specifying Friday-afternoon delivery. I'm not sure why, unless the sender knew Arthur would be away and Elyse would be at the gym. I'm pretty thrown, and I don't want to discuss this with anyone before I talk to you. Jill's on the phone dealing with a client. Can you meet me somewhere?"

"I'm at Lane's, using his computer to run down some leads while he's in the Poconos. I'm alone. Here's what I want you to do. Slide the package into a Ziploc, just in case there are any discernible fingerprints on it—which I doubt there are. Then tell one of the security guys inside the apartment that you're running out to do an errand—*with* your bodyguard. That way, Jill won't be alarmed when she hangs up the phone and comes looking for you. Grab the package and head over here."

"I'm on my way."

"Morgan," Monty added firmly. "I meant the part about taking your bodyguard. You're not going anywhere alone."

"Believe me, I don't intend to."

TWENTY-SEVEN

Monty read the Post-it, handwritten note, and business card—not once, but twice. Then he glanced at the Tyvek. There was no return address.

He raised his head and looked at Morgan. "I assume this is your mother's handwriting?" he asked, pointing to the card and the note.

"Yes." Tears clogged her throat.

A nod. He patted her arm, lowering his head to study the items again.

The business card had Lara's name, and the address and phone number of her Brooklyn shelter printed on it. Beneath the address, she'd scribbled her home number. The note wrapped around the card was bent, and the words had faded a bit with time. But they were definitely visible.

J—Call anytime—L.

"J," Monty muttered. "I wonder who that is." He glanced at the Post-it, obviously penned recently—judging from the ink smear—and in a different, but also feminine handwriting.

There was no salutation and no signature. It simply read, *Your mother once helped me. I'm returning her kindness by helping you. Look close to home. Trust no one.*

"I called the messenger company," Morgan supplied. "It's downtown on West Twenty-second Street. They said a woman dropped off the package with specific instructions to deliver it to me at the Shores' apartment between noon and five today. She was wearing a hooded black coat and sunglasses. Which means we have no description. And she paid by cash."

"Great," Monty said drily. "So much for increased security measures. She could have been dropping off an envelope of anthrax. What sender's name did she provide?"

"Jill's. So that does us no good, either."

"Someone went to a hell of a lot of trouble to get this to you—and to remain anonymous doing it."

Morgan raked a hand through her hair. "The only reason for her to do that would be because she knows something about who killed my parents, and because she's terrified to come forward."

"Or because she was hired to lead us on a wild-goose chase."

"Huh?" Morgan's brows arched in puzzlement.

"The timing is interesting," Monty noted. "But before we get into my theory, let's explore yours. Say that whoever sent this heard about the break-in at your house, and that she has reason to tie it to the murders. Adding all the pieces together, she became afraid for you—afraid enough to come forward. But anonymously, because she's also afraid for herself. Makes sense." Another glance at the Post-it. "Let's focus on the 'close to home' reference. If you're right, that's a pointed warning with some ugly implications. If you're wrong, it's an equally pointed diversionary technique orchestrated by a perp who feels the walls closing in on him."

"That's the wild-goose chase you're referring to," Morgan concluded. "But who's the puppet who delivered the message and who's the puppeteer initiating the chase?"

"Don't know the puppet. Might know the puppeteer."

Morgan made a frustrated sound, then called Monty on the carpet. "Okay, I've been patient. Now I want an explanation. You know something. I sensed it yesterday and I'm sure of it now. What is it? And in full sentences, please."

"Yes, ma'am." Monty gave her a crooked grin, trying to soften the blow she was about to be dealt. But she was the client. She had a right to know. "It's possible Arthur spent some time with another woman the night of the murders. If so, she's a new lead. Suspect, witness, woman scorned—anything's possible. Maybe this is from her. Or maybe it's from someone who knows about her."

Morgan was staring. "What are you talking about? Arthur was at the Kellermans' party the night of the murders. He was with Elyse. How could he have hooked up with another woman? And, even if he did, why would she want to kill my parents?"

"I can't answer that. Not until I find out who she is and what her agenda was. For now, all I have are gut feelings and seemingly disconnected pieces to this puzzle."

"I want to hear all of them, starting with why you suspect Arthur was with another woman that night."

Monty filled her in on Lane's discovery, showed her the color prints with the zoomed shots of Arthur's neck clad in two different dress shirts.

"This doesn't make sense," Morgan said, having reviewed the prints three times for confirmation. "Arthur's no saint, but he's not about to slip out of his in-laws' party just to have sex with some woman. He has more than ample opportunities for that."

"True. But when sex is involved, men rarely think with their heads. Either way, I need an explanation for the shirt change. And if Arthur was with someone that evening, I need to know who and when."

It was the "when" that struck home.

Morgan's eyes widened. "When you said you might know the puppeteer—you're not implying that Arthur is a suspect?"

"I'm not implying anything. I'm stating that everyone who knew your parents has to account for his or her whereabouts between the hours of seven and eight on the night of the murder. If Arthur was away from the party during those hours, then, yes, he has to provide an alibi."

"Have you talked to him about this?" Morgan asked woodenly.

"Not yet. But I did talk to Elyse. She had a hard time keeping it together when I showed her the photos."

"I can imagine. Is that why you wanted to see her alone yesterday?"

"Yup."

"No wonder she was such a mess after you left. Monty, don't rub her nose in Arthur's indiscretions. It's painful enough as it is."

"I'm hunting down a killer. That takes precedence over being sensitive to a wife with a cheating husband. I'm sorry. But that's the way it is."

Morgan searched the hard lines of his face. "You were hunting down a killer seventeen years ago, too. That didn't stop you from being compassionate."

"You were a helpless, traumatized child whose entire world had been shattered. Elyse is a full-grown woman who's chosen to stay in a complicated marriage. Defenseless victim. Victim who allows herself to be victimized. There's no parallel."

"Fair enough," Morgan had to acknowledge.

"I'll set up a meeting with Arthur for tomorrow morning. I need some answers. Once he provides them, I'll have a better idea where we stand." Monty frowned, his gaze returning to Lara's business card and note, and the Post-it that had accompanied it. "Any way you look at it, this note was written by your mother and the business card it's wrapped around was meant for the recipient, not just plucked off a reception desk. People don't scribble their home phone numbers on random business cards."

"The logical assumption is that they were meant for one of the women my mother worked with at the shelter." Morgan chewed her lip. "Maybe Barbara would know."

"Barbara. She's the woman you mentioned at that counseling center—Healthy Healing."

"Yes. She knew my mother—and the women she worked with—very well."

"I want to talk to her."

"It's after five. But I'll see if she's still in her office." Morgan opened her cell phone and punched in the number for the Healthy Healing Center. She reached Jeanine, explained the situation, then agreed to hold on. Covering the mouthpiece with her hand, she murmured to Monty, "Barbara's away until tomorrow night. I spoke to her assistant and explained how important this is, and that it concerned my mother. Jeanine is trying to reach Barbara on her cell phone to make special arrangements." She tugged her hand away from the phone. "Yes, Jeanine? Sunday would be great. Please thank her. She can call me anytime tomorrow tonight, no matter how late, to nail down a time and place." Morgan hung up.

"Sunday?" Monty's brows raised. "That's pretty dedicated."

"That's Barbara."

"Good. So I'll have a busy weekend. Arthur tomorrow and Barbara on Sunday."

"I don't want to be there when you interview Arthur."

"You shouldn't be. No one should. This is a private conversation. Arthur and I will find a private place to conduct it."

"I'm not sure I want to be there when he gets home, either."

The sound of a key turning in the front door lock interrupted their discussion.

"I think your solution is about to walk through that door," Monty replied.

An instant later, Lane strolled in. He saw them, stopped, and blinked in surprise. Then he nonchalantly leaned back outside, glanced at the number on his building, and gave a decisive nod. With that, he reentered the brownstone, plopped down his camera bag, and shrugged out of his parka. "This *is* my apartment," he announced. "I was just checking."

"Sorry," Morgan said with a rueful grin. "I didn't mean to invade your space. Something came up and I needed to see your father ASAP. He was working here. So I showed up in a panic."

"No apology necessary." He winked. "You're the intruder I could get used to coming home to. No offense, Monty."

"None taken."

"And why the panic?" he asked Morgan.

She sighed. "It's a long story."

"You can fill Lane in after I cut out of here." Monty stood up and stretched. "Which I'm about to do. I got what I needed. Thanks for the use of your computer."

"No problem. But what was so urgent that it couldn't wait till you got to your office?"

"A pressing telephone-number search." From behind Morgan's back, Monty shot Lane a "later" look. "How was the skydiving?"

"Incredible." Lane got the message and went with Monty's subject change. "Great form, great weather, great footage." His gaze flickered to Morgan. "But I was ready to head back. So was Arthur. And Jonah's a little under the weather, so even he'd had enough. Obviously, I missed something significant at this end."

"We haven't found the killer. Anything less than that doesn't count as significant." Monty grimaced. "Puzzling, yes. Complicated, definitely. As they say, the plot thickens. In any case, I'm outta here. I've got a ton of paperwork to go through. I'll do that at home. I've barely seen your mother all week. And I'll call the congressman on my cell while I drive." He gathered up his stuff. "Morgan will bring you up to speed. Tonight's yours. But tomorrow, I'll need you. All day long. So clear your calendar."

"Consider it done."

"I'll call you in the morning when I'm heading back into the city." Monty grabbed his coat, glanced back at them as he headed toward the door. "O'Hara's outside?"

"In a car across the street," Morgan supplied. "I promised you I wouldn't go anywhere without my bodyguard and I haven't."

"Good girl. Anyway, I'll stop by his car on my way out, tell him to take the night off. I doubt you'll be needing his services before morning." Monty waved as he walked out. "See you."

The door shut behind him.

Morgan's gaze darted to Lane's, color tingeing her cheeks. "I never said anything about spending the night."

"I know." Lane came over and tipped her chin up. "But you have to admit, it's a good idea." He kissed her, then raised his head, studied her expression. "Unless you don't want to."

She smiled, and for a moment she felt giddy, happy. In contrast to the past day's gravity, it was like the weight of the world had been lifted off her shoulders, however temporarily.

"Don't want to," she repeated. "Funny, that doesn't seem to be a phrase I'd associate with whatever's going on between us."

"Good point." Lane kissed her again, this time pulling her close, gliding his fingers through her hair. "I couldn't stop thinking about you today," he murmured when the kiss finally ended.

"You sound surprised."

"I am. This is all new to me."

"I know." Morgan rested her forehead against his sweater. "And it's scary to me."

"I know." Lane was quiet for a moment. "We have a lot to talk about, don't we?"

"Yes."

"Plus, I want to hear about what freaked you out enough to race over here to see Monty."

"And I want to discuss those color prints you made of Arthur, and their possible implications—the gist of which Monty just laid out for me and now plans to lay out for Arthur. That's why he's calling him, and why I'm preparing for fireworks."

"Wow." Lane loosened his grip around her waist. "You *have* had a hectic day. Tell you what. I'll open a bottle of wine and get a fire going. You grab some blankets from the hall closet and join me in the living room. We can unwind, and talk." A frown. "Unfortunately, my fridge is pretty empty."

"Do you have bread?"

"Sure."

"How about peanut butter and jelly?"

"Yup. Standard fare."

"Cans of soup?"

"Better—I have a quart of Rhoda's chicken soup that I picked up yesterday for when I got home tonight."

"Perfect. You take care of the ambience. I'll do dinner. It'll be a gourmet feast of PB and J and homemade soup. What could be better?"

"At the moment, I can't think of a single thing."

A HALF HOUR later they were sprawled on blankets in front of the fire, munching on sandwiches, spooning up soup, sipping wine, and talking.

Lane listened intently while Morgan described her surprise package and what it contained.

"Seeing your mother's note and card—it must have hit you hard," he surmised.

"It did. I'm counting on Monty to figure out what it means. He's running with a couple of different theories." Morgan dipped her spoon into her soup, stirring it around. "He's planning on pinning Arthur down tomorrow, asking for an explanation and an alibi. I'm not looking forward to the results. Arthur's going to bust a gut."

"It'll be difficult. But it'll clear up a lot of questions. And if all that was involved was an affair, it'll be business as usual. Monty will corroborate Arthur's story, then verify that the woman in question can account for her whereabouts during the time of the murders. If all that checks out, it'll be a done deal and Monty will keep the whole thing under wraps. The only people who will know about it are us and the Shores. If it's Elyse you're worried about, I'm sure she won't be shocked. She knows who she's married to."

"You're right. She does." Morgan raised her chin and stared straight ahead, watching the crackling flames of the fire. "I could never accept that, never live that way," she heard herself say. "To me, marriage is more than blind, passionate love. It's a union—a union that includes fidelity. Not the kind you offer because you have to. The kind you offer because you want to."

"True. But that's not always the hard part," Lane answered quietly. "Even with unwavering fidelity, marriage is a huge, complicated commitment. And you're right—love's not enough to make it work. I saw that with my parents. They were crazy about each other. But they were also very different people. They wanted and needed entirely different things. That pulled at their marriage until it frayed, then finally snapped." He paused. "On the other hand, they never stopped loving each other, and one day they realized that mattered more than the differences. So who knows?"

"Maybe no one. Maybe it's all about taking chances. Huge, complicated chances, as you just pointed out." Morgan swallowed, dropping her gaze to the blanket. "I'm not sure I'm up for something of that magnitude. What's worse is that the description you just gave of your parents' contrasting personalities sounds disturbingly like us. Which probably means we should walk away now, while I'm still in one piece. Much longer, and it'll be too late."

"It's already too late," Lane countered. "Walking away's not an option. Not for me. I'm in too deep—*way* too deep."

His words swirled through Morgan like an aphrodisiac. "So am I," she admitted. "You have no idea how deep. So what do we do?"

"We see it through. We trust our instincts. We shove dinner aside and go upstairs to bed." He was following words with actions, pushing away bowls and plates and rising to his feet. "We spend the rest of the night blocking out all the vast unknowns and losing ourselves in each other. Then we deal with the rest as it comes. How's *that* for a plan?" He held out his hand to her and waited.

Morgan drew a sharp breath, exhaling in a rush. It was no use. She couldn't fight these feelings. Come hell or high water, they were here.

Placing her fingers in his, she scrambled to her feet. "Plan approved."

IT WAS SNOWING lightly as Monty's Corolla turned onto the Taconic State Parkway and toward home.

Reflexively, he clicked his wipers on, his mind preoccupied with the case's most recent developments. He was counting on Barbara Stevens and Arthur Shore to fill in some blanks.

The congressman had sounded strained and pissed off at Monty's demand for an early morning meeting. Especially when he'd heard it was personal. His reaction could have been rooted in fatigue and stress. Or it could have been rooted in guilt.

Monty was so deep in thought that he scarcely noticed the BMW 325i that barreled down the entrance ramp and onto the Taconic, downshifting as it accelerated past his beaten-up Toyota. It rounded one of the parkway's winding bends and disappeared.

Just how deep did Arthur Shore's involvement run? Monty mused. Fidelity and morality were clearly dispensable in his book. So was honesty, since he'd lied about having spoken to George Hayek since he'd left his job at Lenny's. That could have been at the D.A.'s request. Or not.

Monty was nearing the Route 132 exit, where the road narrowed from three lanes to two when, out of nowhere, a pair of flashing hazard lights appeared, outlining a car that was at a near standstill. It was practically invisible in the snowy evening sky. And Monty was almost upon it.

"Shit!" He hit his brakes, swerving to the left lane, narrowly missing the BMW's rear end.

Still muttering, Monty glanced into his rearview mirror and glared at the other vehicle. He was half tempted to turn on the dome light and give the guy the finger for being such a road menace. But he restrained himself, instead concentrating on accelerating up the incline as he reached the overpass.

His headlights illuminated the falling object a split second before it hit.

Then his front windshield exploded.

Spiderlike cracks gave way to shards of glass that sprayed everywhere. Monty raised his arms to protect his face, simultaneously slamming on the brakes as the car swerved out of control. He managed to hook his elbow into the steering wheel, giving it one hard shove so the car veered to the right, away from the center divider.

The Corolla slid off the road, bouncing down the uneven ground of the wooded decline until it struck a tree and came to a stop.

Dazed but conscious, Monty angled his head toward the passenger seat, and saw the brick lying beside him. A foot or two closer and he'd be dead.

SATISFIED THAT HIS goal had been accomplished, the driver of the BMW slowed his vehicle down, stopping only long enough to pick up the man waiting just under the overpass.

MONTY SWORE, AWARE that there was blood trickling down his jaw. Fragments of glass were everywhere—on the dashboard, the seats, the floor, and all over his parka. His hands had been spared, thanks to his gloves, and he used them now to gingerly brush as much glass off himself as he could.

At that moment, he heard the rumbling sound of another car approaching. The BMW that had been creeping along.

It wasn't creeping now.

Headlights off, its running lights were barely visible as it blew by. Monty tried to make out the license plate, but it was too dark, since the Taconic had no streetlights. As for his own car, it was in no shape to move, much less launch into a high-speed chase.

Ripping mad, he stared after it. Clearly, Morgan wasn't the only one the perp wanted scared off.

Well, the son of a bitch didn't know who he was dealing with.

But he was about to find out.

WEAK MORNING SUNLIGHT was trickling into Lane's bedroom when the telephone on his night table rang.

Morgan made a soft sound of protest, pulling the blanket higher around her shoulders and burying her head in the pillow. After an all-night love-making marathon, she was in no shape to move, much less function.

"Let the machine get it," Lane mumbled, wrapping an arm around her.

"Mm-hmm." Morgan was already drifting back to sleep.

The ringing stopped, then started again.

"Goddammit, Monty," Lane muttered, reaching across Morgan and groping for the phone. His gaze fell on the clock. "It's seven fucking thirty." He plucked the receiver off the hook and crammed it against his ear. "It's Saturday," he said bluntly. "I'm sleeping. And I'm not meeting you till ten. So forget it."

"Lane?" a woman's hesitant voice inquired.

He blinked in surprise. "Who's this?"

"Nina Vaughn, Jonah's mother. I'm sorry to call so early, but we're in the emergency room at Maimonides Medical Center. Jonah's been admitted."

TWENTY-EIGHT

Jonah wasn't doing well.

His parents were doing worse.

Nina Vaughn rushed over to Lane the minute he walked into the ICU waiting room. "They're doing a CT scan," she informed him. "I told them everything you said about Tuesday's skiing accident. The doctors said this could definitely be related." Her voice quavered. "Eddie and I are total wrecks. I should be more helpful; I am a hospital aide. But I work in pediatrics. I don't know anything about sports injuries. And he was in so much pain. We rushed him here by ambulance."

"Pain doesn't necessarily mean a critical injury," Lane tried. "I've torn ligaments and literally seen stars."

Jonah's mother nodded, but Lane wasn't even sure she'd heard him. "At least they're giving him something for the pain," she murmured. "He's more relaxed now. Oh, and they drew blood. We're waiting for the results. Something about a CBC to check for internal bleeding."

Lane nodded. "That makes sense." He turned to greet Ed Vaughn with a handshake. "How are you holding up?"

Jonah's father shrugged, his face drawn with worry. "I'm okay. I just wish they'd tell us something."

"They will." Lane forced a smile. "Hey, I spent half my teen years in the ER for stuff like this. My mother used to say that the hospital should be issuing me frequent flier points."

At that moment, the hallway doors swung open and an orderly wheeled Jonah down on a gurney. He looked lousy—half out of it, pale and scared, and like he was fighting back tears. His parents hurried over, flanking the gurney as it made its way down the hall.

Jonah spotted Lane, and surprise darted across his face.

"Hey." A self-conscious grimace. "Did my mom drag you down here?"

"No, I came to find out how soon you'd be back at work. We've got the congressman's photo essay to finish, remember?"

"I'll do my best." Jonah forced a smile. "But right now, I feel kind of crappy."

"Yeah, I've been there. But it gets better."

"Glad to hear it." Jonah shifted, wincing a little at the discomfort. "Would you do me a favor and call Lenny? He'll need someone to sub for me. I feel bad leaving him in the lurch."

"You're not leaving him in the lurch. You're getting better." Lane walked alongside the gurney until the orderly reached Jonah's ICU room. "I'll take care of it. Anything else you need?"

Jonah eyed his parents' drawn expressions. "Yeah. Convince my parents I'm not gonna die."

"They already know that." Lane winked at Nina and Ed, trying to lift their spirits. "But they're your parents. They worry. That's their job."

"Lane's right," Ed told his son in an encouraging tone. "And your job is to heal fast so we have one less thing to worry about."

"I'll try."

Lane paused outside the room. "I'll be out here," he informed Jonah. "Rules say only one or two visitors at a time. So spend some time with your parents and I'll visit later."

Once Jonah was settled inside with his parents, Lane left the building. First, he called Lenny. Then he called Monty, filling him in on what was going on with Jonah and rearranging their plans. Next, he followed up on an earlier call he'd made to O'Hara, confirming that the bodyguard was back on duty, parked right outside Lane's brownstone where Morgan was staying. And last, he called Morgan, gave her a preliminary update, and made sure she was okay. She sounded warm and drowsy, her voice husky with sleep, and he told her to stay that way until he got home. He found himself smiling as he hung up. **There** was something very primal, very natural—not to mention very **erotic**—**about** her waiting for him in his bed.

He didn't have time to dwell on it.

By the time he got back upstairs, Jonah's parents were reconvening in the hall, poised with nervous anticipation as the doctor treating Jonah strode toward them, carrying his test results. He plucked out Jonah's chart and skimmed it, mentally assessing the compiled data.

"Dr. Truber, what do we know?" Nina asked anxiously.

"First, Jonah's anemic. Normal hemoglobin is above twelve grams, and normal hematocrit is above thirty-six percent. Jonah's hemoglobin is nine grams and his hematocrit is twenty-seven percent. And the CT scan shows that Jonah has a lacerated spleen. The good news is that it appears to be an incomplete laceration, rather than a complete rupture. That means it's possible it will heal itself without requiring surgery. Time will tell. The other positive news is that his vital signs are currently fine."

"So other than monitoring him and waiting, what can we do?"

"Donate blood, in the event that surgery or a transfusion is necessary." The doctor glanced questioningly from Nina to Ed. "Does either of you know your blood type? Because Jonah is AB negative, which is the rarest of all blood types. Less than one percent of the population has it. We need to start the cross-match process right away."

"I'm B positive and Ed is O positive," Nina supplied. Seeing the puzzled expression on Dr. Truber's face, she explained, "Jonah is adopted."

That news clearly didn't make the doctor happy. "That complicates matters. Are you acquainted with any of Jonah's biological relatives?"

"No." Tears slid down Nina's cheeks. "This is so ironic. We were just in the process of hashing this out with Jonah. He's determined to try contacting his birth mother. He's under eighteen, so he needs our permission to do so. We're torn; we understand his feelings, but we want to protect him. What if his birth mother wants no part of him? Jonah's young, vulnerable. We're afraid a flat-out rejection would devastate him. The timing seemed wrong."

"It just became right. For medical reasons, I urge you to initiate the search—immediately."

ARTHUR'S CONGRESSIONAL OFFICE was quiet. It was Saturday morning, and no one was in.

Monty and Arthur made their way into Arthur's private office with the cups of coffee they'd picked up down the street. Arthur pointed Monty to a chair, then sat down across from him. "Okay, Montgomery, you made it clear that this meeting was urgent, and personal. Let's hear it." He frowned as Monty unzipped his parka and lowered the hood, revealing a bunch of facial cuts and lacerations. "What happened to you?"

"I skidded off the road last night and hit a tree. I'm fine." Monty didn't mince words. "A couple of things have come up. We need to address them." He took out the color prints Lane had made and placed them in front of Arthur. "The night the Winters were killed and sometime during the hours of the Kellerman party, you had reason to change your shirt. These are the before-and-after shots. I need to know if you left the party to do so, anyone you might have interacted with during that absence, and what time this took place. Also, if you did leave the party, why didn't you mention it either during the initial murder investigation or now."

Arthur took a sip of coffee. His posture and jaw were rigid, but otherwise he was composed. If he was blown away by Monty's line of questioning, he was hiding it well. "That was certainly blunt and to the point."

"Just procedural." Monty flipped open a notepad, took out his pen, and waited.

"Fine. Then I'll be equally blunt. I never mentioned it because it didn't factor into the investigations, then or now. And there are parts of my life I try very hard to keep under wraps." A humorless laugh. "Not that the tabloids let me."

"So we're talking about an affair?"

"More like the unwinding of an affair. But, yes, I left the party. And, yes, I met a woman."

"Fine. I'm not interested in hearing the details of your sex life, or in sharing them with anyone else. Just give me the who, when, and where. I'll check it all out discreetly, make sure the woman in question has an alibi for the time of the homicides, and then let it go."

"Fair enough." Arthur put down his coffee container and interlaced his fingers on the desk. "Her name was Margo Adderly. She was an intern in my Washington office. We had a brief fling. She wanted more. I didn't. She showed up in New York the week before Christmas. She called, came by my office. I avoided her and her messages. The night of the Christmas party she got pretty insistent. She threatened to barge into the Kellermans' and make a scene if I didn't meet with her. That was the last thing I needed. I didn't see that I had a choice."

"So you met with her."

"At her hotel room, yes. I slipped out of the party with as little fanfare as possible. At first, the visit was civil. She took my jacket, offered me a drink. I turned her down. Not that she would have noticed. She was smashed enough for both of us. I wanted to talk, to get through to her that whatever we'd had was over. She wanted to reignite things, to remind me how good it had been. I tried to explain, but I was getting nowhere. Instead of listening, she was removing my tie. Then I got blunt, maybe even cruel. I told her the relationship was over—in no uncertain terms. I finally got through her drunken haze. That's when things got dicey. She went a little crazy—screaming, throwing things. One of those things was her drink, which she flung at me. Her aim sucked, she was so loaded. Fortunate for me, because she missed, other than splattering my shirt. She threw me out. I went home, changed shirts, and went directly back to the party. The whole incident took maybe forty minutes. The party had barely gotten under way. End of story."

"What time was that?"

Arthur's forehead creased in thought. "Jack and Lara had just left for Brooklyn. So it had to have been around six-thirty. I was drinking champagne with my wife at seven-fifteen."

"You remember the exact time you drank your champagne?"

"Actually, yes. Elyse had been having trouble with the clasp of her watch ever since she got dressed for the evening. I fixed the clasp for her while the server was pouring. So I noticed the time when I put the watch back on her wrist."

"I see." Monty was jotting everything down. "Any idea where I can find this Margo Adderly?"

"Not a clue." Arthur gave an arbitrary shrug. "It was seventeen years ago, and very inconsequential."

"To you, maybe. Obviously not to her."

"She was emotionally distraught, Montgomery. Not homicidal. Plus, if she wanted to kill anyone, it was me. But if you have doubts, feel free to track her down. Start with the D.C. area, since that's where she's from."

"I will." Monty stopped writing.

"So, is that it?" Arthur was getting ready to stand up.

"One more thing. Why did you tell me that the last time you spoke to George Hayek was when he worked for your father?"

Arthur paused, something definitely flickering in his eyes. "I had no idea George was still on your list. Have you determined that he's connected to your investigation?"

"That's a question, not an answer."

"The answer is, I gave you the most candid response I could. Any further information is privileged."

"Ah." Monty rolled his pen between his fingers. "Meaning your friend the D.A. doesn't want it getting out that Hayek was, or still is, a CI for his office."

Inhaling sharply, Arthur settled back in his chair and seized his half-empty coffee container. "I should have gotten the twenty-ounce size. I didn't realize I'd be here all morning." He took another gulp, then met Monty's gaze. "How did you find out?"

"Can't say. Any further information is privileged."

"Very amusing. What do you want to know—and why?"

"Three things." Monty counted off on his fingers. "One—did Hayek call you on July twenty-ninth, 1976, at your office at Kellerman Development and tell you he'd been arrested for running guns for Carl Angelo? Two—did you, in turn, contact Jack Winter and make a deal with him that resulted in Hayek's charges being dropped and his file sealed in exchange for his becoming a CI? And three—as a CI for the D.A.'s office, did Hayek eventually testify against Carl Angelo and help Jack put him away just a few months before Jack and Lara were shot to death?"

Arthur's lips had drawn into a grim line. "Yes, yes, and yes."

"Then you shouldn't have to ask why I'm still interested in Hayek."

"I see why you think Angelo might have ordered the hit on Jack. But how would that involve George?"

"Angelo was in prison. Hayek was free as a bird. Maybe he was offered enough cash to arrange the hit on Jack. Or maybe Angelo wanted to find out who'd been ratting him out and Hayek was scared shitless he'd be made and eliminated. So he killed the only person who knew he was the CI who'd gotten Angelo convicted. I don't know. But I plan to find out." Monty paused. "It's interesting though. Your pal the D.A. is pushing like hell to find out who killed his rising star Jack Winter. Yet he's obviously not in someone's face about this Hayek angle. I wonder why."

"No idea." Arthur polished off his coffee. He looked like he wished it were bourbon. "And now I've said all I can say on this subject. Anything more, you'll have to go to the D.A. directly."

"If that's what it takes, I will."

TWENTY-NINE

Monty met Lane at the Second Street Café, a short cab ride away from the Maimonides Medical Center in Brooklyn, for a quick burger and update.

Lane frowned when he saw his father's face. Monty had given him a brief rundown on the Taconic incident. But his story and the visual didn't match up. "You told me the only damage was to the car. It doesn't look that way to me."

"You wouldn't say that if you saw my Corolla. It needs bodywork, a paint job and a new windshield—not to mention a Super Sucker to pick up all the pieces of glass. Me? My jaw stings and I've got a few pulled muscles. None of it hurts as much as my pride. Your mother needed the truck today. She's getting supplies for the horses. So guess who had to take her little royal-blue bumper car to work?"

"You're driving Mom's Miata?" Lane's lips twitched.

"Wipe that smirk off your face."

"I'll try. But it won't be easy. The image of you—" Lane broke off at the murderous gleam in Monty's eyes. "Okay, okay, I won't goad you anymore." He sobered. "No clue on who was driving that BMW?"

"Nope. But whoever it was was a hired hand. As for the car, it probably belongs to the scumbag he's working for—the *real* perp we want." Monty gave Lane a questioning look. "In the meantime, how's Jonah doing?"

"He's got a partially ruptured spleen. Plus, he's got a rare blood type, so they're scrambling to find a donor—just in case. He's adopted, which means that neither of his parents fit the bill and there are no known siblings to turn to. So he's scared. And his parents are a mess. That's why I'm more time pressed than I planned."

"Don't worry about it." Monty waved that away. "If you want to hang out a little longer at the hospital and put the Vaughns at ease, do it. I've got enough to keep me busy for a few hours." His forehead creased. "Where's Morgan during all this?"

"At my place, sleeping. It's probably the first good rest she's had in weeks. I checked in with her on my way over here. She sounds half out of it, and more than happy to relax till I get back. O'Hara's stationed outside my building, and I made sure to set the alarm and double-lock the door when I left. So everything's cool at that end." A scowl. "Everything except my plan to spend the morning with her."

"Spend the night instead. Jonah's condition will stabilize, so his parents will be calmer. I'll be out of your hair—assuming you spend the rest of the afternoon and evening enhancing those crime-scene images. And Morgan will be a hell of a lot more relaxed at your place than at the Shores'. The tension there isn't going to be easing up anytime soon."

"Let's hear the details," Lane said the instant the waitress had taken their orders and disappeared. "What happened during your meeting with Arthur? And why the urgent computer search at my place yesterday? I assume it had something to do with your meeting with Charlie Denton."

"Yeah." Succinctly, Monty repeated the outcome of his meeting with Denton, then went on to relay the gist of his conversation with Arthur.

He provided Lane with the facts, omitting the personal details behind Denton's falling-out with Arthur. He had confidence in Lane's deductive skills. As a result, he simply let him draw his own conclusions.

"So you were right about Hayek being a CI for Jack Winter," Lane commented thoughtfully as soon as Monty was through.

"Yeah, and about Arthur orchestrating the deal between Hayek and the D.A.'s office."

Lane eyed his father, processing everything he'd just been told, and all the implications that went along with it. "That doesn't tie Hayek to the murders."

"I didn't expect it would. But it does tie Hayek to Arthur Shore. And not just as teenagers who Lenny took to the movies so Hayek could have brotherly companionship and a father figure. Arthur and Hayek had some kind of association seven years after Hayek left Lenny's. Who knows how long that association lasted and how deep it ran?"

Brows drawn together, Lane mentally contemplated his father's reasoning. "I'm not sure where you're going with this."

"Me, either. But either Arthur's sitting on something, or the D.A.'s sitting on something." A quick, pointed glance at his son. "Brace yourself. I might be twisting your arm on the Hayek issue again. But for now I'll let it be. The rest of my conversation with Shore gave me more food for thought."

"He came up with an explanation and an alibi."

"*Too* good an explanation and *too* convenient an alibi."

"You think they were staged?"

"Or at least rehearsed. It's obvious Elyse Shore prepped her husband for what was coming. She loves the guy; you gotta give her that. She protects him even at the cost of her own self-respect. I have some feelers out on this Margo Adderly. How much do you want to bet she's either untraceable or unreliable?"

"You think Arthur paid her off?"

"Nah, more likely he did a walk down memory lane, recalling his sexual conquests of that year, then settled on someone who's a druggie or an alcoholic and can't remember what she had for breakfast, much less what time she threw a drink in Arthur's face seventeen years ago. All I know is that he was too prepared and too composed when I hit him with that line of questioning. He didn't lose his cool until I mentioned George Hayek's name. Before that? He had it all down pat, right to the time on Elyse's watch."

"Monty, it's beginning to sound more and more like you think Arthur Shore was involved in these homicides."

"I think he's involved in something. I just don't know what. If Denton's right, then that whole 'my closest friend' reference Arthur uses when he describes Jack Winter is a crock. More likely, they were the equivalent of in-laws in a marriage. Their wives were best friends, so they got along out of necessity. And, of course, they cut that Hayek deal together. So I'm sure they were on civil terms. But it sounds like Jack Winter was an ethical guy who thought Lara's best friend was getting the royal shaft from her husband. That can't have bred good feelings between them."

"Even if that's true, it's hard to believe that even a fierce disagreement over moral choices could lead to murder. Plus, there's another flaw in that theory—Elyse. She knew about her husband's affairs, probably from the beginning. She accepted him anyway. And her father was one hundred percent behind his son-in-law. So it's not like Arthur would have lost either his wife or his financial backing if Jack took the facts to Elyse."

"Assuming that's all Jack took to her. Maybe this isn't about infidelity. Maybe it's about something a lot more substantial. Even illegal. Now, *that* would be both a marriage and a career breaker."

"You're back to Arthur's ties to Hayek." Lane blew out a breath. "I'm up against a wall on this one, Monty. If my source is lying to me, he's not about to admit it, or change his story."

"True. Which means that if getting more detailed dirt on Hayek is what's necessary, it won't be coming from channels—yours or mine. Denton's not any more willing to talk than your source is. When I called him back, gave him Hayek's name as the CI he'd help me figure out, he was thrilled—at first. What A.D.A. wouldn't be? Hell, to be able to link a rich, possibly shady international arms dealer who sells weapons to foreign governments with the Winters' double homicide? Denton would be front-page news for a week."

"Then you dropped the other shoe and told him that Arthur Shore had played an instrumental part in Hayek being recruited by the D.A.'s office."

A corner of Monty's mouth lifted. "Denton nearly choked on his coffee. Needless to say, he won't be running with this lead. He likes his job too much. So Hayek will be our problem. You and I will tackle it as a last resort."

"In other words, we'll save the risky, balls-out approach for last."

"Exactly." Monty drummed his fingers on the table. "Let's talk about the package Morgan got yesterday. It's either a breakthrough lead or a pile of BS meant to throw me off track. Who is this woman who sent it, and how is it that her timing is so perfect?"

"You don't think it could be Margo Adderly, do you?"

"The thought crossed my mind. But that would be too easy. And Arthur's too smart to give me the name of someone who sought out Lara's help."

"Maybe he didn't know about it."

"Maybe. But I doubt it. Then again, I'd be thrilled to be wrong. I can't wait to talk to Barbara Stevens tomorrow."

"And I can't wait to get back to those images." Lane's determination resurged, full force. "In fact, given the direction your investigation is headed, I'm going to see if Morgan has the negatives of all the shots taken at the Kellermans' Christmas Eve party. Now that you got Arthur's rendition of what went on, let's see if I can enhance any photographic details that would help us prove or disprove his story."

"Such as?"

"Such as I'll know when I see it. I keep telling you, image enhancing isn't an exact science."

Monty scowled. "And that's supposed to make me feel better? Because it doesn't. Not with the escalating threats to Morgan."

"Nothing's going to happen to Morgan," Lane stated emphatically. "I won't let it. But the more in sync I am with the victims' states of mind and relationships, the better the big picture I have, and the more likely I am to spot a discrepancy. It's there, Monty. I can feel it in my bones. I just have to find it. And I will."

"Fine. But we'd better hurry. Because my gut tells me time is running out."

LANE PUT DOWN the magazine he'd been reading when Jonah woke up. "Hey. Have a nice nap?"

Jonah still looked pale and weak. "Hey," he replied groggily. Awareness returned in slow increments. "How come you're babysitting?"

"I'm not babysitting; I'm giving your poor parents a chance to get some coffee and stretch their legs. They've been glued to your bedside for hours."

"Hours? What time is it?"

"Two-fifteen."

"You've been here all this time?"

"Relax. I met my father for lunch. He says to get well soon, by the way. I stopped by here on my way home to check on you. Oh, and expect a visit from Lenny. When I called him and explained what happened, he told Rhoda and the two of them immediately started packing up a care package for you and your parents. I'm not sure the doctor will let you eat deli, but I didn't have the heart to tell Lenny that. So whatever's left over, the staff can enjoy."

"Lenny's great." Jonah gave a weak smile. He turned to look at the various pieces of medical equipment around him. "How am I doing?"

"According to the last results, you were holding your own."

"But I'm still bleeding internally."

"That's what lacerated spleens do. Don't worry."

"I'm not. I'm just thinking that I might need a transfusion. Isn't it best to get those from family members?"

"Most of the time, yes. But there are exceptions."

Jonah angled his head so he could see Lane. "You're probably wondering why I'm asking these questions. It's a good time for me to tell you, because it'll also explain why I said there was some heavy stuff going on at home."

"You're adopted," Lane said matter-of-factly. "I was there when your parents told the doctor. They said you were pushing them to contact your birth mother. Well, you're getting your wish—even if you did go to dramatic lengths to make that happen."

"Yeah, who knew that crashing into that tree would help my cause? Then again, nothing short of that was going to get my parents to agree to help me."

Lane leaned forward. "Don't be too hard on them. They're only trying to protect you."

"I know. And maybe I'll be sorry I ever started this. Maybe my biological mother is a crack whore, and my father is a pimp. But I need to know who I am, where I came from. Can you understand that?"

"Sure. Just remember, no matter what happens, who your real parents are. They're the two people who've been glued to this hospital since dawn, waiting to hear the news that you're better, who've been there your whole life, and who are busting their asses to find someone they didn't want to find in the event her blood and yours are compatible. I'm no expert on parenting, but I don't think it gets any more devoted than that."

"You're right." Jonah shut his eyes and sighed. "I feel bad for upsetting them. They're the best."

Lane rose as Nina Vaughn hurried back in. "He's awake?" she asked.

"Yup." Lane pointed. "We were just talking about you, hoping you and Ed were getting a break, maybe something to eat."

"No need to worry about that." Nina glanced at her son, looking as close to smiling as Lane had seen her all day. "Lenny Shore is here. He's got bags of food that are bursting at the seams. The ICU nurse said he can come in, but only for a few minutes and only if you're up to it."

Jonah's lips curved. "I'm up to it."

Two minutes later, Lenny hustled into the room, two bulging brown shopping bags in his hands. "How's the patient?" he demanded, eyeing Jonah. "Pale. Hurting. Half out of it. I've seen the look a hundred times. Arthur was a jock in high school. The ER was our second home. ICU was our third."

Lane chuckled. "What did I tell you? It's a male thing."

"Don't be such a big shot," Lenny chided. "Monty and I have compared war stories. Whose son caused the most gray hairs. There was no clear winner."

"Congressman Shore is a natural athlete," Jonah protested. "I can't imagine him ever taking a fall—especially a dumb one like mine."

"Trust me, he did. A lot of them. But he never let them stop him. He fought his way back from every injury. Shaken not stirred, we used to call him. Like one of James Bond's martinis. You'll be the same way."

"You're a Bond fan?" Jonah asked.

"Big-time. Arthur and me. We never missed a movie when he was a kid. Now we have the whole DVD collection."

"Me, too," Jonah replied. "Q's my favorite. Talk about a genius—his gadgets are too cool. And Bond masters every one of them. That guy's good at everything. He never screws up. And he's never a klutz." A rueful grin. "A lot more like the congressman than like me."

"You're a special kid, Jonah," Lenny retorted. "Just take a look around and see how many people feel that way. Then maybe you'll believe it."

With that, he plunked down the bag on the table near Jonah's bed. "Rhoda packed everyone's favorites. Pastrami, liverwurst, onion and mustard for the patient—along with a quart of her matzo-ball soup, of course. Roast beef with the works for Ed. And chopped liver and corned beef for Nina." He unpacked each foil-wrapped sandwich, one by one. "There's also sides of coleslaw, potato salad, and Rhoda's noodle pudding and chopped liver. Plus a nice, plain sponge cake and a not-so-plain chocolate cake. And last, a variety of Dr. Brown's sodas—cherry, cream, and root beer. Did I leave anything out?"

"Yeah," Lane said drily. "The fifty Bar Mitzvah guests who go along with it."

Lenny grinned, not the least bit put off by the comment. "So we overdid a little. It's good for them. Especially Jonah. He needs his strength." A questioning glance in Jonah's direction. "What's the latest from the doctors?"

"I have a lacerated spleen. It's better than a ruptured one but not as good as an untorn one. We don't know yet if I'll need surgery or if it'll heal itself. In the meantime, the doctors are keeping an eye on the internal bleeding to see if I'll need a transfusion. The problem is, I have a rare blood type."

"That's not a problem. That's what parents are for." Lenny waved away the obstacle as he continued to try fitting all the food he'd brought on the table. "They'll get tested and whichever one of them has your blood type will donate as much as you need."

"I wish it were that simple," Nina murmured.

Lenny's brows drew together. "It's not?"

"I'm adopted," Jonah informed him. "So neither of my parents is AB negative. Almost nobody is. The doctor told me that only half of one percent of the world is AB negative. So we're trying to find my birth parents."

"Well, if being adopted means getting parents like yours, then I'd say you're a lucky guy. As for that malarkey the doctor handed you, AB negative's not so rare. I have it, too."

"Really?" Nina jumped on that. "Lenny, if that's true, would you mind being tested to see if your blood and Jonah's are compatible?" Seeing Jonah's mortified expression, she hurried on. "Honey, we're not discontinuing the search for your birth mother. We've already contacted the adoption agency to see what our options are. But if you should need blood before we find her, then at least your father and I could rest easier."

"I'd be glad to help," Lenny said. "But first I better talk to my cardiologist. He can talk to your doctor, make sure it's okay for me to donate blood to Jonah." A grimace. "I'm probably worrying too much. But better safe than sorry. I've got this thing with my heart. Atrial fibrillation—a big name for a not so big problem. I'm on medicine called Coumadin. It thins my blood, keeps it from coagulating. But, hey, blood is blood, right? And obviously Jonah's and mine are premium specimens, being that they're so rare." He finished setting up lunch, then straightened and gave Nina a comforting look. "I'll make that call right away, and let you know what happens. If the doctors give the okay, I'll be back here later today with my sleeve rolled up."

"Thank you so much," Nina said fervently.

"You want to thank me? Eat your sandwich. When I come back to give blood, I expect to see every drop of that food gone."

LANE WAS A BLOCK away from home when his cell phone rang.

He glanced down, saw his father's number on the display.

"Hey," he greeted. "I'm about to walk in my front door. I'll check on Morgan, then fire up my equipment and get started on the negatives."

"That's not why I'm calling," Monty replied tersely. "I located Margo Adderly and tapped out on what she has to offer."

"Already?"

"Yeah. All it took was a simple Web search."

"So she's in D.C.?"

"Yup. Six feet under."

THIRTY

Barbara Stevens came into the office on Sunday specifically to meet with the private investigator Morgan had hired. She'd never met with a PI before, nor had she ever been put in the position of compromising the confidentiality she offered her clients.

But this time was different. This time it meant trying to catch a killer—Lara's killer.

For that, she'd push her ethics to the limit. She wouldn't blindside her client. She'd contact her, ask for her understanding—and an explanation. Then she'd act accordingly.

When Barbara had reached Morgan last night to set up this meeting, Morgan had told her about the events of the past week. So Barbara had a pretty good idea which client it was.

Consequently, she'd come in early to review the particular file she had in mind. Then she'd make the necessary phone call.

It never dawned on her that the client in question would call her first.

AN HOUR LATER, Monty bounded up the front steps to the Healthy Healing Counseling Center. He rang the bell, and Barbara Stevens let him in immediately, introducing herself and taking his coat. She seemed warm, gracious, and terribly troubled—especially when her gaze shifted to the Tyvek in his hand.

"I appreciate your seeing me on a Sunday," Monty began. "I wouldn't have barged in on your day off if this wasn't so important."

"Actually, your timing is perfect. A client of mine just arrived. She'll be joining us for this meeting."

"Huh?" Monty stared.

"Trust me, Detective. She'll be able to answer your questions far better than I. Ironically, you were next on her call list. I saved her the time and trouble. She needs you as much as you need her. Come. She's waiting in my office."

Mystified, Monty followed Barbara through the reception area and to the adjacent office.

He walked inside and did a double take as the tall, slender woman in the chair adjacent to Barbara's desk rose, raking a hand through her red-gold hair and regarding Monty with wide, frightened eyes.

"Hello, Detective," Karly Fontaine said. "I'm so glad you're here. I was about to call you when Barbara told me you two had an appointment. So I raced over. I desperately need your services. I'll pay you whatever it takes."

The Karly Fontaine standing in front of Monty bore little resemblance to the polished executive he'd met with at the Lairman Modeling Agency. Her face was devoid of makeup, her hair was simple rather than styled, and she wore a casual fleece sweatsuit and sheepskin boots. She looked ten years younger, and like a lost girl.

"You want to hire me," Monty replied, purposely remaining detached until he'd assessed the situation. "That's unexpected. But judging from what Ms. Stevens just told me, we have a common interest. Which, to me, can only mean that your sudden desperate need for my help has some connection to Monday's hit-and-run."

"Not just to the hit-and-run—to the entire investigation you're conducting for Morgan Winter."

"Very cryptic. You're going to have to do better than that if you want me to take on your case. I'm a full-disclosure kind of guy."

"Good. Full disclosure's what I need, along with a private detective who's smart enough, good enough, to offer protection and resolution." Karly folded her arms across her breasts, rubbing her shoulders as if to bring warmth back into them. "I'll start out by saving you the trouble of questioning Barbara about that Tyvek you're holding. I sent it to Morgan. The business card's Lara's. The note, she wrote to me. And the Post-it, I wrote to Morgan. You're welcome to compare handwriting samples, if you don't believe me."

One of Monty's brows rose. Definitely a revelation he hadn't expected. But one look at Karly's face was all it took to convince him. "I believe you. I have a ton of questions, but I'll start with the simplest. If Lara's note was meant for you, then who the hell's J?"

"I am."

"Janice is the name we assigned to Carol—excuse me, to Karly—when she came to Healthy Healing and to Lara's shelter," Barbara explained. "That's how we protected our clients. We never used their real names in our files." She gestured for Monty to take a seat. "Since this is obviously going to take a while, I brewed a pot of coffee. Would you like some?"

"The tallest mug you've got, thanks." Monty sank down into a chair, still studying Karly. "Lara Winter helped you. How? Were you being abused?"

"All my life," Karly replied, in the flat tone of someone who'd survived hell and been numbed by it. "Starting with a string of men who locked me in my room while they had a great time with my mother. And leading up to a sick bastard of a stepfather who sexually abused me from the day he married my mother when I was eleven, to three years later when he tied me up and raped me."

Monty took the mug of coffee Barbara handed him with a nod of thanks. He was far from immune to Karly's story. But he'd seen this sick, vile pattern too many times in the past to be shocked. "Did your mother know?"

"What do you think?"

"I think she either looked the other way and said nothing, or accused you of lying and maligning her loving husband."

"The latter," Karly supplied. "I had to get out. So I ran away and came to New York."

"But the baggage came with you."

"Right. I managed to find every screwed-up guy in the city. I constantly reduced myself to the role of victim. It was a vicious cycle, one I couldn't seem to break, which brings us to the point of this discussion. When I was sixteen, I reached an all-time low in my self-destructive spiral. I fell for a very charismatic, very powerful, very married older man. Talk about getting in over my head. But he was so good to me, so tender. He treated me like I was the most special woman on earth. To me, it was true love. To him, it was a hot, convenient affair."

"To me, it was rape in the third degree," Monty commented. "You were underage."

"I know. But I didn't want to bring him up on charges. I wanted him to love me. Now I understand how stupid that was. But back then, I thought we had a future, that he'd eventually leave his wife for me. I was a star-struck child. My only defense is that I wanted him, desperately, and he said he wanted me. I would have done anything for us to be together."

"And then he dumped you."

"Not just dumped me. Lied to me, paid me off, and ultimately threatened me. When it was just me whose well-being was at stake, I did what I had to and stayed away. But now it involves someone more important than me—my son. I won't let anything happen to him." Karly sank into a chair, pressed a trembling hand to her head. "I thought I'd already paid for my stupidity. But now I'm paying all over again, only worse. The whole damn scenario's come back to haunt me. And the paradox is, the same man who can hurt my son might be the only one who can help him."

Monty held up a deterring palm. "Back up. So you had a child with this guy. And he obviously didn't break out the champagne when you told him you were pregnant."

"Hardly. He gave me ten thousand dollars, told me to get an abortion, head to the West Coast, and go to the modeling school I'd dreamed of attending."

"So you took the money and did as he asked—except that you didn't have the abortion."

"That's where Lara came in. I met her at a coffee shop, and before I knew it, I was spilling my guts to her. She convinced me that I had options. I could have this baby, get the help and support I needed, and either raise it myself or give it to a loving family. Before I decided, I made one more attempt to convince the baby's father to accept us, either to become a family or to make us a part of his life in some capacity. He nearly burst a gut. He grabbed me by the shoulders, stared me down, and demanded to know who'd been putting ideas in my head. I fell all over myself, but I didn't tell him anything. Not that he believed me. He threatened to make me wish I was never born unless I followed through with our original agreement—including staying away from my newfound confidante *and* severing all contact with my current life once I left town."

"Sounds like a real sweetheart."

"I was scared to death. I promised to do as he asked. And I planned to. I even went to the clinic. But I couldn't go through with it. It was *my* child growing inside me. So I went back to Lara one last time. She helped me. She introduced me to Barbara, and Barbara made arrangements for me to stay in a wonderful pregnancy care center until the baby was born, after which he'd be adopted by a loving family through a reputable adoption agency. Part of me wanted to keep him. But after the miserable childhood I'd had, I wanted more for him than a destitute, psychologically screwed-up single mother who was still a kid herself. So I gave him that chance. After he was born, I stayed in New York only long enough to finalize the adoption. Then I got on a plane for L.A. and made a fresh start, knowing my baby was doing the same."

"And that was just shy of seventeen years ago. What made you come back—just the career move?"

"If you're asking if a part of me wanted to be closer to my son, I don't know. I didn't think so at the time. Carol Fenton no longer existed. Karly Fontaine had been offered a fabulous career opportunity, and took it. If there was more to it than that, it was subconscious. But once I got back to New York, yes, the memories swamped me. I started wondering, aching, feeling a sense of emptiness that made me want to reach out and know my child. I had no idea if he and his family were even still living here. I called the adoption agency to see what I could do. I also met with Barbara; that's the meeting I was racing to when that van hit Rachel Ogden. But my hands were tied. Given his age, he'd need parental consent to initiate any contact with me. And even that would be limited."

"You implied your son's in trouble." Something about this story was bugging Monty. "Is that why you wanted to hire me—to find him?"

"No. I've already done that, as of a few hours ago. Actually, he found me, or rather, his adopted parents did. He's in Maimonides Medical Center. He was rushed in with a ruptured spleen. He needs a transfusion. They called the adoption agency in the hopes of finding a biological parent. The agency called me. They knew how eager I was to connect with my son, that I would have done anything to help. But he's got a rare blood type and I'm not compatible."

Jonah. Monty's coffee mug paused halfway to his lips. Her son was Jonah.

"I've got to contact his biological father," Karly was continuing. "I'm the only one who knows who he is. But I'm terrified. The hospital said he could be cross-matched anonymously, but if word leaked out that he had a bastard son—" Her voice broke. "If he could hurt me before, he could destroy me now. Me *and* our son. He's so entrenched in the public eye, he's got the media in his face, and his future on the line. He stands to lose way too much, both personally and politically."

"Jesus," Monty bit out, his mug striking the table as the ugly reality clicked. "Your son's father is Arthur Shore."

"You got it, Detective."

Monty sank back in his chair. The ramifications, the timing, it was all flashing through his mind, one prospect after another. There was no way Arthur knew he had a kid. If he did, he'd have taken some sort of protective, probably legal action, as soon as he found out. But he did know about the pregnancy, and that was one scandal Elyse and her father might not have tolerated.

Karly had left town just a few months after Lara and Jack were killed. In light of what Monty had just learned, that timing no longer seemed coincidental.

"Did you know Lara Winter had been murdered before you left New York?" he asked.

"No." Karly shook her head. "I was in a pretty isolated environment during my stay at the pregnancy care center. I had in-house counseling and childbirth lessons, made half-assed plans for modeling school in L.A., and mostly fought depression. I'm sure everyone purposely kept the news of Lara's death from me. And I never tried to contact her—not after Arthur's threats."

"When did you find out?"

"Last week. When I read about the wrong man being convicted of the double homicide. I saw Lara's name, and I felt ill. I also saw Morgan's name, and I realized that the woman I was working with at Winshore was Lara's daughter. I don't know how I could have missed it; they look so much alike. Probably the reason I never made the connection is that I never knew Lara had a child. We didn't discuss her personal life; only mine."

"So first you found out Lara had a child. Then, when you and I met to discuss the hit-and-run, I told you that that child was raised by the Shores. No wonder you were so thrown."

"I was shocked. Once I realized what a major role Arthur played in Morgan's life, it struck me that maybe he knew I was back in town *and* that I was a Winshore client. That scared the hell out of me. Especially after you pointed out that I could just as easily have been the victim of that hit-and-run as Rachel. If I was the intended target, maybe Arthur was trying to scare me out of town. I know it sounds irrational, but I freaked out. I actually considered resigning my new position and heading back to L.A. The last thing I wanted was trouble. I had a new name, a new look, and a new life. I never thought I'd see Arthur Shore again, much less this."

Monty's forehead creased as he assessed Karly's statement. Something still didn't fit. "If your only fear was for yourself, why did you send this package"—Monty held up the Tyvek—"to Morgan? And why did you warn her not to trust anyone close to her? Obviously, you meant Arthur. Did you suddenly decide he might hurt her?"

"Frankly, I didn't decide anything. But I spoke to Morgan right after her place was vandalized. She mentioned the homicide investigations, and the fact that Arthur's political role placed them all in the public eye. I don't know why, but after the hit-and-run, the break-in just seemed to me like one coincidence too many."

Karly interlaced her fingers, which were still trembling. "I had no specifics, Detective. I never saw Arthur Shore get violent. That doesn't mean he's above doing what's necessary to protect his standing with his family and constituents. I saw the look in his eyes when he threatened me seventeen years ago—and I'll never forget it. When I heard the fear and worry in Morgan's voice, I felt like she should be warned. In the end, it could turn out my warning has no basis. But Lara did so much to protect me; I felt like I owed the same to her daughter."

Monty leaned forward. "I want you to think carefully before you answer this next question. Did you ever, in any of your conversations with Lara, mention the fact that the man you were involved with was Arthur Shore? Ever say anything that could make her suspect it was him—like the fact that your lover was an assemblyman, or that he had a wife named Elyse—anything?"

"I don't have to think. The answer is no."

"You're *that* sure?"

"Definitely." Karly reacted to Monty's dubious tone with an explanation. "I know exactly where you're going with this, Detective. I've gone there myself a hundred times this past week, racked my brain over and over since you and I talked. I'm fully aware that if Lara had realized Arthur was the man who impregnated and dumped me, she'd either have confronted him or gone straight to his wife. Now I know that not only was his wife her best friend, but the Shores were obviously Morgan's appointed guardians. Lara would never have been able to stay silent, even if it meant breaking my confidence. Nor would I have blamed her. She had a child to protect. But it doesn't matter. Because I never said a word. Arthur was a public figure. I was way too afraid to ever let his name or any reference to him slip out."

"That's a moot point. Lara knew." For the first time, Barbara interrupted. Her voice was rough with emotion, and when Monty turned toward her, he saw that she looked positively ill. "She never had to wrestle with whether or not to break your confidence. She was aware of the man's identity from the beginning."

"She told you that?" Monty demanded.

"Not his name, but that she knew him—yes." A hard swallow. "It all makes horrifying sense now."

"Go on," Monty urged.

"Lara burst in here one day the summer before she died, more upset than I'd ever seen her. She said she'd walked in on something she wished she'd never seen. Evidently, she'd dropped by the office of a man she'd known for years, and found him having sex with a girl she was fairly sure was underage. Neither of them had spotted her, and she'd ducked out before they did. She didn't know what to do. She did tell me the man was married, and that announcing what she'd seen would destroy his family, especially if it turned out that the affair was statutory rape. And then there was the girl he was involved with. Did she know he had a family? Did she know she was being used? And was she old enough, mature enough, to make those calls?"

Barbara paused to compose herself. "Lara couldn't let this one go. She followed the girl from this man's office to a coffee shop. She struck up a conversation, and found out all the sordid details Karly just filled in for us."

"You're saying our meeting wasn't an accident?" Karly asked.

"Far from it. Lara wanted to hear your take on the relationship. And when she got it, she was livid—not with you, with *him*. I tried to get her to open up to me, but she said the only person who could help her with this dilemma was Jack. So she went home and discussed it with him. The next thing I knew, she brought you here for counseling. When I managed to pull her aside, talk to her alone, I asked her what Jack had advised. She said they'd been arguing over what the right course of action was. But they agreed on one thing—that they couldn't turn their backs on the situation— for a whole host of reasons. Now I understand what those reasons were."

"Oh God," Karly breathed. "If Lara decided to go to Arthur . . . If he knew . . ."

"Then we have a possible motive," Monty finished.

"What about an alibi?" Barbara questioned. "Do we know where the congressman was the night Lara and Jack were killed?"

"Yes and no. We have some inconsistencies. We're working on clearing them up. But we have to approach this with a level head and with all the facts in our possession. Remember, we're talking about murder here. Not sex with a minor or harassment, no matter how menacing the threats. Would Arthur kill two people to protect his secret? Especially when one of those people was his wife's best friend, and when killing them would mean orphaning their ten-year-old little girl?" Monty's lips set in a grim line. "Right now, there's only one person who can answer that."

"Oh, please, no—not yet." Karly leaned forward, grabbed his arm. "If you go to Arthur with this story, you'll have to tell him where you got it."

"I'm sure Detective Montgomery will make sure you're protected," Barbara soothed.

"I don't give a damn about me. Not right now. Right now, all I care about is convincing Arthur to go through the cross-match process. I need to know if his blood is compatible with my son's. I need Detective Montgomery's help twisting his arm. As it is, Arthur is going to be livid that I went ahead with the pregnancy, and that I'm now asking for his help. If he's blindsided with our suspicions first, I can kiss any cooperation from him good-bye."

"I agree," Monty surprised her by saying. "Your son's health comes first. Besides, I'm not ready to confront Arthur with any accusations—not without concrete proof. So let's hit him with the news that he's a father, and save anything related to the homicides for later." Monty turned to Karly. "You're going to have to face him. You know that."

A tight nod. "I know."

"The good news is, you don't have to do it alone. I'll be there. In fact, I'll be there first. You'll make an entrance. Nothing beats the element of surprise. Give me a few hours to set things in motion. Then we'll spring this on him." A quick glance from one woman to the other. "I can't stress enough that not a word we've discussed leaves this room. Understood?"

"Absolutely," Barbara agreed at once.

"I certainly won't be blabbing," Karly assured him. "But do you really think we can persuade Arthur to get his ass over to the hospital and give blood?"

Normally, Monty would have explained that there were all different methods of persuasion. But in this case, it wasn't necessary.

"Karly, when you spoke to your son's adoptive parents, did they give you their names?"

"Nina and Ed Vaughn—why?"

"Because I know your son. His name's Jonah. He's a great kid. The more ironic part is that Arthur knows him, too. And he likes him."

"Are you serious?" Karly gasped.

"Serious as a heart attack."

"How? Through whom? Since when?"

"That's a long, complicated story. I'll get into it later, when I see you—which I will." A smug spark lit Monty's eyes. "Give me those few hours to organize things. Then head over to my office, say around five o'clock. The address is on my card. Not only are we going to spring this on Arthur Shore tonight, but we're going to get exactly what we want from him."

THIRTY-ONE

Monty's adrenaline was pumping when he arrived at Lane's.

Morgan answered the door when he knocked. She waited for him to identify himself, then double-checked that fact by peeking through the peephole, just to be on the safe side. Clearly convinced, she unlocked and opened the door.

"Nice precautions," Monty praised, striding in and shrugging out of his parka. "I'm proud of you."

"Thanks." Morgan eyed him speculatively and frowned. It was the first time she'd seen Monty since his run-in with the falling brick. "Lane said you were fine. But some of those facial cuts look pretty deep. Are you sure you're all right?"

"Just pissed. And even more determined to nail our perp's ass to the wall." He tossed his jacket on a chair.

"You're certainly fired up," Morgan observed. "Did Barbara provide any answers?"

"It was a very productive meeting." He paused, studied her expression, then frowned. "You look lousy. Did something happen?"

"Jonah's latest CBC wasn't great, which means he's losing blood. His vitals are holding, so there's no immediate rush for surgery, but the doctors want to do a transfusion, see how it goes. Unfortunately, the only compatible donor is Lenny, and he's not their prime choice. He's got a heart condition and he's on a blood-thinning drug."

"So *Lenny* has the same blood type as Jonah. Interesting. Well, I might have an alternative. We'll know tonight. Keep your fingers crossed."

"What's going on?" Lane stepped out of the photo lab.

"I could ask you the same thing."

"Morgan's been rummaging through her parents' memorabilia," Lane replied. "She just found the negatives from the photos taken at the Kellermans' party. Fortunately, Elyse left them in the packet of photos she had developed after the initial trauma of the murders was over. In the meantime, I've been enhancing more of the crime-scene shots. I did find one interesting thing. There's a round circular spot on the floor where something was definitely removed. It's about a foot in diameter and it's near the door. Probably a Spackle container or trash receptacle of some kind. The basement's a pit—filthy, dusty, loaded with stones and debris. Yet that one space is clean as a whistle."

"Someone got rid of the container at the murder scene." Monty was already heading in the direction of the lab. "Yeah," he confirmed, having bent over to study that section of the enhanced photo. "The killer must have tossed something in there that would have given him away, so he got rid of the whole thing."

"Monty," Morgan interrupted, hovering in the doorway. "You never answered my question. What did Barbara tell you?"

Monty cleared his throat. "For now, all I can tell you is that I know who sent you that Tyvek. It wasn't BS; it was meant to protect you—a way to reciprocate the kindness your mother showed her."

Frustration flashed across Morgan's face. "Monty, I'm your client. I'm the one you're supposed to be open with."

"I'm being as open as I can, under the circumstances. This situation is complicated. Once again, I'm going to have to ask you to trust me."

Clearly, she was fighting back tears. "Give me something. Anything."

A long pause. "Remember what you told me about your mother's final journal entries? The ones she made during the last few months of her life?"

"Of course."

"Go read them again."

Morgan waved her arm in a helpless gesture. "I don't have to. I remember every word. They pertained to only two women she was fighting to help—Olivia and Janice."

"Right. One had a happier ending than the other. If I recall, the latter one consumed all your mother's time, and journal entries, at the end."

"Janice," Morgan said.

One dark brow rose pointedly.

"Janice—J." Morgan got his message, and her eyes widened. "You're saying the woman who sent me that package is the one whose stepfather raped her? The one who got involved with some older guy and wound up pregnant and abandoned?"

"No. *You're* saying it."

"And you talked to Barbara about her." Morgan raked a hand through her hair. "Barbara knows her real name. She told me she keeps that on file with the client's original registration form. Knowing you, you found a way to get that name. Dammit, Monty, I need to know who she is. I need to find her, to talk to her. She was the last person my mother mentioned in her journal. Which means she was one of the last people to speak with her before she died. And she must have had a reason for warning me—"

"I already spoke with her," Monty interrupted. "I know her reasons. They're being addressed. Hang tough, Morgan. I know how hard this is for you. But it's going to pay off. Just bear with me. I have to follow through on a lead. I'm doing that tonight. If everything goes as planned, I think I can convince her to talk to you. Right now, she's afraid. If we push too hard, we'll lose her. Leave this in my hands."

Morgan lowered her gaze, seeking control. Then she nodded. "Okay."

Her lashes lifted. "Just tell me one thing. Did you find out anything more on Arthur? All Lane would tell me is that your meeting was civil. That's reassuring, but not informative. I need to know if Arthur was involved in any way—directly or indirectly—with why my parents were killed."

"I can't answer that."

A glimmer of stark fury glinted in her eyes, which faded into a bleak, hollow emptiness. "You just did." She turned around and walked out of the photo lab.

The instant she was out of earshot, Monty seized Lane's arm. "You've got to get some evidence off those negatives. Both sets—the crime scene and the Kellerman party. Also, find out where George Hayek was during the hours the Winters were killed. I don't give a damn how you do it. Tell your CIA pals that your father—the ball-breaking, pain-in-the-ass ex-Brooklyn-detective-turned-PI—digs in like a leech when someone gets in the way of his murder investigations. Tell them I'm not going away. I get it that they need to maintain the world's balance of power. Well, I just need to catch one killer. If Hayek knows something, or did something, I want it. And I'll find a way to get it. I can do that quietly and with their coopera-tion, or I can do it noisily on my own."

Lane's jaw tightened. "You're going balls-out. That means you've got something."

"No question. Now I need proof to back it up. So go back to the crime-scene photos. Think through the mind of Arthur Shore or George Hayek. Look for something that would tie one of them to the scene. It's got to be there. As for the party, look for something that narrows down the time frame on Arthur's disappearing act. Oh, and Lane." He met his son's gaze. "This case is about to come to a head, and then play out hard and fast. It's going to be tough on Morgan. She'll need you."

Not a heartbeat of hesitation. "She'll have me."

IT WAS 5 P.M.

Arthur's limo pulled up in front of Monty's office. The limo driver started to get out, but Arthur wasn't waiting for assistance. He threw open the door, left the vehicle, and went striding up the steps to the front door.

Monty let him in, gesturing for him to have a seat in the office's sitting area.

"Drink?" Monty inquired, having just opened a bottle of beer for himself.

"No. Answers." Clearly, Arthur was pissed. He perched at the edge of the settee, not even removing his overcoat. "I'm sick of your yanking my chain, Montgomery. First, yesterday's inquisition. Now today's cryptic summons. You said there was a break in the case. Let's hear it. My family's waiting for me."

Standing behind the club chair, Monty took a healthy swallow of beer, then propped his elbows on the chair's headrest, intentionally remaining on his feet. "I realize it's Sunday. If this weren't important, I wouldn't have asked you to drive to Queens. As for the inconvenience, I felt we should have this talk in private. That way, you can decide how you want to break the news to your wife and daughter."

That elicited an instant flash of concern in Arthur's eyes. "Is Morgan all right?"

Pensively, Monty assessed Arthur's reaction. "You really care about her, don't you?"

"What kind of question is that? Of course I care about her; she's like a daughter to me."

"I believe you." Monty found the entire situation fascinating. Regardless of the cause—be it guilt or bona fide affection—Arthur's paternal instincts toward Morgan were real. "She's fine," Monty assured him. "She's with Lane."

Some of the tension eased from Arthur's body. "They've become very close these last few weeks. I'm glad. Lane's a good guy."

"I think so." A pause. "Actually, to say Morgan's fine is an oversimplification. *Physically*, she's fine. Emotionally? Psychologically? She's hanging on by a thread."

"That's been my concern from the start. It's why I didn't want her plunging headfirst into this." Arthur frowned, looking a little less irked at having been sent for. "I apologize for jumping on you. Whatever you found out is obviously serious. It's best that I deal with it first. Does it involve that grotesque break-in at Morgan and Jill's place?"

"Huh?" Monty's brows drew together. "Oh, when I said there was a break in the case, you thought I was referring to the Winters' case. Sorry. We got our signals crossed. But now that you brought it up, I did trace Margo Adderly. Unfortunately, the poor woman died seven years ago. Cancer. So I won't be able to get her side of the story you told me."

As Monty spoke, Arthur's expression went from puzzled to annoyed to angry. "What kind of game are you playing?"

"No game. A break in the case, as I said. Just a different case. Are you sure you don't want a drink?"

"No, I don't want a drink." Arthur made a move to rise. "I'm leaving."

"You might want to hold off a minute." Monty angled his head toward the back room, which he used for storage. "Karly, come on in," he called. "We're ready for you."

Shoulders squared, head held high, Karly marched into the sitting room. She looked as she had when Monty first met her—put together, impeccably groomed, designer slacks and sweater—a class act.

Clearly, Arthur didn't recognize her. "Karly," he repeated, rising on instinct. "As in Karly Fontaine—the woman who reported the hit-and-run?"

"One and the same," Monty supplied.

"Then this *does* concern Morgan." Arthur stuck out his hand. "I'm glad you weren't hurt. It's nice to meet you."

"Oh, you've met." Monty looked amused as Karly eyed Arthur's hand as if it were a dead mouse, making no move to clasp it. "Although her hair was darker and longer then, and she couldn't afford an outfit like the one she's wearing now. So I'll refresh your memory. This is Carol Fenton. The woman you impregnated, paid off, and booted out seventeen years ago. Ring a bell?"

Arthur was working like a demon to retain his poker face. "I don't know what you're talking about."

"Sure you do. What you don't know is that Carol—Karly—opted to have the baby rather than the abortion. She had your son, put him up for adoption, and had no idea who he'd become or where he was—until now. And, before you ask, this isn't an extortion attempt. Karly doesn't want a dime. Quite frankly, she never wanted to see you again, even after her career brought her back to New York. But circumstances have changed all that."

"What circumstances?" Arthur managed, his jaw working a mile a minute.

"Remember Jonah Vaughn—you know, the great kid who's Lane's assistant and who you taught how to heli-ski the other day?"

"Of course—so?"

"I'm sure Lenny told you that Jonah's in the hospital with internal bleeding and a lacerated spleen. He's also got a rare blood type, one that's hard to find a compatible match for."

"Yes, he told me. I wish Jonah the best. Why are you telling me this?"

"Because, wouldn't you know it? It turns out Jonah is your natural son. Small world, huh? Problem is, Karly's blood is A positive—and not a match with Jonah's AB negative. So that leaves you."

"I . . ." Arthur's mouth opened and closed a few times. "I won't be blackmailed into any admissions, much less—"

"This isn't blackmail. It's a negotiation. Here are your options, as I see them. One: You can get tested anonymously. We'll arrange for a technician to come to your home, your office, wherever you want, and draw your blood. Hopefully, you'll be AB negative and the cross-matching will say it's a go. Jonah needs an immediate transfusion. His blood count's low. If you're compatible, you'll provide that transfusion, or as many transfusions as are necessary to help your son. In return, Karly will sign a confidentiality agreement, promising to keep your identity a secret."

Monty paused to take a quick swallow of beer. "Option two," he continued. "You can refuse, risk Jonah's life, and Karly will release the entire story to the press. She'll begin with your sexual involvement with a minor—which was statutory rape, by the way—and conclude with the fact that you're now willing to let your own son die. As an aside, statutory rape, given that Karly was sixteen and you were way older than twenty-one, is rape in the third degree, which is a class E felony. It would have been punishable by three or four years in prison, except that it has a five-year statute of limitations. That having been said, you might escape criminal prosecution, but I doubt Congress would want a statutory rapist around.

You'd be forced to step down, your family would suffer pain and humilia-
tion . . . I don't know, Congressman. Option one sounds pretty good to
me. Of course, the choice is yours."

"Who else knows about this?"

"Just us and Karly's counselor, who's bound by client privilege. Karly
didn't involve a lawyer yet; she's willing to let yours draw up the necessary
papers."

Arthur gave a humorless laugh. "Very gracious. Unfortunately, all this
is going to leak out anyway. Some smart-ass reporter will lie, steal, or claw
his way into the hospital database, get what he needs, pay off the right
people until he gets all the essential pieces, and before long this story will
be front-page news."

"You're probably right." Monty didn't insult Arthur by refuting his
statement. "But if you offer a blood sample of your own volition, then provide a transfusion if it's medically possible, the only things that smart-ass
reporter can dig up is the fact that years ago you committed an indiscre-
tion, had a child, and made sure he was adopted by a loving family. Karly
will back up that claim. So it will seem like you two made that decision
together. She'll also say you had no idea she was underage. That entire
backstory will be eclipsed by the fact that you'd be coming forward now to
save your child's life. Hell, you'd come off like a hero."

"Tell that to Elyse."

"Your family's another story. I'd suggest filling them in immediately, so
they're prepared. For what it's worth, I think your wife would forgive you
anything. But the way you handle her, Jill, and Morgan is up to you. So
what's the verdict?"

Bitterness glinted in Arthur's eyes. "What do you think? I'll have the
papers drawn up first thing tomorrow."

"Please, Arthur." Karly spoke up for the first time, her body taut with
suppressed anger, but her tone emanating the selfless plea of a mother. "His
anemia's getting worse. If the wound doesn't heal on its own, he'll need
surgery. Can't you reach your attorney tonight?"

"Probably not." Arthur's gaze shifted to Karly. "But I'm not a monster. I
won't jeopardize Jonah's life for a piece of paper. The legalities can wait

until morning. I'll start the cross-match process tonight." He turned back to Monty. "Give me an hour to talk to my family. Then send a medical tech over to my apartment. He can draw blood and rush it to the hospital. I can already tell you I'm AB negative. So, barring any unforeseen complications, Jonah will have his transfusion."

THIRTY-TWO

Lane was distinctly uneasy.

An hour ago, Arthur had swung by his brownstone, features drawn
and tight, and requested that Morgan come with him to his and Elyse's
apartment for a family discussion. Lane had almost blocked Morgan's path
when she left, but that wasn't his place, nor did he want to tip Arthur off
to just how suspicious of him he was. So he stood aside, watching Morgan
ride off in Arthur's limo, wondering what the hell was going on and when
she'd be back.

He tried Monty's cell phone. Voice mail. That meant he was still following that lead. Damn.

Lane left a terse message, then hung up to wait—again.

He was already itching for his other callback, the one that would
come on his secure line. He'd initiated that particular call not only because of Monty's request, but because he'd spent the day contemplating
possibilities.

It was something Lenny had said during his visit with Jonah. Something about Arthur. Innocuous in and of itself. But when combined with the rest of the puzzle, it could be a connecting piece.

"Shaken not stirred. That's what we used to call him. Like one of James Bond's martinis."

"You're a Bond fan?" Jonah had asked.

"Big-time. Arthur and me. We never missed a movie when he was a kid . . ."

That struck a chord in Lane's head; snippets of the conversation he'd eavesdropped on that day at Lenny's. Monty had questioned Arthur about Hayek. Arthur had responded by saying that Hayek had joined him and Lenny on their father-son trips to the movies.

Father-son trips to the movies. No doubt that included seeing their mutual favorite: "Bond. James Bond." And one thing all Bond enthusiasts knew was that 007's weapon of choice was the Walther PPK.

From the get-go, Monty had been puzzled by the use of a Walther PPK to kill Jack and Lara Winter. Lane could still remember his father's preoccupation over the odd choice of weapons.

Maybe not so odd after all.

"George never forgot the breaks my father gave him," Arthur had said. *"His loyalty ran deep."*

Just *how* deep was the question. Deep enough to save Arthur's ass when he got in way over his head? Especially when Arthur had saved *his* ass when he was facing gunrunning charges?

A good chance the answer was yes.

Lane had picked up the secure phone in his photo lab and punched in the usual number.

"Yeah." The standard greeting.

"Listen, we have a situation here," Lane had stated flatly. "You know what my father's like. He's all over this murder investigation. And Hayek's name is screaming in his ear." Succinctly and sans emotion, Lane repeated Monty's earlier diatribe. "As you can see, he's not going away. That can only end up making trouble for all of us. So here's a suggestion. Contact Hayek. Ask him three specific questions. Get me the answers. If they check out, my father will be satisfied, and you won't be hearing from me about this again."

Silence. Then: "Your father's a pain in the ass. No promises. Give me the questions."

"Where was Hayek on December twenty-fourth, 1989, between seven and nine P.M.? Prior to that date, did he supply someone with a Walther PPK? And did he hire someone to trash Morgan Winter's brownstone last Wednesday night and run my father off the road two nights later?"

"Hayek's not going to confess to murder. And we're not asking him to."

"I don't think it'll come to that. I think he'll have an alibi. And I think he'll remember it. If he doesn't, that'll be our problem. And if it turns out he's guilty of anything short of murder, grant him immunity. He's your contact. You need him. My father doesn't. All he needs is the information Hayek possesses. Believe me, Monty doesn't want anyone but the killer. Help us get him. You'll keep what you want, and I'll owe you one."

Another long pause. "I'll let you know."

Click.

That had been hours ago. Damn, Lane wished he had his answers.

Frustrated, he channeled his energies into something productive.

He pulled up the digitized negatives of the Kellermans' Christmas party on his monitor. Time to focus on those, give his mind a break from the crime-scene shots in the hopes that a little space would grant him new perspective.

Now that he knew Arthur had worn two different shirts during the course of the evening, he concentrated on that visual detail. It was easy to differentiate the before-and-after shots, since the images were in sequential order. In the majority of the shots in which Arthur was present, he was wearing the second shirt. That fact supported his claim that the inopportune need for a change of clothes had come early in the evening.

Turning to the first shots—the one in which Arthur was wearing shirt number one—Lane focused on those depicting the Winters and the Kellermans together. Once again, he was struck by the level of tension their body language conveyed. There was definitely something going on here, some really bad feelings between "friends."

He turned his attention to the next image—the first one Arthur appeared in after the shirt change. The photo was of Elyse and Arthur, standing alone together in front of the panorama of windows, raising their flutes of champagne in a toast. Judging from their full glasses and enthusiastic poses, Lane would guess it was the initial toast of the evening. Made sense, both sequentially and in conjunction with Arthur's story. The champagne moment was just as he'd described. New shirt. Arm around his wife's shoulders. The political guest of honor and his lovely spouse. Arthur's hand was wintry red, a clear sign that he'd just been outside. His rosy cheeks confirmed that, as did his hair, which was visibly windblown. Clearly, he'd just returned from his mystery jaunt.

From behind the happy couple, Lane spotted what appeared to be a reflection in the window—a tall, narrow, wood-toned object. Frowning in concentration, he tweaked the image.

A grandfather clock.

As expediently as possible, Lane zoomed in on the clock's reflection. He then reversed the image and adjusted the shadow, midpoint, and highlight levels, until he could clearly make out where the hands were pointing.

Eight forty-five. An hour and a half after Arthur had claimed he'd returned to the party.

For a moment, Lane sank back in his chair, absorbing the significance of what he was seeing. It wasn't unshakable proof. But it was a big step in that direction.

He wished Monty would call.

More important, he wished Morgan would call, let him know she was okay. The idea of her being with Arthur Shore—even with Jill and Elyse there—was making him increasingly uneasy.

The phone rang shrilly, making him start. But it wasn't his cell. It was his secure line.

He snatched it up. "Montgomery."

"Hayek was in Vegas on Christmas Eve 1989, sharing the holiday with a lady friend," his contact informed him. "He was there from the twentieth of December to the day after New Year's. Our surveillance records confirm it. So forget the homicides. Not only didn't he commit them, he didn't know what the hell I was talking about."

"Got it."

"He only bought one Walther PPK, and it was thirty-some-odd years ago. He bought it for his boss, to protect him from a string of local robberies. Who might or might not have borrowed that gun, he has no way of knowing. And, yeah, he did arrange for a couple of recent scares, one at the brownstone you mentioned and one on the Taconic Parkway, but only because he was pressured into doing so. Seems he was warned that his CIA asset status could be changed overnight into a liability status. Guess that's an easy threat to make when you're a congressman with friends in high places. Friends like the director of the CIA."

"Yeah." Lane heard everything that was, and wasn't, being said. "Can I use any of this?"

"Nope. Just to move that pain-in-the-ass father of yours in the right direction. Tell him he's got his answers. Time to get off our backs and go find his killer."

"I'll tell him."

"This subject's now permanently closed."

MONTY DROVE KARLY home so he could prep her on what to expect next and how to handle the press when they figured things out.

She got out of his car after they exchanged promises to keep each other apprised the second either of them heard any news. She had tears in her eyes as she thanked him. Then she gathered up her purse, climbed out, and walked into the lobby of her lovely Upper East Side apartment.

Monty eased away from the building, pulling over to the next fire hydrant and shifting the car into park. He needed some time alone to think. His mind was crammed with the day's events. Karly Fontaine's crisis might be on the verge of resolution, but the ramifications of what Monty learned today had shoved his investigation of the Winter homicides into overdrive.

Arthur Shore was a piece of work. He'd stood there in Monty's office— ninety percent politician and ten percent human being—as he watched his world teeter and struggled to right it. The ten percent was that tiny, redeemable part of Shore that cared about family, the part that had raised Morgan as his own and now wanted to save the life of a son he never knew he had. Of course, it didn't hurt that his actions would give a huge boost to his popularity. Any way you sliced it, Shore stood to win big from playing the hero.

But what about seventeen years ago? Back then, he'd have been screwed any way he turned. Nothing good could have come from Karly's pregnancy. And with a young family and a career that was just beginning to skyrocket, his entire life would have gone up in smoke if Lara and Jack had called him on the carpet.

That provided a hell of a motive to keep them quiet.

Monty rubbed the back of his neck, torn about what to do next. He was just a mile away from Lane's place. He should go there, talk to him. He knew Lane was waiting on pins and needles. How could Monty blame him? Lane had no idea what was going on. He, on the other hand, did. But he wasn't at liberty to reveal the details. Hopefully, Morgan would solve that problem for him—and soon.

So, yeah, he was stalling. Which sucked, not only for Lane but for himself. He was itching to get on with this investigation and move the process along, armed with the newly discovered info on Arthur. But he couldn't do that, not without providing Lane with an explanation he wasn't authorized to provide.

Like it or not, his hands were tied.

His cell phone rang.

So much for stalling. It was Lane.

He punched on the phone. "Hey. I got your message."

"Then why didn't you return it? And why didn't you answer in the first place?"

"I was in a meeting. I turned my phone off."

"Great. I need to speak with you."

"I know." Monty cleared his throat. "Based on what's been going on at my end, I'm not surprised about Arthur collecting Morgan for a family meeting. It's nothing to freak out about."

"Can you be a little more specific?"

"No. But I'm sure Morgan can. Have you heard from her?"

"Finally. O'Hara's bringing her over in ten minutes."

"Good."

"That's not the only reason I'm calling." It didn't take a psychic to figure out that Lane was irked by his father's cryptic response. "I made that call you asked me to, and applied some pressure. I've got your answers, plus one. I also found something in one of the party photos that contradicts Arthur's time line."

Monty's hand was already on the gearshift. "I'm on my way."

"No, you're not." Lane's words stopped him in his tracks. "I want some time alone with Morgan. She and I need to talk. I realize that's not *your* agenda, but it is mine. Life happens. You're the one who got me involved in this investigation. And now I *am* involved, far deeper than I expected. So this time we're playing it my way. I need an hour, maybe two. Then I'll call you and you can come over."

Comprehension struck, clear as glass. So did frustration. "I hear you. But I'm less than a mile away from your place and—"

"I've got a lead for you to run down that should fill the time. Call Lenny Shore. Buy him a cup of coffee. Find out where the gun he used to keep at the deli went, and how long it's been missing."

"What gun?"

"That was the 'plus one' I was referring to. Remember the individual you wanted me to check into more thoroughly?" Lane kept his reference intentionally vague.

"Right." Monty got the message, and the Hayek reference, no problem.

"Seems that about thirty years ago he gave his boss a gift. Something to keep an 007 aficionado safe. A Walther PPK."

"Holy shit." Monty sucked in his breath.

"I'll fill you in fully later, face-to-face. In the meantime, it should be interesting to find out if the gun was 'borrowed.' And, if so, why didn't Lenny report it?"

"Consider who supplied it. If the gun was hot, Lenny probably didn't want to get his employee in trouble."

"Makes sense," Lane acknowledged. "Incidently, you know we can't use this—not officially."

"I assumed not. But it'll steer us toward things we can. I'll call now. Maybe he'll still be at the deli, cleaning up."

"Good. And, in the meantime, I'll take care of things at my end." Lane paused. "Monty, don't think for a minute that I don't want the real killer as much as you do. But this isn't just about a case for me. Not anymore."

"I get it. Probably better than you think." A corner of Monty's mouth lifted. Lane was every bit his father's son. He'd been fiercely single. Now he'd be fiercely a couple. "Do your thing, daredevil. Good luck. I'll wait for your call." A chuckle. "If I finish up with Lenny before I hear from you, I'll use the time to call your mother. This news will make her day."

"I'm sure. Later, Monty."

"Yup—later. And Lane? Nice work."

MONTY ENDED THE call, rummaging through his car until he found an old take-out menu from Lenny's with the deli's phone number and operating hours on it. Sunday night—open till eight. It was a little past that now. No doubt, Lenny would still be there.

As he stared at the menu, Monty contemplated this unexpected twist. The Walther PPK had never made sense before. Suddenly it did. And if Lane was right—the scales against Arthur were about to be tipped even more.

THIRTY-THREE

Morgan's face was sheet white when she hurried up the steps to Lane's brownstone.

Having been pacing around waiting for her, Lane opened the door before she reached it. He waved to O'Hara that all was well as he let Morgan in, shutting the door behind her.

She blew by him, shock and indignation vibrating through her, then came to a halt in the living room, her back to him.

"Morgan?" Lane went over, gripped her shoulders, and turned her around to face him.

Her pained gaze searched his face. "Did you know?"

"Know what?"

"That Karly was Janice. That Arthur was her lover. That Jonah is their child."

Lane did a double take. "Jonah is Arthur's son?"

"Yes." Some of the tension abated. "You really didn't know?"

"Not a clue." Lane's mind was racing. "But now I understand why

Monty was so guarded on the phone. He must know. And he wanted me to hear it from you."

"Oh, he knows." Morgan told Lane about the meeting Monty had orchestrated at his office. "According to Arthur, Karly hired your father to make sure he fulfilled an obligation he would have fulfilled anyway if he'd known Jonah was his son."

"Sounds touching."

"Right." Morgan's fists clenched at her sides. "Do you know how much self-control it took for me to sit there and listen to Arthur paint himself as the victim in all this? Remember, I read my mother's journal entries. I know what really happened between him and Janice—*Karly*. I know how old she was, how much she wanted her child *and* its father, and how devastated she was when the man she loved blackmailed her into getting an abortion and getting out of town. The whole thing makes me sick."

Lane guided Morgan over to the sofa and gently pushed her into a sitting position. Then he poured a glass of wine and brought it over.

"Here. This'll help." He put the goblet in her hand. "What can I do?"

Morgan tipped back her head, looked up at him. "You're doing it." Tears glistened on her lashes. "I watched Elyse crumple before my eyes. It was heartbreaking. But you know what? I think she knew about Karly—just like she knew—knows—about all his women. She barely flinched during that part of his grand confession. It was only when he announced he had a son, and that Jonah was that son, that she fell apart."

"What about Jill?" Lane asked. "How did she handle it?"

"Jill's amazing. She sat very quietly while her father talked. She was fighting back tears. But her only concerns were Elyse and Jonah. Do you know she actually interrupted the discussion to call the hospital and see how Jonah was doing? It's like she already feels a bond and a responsibility to him. Clearly, she doesn't take after her father." Morgan's tone was laced with bitterness, and she paused, making a concerted effort to let it go. "Anyway, I believe she'll be relieved when the truth leaks out. Then she can really reach out, get to know her half brother. That's just Jill. She's got the biggest heart I've ever seen. And right now, it's breaking for her mother."

"I can understand that."

"Me, too." Shakily, Morgan raised her glass to her lips. "Thanks for the wine," she murmured, taking a sip. "God knows, I need it."

"You've had a rough couple of hours." Lane lowered himself to the sofa cushion beside her. Wrapping an arm around her, he tugged her head to his shoulder, threading gentle fingers through her hair.

"Rough is putting it mildly," she murmured. "I feel like I'm in the Twilight Zone. And the night's still young. I have a call in to Karly, asking her to get back to me as soon as she's up to it. And Jill's on standby, ready to let me know the results of the cross-matching the instant they have them."

"I checked in with the hospital about five minutes before you arrived," Lane reported. "Jonah's holding his own. He's not great, but he's not worse, either."

"Well, steps have been taken to remedy that. Arthur's blood sample is on its way. We should know soon." Morgan set down her glass of wine and kicked off her boots, curling up with her cheek pressed against Lane's sweater. "I feel like I'm on a roller-coaster ride that's never going to end. It's one steep drop after another."

"It only seems that way because the ride's still going. But it'll stop. You'll get off. And the world will right itself again."

"Maybe eventually. But not yet." Morgan twisted around, looked Lane straight in the eye. "Truth time. You're privy to almost everything Monty knows. I need answers. Are there any more red flags that might tie Arthur to my parents' murders?"

This was the moment Lane had been dreading. He'd known it was coming. And he hated what his answers would do to her. But he wouldn't lie. She'd been lied to enough already.

"Yes," he responded. "There are. Too many to suit me. Right now, I've got some specifics Monty doesn't, and I suspect the same is true in reverse. He's coming over here later, and we'll pool our information. But even without combining two sets of facts, there's just too much smoke for me not to believe there's fire."

Morgan's jaw set as she visibly steeled herself. "Tell me everything."

"The night your parents were killed, Arthur was gone from the Kellermans' party for a while," Lane relayed quietly. "The woman he told Monty he was with has been dead for seven years, so she can't corroborate his story. And to make matters worse, the hours he gave us for his vanishing act don't coincide with what I'm seeing in the enhanced photos."

"Which is?"

Lane explained about the reflection of the grandfather clock and the discrepancy it presented.

"So if you're right, Arthur has no alibi for the time of the murders."

"That's the gist of it."

Morgan swallowed hard. "What else?"

Here, Lane had to tread carefully, because of the restricted nature of his projects and his sources. "Over the years, I've had occasion to take on covert photographic assignments. I made a strategic phone call tonight to one of the clients affiliated with those assignments, and I got some off-the-record answers."

"Off-the-record?" Her brows arched. "What does that mean?"

"It means I have faith in my sources."

She studied him for a moment, then nodded. "Okay. What answers did your sources give you?"

"That Arthur pulled the strings when it came to orchestrating the B and E at your brownstone and the hurling of that brick at Monty's car. He called in a few favors from someone who could arrange both—and the hit-and-run, which my guess was really a swerve-and-miss that went bad."

"He was trying to scare me enough to call off the investigation."

"Exactly."

"He's always encouraging me to back off. Of course he claims it's because he's worried about my state of mind. But if you're right, it's *his* ass he's worried about." Morgan raked a hand through her hair. "Let's cut the semantics. You don't think Arthur was peripherally connected with the murders. You think he was an active participant."

"What I think is that there's one more piece of information you should have. Thirty years ago, one of Lenny's employees gave him a gun to keep at the deli for protection. It was a Walther PPK."

Morgan paled. "That's the kind of gun that killed my parents."

"Yeah."

"God." Morgan pressed the heels of her hands against her eyes. "This just keeps getting worse."

"The problem is, it's all circumstantial." Lane paused. "We still need a concrete motive. There are pieces missing. The question is, how many of those pieces can Monty supply, and how many did he learn, in confidence, from Barbara?"

Before Morgan could reply, her cell phone rang.

She grabbed it. "Hello?"

"Morgan? It's Karly." Her voice sounded faraway, and there was a hum of human voices, interspersed with louder intercom pages in the background. "I'm at the hospital. The cross-match is done; Jonah and his father's blood are perfectly compatible. Jonah will be getting a transfusion within the hour." She sounded weak with gratitude and relief, and Morgan wasn't far behind.

"Thank goodness," she breathed. "Is he okay?"

"He will be now." Karly hesitated. "I got your message. I didn't want you to think I was blowing you off. But the Vaughns have arranged for me to meet Jonah after the transfusion. And I just couldn't pass up—"

"Of course not. You need to be there. I understand." Morgan leaned forward. "Karly, we can talk later. For now, just tell me this. Did my mother know . . . everything?"

"Everything and everyone who was involved," Karly confirmed. "I had no idea of that myself until today. She knew. Your father knew. What they did about it—that I don't know. Talk to Detective Montgomery. Tell him he has my permission to share whatever he needs to with you. Hopefully, that'll be enough to get you your answers. Then, after Jonah's blood count is up, and he and I have had a chance to visit, I'll sit down with you and fill in all the details. Maybe by sharing my experiences with Lara, I can bring you a little peace, maybe even a little joy." A pause. "Your mother was a wonderful person. You should be very proud."

"I am. Thank you, Karly. And have a wonderful first talk with your son."

Morgan punched off the call and turned to Lane. "That's one step closer to a motive. My mother knew the identity of the man Karly was involved with." A weighty sigh. "The good news is, Jonah's getting his transfusion. Arthur's blood matched his. Hopefully, that's a first big step toward complete recovery. Karly also said we should ask your father whatever we want answers to. Which means Monty met with her at some point, and she filled in some blanks. So maybe we can put our heads together."

Breaking off, Morgan gave a dazed shake of her head. "I still can't believe what I'm saying. The idea of Arthur killing my parents . . . I'm torn between denial and shock. Stuck somewhere in numb."

"Let's assemble all the evidence. That'll make it easier for you to work through your feelings. And you won't have to do it alone," Lane assured her.

A nod. "That reminds me, when is Monty coming?"

"In a little while. He's talking to Lenny about the gun. Plus, I asked him to stay away for a while. You and I need a chance to talk—alone."

Morgan didn't pretend to misunderstand. "You're right. We do."

"I'm not just referring to the case."

"I know." She forced a smile, striving for some levity. "Maybe I should give you a Winshore client profile to fill out. We can find out if we're compatible."

"I don't need to compare profiles for that."

"That's the problem. You probably don't—not for the kind of relationship you're used to—"

"What makes you so sure that's the same kind of relationship I want now?"

"I'm not sure of anything—except that it takes a lot more than passion and some inexplicable pull, however powerful, to build something solid and real."

"I agree."

Morgan gave a hard swallow. "It's been less than two weeks."

"Some things happen fast. And hard. That doesn't make them any less real. Not even your boutique social agency can account for human emotion."

"You're not making this easy."

"I'm not trying to."

"Lane . . ." Morgan struggled to address the very tangible, very real obstacles in their path. "There's so much I don't know about you."

"Fair enough. My favorite color used to be blue. Now it's green. I've never seen anything as amazing as the color of your eyes. My favorite food is a fat, juicy burger, medium rare—which I think you guessed. My favorite city is New York; I appreciate it more every time I'm away. My favorite holiday is Christmas—I get to hang out with my family, and my brother-in-law's horse farm is a sprawling piece of heaven. My sisters are my soft spot; I'd kill for them. My favorite—"

"Stop." Morgan interrupted him quietly. "Those aren't the things I was talking about. I meant *you*—the total human being beneath the sexy exterior."

"Sexy's good." He gave her a crooked grin, but the look in his eyes was serious. "You have questions? Ask."

"Ask. Where do I begin? With your independence, your craving for excitement and adventure, your wanderlust?"

"Those are personality traits, not secrets."

"Personality traits that affect your outlook on life, and the way you live it."

"You're right. But there are many different outlets for excitement and adventure."

"What about independence and wanderlust?"

"Those thrive when there are reasons to leave. They fade when there are reasons to stay."

Morgan was fighting to see this through, not to cave before she did. "Fine. Let's get back to those different outlets for excitement and adventure. Bad enough you jump out of planes, relish doing photo essays that put you in warring countries or at the heart of natural disasters, and that you probably plan on climbing Mount Everest at warp speed to earn you a place in *The Guinness Book of Records*. I haven't forgotten what you said earlier. Top secret clients, strategic phone calls, photo assignments that you're clearly not at liberty to discuss. Who else do you work for besides *Time*? The FBI? CIA? Homeland Security?"

Lane was silent for a moment.

"My God, you *do* work for them." Morgan stared.

"*Did*," Lane corrected. "It was starting to lose its appeal long before you came into my life. All of it—the vagabond existence, the twenty-four/seven fieldwork, and yeah, the realization that life is short and that I'm not going to be here forever. As for the nature of the assignments, suffice it to say they're classified. That's the best answer I can provide. And *not* because I'm hiding anything from you. But because, like you, I respect my clients' confidentiality."

"Wow." Morgan exhaled sharply. "I keep discovering new facets to the life of daredevil Lane Montgomery. Is there any risk you *haven't* taken?"

"Actually—yes. A biggie." He leaned forward, framed her face between his palms. "I haven't admitted I'm in love with you. Well, I am. Head over heels, this-only-happens-in-the-movies, what-the-hell-am-I-doing in love. And given the inquisition you're subjecting me to, your own emotional baggage, and my total lack of experience with what I'm feeling, I'm floundering. Also, given how badly I want this, I'm terrified. Is that vulnerable enough for you?"

"Yes. No. I . . ." Tears glistened on her lashes. "You're not as vulnerable and terrified as I am. I'm walking out on a limb—with no net to break my fall—and I can't seem to stop myself. I'm falling anyway."

"I'll catch you." Lane's thumbs captured her tears, wiped them away. "Just tell me you love me."

"I do. Irrationally, but undeniably." She squeezed her eyes shut. "I must be insane."

"Lucky me." He lowered his head and kissed her.

"We have so much to work out," she murmured.

"And all the time in the world to do it in." He waited until he felt her physical response, her lips softening and parting under his. Then he lifted her onto his lap and deepened the kiss.

"In the long run, maybe." Morgan smiled against his mouth, even as her arms tightened around his neck. "But right now, we've got less than an hour. Monty's coming over, remember?"

"Only too well." He drew back, tipped up her chin so their gazes locked. "We'll take this to the bedroom later. But for now, just so we're both clear on where things stand, what we have is for real. It's also forever. I'm not letting you go."

"Sounds like a certainty to me," she whispered. "I thought we agreed that life is tenuous, and that security is never a guarantee."

"We just changed our minds."

LENNY UNLOCKED THE door to the deli and let Monty in. He was still wearing his apron, and he'd obviously been in the process of cleaning up.

He gestured for Monty to have a seat at the counter. Automatically, he put a cup of coffee and a slice of honey cake in front of him. Then he walked around behind the counter, facing Monty directly and motioning for him to eat.

Monty complied, studying Lenny's demeanor and wondering if it was possible the older man had an inkling that Monty had asked to meet with him armed with questions that might incriminate his son. Lenny certainly wasn't himself. He was visibly upset, his expression grim and his gestures nervous as he twisted his initial ring around and around on his finger.

"I'm worried about my boy, Monty," he began. "He told me some things tonight that really threw me for a loop. I'm guessing that's why you wanted to see me."

So *that* was the reason for Lenny's skittishness. Arthur had apparently squeezed in a quick chat with Daddy. Monty had no idea what the congressman had said, but on the off chance that he'd made some grand confession to his father, no way should it come out like this. If Lenny spilled his guts without counsel present, Arthur's lawyer would find a way to have the information thrown out, or declared as hearsay.

"Lenny, I don't know what Arthur told you, but you shouldn't be telling me about it, not without proper representation. Maybe you should call a lawyer."

Lenny blinked. "A lawyer? What would I need with a lawyer? This is personal. I'm not suing anyone. Besides, if I need a lawyer, I have Arthur. He graduated from Columbia, remember? And Yale before that."

"I remember." Monty waved his hand in a gesture of noncomprehension. "Okay, you lost me. Why is it you think I'm here?"

"Jonah." Lenny stared at the carnelian stone on his ring, traced the etched lines that formed the letter *L*. "Arthur just told me he's my grandson. He also told me you were there when he found out from that woman."

"That's true. But what happens from here is none of my business. It's certainly not why I wanted to see you." Monty opted to drink the coffee after all. "Besides, Jonah already has a great set of parents. Once his medical condition is resolved, things can go back to the way they were before."

"It's more complicated than that. The kid involved isn't just some faceless name. It's Jonah. I *know* him. He works for me. I just visited him in the hospital. I—" Lenny broke off, and there were tears in his eyes. "He's my flesh and blood."

"I'm sure this hit you hard." Monty couldn't help but empathize with the guy. "When did you speak with Arthur?"

"A few minutes ago. He'd just finished telling Elyse and the girls. There was someone at the apartment, drawing a sample of Arthur's blood. Jill was trying to calm her mother. Morgan was in bad shape, too. Arthur said she'd left for Lane's."

Mentally, Monty added on an extra half hour before showing up on Lane's doorstep. Morgan and his son had a lot to discuss.

"I'm sorry," he said aloud. "I'm sure this came as a shock to all of them. But they're strong women. They'll hold up."

"They'll have no choice. Arthur's an important man. He's a powerful congressman with a major piece of legislation on the table. Those slimeballs at the press hound him like crazy. You can be sure this news will leak. That's why he called me right away. He wanted me to hear it from him."

"I can understand that."

"I'm still in shock. I have to go home and tell Rhoda. I'm not sure how either of us will handle it. But that's our problem. We'll do whatever we have to to support our son. He's a great man, destined for great things. And now, besides the wonderful family he already has, he'll have a son in his life . . ." Lenny cleared his throat. "Anyway, I don't know why you asked to see me. But I'm glad you did. Because I have a few things to say."

"Okay, shoot."

"You and I have known each other a long time, Monty. We've shared lots of family stories, pictures, proud milestones in our kids' lives. You're a good father, and I know how much your children mean to you. Well, mine means just as much to me. So please—stop doing this to my boy."

Monty stared. Evidently, Arthur had handed his father a pile of crap that painted Arthur the hero and Monty the villain.

He'd have to tread carefully. To Rhoda and Lenny, Arthur was the sun and the moon and the stars. Monty couldn't tarnish that image—not if he wanted to keep Lenny on his side and get the information he came for.

"I respect the hell out of you, Lenny," he said. "As a man and a father. I'm not looking to cause you any grief. But, frankly, I have no clue what you're talking about. What is it you think I'm doing to Arthur?"

"Jeopardizing everything he cares about—his career, his family. Taking a stranger's word over his. Tearing him up inside. You should have heard his voice tonight. It's like he was drowning. I swear, Monty, I've never heard him in so much pain. I don't know how this Karly woman found you, what she told you, or why you got involved, but you're being way too hard on Arthur. He's taking responsibility for his son—a son he never knew he had. He's doing the right thing. He's already supplied a blood sample. He's waiting for the results. If it's medically possible, he'll give Jonah his transfusion. So back off. Whatever you're pressuring him with, stop."

So that was Arthur's game. Telling his father he'd never known about Karly's pregnancy and that she was springing the whole enchilada on him at crisis time. Telling him that Monty had joined Karly's cause, and was putting him behind the eight ball because of it.

"You know me better than that, Lenny. I'm not into social scandals. I'd never threaten Arthur's political future or his family because of an illegitimate son he just found out he has." Monty played this with supreme caution, determined not to antagonize Lenny and push him away. "I respect the fact that he's taking responsibility for Jonah. Aside from that, I'm out of the picture. If Arthur senses pressure, it's because I asked him a bunch of questions. I'm busting my ass trying to solve the Winters' homicides. Which is also why I'm here tonight. Not to talk about Jonah. To talk about George Hayek."

"George Hayek?" Clearly, that came at Lenny out of left field. "I already told you everything I know about him. Why is his name coming up again now?"

"The same reason it came up the first time. I've got outstanding leads to follow up on. I'm pounding every one of them into the ground." Monty took a bite of honey cake. "For example, did Hayek ever give you a gun?"

This time Lenny jumped. "A . . . gun?"

"Yeah, you know—a pistol, a revolver, whatever."

"Right." Lenny stopped fiddling with his ring. Grabbing a damp cloth, he began mopping the counter. "Now that you mention it, yes. It was so long ago, I'd almost forgotten. But he did give me a gun. He was trying to help. There'd been a string of robberies in the neighborhood. Rhoda was a nervous wreck, and I did a lot of bitching and moaning. George got worried. So he gave me a pistol, just in case. If you're going to ask me if it was hot, I have no idea. George just—"

"I don't care if it was hot," Monty interrupted. "I care what kind of gun it was. Do you remember?"

"Sure." Lenny's gaze was fixed on the counter he was wiping. "It was a Walther PPK. George knew I was a big Bond fan. That's why he chose it. He was a really good kid, Monty. I can't imagine him being involved in anything like murder . . ."

"Those murders happened more than twenty years after George worked for you. It's possible you didn't know him or what he was capable of anymore. By the way, what happened to the gun?"

"What?"

"The Walther. What happened to it?"

"I . . . It was stolen. I'm not sure when. The day George gave it to me, I stuck it in a drawer and forgot about it. One day I looked for it and it was gone."

"A drawer—which drawer? Was it locked? And who else knew the gun was in there?"

Monty's rapid fire was having the desired effect. Lenny was clearly unnerved, his gaze darting about as he groped for a reply.

"The drawer under the register," he said finally, gesturing in that direction. "I kept it there with the bigger money, like hundred-dollar bills.

Usually, I locked the drawer. I guess sometimes I forgot. Anyone behind the counter could have seen it."

"What about your family—Rhoda, Arthur? Did you tell them about the gun?"

"They knew about it. They weren't happy."

"I don't blame them. Guns can be dangerous. You said one day the gun went missing. What else was taken?"

"The cash that was with it."

Monty whistled. "That must have been a lot of money back then. Did you report the burglary to the cops?"

"No. I was afraid it would get George in trouble, since he's the one who got me the gun."

"So he was still working for you when the theft happened?"

"I—I guess so."

"There's an easy way to make sure. Let's ask Anya."

"What?"

"Anya. Your waitress. She's worked for you for twenty years. You just said that anyone behind the counter could have seen the gun. Well, Anya sees everything that goes on in this place. Nothing escapes her eagle eye. If there were a pistol in that drawer, she'd know. She'd also know if it disappeared. On the other hand, if the gun was taken back when Hayek worked here, that would be—let's see, thirty-eight or thirty-nine years ago—way before Anya's time. In which case, she'd know nothing about it. So let's give her a call and ask her. That'll solve the mystery, maybe even narrow down the timetable."

"I suppose. But it's late. And I really don't want to involve anyone else in this." Lenny stopped mopping the counter and planted his palms on it, leaning forward to use the counter as an anchor. "Maybe the gun wasn't taken when George was here. Maybe it disappeared later. My memory's not what it used to be. But I do remember that I never got a permit for it, and I didn't want any trouble with the cops."

"Makes sense." Monty polished off his coffee and his honey cake. "Okay then, let's leave it at that." He rose. "Good luck with Jonah. I hope things work out so you can have a real relationship with your grandson."

"Monty." Lenny stopped him as he turned to go. "Do you really think

George had something to do with the Winter murders? Do you think he came back and took the gun?"

"You mean the kid who never stole a dime from you and thought of you as a second father?" Monty shrugged. "If so, he really did a one-eighty. Either that, or he had you snowed from the start. There are people like that. And they're capable of just about anything."

Usually, I locked the drawer. I guess sometimes I forgot. Anyone behind the counter could have seen it."

"What about your family—Rhoda, Arthur? Did you tell them about the gun?"

"They knew about it. They weren't happy."

"I don't blame them. Guns can be dangerous. You said one day the gun went missing. What else was taken?"

"The cash that was with it."

Monty whistled. "That must have been a lot of money back then. Did you report the burglary to the cops?"

"No. I was afraid it would get George in trouble, since he's the one who got me the gun."

"So he was still working for you when the theft happened?"

"I—I guess so."

"There's an easy way to make sure. Let's ask Anya."

"What?"

"Anya. Your waitress. She's worked for you for twenty years. You just said that anyone behind the counter could have seen the gun. Well, Anya sees everything that goes on in this place. Nothing escapes her eagle eye. If there were a pistol in that drawer, she'd know. She'd also know if it disappeared. On the other hand, if the gun was taken back when Hayek worked here, that would be—let's see, thirty-eight or thirty-nine years ago—way before Anya's time. In which case, she'd know nothing about it. So let's give her a call and ask her. That'll solve the mystery, maybe even narrow down the timetable."

"I suppose. But it's late. And I really don't want to involve anyone else in this." Lenny stopped mopping the counter and planted his palms on it, leaning forward to use the counter as an anchor. "Maybe the gun wasn't taken when George was here. Maybe it disappeared later. My memory's not what it used to be. But I do remember that I never got a permit for it, and I didn't want any trouble with the cops."

"Makes sense." Monty polished off his coffee and his honey cake. "Okay then, let's leave it at that." He rose. "Good luck with Jonah. I hope things work out so you can have a real relationship with your grandson."

"Monty." Lenny stopped him as he turned to go. "Do you really think

George had something to do with the Winter murders? Do you think he came back and took the gun?"

"You mean the kid who never stole a dime from you and thought of you as a second father?" Monty shrugged. "If so, he really did a one-eighty. Either that, or he had you snowed from the start. There are people like that. And they're capable of just about anything."

Usually, I locked the drawer. I guess sometimes I forgot. Anyone behind the counter could have seen it."

"What about your family—Rhoda, Arthur? Did you tell them about the gun?"

"They knew about it. They weren't happy."

"I don't blame them. Guns can be dangerous. You said one day the gun went missing. What else was taken?"

"The cash that was with it."

Monty whistled. "That must have been a lot of money back then. Did you report the burglary to the cops?"

"No. I was afraid it would get George in trouble, since he's the one who got me the gun."

"So he was still working for you when the theft happened?"

"I—I guess so."

"There's an easy way to make sure. Let's ask Anya."

"What?"

"Anya. Your waitress. She's worked for you for twenty years. You just said that anyone behind the counter could have seen the gun. Well, Anya sees everything that goes on in this place. Nothing escapes her eagle eye. If there were a pistol in that drawer, she'd know. She'd also know if it disappeared. On the other hand, if the gun was taken back when Hayek worked here, that would be—let's see, thirty-eight or thirty-nine years ago—way before Anya's time. In which case, she'd know nothing about it. So let's give her a call and ask her. That'll solve the mystery, maybe even narrow down the timetable."

"I suppose. But it's late. And I really don't want to involve anyone else in this." Lenny stopped mopping the counter and planted his palms on it, leaning forward to use the counter as an anchor. "Maybe the gun wasn't taken when George was here. Maybe it disappeared later. My memory's not what it used to be. But I do remember that I never got a permit for it, and I didn't want any trouble with the cops."

"Makes sense." Monty polished off his coffee and his honey cake. "Okay then, let's leave it at that." He rose. "Good luck with Jonah. I hope things work out so you can have a real relationship with your grandson."

"Monty." Lenny stopped him as he turned to go. "Do you really think

George had something to do with the Winter murders? Do you think he came back and took the gun?"

"You mean the kid who never stole a dime from you and thought of you as a second father?" Monty shrugged. "If so, he really did a one-eighty. Either that, or he had you snowed from the start. There are people like that. And they're capable of just about anything."

THIRTY-FOUR

Monty was sitting in a bar, nursing a Michelob, when Lane called, gave him the green light to head over.

In five minutes flat, Monty had paid the tab, jumped in his car, and was flying uptown to Lane's place.

Once inside, he paused only long enough to scrutinize Morgan, who was sitting on the sofa, sipping a glass of wine. "You okay, sweetie?"

She smiled slightly at the unexpected term of affection. "I'm not sure. Ask me again when the numbness wears off."

"I will. But you'll be fine. You were a tough kid. You're a tougher woman. And we're almost there."

With that, he perched at the edge of a leather club chair, turning his attention to his son. He listened intently to what Lane had to tell him—Hayek's alibi, his being blackmailed by a congressional friend into arranging the break-in and hit-and-run scare tactics aimed at Morgan, and the brick-throwing warning aimed at Monty, plus the whole Walther PPK story, including how Lane had come up with the idea of pursuing it.

"Great detective work," Monty praised. "You're definitely my kid." His restless gaze shifted toward the photo lab. "Show me the time discrepancy you found." He followed Lane into the lab and over to the computer, peering over his shoulder as Lane pointed out the grandfather clock, the time, and Arthur's cold-reddened skin and windblown hair.

"That gives us opportunity," Monty pronounced. "The Walther PPK gives us means. As far as motive . . ." He hesitated.

"I spoke to Karly," Morgan supplied, having come in to hover in the doorway. "She told me my mother knew it was Arthur who'd impregnated her. She said I should give you permission to tell me everything."

"Good." Monty looked sober, but relieved. Quietly, he relayed everything he'd learned when he visited Healthy Healing, including Barbara's description of the quandary Lara was facing—and how she'd reacted to it.

"So both my parents were going through moral crises," Morgan murmured. "That explains the tension in the house, and their eagerness to whisk me away from the Kellermans' party ASAP, instead of giving me time to play with Jill. They probably couldn't stand the sight of Arthur. And, knowing them, they could never have lived with themselves if they'd stayed silent." Morgan's chin came up. "So you've now got your motive."

"What about the Walther PPK?" Lane asked. "Did Lenny confirm Hayek gave it to him?"

"He more than confirmed it. He started twitching when I pressed him on it. He fell all over himself, explaining and contradicting his explanations."

"So you think he knew. That it wasn't Hayek he was protecting, it was Arthur."

"I think Arthur Shore is an incredibly charming and charismatic guy who has a wife and parents who'd do anything for him—including covering up a murder. That's why Elyse conjured up that whole scenario about the telephone hang-ups and the van. She was throwing me off track. I also have a hunch she knew Karly—Carol Fenton—was back in town. Remember, she's had PIs swarming around Arthur for years. And she asked me lots of questions about Karly when we talked. I think she was worried I'd supply Arthur with enough details to figure out that his old flame was in town."

A slight gasp escaped Morgan. "You don't think Arthur knew the

THIRTY-FOUR

Monty was sitting in a bar, nursing a Michelob, when Lane called, gave him the green light to head over.

In five minutes flat, Monty had paid the tab, jumped in his car, and was flying uptown to Lane's place.

Once inside, he paused only long enough to scrutinize Morgan, who was sitting on the sofa, sipping a glass of wine. "You okay, sweetie?"

She smiled slightly at the unexpected term of affection. "I'm not sure. Ask me again when the numbness wears off."

"I will. But you'll be fine. You were a tough kid. You're a tougher woman. And we're almost there."

With that, he perched at the edge of a leather club chair, turning his attention to his son. He listened intently to what Lane had to tell him— Hayek's alibi, his being blackmailed by a congressional friend into arranging the break-in and hit-and-run scare tactics aimed at Morgan, and the brick-throwing warning aimed at Monty, plus the whole Walther PPK story, including how Lane had come up with the idea of pursuing it.

"Great detective work," Monty praised. "You're definitely my kid." His restless gaze shifted toward the photo lab. "Show me the time discrepancy you found." He followed Lane into the lab and over to the computer, peering over his shoulder as Lane pointed out the grandfather clock, the time, and Arthur's cold-reddened skin and windblown hair.

"That gives us opportunity," Monty pronounced. "The Walther PPK gives us means. As far as motive . . ." He hesitated.

"I spoke to Karly," Morgan supplied, having come in to hover in the doorway. "She told me my mother knew it was Arthur who'd impregnated her. She said I should give you permission to tell me everything."

"Good." Monty looked sober, but relieved. Quietly, he relayed everything he'd learned when he visited Healthy Healing, including Barbara's description of the quandary Lara was facing—and how she'd reacted to it.

"So both my parents were going through moral crises," Morgan murmured. "That explains the tension in the house, and their eagerness to whisk me away from the Kellermans' party ASAP, instead of giving me time to play with Jill. They probably couldn't stand the sight of Arthur. And, knowing them, they could never have lived with themselves if they'd stayed silent." Morgan's chin came up. "So you've now got your motive."

"What about the Walther PPK?" Lane asked. "Did Lenny confirm Hayek gave it to him?"

"He more than confirmed it. He started twitching when I pressed him on it. He fell all over himself, explaining and contradicting his explanations."

"So you think he knew. That it wasn't Hayek he was protecting, it was Arthur."

"I think Arthur Shore is an incredibly charming and charismatic guy who has a wife and parents who'd do anything for him—including covering up a murder. That's why Elyse conjured up that whole scenario about the telephone hang-ups and the van. She was throwing me off track. I also have a hunch she knew Karly—Carol Fenton—was back in town. Remember, she's had PIs swarming around Arthur for years. And she asked me lots of questions about Karly when we talked. I think she was worried I'd supply Arthur with enough details to figure out that his old flame was in town."

A slight gasp escaped Morgan. "You don't think Arthur knew the truth, do you? And that because of it he really targeted Karly for that hit-and-run?"

"In this case, no. Judging from the white shock on Arthur's face when I told him Karly was Carol, I don't think he had a clue she was in New York. I think it was just a sick coincidence. In my opinion, that scare tactic was aimed at you. You were early, Rachel was on time, and your two descriptions match. As for Karly, she just happened to be there. The fact that she was also a client of yours turned out to be a plus—especially after the double screwup Hayek's guy made. Not only did he mistake Rachel for you, he actually hit her. I doubt that's what Arthur had in mind."

"So where do we go from here?" Morgan asked, folding her arms across her breasts. "Do we have enough for an arrest?"

"Nope," Lane supplied for her. "It's all circumstantial. Arthur's attorney would take it apart."

"Not if there were a witness who could place Arthur at the scene of the crime," Monty said. "A witness who heard him arguing with Jack and Lara in the basement of the women's shelter that night. If we had that, he'd be toast."

Lane spun around in his computer chair. "Where the hell did you find this witness?"

"I didn't. But Arthur doesn't know that." Monty whipped out his cell phone.

"Who are you calling?" Morgan demanded.

"Karly Fontaine." A corner of Monty's mouth lifted. "Your Winshore holiday party is Tuesday night, right? At Elyse Shore's gym?"

Morgan nodded.

"Good." Monty punched in Karly's number. "I want the entire Shore family there, including Lenny and Rhoda. If Karly agrees to help us out, this is going to be one memorable occasion."

TUESDAY NIGHT TURNED out to be cold but clear.

Darkness had fallen and frost glistened on the trees when the Winshore holiday party began promptly at seven.

Elyse's gym was a glittering wonderland, filled with the decorations Jill had insisted on hand-making and hanging herself. Morgan hadn't argued. She understood that for her friend, creating this fantasy world was therapeutic. Hearing people's exclamations, seeing their excitement, brought her as much joy as it did them.

Everyone looked stunning—lots of stylish Armani suits, fashionable "little black" Nicole Miller dresses and elegant Vera Wang cocktail dresses for the women, and sophisticated Joseph Abboud and Brioni suits for the men. Laughter rang out as small groups and the occasional twosome got better acquainted, and the tinkling of the bell over the front door signaled the arrival of more and more attendees. Servers weaved their way through the room—which had been cleared of all exercise equipment—carrying trays of sumptuous hors d'oeuvres and frothy goblets of rum-spiked creamy eggnog. A string quartet was stationed in one corner, completing the holiday atmosphere with their lovely strains of seasonal music.

It was all just as Morgan and Jill had planned.

Except that Morgan felt like throwing up.

Maneuvering her way through the room in the sexy black velvet Prada cocktail dress she'd bought specifically for this occasion, she felt surreal, as if she were standing outside herself and watching herself perform. It took every ounce of strength she possessed to keep up the pretense, milling through the room, welcoming clients and guests alike, making idle chitchat, and urging everyone to enjoy the festivities.

Jill looked a little strained, too, although her natural cheeriness overcame her tension. Wearing a sky-blue vintage embroidered flapper dress that swirled in concert with her as she moved around the room, she spoke to each and every guest, made sure they were having fun.

Then again, all Jill knew was what her father had told her the other day, plus the fact that Jonah had received his transfusion and was well on his way to recovery. Jill was waiting for the news of Jonah's paternity to leak, after which she had high hopes of getting to know her half brother.

Elyse and Arthur were, as always, the consummate political couple. With enough undereye concealer, Elyse had managed to camouflage the puffiness caused by crying and lack of sleep. In a stunning ivory Valentino skirt suit, she strolled the room on Arthur's arm, meeting and greeting and operating on autopilot. Lenny and Rhoda were there as well, bursting with pride about their family's accomplishments. Their son was a rising congressional star, their granddaughter and adopted granddaughter's company was hosting this chichi event, and everyone was commenting that Rhoda's chopped liver was every bit as good as the imported pâté being served here tonight. So what could be better?

Monty hadn't arrived yet. Neither had Karly, who knew her arrival would cause a world of tension for Arthur and, unfortunately, for Elyse. So she was timing it just so, on Monty's instructions.

Pausing to pick up a glass of eggnog, Morgan perused the room, wishing Lane would arrive. He'd promised to get there as soon as possible, but he was focused on one of the crime-scene photos, and wanted to see it through first.

Privately, Morgan suspected he'd just figured it was best to study the most graphic photos when she wasn't there. Maybe he was right. The last thing she needed was more horrifying images to exacerbate her nightmares. They'd already grown to epic proportions.

But whatever he was looking at, she wished he'd hurry.

WHAT LANE WAS looking at were the same images that had been bothering him all week—the first close-ups taken of the Winters' bodies. Initially, he'd focused on the areas around each body, hoping to find minute details in the shadows. That hadn't happened. Instead, he'd noticed some flash glare in the close-ups of the blood around Jack Winter's body. At first, he'd figured the CSI tech was either inexperienced or careless. But the glare repeated in several shots. Same locations, same intensity. All the other pictures were properly exposed, despite the difficult lighting conditions. It didn't make sense.

Bugged by the discrepancy, Lane applied his PhotoFlair filter to those specific areas. Originally developed by NASA, the Photoshop plug-in was nothing sort of amazing. Interesting, he noted. Not all the bloodstains in the same pictures appeared to have the same reflective quality. Some of the stains appeared fresh, as if still wet. And they were scattered in a random pattern, not pooled tightly around the body.

Something felt wrong.

On a hunch, Lane picked up the phone and made a quick call. He'd just finished leaving a message, when Monty walked into the photo lab.

"I'm leaving," he announced, awkwardly looping his tie. "Karly should be there by now. With any luck, we'll pull this off. Are you coming?"

"Not yet. I'm waiting for a return call."

"It had better come soon. Or you'll miss all the excitement." Monty frowned as he made his third attempt to tie his tie. "Dammit. Have I mentioned how much I hate these?"

"Seven or eight times." Grinning, Lane stood up and walked over. Smoothly, he knotted his father's tie. "Too bad you weren't paying attention when Mom taught me how to do this."

"Yeah. Right." A curious glance at the monitor. "What is it you're working on so intently?"

"The first crime-scene photos. Some of the blood around Jack Winter's body looks wetter than the rest."

"I remember." Monty shrugged. "There were a couple of wet spots. But both victims bled out. The drying process happens as the blood is exposed to air. It's not unusual to see some differences."

"It's the pattern of the differences that's bugging me. The wet blood is in random splatters. And where they're located . . . it's just not sitting right with me. That's why I made that phone call. I've got an old college buddy who's now a hematologist. I want his take on this."

"Hey, if you've got a gut instinct on this, go with it," Monty said. "But don't take too long. Morgan's gonna need you. Besides . . ." A hint of a grin. "She's a knockout in that black dress—what little of it there is. It's got no back, no straps, and a neckline that's way too low to leave her alone in a roomful of horny men."

Lane shot his father a look. "I'll be there in a half hour. If anyone comes near her before then, pull out your Glock and shoot to kill."

THE PARTY WAS in full swing when Monty arrived.

He handed his overcoat to the attendant at the door, accepted a glass of eggnog and a plateful of his all-time favorite hors d'oeuvre—pigs in a blanket.

"Detective Montgomery." Jill Shore happened to be standing close by when he appeared. She looked surprised, and a little uncomfortable, at seeing him. "I didn't know you were coming."

He flashed her that magnetic smile that Lane had inherited. "Morgan invited me," he explained. "I think she took pity because, with all the overtime I've been putting in, I haven't seen my wife all week. Also, aside from the couple of meals I've had at your grandfather's deli, I haven't eaten anything that's not out of a can."

Jill's natural grace took over. "That does sound pretty bleak."

"It is. These pigs in a blanket look like a five-star gourmet feast." Sobering, Monty lowered his voice to a quiet undertone. "Please don't worry. I'm aware the walls have ears. I'll act accordingly."

Gratitude flashed across Jill's face. "Thank you. And happy holidays."

"The same to you." Monty paused, feeling like a shit for misleading her into thinking his motives here were strictly celebratory. Jill Shore was a warm, likable young woman. She didn't deserve the fallout she was about to endure. Justice or not, the whole thing sucked. "I'm sorry your family's been turned upside down," he heard himself add.

"I know you are." Jill reached out and squeezed his arm. "But I also know you're helping Morgan. She's part of my family, too. So enjoy Winshore's contribution to the season. Eat, drink, and be merry."

"No need to ask twice." Monty gave her a paternal wink, then headed off to the left. He'd spotted Morgan, who was standing in a less hectic niche, chatting with Karly. Karly's high color said she'd either just arrived or she was very nervous. Probably both.

"Ladies," he greeted. "You both look beautiful."

"Hi, Monty. You look very handsome yourself." Morgan's gaze flickered past him. "Is Lane with you?"

"He had a few loose ends to tie up. He'll be here within a half hour."

"Hello, Detective." Karly smoothed a fold of her black chiffon Chanel cocktail dress. "And thank you for the compliment. You can never get too many of those."

Actually, now that Monty was seeing Karly close-up, he had to rectify his original assessment. The heightened color was definitely from the winter chill. Rather than nervous, she looked determined, a purposeful glint in her eyes as she readied herself to right a heinous, seventeen-year-old wrong.

"How did your visit with Jonah go?" Monty asked quietly.

That elicited a spontaneous smile. "He's a terrific kid. Smart, talented, and with a great future ahead of him. Speaking of which, he talks about your son as if he walks on water. He's obviously been an amazing mentor."

"He likes Jonah—his photographic instincts, his drive, his energy. Between you and me, he thinks he's going to be a world-class photographer." Monty glanced at Morgan, who was definitely pale and on edge. "Hey," he said, calling for her attention. "I'm supposed to find out if any of the guys have hit on you. I have orders from Lane to shoot first and ask questions later."

Morgan's lips quirked. "You always know how to make me smile."

"I wasn't kidding. Lane's become very possessive these days." Without changing expressions or altering his demeanor, Monty asked, "Where's Arthur? Has he spotted me yet?"

"He and Elyse are diagonally to your right and halfway across the room," Morgan supplied, all humor having vanished. "And I don't think so. There's a small cluster of guests blocking his view."

"How many guests?"

Morgan counted. "Five."

"Can you go over there and join them, shift the group over a little so he'll have an unimpeded view?"

"I can try."

"Good. Do it." Monty's gaze shifted back to Karly. "Do you have a clear view of him?"

"Yes," she supplied, after a quick check.

"Don't look directly at him. Just keep him in your peripheral vision. Keep making idle chatter until Morgan's done her job. Once Arthur sees us, glance around, like you want to talk to me in private. Then pull me aside—but not out of his line of sight. Act like you have something vital to discuss, like we're having a heated conversation. It shouldn't take long—maybe five or ten minutes. Take your cues from me. Once our conversation's over, go mingle. Enjoy yourself, but keep up a certain level of tension, in case any of the Shores are watching you. Remember, they all know who you are now, and the part you played in Arthur's life. The rest is up to me. Any questions?"

"I don't think so." Karly drew a slow, calming breath. "I'm good to go."

"Morgan?" Monty arched a quizzical brow. "Ready?"

"Ready as I'll ever be."

Her pallor had intensified, and there was a pained moment-of-truth awareness in her wide green eyes. It wasn't hard to figure out she was holding on by a thread—and that at any moment that thread could unravel.

Monty frowned. "We can do this without you."

"No." She gave a hard shake of her head, visualizing her mother and father, and finding the necessary strength to secure the justice they deserved and, by doing so, the closure she needed. "I'm on my way."

LANE PRESSED ON while waiting for the callback from his hematologist friend.

Four of the bloodstains on the concrete floor were wetter than the others, all in proximity of Jack Winter's body. Interestingly, there was also one other bloodstain, with the same glistening consistency, on Jack's face.

Lane zoomed in. The cement chips and stones had done a number on Jack's face, as had the fight that preceded it. The cuts and gouges were on the right side of his face, which suggested that was where he'd landed when he hit the floor. The contusion from the gun was on the left side of his head.

The odd part was that there was a wet blood splotch on the left side of his face, directly below the cheekbone. So he must have gotten that during the fight. But why would that have dried more slowly than the gashes sustained afterward, during the point of impact with the floor? If the perp had knocked him down, then grabbed for the gun, he wouldn't have waited to slug Jack again. He'd simply have shot him before he could regain his strength and strike back. The execution-style position confirmed that.

So why the differing blood consistency?

Lane zoomed in closer, focusing on that spot on Jack's left cheek. In addition to the odd splotch, there were several bruises in the area, plus a rivulet of dried blood from his nose—all signs of a fistfight. When Lane applied his PhotoFlair filter, several blood splatters and a previously un-noticed mark came to the forefront. The mark itself wasn't jagged. Actu-ally, it looked etched—two straight, distinct perpendicular lines—a longer vertical line and a short horizontal line at the base that jutted left. Lane found himself wondering what could have caused that particular shape—a knife? A razor blade? It had to be something specific.

His gaze returned to the shiny splotches of blood, which were just below the gash. Something was odd. Upon point-blank inspection, Lane could see that it was, in fact, a series of four small splotches, all in a row, forming a distinct pattern despite their random appearance. Four irregularly shaped ovals, roughly one inch apart.

Fingerprints.

No. Knuckle prints.

THIRTY-FIVE

Monty stopped the server who was passing by, and helped himself to two baby lamb chops with mint jelly to go along with the three mini-quiches and four more pigs in a blanket he already had on his plate. He was just being practical. The food was great, he was starved, and he needed his energy for the tête-à-tête he was about to have.

Plus, he was having too much fun watching Arthur Shore squirm to rush things.

Ever since the congressman had seen Karly pretending to spill her guts to Monty—her body taut with anxiety, Monty's features focused and grim as he fired terse, intentionally drowned-out questions at her—he'd been in freak-out mode. He obviously knew some damning information had been exchanged. Monty had made sure to drive home the fact that Arthur was the subject of that damning information by instructing Karly to edge a few quick, furtive glances in his direction while she spoke.

Now it was a waiting game, one Monty was taking full advantage of.

The longer he waited, the testier Arthur was getting. And it was a lot more fun being the hawk than the prey.

In the end, it was Monty's eye contact with Morgan that made him act. She was standing off by herself, looking on the verge of collapse, and pretending to be overseeing the servers.

Monty strolled over, leaned past her to set down his empty plate, and muttered, "It's time. I'll use one of the yoga rooms in back, so it stays private. You hang tough. Lane should be here any minute."

"I'll try." Her hands were trembling, and she kept glancing over at Jill. "In some ways, this is even a bigger nightmare than the original one. A faceless killer is easier to live with than a man you thought of as a second father. As for Jill—I don't know how she's going to get through this. Elyse, either. I realize she's been covering up for him, but infidelity's one thing. Murder is another. I'm sure she's in denial. I pity her. And Jill . . ." Morgan's voice trailed off.

"They're not alone," Monty replied flatly. "You were. They have each other and you. You had no one. They're adults. You were a child. What you lived through was hell. Death is permanent. Prison's not."

"You're right. It isn't." Morgan reached over for two icy bottles of water. She handed one to Monty, and uncapped one for herself. "Thanks for the verbal slap in the face. Good luck."

LANE WAS STARING at the blood splotches on his monitor when the phone rang.

The caller ID said *private*. Lane grabbed it on the first ring. "Hello?"

"Lane? It's Stu McGregor." In the background were the distinct medical center sounds and intercom pages of a hospital. "My service said you needed some urgent information."

"Stu, thanks for getting back to me so fast. I'm fighting the clock on a criminal investigation, and I'm stumped on a blood issue. It truly is time critical, or I wouldn't be jumping on you like this."

A chuckle. "I should have known you'd be up to your ass in intrigue. Okay, tell me what you've got."

As thoroughly and comprehensively as he could, Lane explained what he was seeing in the photos on his monitor. "What it doesn't explain—at least not to me—is the glossy consistency of the blood. It dried under the same set of environmental circumstances. So what could cause some blood to dry more slowly?"

A pensive silence. "Okay, this is just speculation on my part, since I obviously have no firsthand knowledge of either person involved or his medical history. But what if you're looking at bloodstains from two different sources—the victim and the killer? Following that logic, I'd say one of them is on some kind of anticoagulant. Those are taken under certain medical conditions in order to reduce the risk of blood clotting."

"So they thin the blood, like aspirin does."

"Differently. Aspirin thins the blood and keeps it flowing properly through the arteries. Warfarin, the anticoagulant I was referring to, reduces clotting in lower-pressure areas, like the legs, where the blood is stagnant. I don't think aspirin alone would explain the liquidlike appearance you're talking about. For that kind of sticky consistency to be present, I'd suspect the patient was on warfarin. That's prescribed when a patient has either an artificial heart valve, deep vein thrombosis, atrial fibrillation, or in some cases after heart attacks or strokes—"

"Wait," Lane interrupted. Everything inside him ran cold as Stu's words struck home.

I've got this thing with my heart. Lenny's words, spoken in Jonah's hospital room. *Atrial fibrillation—a big name for a not-so-big problem. I'm on medicine . . . it thins my blood, keeps it from coagulating.*

"Did you say atrial fibrillation?" Lane asked.

"Yes. In layman's terms, that's an irregular heartbeat. In chronic cases, the blood doesn't flow quickly enough from the heart, making it more likely that clots will form. If that happens, and a clot is pumped from the atria to other parts of the body—kidneys, intestines—major problems can occur. And in the worst-case scenario, if the clot is pumped to an artery leading to the brain, it can cause a stroke."

"And you said the drug prescribed is warfarin?" That didn't ring a bell. It wasn't the name Lenny had used. And before he jumped to an unthinkable conclusion, he had to be sure. "Is that the only anticoagulant of its type on the market? Or is it known by any other name?"

"The most common brand name is Coumadin."

Coumadin. That was the drug Lenny had mentioned.

Lane was beginning to feel sicker by the minute. "How long has Coumadin been on the market?"

"Let's see—President Eisenhower was given Coumadin after his heart attack in 1956. It's been prescribed on a regular basis ever since. Does that answer your question?"

"Unfortunately, yes. Is Coumadin prescribed long-term? Could it be taken, say, for seventeen years?"

"Sometimes for life. One important caveat—patients taking Coumadin *must* get their blood levels checked, at least monthly. The therapeutic window—the difference between the dose necessary to adequately slow the anticoagulant process and the dose that would cause spontaneous bleeding—is very narrow. So the dose must be carefully monitored and adjusted."

That triggered another memory. Lenny. At the deli last week. Nicking himself while slicing a sour pickle and bleeding way too much for a simple cut. And Arthur, nudging him to have his blood tested, explaining to Lane and Monty that his father was on blood-thinning medication and was supposed to get his levels checked every month, doctor's orders.

Shit.

"Lane?" Stu prompted. "Are you still there?"

"Sorry. Yes, I'm here. Thanks for getting back to me so quickly, and for being so precise with your answers."

"They clearly weren't the answers you wanted."

"No. But they had to be gotten. I appreciate it, Stu. Oh, and happy holidays."

Lane hung up and just sat there, still struggling to process the implications of what he'd just learned.

The wet blood on the floor. The shiny bloodstained knuckle prints on Jack's face. Both Lenny's.

Lenny. Warmhearted, jovial Lenny. The guy who welcomed everyone into his deli. The guy who'd do anything for anyone.

The guy who'd do even more than that to protect his son.

Shoving back the chair, Lane rose. He had to get over to Elyse's gym, to be there when Monty was putting the screws into Arthur. Because there were pieces of this puzzle that only he could supply.

He was about to flip off his monitor, when the zoomed photo of Jack's cheek caught his eye, the vertical and horizontal lines, so exactingly perpendicular, etched into Jack's skin like the mark of Zorro.

And suddenly it made sense. It *was* a mark, however unintentional, just like Zorro's. An initial. In reverse form, because it had been carved into Jack's face by a punch. But when viewed as a mirror image—it was the letter *L*.

THE YOGA ROOM was dark, removed from the main section of the gym. Which made it perfect for what Monty had in mind.

He led Arthur Shore down the hall, opening the door and assessing the congressman's demeanor as he blew by Monty and into the room. Stance rigid, anger emanating from every pore, Arthur was the essence of a man about to be wrongfully accused.

He stopped in the center of the room, waiting as Monty flipped on the lights. With the room illuminated, Monty could see that Arthur's eyes were ablaze, his body language confrontational. But beneath that great show of bravado, Monty could sense the fear, the worry. Congressman Shore was sweating it—and nobody deserved it more.

With visible irritation, Arthur glanced around. The yoga room was furnished with nothing but a mauve rug, soothing landscape paintings, lavender candles, and a dozen purple yoga mats.

"Grab a Lifecycle," Monty urged, shutting the door behind them and pointing to one of the bikes that had been lined up against the wall in here to clear the gym for the party. "From what I hear, the seats are pretty comfortable."

"I'll stand." Arthur folded his arms across his chest. "Fine. Once again, you've dragged me off for some clandestine talk. What's this one about— Jonah?"

"Nope." Monty remained standing as well, although he perched his bottle of water on a Lifecycle seat and leaned his elbows on the handlebars. "This one makes your statutory rape seem minor in comparison. That's why

I picked this room, stark though it is, to talk. I wanted maximum privacy—not out of respect for you, but out of respect for your family."

"Ah. Another ugly insinuation session."

"No insinuations. Truths. Facts about the Winter double homicide. But you already knew that. It's the reason you excused yourself and came with me. It's also why you're scared shitless. Well, you should be. I'd bet my entire pension on it. In fact, I'd donate it to your next campaign. And since there's a snowball's chance in hell I'd do that, you should realize how sure I am that I'm right."

Monty's jaw tightened, and he leaned forward, his hands gripping the Lifecycle. "While you've been sending me on wild-goose chases, I've been accumulating facts. For example, your ongoing friendship with George Hayek. You really had the poor guy going; he believed the crap you gave him about scaring Morgan off for her own good. You even threatened to use your influence in high places to alter his government status, just to ensure his cooperation. You got it, too. Maybe a little bit too much. You didn't plan on Rachel Ogden being hit by that van, did you? In fact, you didn't plan on Rachel Ogden at all. You wanted to scare Morgan. When that didn't do the trick, you had Hayek send some punk over to trash the brownstone and leave that frightening display on Morgan's bed. Incidentally, smart move getting both girls out of the house that night. Ordering me to put extra security on them, then having them stay at your place while the dirty deed was done. Nice plan. The final touch was good, too. Having Hayek send a few thugs to smash my windshield and run me off the Taconic. It didn't faze me—other than the damage they did to my car—but it did upset Morgan."

A red flush was creeping up Arthur's neck. "You're crazy." He groped inside his jacket pocket, reaching for his cell phone. "I'm calling my lawyer."

"Don't waste your time." Monty waved away the idea. "Wait until it matters. This isn't an official interrogation. I'm a PI now, remember? Not a cop. Miranda rights don't mean squat to me. This is personal. When I turn that evidence over to the D.A.—the one who's itching to convict Jack Winter's *real* killer—*then* call your lawyer. You'll need him."

Arthur's hand slid back to his side. "What evidence?"

"Ah, I've captured your interest. Let's see. How about a grandfather clock that contradicts the time you said you were missing from the Keller-man party by an hour and a half? How about the fact that you were actu-ally MIA during the precise time Jack and Lara Winter were being killed? Oh, and by the way, you know that alibi you gave me? You should have been a little more thorough in your research. Nice job finding someone who fit the profile of an Arthur's Angel and who's now conveniently dead. Unfortunately, you didn't dig deep enough. Margo Adderly had a family. I located her sister. She's lived in Manhattan for twenty-five years. Every Christmas Eve, she and Margo got together at her place, including the Christmas Eve in question. So Margo might be dead, but her sister just shot your alibi to hell."

A muscle was pulsing at Arthur's temple.

"No response?" Monty inquired. "That's okay, I've got enough to say for both of us."

He paused to take a quick swig of water. "Let's get back to George Hayek. Fascinating that years ago he gave your dad a Walther PPK—one that was cooperative enough to vanish sometime after the murders. Fair warning, by the way. Lenny was a wreck when I questioned him. I have no doubt he'll crack on the stand and blurt out whatever he knows. I'll have to remember to stress that to the D.A. As for Elyse—too bad she can't be called to testify against her husband. She'd crack, too. You know, the whole BS story about telephone hang-ups, being followed, seeing that van? She'd throw herself in front of a speeding train for you. That's why she accepted the whole Carol Fenton fiasco, right up through the pregnancy. Of course, like you, she didn't know about Jonah. She thought Carol had the abor-tion. She also didn't expect you to kill to protect your secret."

Exhaling sharply, Monty gave a sympathetic shake of his head. "That must have been the toughest part for her to live with. Her best friend from college. Murdered by you. Talk about guilt. I can't imagine the demons your wife's had to fight all these years. Tell me, did raising Lara and Jack's daugh-ter help? Did it make you feel like you were off the hook just a little?"

"Shut up," Arthur snapped. "Elyse and I love Morgan. We raised her as our own."

"I rest my case."

"You don't *have* a case." Arthur's eyes were blazing. "You have a pile of circumstantial crap. Who I *wasn't* with, where I *wasn't*, doesn't matter. You need to prove where I *was*."

"I can do that, too." Monty jerked his thumb toward the gym. "What would you say if I told you I just found out that one of the guests Lara invited to that fateful Christmas party showed up early? What if I said that when she arrived, that guest heard Lara and Jack arguing downstairs with a man whose voice she recognized intimately—yours?"

Beads of perspiration were beginning to dot Arthur's forehead. "You're lying. If that were the case, she'd have come forward sooner."

"If she'd known what had happened, she would have. But she didn't. She was sequestered away, having her baby, then hopping on a plane and getting the hell out of New York, cutting all ties with her old life—on your orders. She's been in L.A. all this time, with no idea the Winters had been murdered and there was a killer at large. She was transferred back here several months ago. And she first heard about the murders and the wrongful conviction when the news broke. She read that Lara had a daughter named Morgan, put two and two together, and after the hit-and-run, came to me with what she knew. That gives us motive, means, and opportunity." Monty's lips thinned into a cold, grim line. "Game, set, match."

LANE BURST INTO the gym, not even bothering to remove his coat, just blowing by the attendant and into the room. He and Morgan spotted each other simultaneously, and he covered the distance between them in long strides, gripping her shoulders tightly.

"Where are Monty and Arthur?"

"In the yoga room." She pointed, her eyes wide and questioning. "Having it out. They've been in there for almost half an hour."

Scrutinizing the room, Lane found the man he was looking for.

"Morgan, I want you to think," he said. "Who provided the food for your mother's Christmas party at the shelter that night?"

"I don't have to think. Lenny did. Or at least he would have if—" Her breath caught as Lane grabbed her hand, pulled her through the room. "What's happened? What's going on?"

"You'll see." He stopped in front of Lenny and Rhoda, who were chuckling with a couple of guests. "Lenny, can I see you for a minute? It's important."

Lenny's brows rose in surprise. "Of course." A hint of apprehension. "It isn't . . . Nothing happened to . . ."

"Jonah's fine," Lane answered quietly. "Almost ready to go home. Now, please, come with me." He glanced at Rhoda and the others, forcing a natural and apologetic smile. "Excuse us. I have to borrow Lenny for a few minutes."

"Take him," Rhoda said with an affectionate grin. "It'll give me a chance to talk for a while."

Lane clapped a hand on Lenny's shoulder, guided him toward the yoga room, his other hand still tightly clasping Morgan's.

"What's this about?" Lenny looked totally confused, and a little wary. "Where are we going?"

"To join Monty and Arthur. They're talking."

They reached the door. Lane twisted the knob and pushed the door open. Both Arthur and Monty whipped around to stare at them.

Lane prodded Lenny in. After that, he paused in the doorway for a heart-beat of a second, turning his back to the room and speaking softly to Morgan. "I'm sorry, sweetheart," he murmured. "You have no idea how sorry."

Before she could reply, he led her inside and shut the door with a firm click.

"Lane," Monty began. "We're right in the middle of—"

"I know what you're in the middle of. I'm just here for the ending." He glared at Arthur, stared him down. "Let me guess. You denied everything. Even in light of all the evidence Monty presented."

"You're damned right I denied it," Arthur responded, pain and anger flashing across his face as he saw Morgan. "You brought Morgan here? You filled her head with this garbage? How could you subject her to—"

"Cut the crap, Arthur," Lane interrupted. "You're in way too deep to play the loving surrogate father. So, for my own edification—and Morgan's—were the murders planned? Or did they just happen? Were you an accomplice? Or just the cleanup committee? Which one of you brought the gun—you or your father?"

Arthur's mouth opened, then snapped shut.

"His father?" Morgan asked weakly.

Lane glared at Arthur with utter disgust. "Does it give you some sick sense of power to know your father is so blind to who you really are that he'd kill to protect you? That two amazing human beings were murdered because you knocked up an underage teenager and wouldn't face the consequences? That Lenny refused to *let* you face the consequences or even to listen to Lara and Jack?"

Everyone was staring at this point, even Monty.

Squeezing his eyes shut, Lenny made a tortured sound deep in his throat. "Lane, please. Don't do this. Not in front of Morgan. I can't bear for her to hear it. She was a child . . . a little girl . . ."

"Dad, be quiet," Arthur commanded. "They've got nothing. They're fishing."

"I wish I was." Lane fought the urge to punch Arthur's lights out. "I have proof, Arthur. Physical evidence." He pulled out the prints, one by one, then knelt down and slapped them onto the yoga mats. "The imprint of Lenny's gold initial ring on Jack Winter's face. His blood on the floor from the fistfight, and his bloody knuckle prints on Jack's face. See the wet, sticky consistency? That's because Lenny's blood is slow to coagulate because of the Coumadin he takes for his atrial fibrillation. Today's DNA testing is balls-on accurate. It'll prove the blood is Lenny's. Then there's this clean, round space where an empty bucket of Spackle was removed—right here." Lane pointed. "That's where Arthur threw his bloody shirt after he mopped up Lenny's face and hands, wiped his prints off everything, and made it look like the Winters had been killed during a random burglary."

Lane heard Morgan's gasp, felt her violent trembling as she hovered beside him. But he couldn't quit, not yet. Not until he had both confessions he'd come for.

He shot a quick look at Monty. "Another bit of evidence for you. I gave Anya a call on my way over here. Like us, she knows how conscientious Lenny is. His deli's always open, even on Christmas day. Well, she distinctly remembers just two days he called in sick during her entire twenty years at the deli. Guess when those days were? Christmas day and the day after, 1989. She remembers because it was right after his son's friends were killed. But he didn't look good when he came back—his face had cuts and bruises on it. He said he fell. I say he was beaten up in a fight with Jack Winter, who was defending his wife's life and his own."

By this time Lenny was openly weeping, his hands covering his face as if he couldn't bear the shame or the sorrow. "It shouldn't . . . I never meant . . ."

"Dad!" Arthur barked out again.

Lane turned back to Arthur, shook his head in utter disbelief. "You don't even feel remorse, do you? You certainly didn't then. You just plucked the valuables off Jack and Lara's bodies, chucked the Walther PPK in the Fountain Avenue dump, and went back to a goddamned Christmas party being held in your honor. Like nothing ever happened. You didn't miss a beat."

"He did," Lenny chimed in, defending his son to the last. "You should have seen him when it happened. The whole time he cleaned up, tried to cover for me, he cried like a baby. Then, when the cops were called, he was the first one at the scene. Dear God, Lane, neither of us knew Morgan was upstairs. We never imagined she'd be the one who'd find them. And when we realized she had, when Arthur saw what it had done to her, it tore his insides out. Mine, too. From that moment on, she became a Shore. She still is. In our hearts, she's Arthur's daughter and my granddaughter. We swore nothing would ever hurt her again. And we kept our promise. All these years, we've tried to make up for what happened—even though we knew nothing really could. But Elyse is a wonderful mother. And Jill is a sister in all ways but blood. We all cared for her, sheltered her, loved her, and—"

"*Shut up! Just shut up!*" The words exploded from Morgan's mouth, from her heart and her soul, as she stared at this man—these two men— she didn't know and couldn't stomach.

"Morgan . . ." Lenny reached out to her. "Please try to—"

"No." She jerked away as if he were a loathsome monster. "No more excuses." Her voice sounded rough, unsteady, nothing like her own. "No more words of affection. No more pleas. No more remorse. The truth. Lenny, how much of this was you? How much was Arthur? Who's lied to me more? Dammit, I want the truth. Tell me what happened that night. You owe me that much."

"Morgan." This time it was Lane who interceded, taking her cold hands between his. "Are you sure you want to—"

"Yes. I'm sure."

"Let her be, Lane," Monty said. "She needs closure."

Lane nodded, but didn't release her hands, determined to show her she wasn't alone.

"I'm calling our lawyer," Arthur announced, whipping out his cell.

"Call whoever you want," Lenny replied bleakly. "I'm telling Morgan what she wants to know. It's over, Arthur. And you know what? I'm glad. I can't take it anymore—not even for you."

Ignoring his son's protests, he turned to Morgan, making no further move to touch her. "I never planned to hurt them. I went to deliver the food. The gun was just for protection. It was Christmas Eve, it was nighttime, and it was a lousy section of Brooklyn. I went in through the basement door. Arthur and your parents were down there, arguing. Your mother was accusing Arthur of being a coward and of cheating on Elyse with a teenage girl. She told him she'd seen him with her own two eyes, and that she couldn't stay silent, knowing everything she knew. Arthur told her to butt out, to stop trying to heal the world, and to keep her mouth shut or he'd sue her for slander."

Remembering, Lenny gave a hard shudder. "That set your father off like a firecracker. He called Arthur a sick bastard and a rapist, and said he'd make sure he was prosecuted and put away for statutory rape. He said that when he was through, Arthur's marriage would be destroyed, and his career would be over."

Lenny wiped a palm across his face. "I couldn't believe he was saying those things—not about my boy. I couldn't keep quiet. I yelled at him to shut up, to leave my son and his family alone. Arthur denied everything—again and again—but they wouldn't believe him. Lara kept calling him a liar and a cheat, and Jack kept threatening him with criminal prosecution.

"Then, out of nowhere, Jack announced that they were changing their wills so Arthur could never raise Morgan. He said their feelings for Elyse no longer outweighed the fact that Arthur was barely one step better than a pedophile. Arthur went crazy. He started throwing things, swearing he was innocent, that they were just out to ruin him. That tore out my heart. I didn't know what to do. So I pulled out the gun and started waving it around. I'm not sure what I hoped to accomplish—maybe to scare Jack enough to take back his lies and his plans to ruin Arthur. Lara must have thought I meant to use the pistol, because the next thing I knew, she was swinging a two-by-four at me. I never meant to shoot her. I'm not even sure if I fired the damned thing or if it just went off—I didn't even know how to use it. But what difference does any of that make? One minute Lara was swinging the board at me, the next, she was lying on the floor . . . and there was blood everywhere . . ."

Lenny had to pause to control his sobs. "Jack lunged at me like a wild animal. We fought. I whacked him on the side of the head with the gun. The gun went flying off somewhere. But Jack and I kept fighting. I punched him hard in the face. At some point, we tripped over a bucket, and went down. Jack fell on his face. All I could think was that I had to stop him, to keep him from hurting Arthur. But I was a lot older than he was, and I was getting tired. I just knelt there, trying to breathe, trying to get past the shock of what I'd done."

"What about Arthur?" Monty asked. "Where was he through all this?"

"First he rushed over to Lara. He checked her pulse to see if maybe she was still alive. But it was too late. She was gone. He looked lost for a minute, like a kid who didn't know what to do. Then—" Lenny broke off, clearly aware that whatever he said next could do nothing but incriminate Arthur.

"Then he realized that the only way to save his ass—and yours—was to finish what you'd started," Monty deduced. "So he found the gun on the floor. He picked it up and crossed over to where Jack was lying, facedown and dazed. He had to move fast, before Jack came around and reacted. So he convinced you that the only way he could protect you from the crime you'd just committed and to silence Jack's lies was to kill Jack, too. You were so out of it by then, you didn't even know which end was up. But Arthur did. He knew exactly what he was doing when he aimed that gun and fired two shots into the back of Jack Winter's head. After that, the rest was pretty much as Lane described. Except that your son had two sets of fingerprints to wipe off that gun, not one."

"God help me . . ." Lenny bowed his head.

"*You shot my father in cold blood?*" Morgan wrenched her hands out of

Lane's. Trembling with rage, she slapped Arthur across the face with every ounce of strength she possessed.

His head snapped sideways from the impact, and when he turned back, there were angry marks where her fingers had been. "Morgan . . ."

"Don't say my name. Don't even speak to me. Not now. Not ever. Lenny is pathetic. But you . . . you're an animal. A cowardly, hypocritical, inhuman . . ." She sucked in her breath, still staring him down. "Who else knows?" she asked in that same odd, stony voice. "Does Elyse?"

"I have no answer for that," Arthur replied tonelessly.

"You have no answers for anything," Monty noted. "Just sick lies and an even sicker sense of retribution."

"That's not what I meant." Arthur's jaw was working. "What I meant was, Elyse and I never discussed it. It was better that way. Did she figure it out? I'm sure she suspected something. One thing's for sure—she's never been the same since that night."

"And Rhoda?"

"My mother knows nothing. Neither does Jill. They wouldn't have been able to live with it."

"Jill," Morgan repeated, a tremor in her voice. "This is going to break her heart."

"It'll mend," Monty assured her gently. "Jill's strong. And you're stronger. Plus, she's not alone. And this time, neither are you." He watched as Lane came up behind Morgan, planting his hands firmly on her shoulders and easing her back against him. No words were necessary.

Satisfied, Monty whipped out his cell phone. "I'm calling the cops. Oh, and Arthur?" He shot the congressman a look. "Now would be a good time to call your lawyer."

EPILOGUE

Six months later . . .

Morgan stared out the passenger window of Lane's car, watching the sun reflect off the East River as they crossed the Williamsburg Bridge and headed into Brooklyn.

It was hard to believe that half a year had passed since her foundation had been ripped out from under her, and her world had been turned upside down—again.

She glanced down at her engagement ring—a square-cut diamond, simple, classy, and elegant. Lane had slid it on her finger on the first day of spring. The perfect time for new beginnings, he'd said.

They hadn't set a wedding date. Not yet. She wasn't quite ready. Not when there was so much still unresolved, both emotionally and legally.

The charges against Arthur had yet to be filed. Monty was pushing for second-degree murder, but he had his work cut out for him.

The team of defense attorneys Arthur had hired was the best. Following their advice, he'd stayed totally silent while his attorneys' motions were flying. Motions to dismiss. Motions to change venue. Motions to you-name-it—they were all flooding the court. Indicting him on anything more than covering up a crime was going to be tough, since all the physical evidence implicated Lenny, who was being charged with second-degree manslaughter. Between his age, his standing in the community, and his plea of self-defense, Arthur's attorneys were confident they could keep Lenny's sentence to a minimum, with no jail time. The story they were going with was that Lara had been killed by a bullet accidentally fired when Jack brutally assaulted Lenny, after which Lenny had shot Jack out of fear for his own life.

Part truth. Part lies. Altogether believable.

It didn't matter what Arthur said. Morgan knew the truth. So did the rest of the family. And they each fought to cope in their own way. But Lenny was a broken man. It was Rhoda who held him together. She kept the deli open and running—for his sake, for her own sake, and for their customers' sakes. It kept her hands busy, her mind occupied, and her customers happy. Besides, Jonah was working longer hours now that summer vacation was here, and it did Rhoda a world of good to spend time with her grandson.

Jonah valued the relationship building as well, particularly the one with his biological mother. His parents fully supported his efforts, and did everything they could to make Karly feel like a welcome addition to Jonah's life.

Despite everything that had happened or maybe because of it, Winshore was thriving, since the unintended publicity of the current scandal brought in new clients by the droves. Hard work was the best medicine Morgan could ask for. It kept her focused and gave her a sense of purpose.

So did Lane.

He was the one who ultimately convinced her that while the past would always be part of her, it didn't have the power to control her—not unless she let it. Life, as he taught her, was like art. Rarely black-and-white. Mostly shades of gray.

"You're awfully quiet," Lane observed now, accelerating slightly and turning onto Atlantic Avenue.

"I'm wondering what this meeting is all about." Morgan shot him a questioning look. "Are you sure Barbara didn't say why she wanted to see us?"

"Positive." He kept his eyes on the road. "She sounded rushed. When I told her you were in the shower, she just asked if we could run over for a half hour. I knew you'd say yes, so I said it for you."

"But we told your parents we'd be up at the farm in time for lunch."

"We will be. Besides, I wouldn't worry about being missed. Devon and Blake are already up there. My parents will be hovering over Devon like EMTs, making sure she's eating, taking it easy—the works. Monty will probably have the truck engine idling, in case the baby decides to show up three weeks early. Believe me, they'll be plenty busy."

Morgan smiled. "You're about to become an uncle. That's pretty exciting."

"Yup. I can't wait." Lane slowed down and made a right, then another, until he swung onto Williams Avenue.

"This isn't the way to Healthy Healing," Morgan observed in a wooden tone.

"I know." He continued driving toward the very building she most dreaded and had avoided revisiting all these years.

"Lane . . ." she managed.

"It's okay." He reached over, squeezed her hand. "Trust me."

She'd opened her mouth to reply, when he pulled up in front of their destination—and her mouth snapped shut, her eyes widening in astonishment.

The three-story brick building had been totally restored, its white plaster-trimmed windows numerous and expansive, its twin banisters flanking a bluestone path and stairs, and its fence enclosing a small playground/backyard. The front door was solid cherry, and over it hung a brass plaque that read: THE LARA WINTER WOMEN'S CENTER.

Morgan stared. "I don't understand."

"You will." Lane pressed a key into her hand. "It's a gift from me to you."

She glanced from the key to Lane, comprehension slowly dawning. "You bought the building?"

"Good guess." A crooked grin. "It worked out well all ways around. The thrift-shop owner relocated a few blocks away, and the landlord liked my offer enough to accelerate the transfer of title. I hired the construction workers; Barbara hired the staff. The doors open in a week. We just need your final okay. Which is why we're here—to get it." Lane got out of the car and walked around to offer her a hand. "Come on. Let's take a look."

She did as he asked, placing her fingers in his and walking up the front steps. It took her three tries to unlock the door, her fingers were trembling so badly.

Stepping inside, she sucked in her breath, taking in the parquet floors and soothing aqua walls. There were three distinct sections—a semicircle of chairs that was clearly the women's conversation center, a small room filled with toys and books for child care, and a card table, set up with jars of Snickers and Milky Ways in the center.

On the wall just inside the front entranceway was a framed photo that Morgan knew like the back of her hand—the beloved and final photograph she'd taken with her parents, dated November 16, 1989, with the words *Jack, Lara, and Morgan* calligraphied at the bottom in her mother's hand.

It was just like the original. Only better. Because it had been enlarged and enhanced, cropped with absolute precision. It was as if her parents were right there in the room with her—and with all the other women who'd now walk through these doors for support and camaraderie.

Tears glistened on Morgan's lashes. "I . . . I don't know what to say."

"Don't say anything," Lane replied. "Spend a few minutes alone with your parents. I'll be waiting outside." He turned to go.

"Lane." Her voice was watery. "I love you."

"I know. I love you, too." With a quiet click, the door shut behind him.

Morgan stood still for a moment, just staring at the photo and letting its impact sink in. Essentially, it was the same photo she'd been staring at night after night, drenched in sweat from her nightmares.

This experience was different. Hanging here, in this center dedicated to her mother, the photograph was no longer a prelude to death. It was a living testimonial. A celebration of her parents; a fulfillment of their dreams.

A way for them to endure.

This building was no longer the embodiment of a nightmare.

It was the embodiment of hope, a promise for the future—everything Lara had wanted and worked for.

Her throat tight with emotion, Morgan ran her fingertips over the wooden frame, the glass casing that protected the photograph beneath. A sanctuary, she thought, tracing every beloved line of her parents' faces. This center was a sanctuary. Not only for the women in desperate need of refuge, but for her. It was a meaningful, tangible place for her to come and to be. To visit, to help out, to feel that precious connection to her parents.

They weren't lost to her. Thanks to Lane's gift, they never would be.

Turning, Morgan walked slowly around the room, feeling her parents' presence with every step she took, and letting the memories flood back. She smoothed her palm over the card table, smiled at the candy bars that would soon serve as winnings, and felt a sense of inner peace that, until now, had eluded her.

That's what Lane had brought to her life, she acknowledged. He'd taught her to accept and give love again—not half measure, but fully and without reservation. He'd taught her to trust. And he'd taught her that love meant risk. It sometimes meant pain. But a life without risk—worse, a life without love—was no life at all.

Finally, and for the first time, she could put the past to rest. Her parents weren't gone. They were with her—always. And their legacy would live on at the Lara Winter Women's Center.

On that thought, Morgan retraced her steps to the doorway. She paused to gaze at the photo again, silently acknowledging her feelings, saying good-bye and yet knowing it would never really be good-bye.

Then, with a tranquil smile, she left, closing the door behind her.